MW00626890

Malverne Manor

Malverne Manor

HELEN YORK

PUBLISHED FOR THE CRIME CLUB BY
DOUBLEDAY & COMPANY, INC.
GARDEN CITY, NEW YORK
1974

All of the characters in this book are fictitious, and any resemblance to actual persons, living or dead is purely coincidental

Library of Congress Cataloging in Publication Data

York, Helen.
    Malverne Manor.

    I. Title.
PZ4.Y62Mal [PS3575.06]   813'.5'4
ISBN 0-385-09654-2
Library of Congress Catalog Card Number 73–14058

To the memory of my brother
ELMER YORK
July 10, 1921–January 11, 1972

Malverne Manor

CHAPTER 1

I stopped suddenly in the road. I'd been hurrying because of the cold wind and threatening rain, but now that I'd come around a bend in the road, Malverne Manor abruptly came into view and, looking up at the manor house, I remembered all at once what Amy had written in the letter I received the day before. . . . "You must come in secret or they will turn you away."

Glancing over my shoulder to the village in the distance, I wondered whether it wouldn't be more sensible to return to the Three Crowns Inn. I could inquire there about Malverne Manor, perhaps engage the help of the local constable.

There'd been a number of things in Amy's letters from the manor that had caused me to wonder whether Amy wasn't holding back, whether, indeed, the situation at Malverne Manor wasn't more serious than she'd intimated. Only in that last letter did she stress the urgency of my coming to the manor. I was immediately on my way. Although Amy and I were not sisters but cousins, I'd always felt a sisterly responsibility toward her.

Despite her emphasis upon the secrecy of my arrival, I remained standing in the road, hesitating, my eyes on the village in the distance. It seemed wiser, I thought, to return to the inn, make some inquiry there about Malverne Manor.

But, no, that wouldn't do. Amy had stressed that I come in secret, warning me in her letter that "Even so, they will probably turn you away."

I continued up the road, walking quite fast now because of the splatter of raindrops and the dark-gray threatening sky. A crash of thunder made me start. The slashing noise startled me so badly I came to a jarring halt, then I began to hurry even more. The scattered raindrops had whipped into a pelting rain. In a short while my bonnet was soaked, my shoes wet, my shoulders cold from the dampened cloak.

Rushing toward the manor house, I thought how all along I'd felt Amy's decision to come to Malverne Manor had been a mistake, that she never should have listened to Lady Bellingford. It was she who'd urged Amy to go to Malverne Manor.

Yet, Amy's early letters from the manor indicated that all would go well in the end. There were little worries interspersed in her news, but no cause for alarm. When Sir Edmond arrived at the manor from Scotland, Amy assured me, the wedding would take place even though Lady Edythe, his widowed aunt who made her home at Malverne Manor, seemed displeased. . . . "What's it to me?" Amy had written. "When Edmond and I are married, I will be mistress of Malverne Manor and Lady Edythe will no longer be living here."

Those early letters from the manor were mostly joyful letters with much reference to the wedding soon to take place. "You, of course, Claire, will be my maid of honor," she'd written from London and again when she arrived at Malverne Manor. In every letter she described the manor house and gardens in great detail. Any reference to Lady Edythe was glossed over.

But the letter of the day before was different. For the first time, she'd expressed an outright fear of not only Lady Edythe but of Mrs. Hopkins, the housekeeper. "When I am mistress of Malverne Manor, I shall dismiss her," she'd written.

She'd ended the letter with "You must come to the manor without delay, Claire, and you must come in secret or they will turn you away. Even so, they will probably turn you away. You can stay at the Three Crowns Inn in the village where the coach stops, then walk from there. It will take you less than an hour. As you must have deduced from my letters, I've had reason to be uneasy from the day I arrived at the manor but now the situation has become more serious. If you don't come—— Oh, I cannot imagine your not coming, Claire. You must."

Now, hurrying up the drive that led to the manor house, my only thought was that, indeed, Amy had exaggerated the problem, that my premonition of danger was unfounded.

I was halfway up the long, curving drive when the rain clouds burst open with a fury. By the time I reached the front door, I was out of breath, my cloak was drenched, and I was trembling from the cold. I leaned for a moment against the door, waiting for my breathing to steady itself before reaching for the bellpull.

I soon realized that I should have postponed my visit to the manor till the next day, as I'd originally planned. I might have been spared this torrent of rain. But when the coach, after an exhausting six-hour journey, had arrived at the Three Crowns Inn, I'd changed my plans. I was travel weary when I arrived at the inn and a light rain was falling, but by the time I'd secured a room and rested briefly, the sun came out. Knowing I had four hours of daylight ahead of me, I started out for the manor. I couldn't imagine my resting that night at the inn with Malverne Manor less than an hour's walk away. The weather had turned favorable. The walk would do me good, I decided.

The changeable April weather, however, turned against me soon after I left the inn. The light spring shower of a short time ago had been only a prelude of what was to come. After I'd walked up the country road for about twenty minutes, the sun disappeared, the wind came up, and with only half the walk to Malverne Manor accomplished, I was thrust into a threatening darkness followed by cold, windy rain.

Now, exhausted and trembling from the cold, I had finally arrived at the manor house, but I stood at the front door, hesitating, secretly wishing that when I pulled on the bell, I would be turned away as Amy had warned I might be. Then I could return to the village and seek help.

Why this vague disquiet? I asked myself. When I'd made the decision to come, I had no fear then, only a firm purpose.

There was nothing else to do at present, I told myself firmly, but ring the bell and hope I wouldn't be turned away. Amy was somewhere in that house and she needed me.

I tugged at the bellpull. The clanging sound echoed faintly within the house. I waited but there was no other sound from inside. I pulled again on the bell.

After another long wait, I finally heard a muffled noise, approaching footsteps, and the jingle of keys. Twice, Amy had remarked about that sound. "It's worse at night," she'd written, "the soft footsteps and the jangle of those keys."

I looked up with a start. The front door opened and a woman in a gray, white-collared servant's dress greeted me with a cheery smile. She glanced past me and I realized she was looking for some mode of transportation. I quickly explained that since the weather had looked promising, I'd walked from the village.

The woman shook her head at my drenched appearance. The next instant she had her arm protectively around my shoulder and, accompanied by solicitous exclamations that I should have had the misfortune to be caught in such a downpour, she hurried me into a room where a fire blazed in the hearth.

I was astonished at this hospitable welcome and even more so when the woman said she was Mrs. Hopkins, the housekeeper, whom Amy had frequently mentioned, first with dislike then with fear. She was a small, plump woman with a round, rosy face and bright black eyes. The dark hair was neatly brushed into a tight bun at the back. When she smiled, her face lit up with a cheery glow.

Mrs. Hopkins whisked me to the marvelous warmth of the fire, chattering all the while. "So you walked all the way from the village," she exclaimed, sounding incredulous, then shook her head, adding, "Well, yes, it is a lovely sort of walk. I sometimes do that. It is too bad, though, that you got caught in the rainstorm. Perhaps you should have postponed your visit to the manor until tomorrow." She paused briefly, flashed her sunny smile. "We were, in fact, expecting you tomorrow."

Expecting? My breath caught. How did she know I was coming?

Before I had a chance to speak, she rattled on: "Lady Edythe will arrive shortly. In the meantime you must warm yourself by the fire." She'd already removed my bonnet and was now removing my wet cloak. "Now the shoes," she said, stooping to help me with them. "You must remove those wet shoes."

She pulled a chair close to the fire, gesturing that I sit. "Lady Edythe might be slightly delayed," she continued, pausing only an instant now and then to catch her breath. "Old Abner simply hates to have the carriage out in the rain," she ran on. "He's quite old. His eyesight isn't what it used to be. He's terribly deaf, too. I can imagine how fretful Old Abner is at this moment, fetching Lady Edythe home in that downpour." She gave me a quick bright smile and I thought in passing that she did not have the provincial speech of a servant.

"But you know how busy Lady Edythe is these days," Mrs. Hopkins explained, her chatter rolling along, not giving me a chance to get a word in edgewise. "Sir Edmond's campaigning keeps Lady Edythe quite occupied, particularly with Sir Edmond still in Edinburgh. But he will be returning to the manor tomorrow and Lady Edythe will not be quite so rushed since Sir Edmond will take over the election campaigning."

She paused for an instant to catch her breath. I gaped at her, trying to follow her rapid chatter, watching her bustling movements all the while she talked, carefully placing my wet things near the hearth. I didn't speak. There was never a pause long enough in her chatter to squeeze in a word of my own. But, then, I didn't wish to discuss Amy with her, not with a servant. I would wait till Lady Edythe arrived.

"I will be back shortly," Mrs. Hopkins was now saying, with a brisk movement toward the door. "I have some things to attend to in the kitchen," she rushed on. "I'll bring you a cup of tea. By the time you've had your tea and warmed your toes, Lady Edythe will arrive."

She flashed her sunny smile and bustled out.

For a moment I stared blankly at the closed door as Mrs. Hopkins' footsteps receded down the hall. Snatches of her runaway chatter crossed my mind, but I put all that aside for the while. I relaxed into the down-cushioned chair, luxuriating in the cozy comfort of the blazing fire. I gazed idly about the room, which I'd barely noticed when I'd entered.

The gold brocade curtains at the tall arched windows caught my eye and I realized all at once that this was the drawing room Amy had described so vividly in her first letter from Malverne Manor.

She, too, had been ushered into this room upon her arrival.

I could easily imagine Amy's delight when she entered this lovely room, how her breath must have caught at her first glimpse of the gold-colored curtains at the tall arched windows. . . . "All the more beautiful," she'd written, "with the firelight shining on them, bringing out the shimmery luster."

That was how the curtains at the two windows near the hearth appeared now with the firelight shining on the gold-colored fabric.

Near a window at the far end of the room stood the rosewood harpsichord Amy had mentioned. Near it was the Chippendale sofa covered in pale blue silk. . . . "—the same kind of pale blue silk as that dress you helped me make. Remember, Claire, how we labored over that embroidered blue sash?"

My eyes traveled along the walls, hung with ancestral portraits and glowing landscapes, to the graceful Queen Anne chair, covered in yellow silk, at the other end of the fireplace.

An enchanting room, just as Amy had described it.

I recalled what she'd written about the garden view from the drawing room windows, and since Mrs. Hopkins was taking her time with the tea, I decided to have a look. My stockings were dry now. I'd make no marks on the carpet. The rain had slacked to a thin drizzle. I'd be able to see the gardens.

When I started to get up, I heard footsteps in the hall and the faint jangle of keys. I again remembered Amy's dread of that sound. A vague discomfort swept over me. Even after Mrs. Hopkins entered with the tea things, cheerfully pleasant as before, and I knew it was only her footsteps I'd heard and the keys pinned to her apron, my hands shook a little and I clasped them together tightly so she wouldn't notice.

I was thankful she promptly launched into her stream of chatter. Her bubbly voice eased the unreasonable discomfort that had seized me. By the time she'd set up the table before the hearth and poured my tea, I could reach for the cup with steady fingers.

"I thought you might like a slice of my fresh-baked bread with butter, to go with the hot tea," Mrs. Hopkins said, beaming at me. "Now I must hurry back to the kitchen to prepare dinner. You enjoy your tea and warm your toes on this chilly evening until Lady Edythe arrives."

She smiled, the plump cheeks pink and shiny. When she once more began to hurry out of the room, I was on the verge of stopping her, to inquire how she knew I was coming. Odd, too, that she never once mentioned Amy.

But I held back. I would not ask her anything, not about Amy or why I came here. I would not discuss the matter with the housekeeper. I thanked her for her kindnesses and let her be on her way to the kitchen.

When I finished the hot, delicious tea and the wonderfully good fresh bread with butter, I went to the window for a look at the gardens.

The garden view was so lovely I uttered a low exclamation of surprise. The rain was now no more than a mist. It bathed the gardens in a delicate veiled beauty, all the colors softened, from the coppery leaves of the tall beech trees to the blush pink of the roses that tumbled over a curving stone wall. The lawns which sloped down to the pond were a plushy green, shrouded by mist that hugged the ground.

In the distance, beyond the pond, I could see the faint outline of the steeple on the village church. I realized then that Amy's bedroom was on this side of the house. This is the view she said she had from her bedroom.

Gazing into the garden, snatches from Amy's first two letters from the manor came to mind, happy letters mostly, with only hints of trouble —Lady Edythe was "cool"; Mrs. Hopkins was "a bother." I wasn't alarmed. I knew how willful and capricious Amy could be. It didn't surprise me that her adjustment to Lady Edythe and Mrs. Hopkins wasn't altogether smooth.

Yet, even those first two letters had left me uneasy enough to bring up the subject with Walter Binson.

After my father's death last year, Walter Binson took full charge of the chemist's shop where he'd worked for my father for three years. It was more or less precluded that soon—probably the following summer —Walter and I would marry.

When I told Walter of my rising apprehension concerning Amy's visit at Malverne Manor and what I'd from the start considered her foolhardy intention to marry Sir Edmond, he objected vigorously to my "interfering," adding, "You know what Amy is like."

I hadn't replied to those first two letters. They'd come in quick succession and Walter and I were quite busy with the chemist's shop, involved in some renovation which Walter said was necessary. After his stern advice not to interfere, I decided to wait awhile, see what the next letter or two had to say.

When the third letter arrived, I'd read it only part way when I resolved to overlook Walter's advice and reply, even ask Amy whether I should come to Malverne Manor. But the letter ended with Amy's emphatic order not to write to her at the manor "because things might be worse then." She'd even underlined the words. "I will let you know when Edmond arrives from Scotland," she'd ended, "and then I want you to come to the manor for the wedding."

I seriously considered going to Malverne Manor then or, at least, writing despite Amy's order not to and Walter's order not to interfere. I particularly didn't like the sound of Amy's warning that "things might be worse then."

But another letter quickly followed, giving no indication of urgency. She wasn't feeling well, was writing the letter in bed. . . . "But I'll be fine soon. I sleep a great deal and I'm sure that will help. Edmond is expected in a day or two. By then I'll be fully recovered."

In her fifth letter—there were six altogether from the manor—she'd expressed very definite opinions about Lady Edythe. . . . "I know she is very much opposed to my marrying Edmond. It's not that she says anything directly to me, but, then, she doesn't consider me important enough to discuss the matter with me. She's waiting for Edmond to return from Edinburgh so she can express her disapproval of me to him. Disapproval of me? Indeed! Claire, I am certain our ancestry is far more illustrious than hers." And, again, the optimistic note at the end of the letter that soon Edmond would return and everything would be fine.

A clatter in the hall broke into my rambling thoughts and I quickly turned away from the window. Lady Edythe had probably arrived. I returned to my chair and hurriedly slipped on my shoes which felt a bit damp but, considering all I'd heard from Amy about Lady Edythe's aristocratic, formal manner, I did not wish to meet the formidable lady in my stocking feet.

There was a babble of voices in the hall as Mrs. Hopkins was apparently explaining my presence. Soon, swift firm steps were approaching the drawing room.

Lady Edythe entered, greeting me with a warm gracious smile. "I am so sorry you got caught in the rain," she said in the same solicitous tone Mrs. Hopkins had used. She inclined her head, regarding me with friendly interest.

She, indeed, was as regal a person as Amy had declared, tall, with an erect bearing. She wore a dress of dove gray, cut on elegant simple lines. The soft gray color enhanced the gray-white hair which was arranged meticulously atop a fine-boned head, held at a slightly arrogant tilt. High, prominent cheekbones intensified the sharp, precise appearance, but the light-brown eyes softened the cool, imperious look. She seemed to be in her early sixties, but the fastidious appearance and graceful movements gave the illusion she might be younger.

"I rather expected you tomorrow," I heard her say, "since it's been threatening rain all day. But I am glad you are here and that Mrs. Hopkins has made you comfortable. I've been looking forward to your visit."

She'd been looking forward to it? Considering Amy's urgency that I come in secret, she surely hadn't told Lady Edythe I was coming. Nor would she have told Mrs. Hopkins. Had Amy's final letter from the manor been read before it was posted? I wanted to ask Lady Edythe how she knew I was coming, but before I could recover from her surprising statement, she'd taken the yellow silk Queen Anne chair opposite me and was now speaking in a casual, friendly manner about the rain and that it would be good for the gardens.

"I was admiring the gardens from the window a moment ago," I said. "I'd read so much about them."

"Oh, yes," Lady Edythe remarked with a smile, "the manor gardens have been written about in considerable detail."

For an instant I wondered what exactly she meant by that. I, of course, was referring to Amy's page after page of garden details, but I had the feeling Lady Edythe and I were not speaking of the same thing. My attention was drawn back to Lady Edythe who continued speaking.

"Sir Edmond," she was explaining, "has found it necessary to be away from the manor the past few days and, as a result, I have been busier than usual with the election campaigning." She smiled warmly, giving me a direct but friendly look. "It is so heartening to see that Sir Edmond has so many loyal supporters in the county. I am certain his election will be a unanimous victory."

So I was going to hear about the county elections again. I recalled

Mrs. Hopkins' innumerable comments about the election campaign as if I, too, should be vitally interested in the subject.

Lady Edythe's gaze rested on me for a moment, the cordial smile widened. "I am so pleased," she said, "that you are willing to help Sir Edmond in his campaign. Are you quite settled now at Hammond House?"

"Hammond House?"

We looked at each other in puzzled silence, then the baffled expression left her face and she smiled, although a bit uncertainly.

"Am I mistaken?" Lady Edythe asked, the cordial voice a trifle strained. "You are not Mrs. Raynord?"

I shook my head, still a bit dazed by this new turn in the conversation. Before I had a chance to speak, Lady Edythe quickly said, "Forgive me, but I don't know all of Sir Edmond's constituents." She'd regained her composure, sitting erect in the chair once more, but there was increased uncertainty in her voice. "I've met most of Sir Edmond's people," she continued in a thin, hesitant voice, "but I haven't met everyone." She smiled faintly. "I'm sorry, but both Mrs. Hopkins and I presumed you were Mrs. Raynord. She was expected today to offer her assistance with Sir Edmond's campaign, but we rather expected her tomorrow since it's been threatening rain all day."

"I'm not Mrs. Raynord," I said. "I'm Claire Atwood, a friend of Amy's."

"A friend of Amy's?" The words were repeated in a voice so low it was barely audible.

"Yes, a friend of Amy's," I said. "When Amy came to Malverne Manor, she——"

"——came here?" Lady Edythe broke in. "To Malverne Manor? But she never arrived."

CHAPTER 2

For a brief, uneasy moment, we looked at each other without speaking.

I decided to remain silent lest I say more than I intended. I waited for Lady Edythe to speak first.

"This friend of yours—this Amy—she did write to me—twice, in fact," Lady Edythe said at last. "She informed me she'd met Sir Edmond in London five months ago, told me she was coming here to Malverne Manor." She smiled, but it was no longer the warm, hospitable smile but a rather fixed, impersonal one.

"To tell the truth, Miss——" Lady Edythe paused, drew herself to a more upright position in the chair. "You said your name was——?"

"Atwood. Miss Claire Atwood."

"Well, Miss Atwood, I was a bit astonished at Amy's letter, informing me she'd met Sir Edmond. He'd never mentioned that fact to me. Then to tell me she was coming here—" There was a pause, a quick intake of breath. "Even when her second letter from London was followed by one from Sir Edmond, explaining he'd met the young lady previously in London five months ago and that she was to be a guest at the manor while he was in Scotland on business—why, even when Sir Edmond's letter arrived, informing me of Amy's anticipated visit, I did not put much stock in it." She braced her back against the chair. The fingers dug into the yellow silk chair arms.

"You see, Miss Atwood," she continued after drawing in a long, slow breath, "Sir Edmond is rather impulsive, overly hospitable at times. He tends to invite guests to Malverne Manor rather helter-skelter when he goes up to London. I couldn't imagine, though, his sending me a guest at this time when he knows how occupied I am with the campaigning for his county election." She dropped her hands into her lap, began to twist a large amethyst ring. "And to send me an incapacitated guest, at that," she added, her eyes downcast.

"I know about Amy's injury," I said. "She'd written me about it from London, explaining her fall from a horse, that she'd injured her foot and her shoulder."

Lady Edythe looked up sharply, as if surprised at my statement concerning the accident. After a prolonged hesitation, she said, "In her second letter to me from London, your friend, Amy, informed me she was on her way to the manor, that she and Sir Edmond were—were going to be married when he returned from Scotland." Her voice wavered, then became brusque. "That, Miss Atwood, was out of the question. I am sure your friend—although I've never met her—is a sweet, lovely girl, but Sir Edmond is practically betrothed to Miss Pamela Wickham of an old county family." The fingers twisted the amethyst ring. She spoke rapidly now. "Sir Edmond is quite a catch. Many young ladies would like to be the mistress of Malverne Manor but, impulsive as Sir Edmond might be, Miss Atwood, he is quite aware of his responsibilities to the manor and to Miss Wickham."

Lady Edythe drew herself erect in the chair, tilting her head back slightly, as if waiting for me to speak, but before I could put my thoughts in any sort of order, she said in a rush of words:

"I am certain your friend, Amy, misunderstood Sir Edmond's casual friendship. He might have even suggested she come to Malverne Manor for a few days' visit. But marriage?" She seemed visibly to shrink from the very suggestion. "Furthermore, Miss Atwood, your friend, Amy, never arrived after all."

"Did Lady Bellingford arrive?" I asked.

"No. No such person came here. Amy did mention that a Lady Bellingford would accompany her." A tiny deprecating smile flicked across her face, as if such a person existed only in Amy's imagination.

"But in Amy's second letter from London," Lady Edythe went on, "she said Lady Bellingford would not be able to accompany her, that she was arriving alone. Something about Lady Bellingford going to the South of France." She stopped abruptly, her voice quivering slightly. "You seemed quite certain a while ago, Miss Atwood, that Amy had come here to the manor. What makes you think she'd been here?"

I quickly retraced in my mind what I'd said—before she'd told me Amy had never arrived at the manor—and I recalled that, luckily, I'd said nothing about Amy having written to me from Malverne Manor. And at Amy's urgent request, I had not written any letter to the manor.

"Amy wrote me from London," I answered, then after a pause, added, "and she asked me to come here to be her maid of honor, that she and Sir Edmond were to be married at Malverne Manor." I hoped the slight pause between the two statements would give Lady Edythe the impression the request to be maid of honor had come only in a letter from London.

Apparently, Lady Edythe did come to that conclusion. "Then Amy changed her mind after writing to you from London," she said. "She's probably still in London." Her voice was composed now; the smile came more easily. "Your coming here was such a dreadful waste of your time, Miss Atwood. If you wish to know more, you will have to ask Amy, and the place to inquire is London, not here."

I gazed at her, my brain spinning with details from Amy's six letters from Malverne Manor. My eyes caught the gold-colored brocade curtains with the firelight bringing out their subtle sheen, the way Amy had described them. I glanced at the harpsichord she'd mentioned, the blue silk Chippendale sofa. I thought of the garden beyond the windows, the curving stone wall with the rambling roses, the pond, the village church spire. Amy saw all these things. She wrote to me about them.

Could it be true, I asked myself, that she'd never been here? Merely read about Malverne Manor? Or heard about the manor and its occupants from Lady Bellingford? From Sir Edmond?

No, it wasn't like Amy to deceive. She'd always been a starry-eyed romantic goose with too much imagination, too much dreaming. But not lies. Besides, what would have been the point of weaving such an intrigue for my benefit?

"I realize this is distressing for you, Miss Atwood," I heard Lady Edythe say. "To come all this way, only to learn that your friend has never been here."

"Yes—yes," I murmured absently. "It—it is rather bewildering."

"What do you plan to do?" Lady Edythe inquired.

"Do?" I looked at her, then at the windows where the rain beat against the glass. The mist had switched to another downpour. I wondered dazedly whether I'd have to walk back to the inn in the rain since it was discovered I was not Mrs. Raynord, the expected and cherished guest.

On the other hand, I debated, it might be safer to return to the Three Crowns Inn. Dare I stay in this house?

But I had to. Amy was here, somewhere in this vast house. Possibly ill. She'd said in one of her letters she wasn't feeling well. The fall from the horse might have been more serious than she had at first thought.

I completely dismissed from my mind Lady Edythe's statement that Amy had never arrived at the manor. How clearly I remembered her description of the bedroom she'd been given. The Cream Lace Room, she said it was called. . . . "There's a tall glass display cabinet facing my bedroom," she had written. "There's a little shepherdess figurine in that cabinet. I often stand in front of that cabinet, Claire, and gaze at that little shepherdess. She looks so much like you, the same gold-brown hair, the large gray eyes. But most of all, the smile, Claire. She has your smile. I've already named her Claire in my mind."

If I could induce Lady Edythe to permit me to stay overnight at the manor, I thought, I'd search for the tall glass cabinet which faced the Cream Lace Room.

"Lady Edythe," I began, "could, that is, could——"

"Yes, of course," she said. "Of course you may stay for the night," she replied, guessing my request, since my eyes were fastened on the windows where the rain beat furiously against the glass.

"You could not possibly walk back to the inn," Lady Edythe continued. "We at Malverne Manor are proud of our hospitality, and I'd rather not send Old Abner and the carriage out in that downpour." She arose slowly from her chair, not quite so erect, appearing somewhat drained. The thin lips formed a smile. "You, no doubt, are rather exhausted after your coach journey, Miss Atwood. Perhaps you would like a supper tray sent up to your room and retire early."

"That is most kind of you. Yes, I am rather tired."

"Then I will have Abner lay a fire in one of the bedrooms immediately. The evening is rather chilly. Mrs. Hopkins will bring you a tray."

A smile came slowly to her face, softening the taut lines that had deepened into her cheeks.

"Mrs. Hopkins makes an excellent chicken broth," she said from the doorway, the warmth returning to her voice. "That will make your fatigue vanish. I'm sure there will be some lovely sweet, too, perhaps one of her delicious apple tarts. You go right on warming yourself by the fire. Your room will be prepared for you shortly."

When she was gone, I gazed into the fire, my thoughts leaping and chasing about like the flames in the hearth. I drew my eyes to the splendid appointments of the spacious drawing room—the heirloom furniture, the beautiful Aubusson carpet, portraits of illustrious ancestors gracing the walls. I recalled how Amy in her letters had marveled at the grand scale of the manor house and the gardens.

And Amy desired to be mistress of all this, the mistress of Malverne Manor. In a way, I was responsible for her fanciful dreams. Not actually due to me but, rather, due to my mother. It all started innocently enough. Neither Amy nor I placed any significance upon it at first.

My mother was French, not English. Her family, like many another French aristocratic family, had fled to England during the Revolution. My mother was fifteen at the time. I'd never heard my mother pine for those grand days when she lived in the Château du Montellarais. When she was seventeen, she'd met my father and was blissfully content to be the wife of a chemist in a small English village. Her early life at the Château du Montellarais, and all its attendant adventures, served merely as the basis for bedtime stories she told me when I was a child. They were far more interesting than stories from books.

My cousin, Amy, who lived in the house the other side of my father's chemist's shop, listened with wide-eyed wonder to these stories which I related to her.

That was all there was to it at first. Amy, two years younger than I, and far more inclined toward the fanciful, enjoyed hearing the "fairy-tale" stories about the Château.

Later, when Amy was about twelve, my mother's French aristocracy came to mean something altogether different to her. I remember her pointing out to me, with a faraway look in her eyes, that since she and I were cousins, then she, too, was of aristocracy. Perhaps since Amy, at the age of twelve, had blossomed into the prettiest girl in the village, with many a young man casting a yearning eye her way, she began to imagine herself in some sort of fairy-tale princess role. Surely the possibility of her being dimly related to French aristocracy had crossed her mind before, but it hadn't been important. Gradually it became almost an obsession.

It was her father's side of the family that was distantly related to my mother. Amy harassed him for information about his ancestry. He laughingly denied any aristocratic connections and was interested only in making a success of the family teashop in the village.

The indifference that Amy's father displayed concerning this ephemeral high-born heritage did not daunt Amy or her mother who, unlike my mother, had always wished for "better things" for herself and her only daughter.

Amy and her mother nurtured the dream. Amy's last name was Chapel, but Amy and her mother soon became convinced it was actually La Chapelle and not English at all. Soon Amy and her mother became a little embarrassed about running a teashop.

When Amy's father died—she was fifteen then—and her mother remarried a year later, the preoccupation with aristocratic lineage was forgotten more or less. Discord in the family superseded all else, particularly since Amy and the stepfather did not get on well.

Then, when her mother died last year, the antagonism between Amy and her stepfather increased to the point where seven months ago she'd fled to London. The final break came when the stepfather harshly accused Amy of carrying on with one of the local swains. This sort of accusation he'd frequently hurled at Amy, reducing her to tears, causing her to flee to our house—my house by then, with both parents dead. I tried to convince Amy that going to London alone was unwise. I even offered to leave the chemist's shop in charge of Walter Binson and accompany her to London till she got settled. But Amy said that was unnecessary. She had no fear of going alone.

I was relieved when her letters began to arrive. She'd secured employment. She'd made friends. She was happy. With her winning, vivacious ways, her lovely looks, I wasn't surprised. When she wrote about her acquaintanceship with a Lady Bellingford, I strongly suspected that Amy had omitted mentioning the village teashop, but perhaps much had been made of her French aristocracy heritage.

Soon after meeting Lady Bellingford, there was the news that she'd met the "dashing and terribly rich" Sir Edmond. Then the astonishing letter from London informing me she was on her way to Malverne Manor "and the wedding would soon take place."

Now, sitting in the drawing room of Sir Edmond's ancestral home, I, for the first time, gave him serious thought. What was he like? All Amy had ever said about him was that he was dashing and terribly rich. How fortunate that Mrs. Hopkins, mistaking me for Mrs. Raynord, had let it slip that he was returning to the manor tomorrow.

Then I would be able to see him, talk to him. If he arrived early in the day, I might still be at the manor. If it were hinted too broadly that I depart for the inn in the morning, I would return to Malverne Manor later in the day.

I was roused from my preoccupation when I heard the light steps in the hall and the jangle of keys. The first awareness of the sound made my back stiffen. I promptly checked myself. I was not going to build up a dread of that sound, I told myself sternly, just because Amy had done so. If I am going to help her, I had better keep a cool head.

Mrs. Hopkins entered, the house keys jingling at her waist. She was as cheerful and friendly as when she'd ushered me into the drawing room and seated me before the cozy fire in the hearth.

"Lady Edythe tells me you will be staying at the manor for the night," she said, launching once more into her rolling, uninterrupted speech, "which is an excellent decision. Now you come with me, Miss Atwood." She gestured briskly and I followed her out of the room. If she was surprised that I was Miss Atwood, not Mrs. Raynord, she didn't show it.

"Abner has laid a fire for you," she continued as we proceeded along the hall. "Your room will be nice and comfy by now. I will be up shortly with a nice little supper tray for you."

Mrs. Hopkins modified her brisk walk when she observed that I couldn't help but gaze all around at the splendid hall which, on entry a while ago, I hadn't noticed.

The hall was spacious, high-ceilinged, the walls a light tawny color which gave it a pleasing appearance. There were contrasting areas of wood-paneled walls and the minstrel gallery was of the same glossy wood. An enormous tapestry of a battle scene hung above the huge stone fireplace.

We'd come to the graceful curving staircase. As we mounted the wide, white marble stairs, I glanced at the portraits along the stair wall.

Which of these illustrious ancestors did the present master of the manor resemble? I wondered. My eyes lit on a balding, rotund gentleman with a mischievous glint in his eye. Is that what Sir Edmond is like?

Or like that other gentleman, the tall, bony fellow standing beside his horse?

When Mrs. Hopkins and I arrived at the top of the stairs, my guessing game with the portraits was promptly forgotten. My eyes searched the upper hallway for the tall glass cabinet with figurines on display. It faced the door to Amy's bedroom, the Cream Lace Room. Mrs. Hopkins lapsed into a rare silent moment and as we walked along, our heels clicking against the parquet floor, I peered anxiously ahead. But there was no glass cabinet of any kind.

"You have been given a pleasant room, Miss Atwood," Mrs. Hopkins said, breaking the brief silence. "It overlooks the orchard. Not that you can see much now, with the sky so dark all of a sudden. But the rain will probably stop soon and the moon might be clear tonight. Be sure you take a look first thing in the morning, Miss Atwood. You will see how pretty the orchard is with all the blossoms." She made a quick gesture. "Your room is in that wing, miss. We go around that corner."

When we turned the corner, there it was, the tall glass cabinet standing against the wall. It was far down the corridor, but even from this distance, in the light of Mrs. Hopkins' candle, I could see there were figurines on the glass shelves.

CHAPTER 3

I couldn't take my eyes off the tall glass cabinet and consequently bumped into Mrs. Hopkins, when she halted suddenly, because we'd come to the room I would occupy.

I apologized for jostling her and she murmured good-naturedly that she could well understand my gazing about, being so taken with the splendor of the house.

"I have been housekeeper here for seven years," she said with a proprietary air as she opened my bedroom door, "and I still catch myself gazing about in admiration at all the beauty of this great house."

We entered a small, comfortably furnished room. Mrs. Hopkins lighted a lamp. The glow of the lamp and the crackling fire in the hearth imparted a feeling of cozy welcome.

The four-poster bed had a blue and white muslin counterpane, and a chair near the bed was covered in the same neat material. There was a small white-painted dressing table with a mirror above it and a chest of drawers, dark wood with brass hardware. A braided rug lay on a highly polished floor.

I sensed that Mrs. Hopkins, standing silently inside the door, was awaiting my sign of approval and I told her it was a pleasant room, which evidently pleased her.

"Now, you freshen up, Miss Atwood," she suggested. "There is a convenient little bath through that door and I've brought you plenty of hot water." She turned to go, then added, "I will be up shortly with a nice supper tray for you."

I listened to her retreating footsteps on the wood floor of the hallway and, as soon as I heard her turn the corner out of the wing, I slipped out into the hall to have a look at the figurines in the glass cabinet, only a short distance from my door.

After I'd gone only a few steps, I heard a door open somewhere. I couldn't tell the direction of the sound nor could I place the location of the footsteps I now heard. I hurried to my room and closed the door, rather expecting the person to walk past my door, but the steps came to a halt somewhere along the corridor and were heard no more.

I decided that for the time being I would content myself with freshening up while the water was hot, and Mrs. Hopkins couldn't come too soon with that chicken broth and the promised apple tart. Despite the tensions and excitement of the day, I was quite hungry.

I went into the small bath, prettily done in yellow and white, complete with hip bathtub. I freshened up with a lovely soap that smelled of lilac and dried myself on a large fluffy towel embroidered with bright yellow flowers.

I'd just fastened my long hair back with a ribbon when a knock on the door told me Mrs. Hopkins had come with the tray.

After she set my supper on a table, which she'd pulled up to the hearth, Mrs. Hopkins did not linger, explaining that she was needed downstairs. "I will bring you some night clothes when I come for the dishes," she said, then hurried away.

I sat before the glowing fire and enjoyed the delicious meal. Lady Edythe had not exaggerated Mrs. Hopkins' culinary skill. The hot chicken broth was hearty and the tastiest I'd ever eaten. There was also a serving of lamb, delicate and tender, and some potato done with cheese and cream. An apple tart, too, as Lady Edythe had promised. That and the hot coffee finished off a superb supper.

When Mrs. Hopkins came later for the dishes, I was still sitting lazily by the fire. I immediately complimented her on the fine supper.

"I am pleased you enjoyed it," she said, gathering up the tray, and putting the small table back against the wall. "Now, I believe you should rest a bit and retire early." She paused at the door to say good night and was gone.

I sat for a while longer at the hearth, almost dozing, then I got up and peered out my door to where the glass cabinet stood.

I stepped into the hallway and listened. Not a sound. It was as if I were the only person in the vast house.

Quietly, looking behind me at intervals, I crept along the corridor to where the glass cabinet stood.

I saw the shepherdess figurine immediately. As Mrs. Hopkins had predicted, the rain had stopped and a clear moon shone through the large window at the end of the hallway. I leaned closer to the cabinet and saw that the little shepherdess did have gold-brown hair. I couldn't tell the color of the eyes, not in this light, but I could see that she was smiling. . . . "But, most of all, the smile, Claire. She has your smile. I've already named her Claire in my mind."

I turned and looked at the door facing the display cabinet, the door to the Cream Lace Room.

I stepped to the door, fully expecting it to be locked, and was surprised when the knob turned in my hand. I opened the door and stepped inside.

Looking about, I could see why it was called the Cream Lace Room. In the clear light of the moon, I could see that the bed's canopy and counterpane were made of cream-colored lace. The room's wallcovering was a creamy silk with a woven lace design. I touched the lace flounces that billowed around a dressing table on which brushes and scent bottles stood, as if the room was being used at present.

I drew my eyes to the windows where the moonlight filtered through filmy lace curtains. A small, exquisite writing desk stood at the window, its graceful lines in keeping with the lace motif of the room.

Remembering the view Amy wrote about, I went to the window and looked out.

The moonlight bathed the gardens with a soft, pearly luster. I could see the curving stone wall with the roses climbing over it. Farther away was the pond. The rippling water shimmered in the clear, moonlit night. Beyond the pond was the church spire.

I turned to leave when I remembered about the picture.

Amy had explained that when she wrote to me and had to hide the unfinished letter, or a completed one before she could have it posted, she had found a fine hiding place. . . . "There is a picture hanging in my bedroom and I can slip the letter behind it, where the letter is safe from prying eyes and fingers. It's a rather pretty picture, Claire. Looks like our village. Smile if you wish, but, yes, sometimes I miss our little village. That's why I noticed the picture immediately. There's even the same kind of wooden bridge, like the one near your father's chemist's shop."

I made a hurried inspection of the pictures on the walls and soon found the right one. Even in the half-darkness, I could see the wooden bridge in the landscape.

I pounced on the picture, groping behind it, but there was no hidden letter there.

After one last look around the room, from the doorway, I crept back to my room and got into the nightgown Mrs. Hopkins had brought. Before going to bed, I went to the window to have a look at the orchard. I'd glimpsed the edge of the orchard from a window of the Cream Lace Room. Mrs. Hopkins said my room gave me a good view of it.

In the silvery light of the moon, the flowering trees were a breathtaking sight; the light-colored blossoms appeared like puffy clouds hovering over the trees.

I stood there for some time, my eyes resting on the moonlit orchard, then straying to the extensive gardens surrounding the vast house. The thought kept repeating itself—Amy wished to be mistress of all this.

I recalled that day when Amy and I went to London, I to take care of some business for my father who was too ill to travel, Amy to buy some fabric for a very special tea gown. We, of course, took in the theater, the ballet, and various London sights, but it was the tea gown that was important. Amy had been invited by her current beau to a tea party at his great-aunt's house and Amy had determined on pale blue silk for the gown, a color which enhanced her delicate blond beauty.

Little did we dream that day that The Alroyd Store, where we purchased the silk, would one day figure so prominently in Amy's life. It came about when, sometime later, Mrs. Alroyd, traveling to London, had stopped at the village teashop with her two young children. She'd lamented that the children's governess had been called home due to her mother's serious illness and now she'd received word the governess would not return and had decided, because of the mother's illness, to seek employment closer to home.

It was the following week that Amy had had her most severe altercation with her stepfather. After the tears had subsided, she informed me of her decision. She would go to Mrs. Alroyd's house in London, to seek the position of governess.

But upon arrival at Mrs. Alroyd's house, Amy learned that the governess's mother had died. The governess had returned.

Where the unexpected return of the governess was a blow, the timely arrival at the house of Mrs. Alroyd's bachelor son proved fortuitous. It was he who suggested that Amy, being so personable, would be a most desirable companion to Grandmamma Alroyd. Mrs. Alroyd agreed. The position was secured.

In her first letter from London, in which Amy explained how she secured the position, the situation itself was slighted over. Young Alroyd was the prime interest, but not for himself. Amy's capsule description was "skinny, homely, and lisps badly." But if the young man was lacking in personal charm, he held the key to the kind of life Amy had been pining for, what her mother considered the "better things" of life.

The second letter from London went into ecstatic detail about a horse show young Alroyd had taken her to, and Covent Garden, and a dinner party with "some titled people," including a Lady Bellingford with whom Amy immediately became friends.

Soon came her most important news of all. At a dinner party in Lady Bellingford's town house, Amy met Sir Edmond. A whirlwind romance developed.

When, according to Amy's breathless-sounding letters, the whirlwind courtship seemed to be edging toward hints of marriage, Amy wrote that Sir Edmond had to return to Malverne Manor, but he would be back shortly.

The "shortly" extended into a five-month period, during which time Amy's correspondence dwindled to a few cheerless letters. Young Alroyd was out of the picture, touring Europe. She'd met someone else during that waiting time, referring to him as "an adventurer" and "merely an interlude."

Then came the letter that, from the first line, was altogether different; it could mean only one thing. Sir Edmond, after a five-month absence, had returned to London.

"It's a pity," she wrote, "that Edmond and I cannot go dancing and partying as we used to. I had a bad fall from a horse recently, injuring my foot and shoulder badly. But how wonderful to have him back."

Then came that astonishing letter telling me she, with Lady Bellingford as chaperone, was going to Malverne Manor. Sir Edmond would be in Scotland on business of some sort and when he returned to the manor the wedding would take place.

I remember how exasperated I was when I read that letter. How like Amy—muddleheaded, foolishly romantic. I shot off a letter to her, reminding her she was not gentry, that it was only wishful thinking, that she did not belong at Malverne Manor.

She replied promptly with a hint she was miffed at my little scold and informed me she was leaving for Malverne Manor the following day, that she'd already written Lady Edythe to tell her she was on her way. Lady Bellingford, she'd added, would not be able to accompany her. Her mother, on holiday in the South of France, became ill suddenly and Lady Bellingford must go to her.

"But it's quite proper for me to go to Malverne Manor," Amy assured me. "Lady Bellingford will be only slightly delayed. She will arrive at the manor before Sir Edmond returns from Scotland."

Now this strange development, I said to myself. Lady Edythe telling me Amy never arrived at Malverne Manor, nor did Lady Bellingford.

I stepped away from the bedroom window with an abrupt movement. Impossible. Evidently Lady Bellingford was detained, had not yet arrived at the manor. But Amy came.

I snatched up my wrapper from the chair near my bed, put it on, and crept out into the hall. I would try a few doors along the corridor. The only room I'd looked into was the Cream Lace Room. I'd heard footsteps in the upper hallway a while ago, heard someone enter a room nearby. It might have been Lady Edythe or Mrs. Hopkins or some other servant. Nevertheless, I would try a few doors.

I slipped into the shadowy hallway, dimly lit by one small oil lamp. I first tried the door of the Cream Lace Room, deciding on one more look. It was empty. No one had answered my knocks.

Moving along the silent, darkened hallway, I tried the next four doors. They were locked. The fifth revealed only a duster-shrouded room. I crept along, trying still more doors. Some were locked, the others empty. No response to my knocks.

When I reached the end of the corridor, I peered into the adjoining wing. It was totally dark. From the far end of the dark, tunnel-like corridor, a faint sound occasionally broke the deep stillness. I did not have the courage to venture into the long, dark hallway. I'd investigate it in the light of day. I hurried back to my room.

I felt tired enough to drift off to sleep immediately. But sleep wouldn't come. My thoughts scurried and jumped about like the dancing shadows cast by the dying fire in the grate.

I thought of the Cream Lace Room, and that lovely writing desk by the window, where Amy, out of loneliness and worry, wrote those six secret letters to me.

I tried to recall the postmarks on those letters, but I couldn't remember. I had no reason then to imprint the postmark on my mind. Were the letters posted from the village where the Three Crowns Inn stood?

Probably. How did she manage to post the letters secretly? She'd injured her foot badly in that fall from a horse. She couldn't have walked to the village. Did they let her borrow a ponytrap to go to the village? The next day, when I returned to the inn, I would inquire about the postal service in the vicinity.

I would also make other inquiries—about Amy's arrival by coach. She'd, no doubt, stopped at the inn if only to be met by Old Abner and the Malverne carriage. Someone at the inn might have seen Amy, remembered her. With her pretty blond looks, Amy was the kind of girl one noticed and remembered.

I would look into the matter the next morning as soon as I returned to the inn. Lady Edythe would, undoubtedly, send me away from Malverne Manor soon after breakfast. Surely she would give me breakfast.

The following morning Lady Edythe did graciously offer me breakfast. She also brought up the subject of my immediate departure from Malverne Manor.

We were having breakfast in a small, sun-filled room, which Lady Edythe said was her favorite room in which to have the first meal of the day.

A cheery place in which to begin the day, I thought, an intimate sort of room because of its small size and sunny appearance. The walls were a cream color; where the morning sun shone on them, they were a warm rosy color. A petit-point carpet of bright field flowers covered part of the burnished oak floor. The small table and honey-oak sideboard all but filled the small oval room. Four wide windows faced the rose garden.

Although I tried to hold my attention to Lady Edythe's conversation, my interest was frequently drawn to the pleasing freshness of the airy sunlit room. It seemed almost a part of the garden beyond the windows, where wide green lawns sloped down to the pond. White roses bloomed near the open windows. The floral scent drifted into the room with each stir of the breeze.

Lady Edythe carried the burden of the conversation, going into length about the election campaign and what a delight it was to meet so many of Sir Edmond's constituents.

She did not mention Amy and I thought it wise not to bring up the subject.

She inquired whether the supper tray Mrs. Hopkins took to my room was satisfactory and did I sleep well. I assured her I slept well and the supper tray was quite satisfactory.

Lady Edythe was aware of my admiring glances at the room and the gardens. She did not appear perturbed at my not maintaining strict attention to her conversation—about the county elections mainly. She was obviously pleased with my silent admiration of the room and the gardens. It was clear that she was as proud of Malverne Manor as if it were all hers.

"It is a superb house, isn't it, Miss Atwood?" she asked, dropping the subject of elections temporarily.

"Yes. It is a beautiful house," I agreed.

"The gardens are lovely, too," Lady Edythe added with a proprietary smile. "I am sorry that I am so terribly occupied with the county campaigning for Sir Edmond, or I would ask you to stay a while."

She lowered her eyes and, after a short silence, her eyes still lowered, asked, "I suppose you will be leaving immediately for home, Miss Atwood? By the way, where is home?"

"Clisty. A rural village. I work there in my father's chemist's shop."

"Oh, then you will be anxious to return to help your father in the shop," she suggested brightly.

"My father died a year ago. I'm alone now but—but I have an excellent manager for the shop. I only help out." I paused, then wondered why I heard myself repeating lamely that I had an excellent manager for the shop.

Was that all I could say for Walter Binson? With no feeling in my voice, no rush of emotion? But Walter Binson and I were going to be married soon, probably this summer. As Walter pointed out, the shop was doing quite well now and we shouldn't postpone the wedding another summer.

"How fortunate you are," Lady Edythe was saying, "to have an excellent manager for the shop."

"Yes, he is—an excellent manager for the shop."

"Your friend, Amy," Lady Edythe continued. "Is she from the same village?"

"Yes, we grew up almost like sisters."

Lady Edythe became thoughtfully quiet and we both concentrated on Mrs. Hopkins' excellent breakfast of crisp bacon, scrambled eggs, and fresh muffins.

"Your friend, Amy," Lady Edythe said abruptly, "she—she had no family, isn't that so? I—I got that impression from the two letters she wrote me from London."

"Her mother died when Amy was sixteen. Like me, she had no

brothers or sisters and there was only a stepfather, but they were never close."

"I see."

A silence fell between us once more. I drank my coffee and looked out the window at the sunny garden or gazed idly at the flower prints hanging on the wall facing me.

Once or twice I glanced at Lady Edythe who'd lapsed into another reflective silence. She certainly belongs in such splendid surroundings, I thought. Everything about her was so appropriate—the serene face; the restrained yet eloquent gestures; the silver-white hair, impeccable in its arrangement; the luxurious blue velvet morning dress, very correct for a cool, breezy morning.

She finally raised her eyes. A smile gentled the sharp, imperious look. "It was a pleasure to have you as a guest, Miss Atwood," she said, "if only for a short time. And I wouldn't hear of your walking back to the inn. I will see to it that Old Abner has you at the Three Crowns Inn in time for the noon coach departure."

"But I'm not leaving."

The smile fled from her face. "Not leaving, Miss Atwood?"

"No, I shall stay at the inn for a while and ask around."

"Ask around?" The words came out in a thin whisper.

"Yes, ask around," I repeated. "Someone might have seen Amy arrive at the inn. She might have got her directions mixed up and got back on the coach or—someone might know something."

"Yes, I see what you mean," Lady Edythe murmured. She was making a valiant attempt to remain calm, to appear disinterested, but her face had become ashen. Once or twice she apparently wished to speak, but the words faded and she opened and closed her mouth in a slack movement of the lips. I thought she was going to become ill.

At that moment Mrs. Hopkins passed by the windows and Lady Edythe turned her head with a jerk. She regained her composure instantly as, I supposed, befitted the gentry.

"I see Mrs. Hopkins is out to cut some roses for the house," she said in a quiet, calm voice. "I'm pleased she's doing it early in the morning. The roses last so much longer when they're cut in the early hours."

It was as if the distressing matter of Amy was closed, as if my decision to remain at the inn to ask questions was no longer a threat.

"Would you excuse me for a moment, Miss Atwood?" Lady Edythe requested, rising slowly from her chair. "Have another cup of coffee. I'll be back for a second cup, too, but I wish to see Mrs. Hopkins briefly about a household matter."

She hurried out of the room and the next instant I saw her walk swiftly past the windows. I did not wish any more coffee and decided to have a closer look at the flower prints hanging on the wall.

As I crossed the room, my eye caught Mrs. Hopkins and Lady Edythe at the far end of the rose garden, engaged in what appeared to be a heated discussion. Lady Edythe had secreted herself, but not too well, behind a hedge. I could see her hands flailing out as she gestured from behind the hedge.

Mrs. Hopkins had her back to me, but her bobbing head and gesticulating elbows indicated that "the household matter" under discussion had much to do with my intention to remain at the inn and make inquiries. Judging from Mrs. Hopkins' frantic gestures, the poor woman probably had to admit now that she'd let it slip the previous day that Sir Edmond was returning to the manor today.

The agitated conversation gradually subsided into an intense discussion, with Mrs. Hopkins leaning forward, listening earnestly while Lady Edythe seemed to be explaining something in detail.

After several bobbings of Mrs. Hopkins' head, Lady Edythe emerged from behind the hedge and, as she briskly started back for the dining room, I forgot about the flower prints on the wall. I quickly resumed my seat and when Lady Edythe re-entered the room, composed now and smiling, I was enjoying my second cup of coffee.

Lady Edythe poured herself a second cup and began to talk to me in a casual, conversational tone about the rose garden. From that subject, she proceeded to make complimentary remarks about the Malverne orchards which will give a good cider yield. That led to a discussion of Mrs. Hopkins' herb garden which Mrs. Hopkins planted herself and which she tends carefully.

Listening to Lady Edythe's leisurely discourse on horticulture, I wondered what verdict she and Mrs. Hopkins had reached behind the hedge.

"Yes, I've seen many a beautiful garden in the county," Lady Edythe was saying in an absent, preoccupied way, "but I believe that the Malverne gardens are the loveliest." She set her cup down and inclined her head toward me. "If you are not planning to return home immediately, Miss Atwood, why stay at that noisy inn? Why not stay here at Malverne Manor? I can see that you are quite taken with the place and it will be a pleasure to have a guest who truly appreciates the beauty of the manor. Besides, Sir Edmond might be returning from Edinburgh later in the day. You could then ask him about Amy. Will you stay, Miss Atwood? You could take the noon coach tomorrow."

I thanked her and said I'd be delighted to stay. "Would it be possible,"

I asked, "for Abner to take me to the inn so I may get my traveling bag? There are some things in it that I need."

It wasn't anything packed in the bag that interested me. I was determined to make a few inquiries at the inn. Lady Edythe was considering my request at length, no doubt guessing my motive, so I hurriedly added, "It isn't really necessary that I have the traveling bag, not if it's an inconvenience."

"No, no, not an inconvenience at all. Old Abner will be occupied this morning, but he will be able to oblige you the early part of the afternoon."

"Thank you, Lady Edythe. That's most kind of you."

"I will be gone all morning," she explained, "visiting Sir Edmond's constituents. You are welcome to enjoy the gardens until Old Abner is free to take you to the inn to collect your things.

"Only one thing, Miss Atwood," Lady Edythe added as she rose to leave. "As you wander about the garden, don't go near the pond. I would advise you to stay close to the house. We've had difficulty lately with the soft soil and loose stones at some places along the banks of the pond and . . . there was a drowning there not long ago, a servant girl. She was warned about the dangerous slippage and that the water is quite swift in some spots and deeper than it seems, particularly after a severe rain, but she ignored the warnings."

"I'll stay away from the pond," I promised. "Thank you for telling me, Lady Edythe."

We parted cordially, she hurrying off on her appointed rounds, I to stroll in the gardens.

I went first to the rose garden I'd seen from the dining room. The scent of roses filled the crystal-clear air. I walked idly along the wide expanse of lawn, stopping frequently to admire the roses, all of them white, ranging from a snow-white to a deep ivory, tinged with pink.

I'd come almost to the pond and, recalling Lady Edythe's admonition, kept my distance, although the pond did not appear the least hazardous.

There was a garden seat under a wide-spreading elm tree and I sat down, gazing at the sparkling pond in the distance where the water tumbled swiftly over rocks; then rushed down toward a small valley barely visible from where I sat. I listened to the small chirpings of birds all around me in the many trees. A lark in some distant tree lifted its voice over and over in a joyful song.

It was a pleasure just to sit in this peaceful, beautiful place. I could imagine what a lively, enchanting place the gardens were when Malverne Manor held its balls and other festivities. For now, I was content to sit in the hush of the garden. After yesterday's tiring journey in the coach and the subsequent strange experiences at Malverne Manor, not forgetting the troublesome rain-soaked walk to the manor, the momentary solitude was welcome.

In a little while, I got up, wanting to find the apple orchard that I'd seen from my bedroom window. As I made my way over the velvety lawns, my eyes traveled across the wide expanse of the manor house, the brick and stone walls tinted a pleasing rosy color by the morning sun, the large arched windows sparkling in the sunlight. I wondered where my room was located. I could not get my sense of location. The house was immense, with a long center structure and two wings.

I turned for a backward glance at the rose garden and, from the slight elevation where I now stood, I saw the pond more clearly, wider than it had seemed at first, rushing with surprising speed to the small valley in the distance. The thatch roof of a cottage, built close to the pond, showed through the trees.

I continued on my way, hoping to find the orchard, but I looked back once more, my eyes lingering on the little valley and the cottage, almost hidden in the grove of trees.

CHAPTER 4

I quickened my steps because, unexpectedly, a chilling breeze cut across my shoulders. The sun, as capricious as yesterday, hid behind puffed-up clouds and a cold wind scudded across the lawns.

Yesterday's fatigue and chilliness, resulting from my long journey by coach and the rain-soaked walk to the manor house, had left their mark. A quiet time in the sun, I hoped, would take care of that. The sun was surely hiding behind a cloud for only a short time.

I came now to a formal garden with neatly clipped hedges in classic arrangements. A weeping willow bowed its branches to a pool where goldfish flashed through the water. Daffodils and hyacinths bloomed in long, straight rows alongside the pool. From here I could see the apple orchard and I hastened in that direction.

I walked about in the orchard where the air was heavy with the fragrance of apple blossoms. I looked up into the trees, idling my way along, then glanced up at the windows of the house and spotted the Cream Lace Room. The lace curtains identified it immediately. My room, then, was not far from it. I decided, as an afterthought, to go to my room for my light wool shawl. The chill hadn't left me and I did not wish to come down with a cold.

I went forward to enter the house through a door directly ahead, then quickly stepped back and looked up at the windows again. Did I see movement at one of the windows? Yes, someone again walked past the windows of what I took to be my room.

I entered the house and looked around, trying to get my bearings. As I climbed the nearest flight of stairs, which I hoped were taking me in the right direction, I was conscious of how still the vast house was.

When I reached the top of the stairs, I again looked about, then proceeded, rather blindly, along the shadowy corridor. When I turned a corner and spotted the tall glass cabinet, I knew I was on the right track and hurried toward my room.

On entering, I stared in surprise. My luggage stood in the middle of the room.

I opened the bag and removed a dress, warmer than the one I was wearing. While I dressed, I considered the reason for the swift retrieval of my luggage. Were they so determined that I stay away from the Three Crowns Inn where I might ask some disturbing questions?

After a quick combing of my hair, I picked up the wool shawl, in case I should need it later, and hurried out of the house into the garden where the breeze had already calmed down and the sun had come out again.

I walked along, following the path of the rushing pond, remembering Lady Edythe's admonition about keeping a safe distance. I hadn't yet reached the small valley but, standing on a grassy rise and looking into the grove of trees near the pond, I could see the cottage distinctly.

I hurried now, my eyes on the cottage, which seemed deserted.

As I approached it, stepping along a weed-choked path a safe distance from the pond, I realized there was someone inside the cottage.

I was almost at the doorway when the door burst open and a tall young man, his hair the color of wheat, brightened by the sunlight, gave me a startled look.

"Well, well," he said, inclining his head and giving me a disarming smile which heightened his blond good looks. "It isn't often I open my door to such a lovely surprise," he continued, the smile lingering.

After I got over my astonishment at his sudden appearance, I explained that I was a visitor at Malverne Manor and was out for a stroll.

"And there is no better place for a stroll than the splendid luxuriant gardens of Malverne Manor," he said in a light, mocking voice.

He hadn't taken his eyes off me, his face alert, the eyes appraising me.

"Come in," he said, with a wide sweep of his arms. "I was just about to have my midmorning tea. I'd be delighted to have such pretty company."

"I'd like that very much. I am a bit tired from all that strolling."

"Well, all the more reason," he exclaimed, ushering me inside, "to come in, sit down, and have a cup of tea."

We drank our tea which was hot and lemony and he told me his name was Brian and that he was an artist. I gathered as much the minute I stepped into the sparsely furnished cottage. An easel was set up, there were paintings leaning against the chairs, and paint things were scattered about the room.

Answering his question about my presence at Malverne Manor, I explained that I was Claire Atwood and that I'd come to the manor to be a bridesmaid to my friend, Amy.

"Only, now it seems that Amy has disappeared," I said to him as he listened to my explanation, his attractive blond head bent attentively toward my chair, the large expressive brown eyes never leaving my face.

"I expected to find Amy at the manor in the midst of wedding preparations," I continued. "Now I am told that Amy never arrived at the manor."

I paused, stirring my tea absently, as he listened intently without speaking. "But I am sure," I said, "that Amy did arrive at Malverne Manor."

He moved abruptly in his chair. "You're *sure?*"

"What I mean is," I went on, realizing I must be cautious in what I said, "—I mean Amy wrote me from London where she was working, telling me she was going to marry Sir Edmond very soon and would I come to Malverne Manor because she wanted me to be her bridesmaid." I paused, conscious of his full attention, then said, "Only, now I'm told she never arrived at Malverne Manor."

"That's true. She didn't. I've been up at the manor house every single day lately and I would know if any guest was present at Malverne Manor. Lady Edythe said she was expecting a young lady named Amy, but she never came."

The room became very still. I turned my eyes from his intent gaze to the window, looking absently at the swaying branches of a lilac bush.

I wondered why I had hoped he'd tell me differently. But from the moment I saw him emerge unexpectedly from the cottage, I was hopeful he would tell me he'd seen Amy. I immediately thought of him as an ally, someone who would be able to help me unravel the puzzle concerning her.

But now it seemed he couldn't help me at all, and the mystery of Amy's disappearance only deepened because for some reason, which at the moment eluded me, I had the feeling that Brian knew more than he cared to tell. It was more than his evasive attitude.

When I looked up again, Brian was regarding me with a quizzical expression.

"It—it isn't possible," I murmured. "Amy must have been at Malverne Manor."

Again, that slightly speculative look crossed his face, but when he spoke, it was in a careless, offhand way. "Why are you so certain she's been here?" he asked.

Before answering him, I bore in mind that I did not know what his connection with Malverne Manor was, that he'd intentionally or unintentionally avoided telling me.

"Because of the letters she wrote to me from London," I replied, "telling me she was coming here to marry Sir Edmond. She'd hardly make up a story like that."

Nor did she make up the story of being at Malverne Manor, I thought, remembering all the bits of information about the house and gardens, not the sort of thing one might find in a booklet describing a manor house but, rather, things she'd observed personally.

But I told Brian none of that, nothing about letters I'd received from the manor. I could not entrust such disclosure to a complete stranger, not knowing yet how he fitted into the scheme of things.

"You shouldn't have taken those letters from London so literally," I heard Brian say. "Your friend, Amy, is probably infatuated with someone else by now and there's another letter waiting for you at home, no doubt, telling you about a new love she's found."

He leaned toward my chair and his voice became gentle and reassuring. "Finish your tea, Claire, and don't look so worried about Amy's adventures. Here you are, fretting about her and, for all you know, she's off somewhere having a marvelously romantic escapade which she'll tell you about in a letter."

He placed his hand lightly on my arm. "I'm sure there is a sensible, simple solution to your friend's disappearance, Claire, and I will help you solve this little mystery if you are worried about it."

"Would you?" I asked, my voice rising with expectation.

"Yes," he answered, laughing, "if you promise to drink your tea while it's still warm."

While I finished my tea, I was deciding whether it would be impertinent to ask what his connection was with Malverne Manor or wait for him to bring up that subject. He seemed to be more than a mere tenant at the cottage and said he was a frequent guest up at the house. His staying at the remote cottage was probably his choice so that he could work at his painting.

"I'm having a showing in a London gallery within two weeks," he said, breaking abruptly into my thoughts. He got up from his chair and began to move about the room, scrutinizing the pictures leaning against the few pieces of furniture in the one-room cottage. "I'm not satisfied. The collection lacks something," he muttered, squinting critically at one of the pictures which struck me as being quite good.

A self-portrait, I thought, would enhance his collection. The unusual combination of gold-blond hair and dark, luminous brown eyes was interesting enough, but there was also a careless sort of elegance about him, along with an engaging smile.

"The picture you're scowling at right now," I said, "looks fine to me."

Brian shook his head, his hands placed behind his back, the head lowered. He continued his critical appraisal of the landscape I'd praised.

"There's something missing," he mused, still studying the landscape. "I'm not at all pleased with the collection. I—" He stopped speaking and swung around to face me. His face lit up with that swift, disarming smile.

"My collection needs a portrait," he exclaimed. He flung his arms out wide then, in one quick stride, came over to my chair and looked down at me as if he'd just now seen me. "Yes," he repeated, "my collection needs a portrait."

"I was thinking exactly the same thing," I said, and before I had a chance to go on, he began to study my face, holding his head this way and that, stepping back and forth and gazing at me from various angles.

"That isn't what I meant," I said.

"Claire," he murmured with a pleased smile, "you are exactly what I've been waiting for."

"You can't be serious," I protested, and I could feel my face flush at his close scrutiny, his eyes roaming my hair, my eyes, my mouth.

"I am going to do your portrait," he announced, as if I hadn't spoken. "A portrait of you will light up my collection like a bright shaft of sunlight."

"Brian, don't talk nonsense," I said, as he continued to study me with an exultant smile. "I'm no beauty. I'm not even pretty."

"Pretty!" he jeered, throwing his arms out impatiently. "Who wants pretty pictures?" he said, laughing. Then his tone changed sharply and he was scolding me. "Don't go underestimating yourself so badly. I'd almost suspect you were fishing for a compliment."

He came over and touched my hair, smoothing it back slightly from my temples, then stepping back, nodding and smiling. "Claire, hasn't anyone ever told you that you are a beautiful woman? Not pretty, nothing so flimsy. You have marvelous hair. You surely know that. You must be secretly vain about it. How could you help it? Those gold highlights will come out beautifully in the portrait." He stepped forward again, his face close to mine, and I could feel the blood rushing to my face once more.

"Stop talking flattering nonsense," I said to him, but he only shook his head and smiled.

"No, not flattery, Claire. I'm banking on your portrait being the winner in my collection." He was back to his intent appraisal of my face. "The eyes are good," he said with a knowing nod. "Like the sea at dawn. An interesting gray, no blue, no green to blur the purity of the color. Yes, the eyes are good. A clear, interesting gray with just the right touch of innocence."

I made another showing of protest but in vain. The next minute he was snatching up easel and paintbox and waving me out to a sunny spot in the garden behind the cottage.

"The light here is very good this time of day," he explained in a brisk businesslike tone, waving me to a wicker chair where he wanted me to sit.

My protests went unheeded; not even when I told him that I would be leaving Malverne Manor at noon the next day, did he pay any attention to my arguments.

I decided finally to indulge him. Perhaps an hour in each other's company and he might come around to explaining his association with Malverne Manor and why Lady Edythe should consider him worthy of those frequent visits up to the manor; then he might casually say something that would prove valuable in my search concerning Amy. I relaxed into the wicker chair, turning my head this way and that at his bidding while he made marks on the canvas before him.

"Lady Edythe won't be back until lunchtime," Brian said after a silent interval during which time he'd concentrated on my face and made occasional jottings on the canvas. "You won't be missed till then. That gives us more than an hour. And don't talk about leaving Malverne Manor tomorrow. I'll need all of the two weeks to do the portrait."

"No, Lady Edythe was quite definite. Abner is taking me to the Three

Crowns Inn in time to make the noon coach tomorrow. Today's sitting will be less than an hour long. You know how busy Lady Edythe is with the election campaign. I don't wish to keep her waiting by being late for lunch."

"Yes, she's been gallivanting all over the county because of that election business for Sir Edmond. Lady Edythe will be so preoccupied visiting Sir Edmond's constituents, she won't even be aware of your presence at the manor, so there's no need for you to rush off tomorrow."

I waited for him to offer some explanation concerning his association with Lady Edythe, but when he still refused to take the initiative, I asked, "How long have you known Lady Edythe?"

He threw his head back and laughed as if I'd told him a rollicking joke. "I've known her for two years," he answered, the uproarious laughter sliding into an amused grin. "Just between you and me," he added with a broad wink, "I'm not that fond of the old girl." He shrugged and grinned once more. "Oh, she's just fine in some respects but—oh, by the way, Claire, would you do me a great favor and not mention my presence at the cottage to anyone up at the house. Lady Edythe and Mrs. Hopkins think I'm still in London. If either of those ladies should learn that I'm back, they'll dream up all sorts of diversions for me, and I came to the cottage to get my collection in shape for the gallery showing. Lady Edythe would begin dragging me around the county on that infernal campaigning and I'll get no painting done." He paused in his sketching and gave me a pleading look. "Please don't give me away. Nobody ever comes to this abandoned cottage, and if you say nothing, I'll have my collection ready in time."

"If you wish," I agreed. "But how, then, will you help me with the puzzling disappearance of Amy? And won't they suspect if they see me going in the direction of the cottage?"

"No, they'll figure you're simply out for a stroll and they have no reason to believe I'm at the cottage. But don't worry about my helping you. You can be sure of that. What's more, Lady Edythe's not knowing I'm back from London will be to our advantage. Something tells me she wouldn't co-operate in our digging into this business of your lost friend, not if your friend, Amy, seemed to have some claim on Sir Edmond. This county election means even more to Lady Edythe than it does to Sir Edmond. Believe me, Lady Edythe wouldn't tolerate any obstacle to Sir Edmond's election victory, and the old girl might have considered Amy an obstacle, although I don't see how this Amy could have claimed she and Sir Edmond were about to be married. He's more or less promised to a young lady living nearby."

"Yes, I know. Lady Edythe mentioned a Miss Pamela Wickham."

"Oh, she's already informed you, has she?" He paused in his sketching and gave me a knowing smile. "Let's go about our sleuthing in secret. We've got ourselves a formidable antagonist in Lady Edythe. And from what I've heard here and there, Sir Edmond has a way of getting himself into awkward situations with young ladies. Amy might have been another awkward situation and Lady Edythe wouldn't want that advertised now, with the county election in full swing."

"But you will help me?" I asked. "You don't think I'm making a fuss about nothing?"

He regarded me silently for a moment then said, "You can count on it. I'll do everything I can."

After that he became absorbed in sketching out the portrait and I sat quietly, wishing he'd stop soon because I was getting a crick in my neck.

When I reminded him that I had to leave, he walked with me a short distance. "This is as far as I'll go, Claire. I don't want anyone from the house to see me. And don't forget your promise," he called to me as I walked away. "It's our secret."

"It's our secret," I called back, then hurried away toward the house.

I found a sunny spot in the rose garden where I could be easily found by Mrs. Hopkins when she came to fetch me for lunch. I sat down in a garden seat which had a convenient back rest. I leaned back and closed my eyes. The crick in my neck hadn't eased and I was disappointed that the tiredness and chills of the previous day hadn't dissipated. The sun on my face and shoulders felt comforting, though, and I sat quietly, almost dozing, hopeful that by lunchtime the lingering discomfort would leave me.

I was roused from my drowsiness when I heard someone approaching.

It was Mrs. Hopkins to tell me it was lunchtime and that Lady Edythe was awaiting me on the terrace where lunch would be served.

After my short interval of relaxation in the sunny garden, I felt better, the chill almost gone, so I was surprised when Lady Edythe's first words were that I appeared unwell.

"Getting caught in that wind and rain yesterday, Miss Atwood, has left its mark," she said, giving me a critical once-over. "The long coach journey has evidently worn you down a bit."

"I'm just a trifle tired, that's all."

"You look flushed. I hope you do not become ill."

All through lunch I caught Lady Edythe's covert glances, and although I had no appetite, I ate heartily, to prove I was not about to become ill.

"It might be advisable, Miss Atwood," Lady Edythe said as we came to the end of our meal, "that you go to your room after lunch and rest. There's a stiff breeze blowing about the gardens. It's not felt here on the terrace because it is sheltered, but strolling about in the open might cause you more discomfort."

"I feel fine," I repeated, making a show of liking the sweet, a wedge of peach pie which, under different circumstances, I would have truly enjoyed. The thought now came to me that I'd said nothing to her about my luggage having been brought up from the inn.

"Thank you for having my luggage brought up," I said. "I appreciate being spared the trip."

Lady Edythe smiled. "I noticed that you were wearing a different dress, Miss Atwood, so I assumed you'd found your travel bag in your room."

"Yes, I went up to my room shortly after breakfast. While I was strolling in the garden, a cool wind came up and I went to my room for my wool shawl. With the luggage there, I was able to change to a dress more suitable for the cool weather."

"I'm pleased that it turned out to be convenient for you, Miss Atwood," Lady Edythe said, inclining her head with a gracious smile. "Now you take my advice and rest, so you don't come down with some indisposition."

"I might lie down for a while. When is Sir Edmond expected to arrive at the manor?"

There was a sharp silence before she replied. She rose from her chair and her voice became crisp, a little too high-pitched. "I don't know when to expect him, Miss Atwood. Now I must be on my way. No, no, don't get up. Finish your coffee." She flashed a quick smile and hurried away.

I remained on the sheltered terrace where the sun felt warm on my back and where there was no wind. I gazed past the low stone balustrade that circled the terrace. The wide sweep of verdant lawn made an appealing view for outdoor dining. The grand scope of the gardens on this side of the house was gentled by small flower beds of tulips and hyacinth. There was a little duck pond nearby and I watched the ducks skim across the water, then waddle out and sit on the grass.

My attention was drawn to a high brick wall past the duck pond. The brick wall probably enclosed the kitchen garden; I presumed correctly because I then saw Mrs. Hopkins, with a basket on her arm, unlatch a gate in the high wall and enter. She was soon followed by a man and, judging from his stooped, doddering walk, it would be Old Abner whom I hadn't met yet.

Abner had left the gate open and I decided to while away a few minutes in the kitchen garden. I didn't think Mrs. Hopkins would mind. But as I approached the gate in the brick wall, I heard loud voices and, thinking an argument was raging, I started to back away when I remembered that Old Abner was quite deaf, and I then realized that the conversation was merely loud not hostile.

Abner was shouting in his shrill voice, informing Mrs. Hopkins that the grafting on some trees in the orchard turned out quite successfully and that Sir Edmond would be quite pleased. Mrs. Hopkins, in reply, shouted back that yes, Sir Edmond would be pleased. There was a lull after that and I called to Mrs. Hopkins from the open gate, asking if she'd mind if I came inside.

She glanced up from a luxuriant bean patch where she was snapping off beans and dropping them into the basket. She seemed pleased to see me and waved me inside, then, in a clear loud voice, she introduced me to Old Abner who poked his wrinkled old face forward to catch my name which had to be repeated.

"Pleasure t' meet 'ee," he then shouted, peering at me with faded blue eyes. He grinned at me, displaying a mouth almost toothless. "Pleasure t' have 'ee for a guest. I wuz a-tellin' Mrs. Hopkins 'ere thut the graftin' them apple trees turned out right. When Sir Edmond comes——"

He seemed ready to launch into a lengthy chat on this subject, but Mrs. Hopkins adroitly stepped in and briskly dismissed the old man, reminding him in a loud, authoritative voice that Lady Edythe was probably waiting for him, so he'd better hurry to the stable and get the chaise ready.

The old man nodded his grizzled head to indicate he understood, then shambled away obediently.

If the apple orchard was Old Abner's proud domain, then the kitchen garden was Mrs. Hopkins'. She was delighted to have the opportunity to give me a guided tour of the vegetable garden, which was a showy success. There were neat rows of beets, carrots, and parsnips, with not a weed in sight. We walked along the flourishing rows of vegetables and came to a corner of the garden where unfamiliar plants grew, and I recalled Lady Edythe's remark about Mrs. Hopkins' herb garden.

"So this is your herb garden," I said. "Lady Edythe mentioned it."

"Oh, she spoke of it?" Mrs. Hopkins said. "Yes, Lady Edythe is rather partial to an herb tea I sometimes make for her when she's been overdoing and can't sleep."

Listening to her, I became aware for the second time, particularly since I'd just heard Old Abner speak, that Mrs. Hopkins did not have the servant's provincial speech. I remembered her telling me yesterday

that she'd been at Malverne Manor for seven years. Then she'd probably come here with Lady Edythe. Had Mrs. Hopkins always been a servant, I wondered.

"Lady Edythe said you were feeling a bit out of sorts," Mrs. Hopkins
said, and I assured her I was only a bit fatigued from the long coach
ride and had come down with a slight chill.

She bobbed her head knowingly. "Come," she urged, stepping carefully along the narrow rows. "I will point out some of the herbs to you.
I use them in cooking and for medicinal purposes," she explained with
an air of authority.

We moved slowly between meticulously weeded rows while she identified the various herbs. "That row," she indicated, "the little plants
that look like parsley, that is chervil. Gives a nice delicate flavor to my
soups. The row next to it is fennel which I use in preparing fish. There,
in the corner, is lady's bedstraw and the tiny row is tansy. Over here,"
she continued, "is bergamot mint. Lady Edythe sometimes likes a refreshing cup of bergamot mint tea."

She went on, telling me how she made chivry butter with chervil and
burnet, then she returned to the green-bean patch where she completed
her chore of picking the green beans, permitting me to help her.

"Come into the kitchen, Miss Atwood, if you have nothing else to
occupy you at the moment," she suggested. "There's a chilling wind
blowing about the garden today and you appear to be a bit indisposed.
You will find the kitchen quite comfortable, not too warm, since I did
the baking early this morning."

I accepted her offer, hopeful that this might be Mrs. Hopkins' way
of letting me know that she was willing to have a little gossipy visit with
me and tell me something about Amy or something about Malverne
Manor, anything that might be helpful to me.

The kitchen we entered was a large, pleasant room. The afternoon
sun streamed through the wide open windows that faced the kitchen
garden. A long, polished trestle table stood in the middle of the room
and bright-colored mats were placed on the slate floor all around the
long table. A huge stone fireplace and brick oven dominated one wall;
an oak sideboard, displaying flower-sprigged dishes, covered most of
another wall.

When I remarked to Mrs. Hopkins about the homey attractiveness of
the kitchen, she complacently folded her arms over her plump bosom.
"Ah, yes," she murmured. "It is my pride and joy. But then, I am most
fond of Malverne Manor." She placed a chair for me near the table and
began to bustle about, explaining that she would do the green beans

first, then she'd make the lemon sauce for the currant cake she'd baked that morning. "For teatime," she explained.

At first we chatted amiably about cooking and baking, a subject, I admitted, I knew very little about and about which Mrs. Hopkins obviously knew a great deal. After a while I decided that I should make some mention of Amy. My complete avoidance of the subject would be as unwise as saying too much.

"If my friend, Amy, had ever come to Malverne Manor," I said, observing a flash of alertness in Mrs. Hopkins' pleasant face, and feeling a twinge of conscience that I had to be devious, "she would have really enjoyed the gardens. Amy was particularly fond of beautiful gardens."

As if my finally broaching the touchy subject had relieved Mrs. Hopkins of a suspenseful anticipation, she uttered a small sigh then said, "Yes, Lady Edythe mentioned the matter to me, that your friend from London, the girl from the teashop, was to be a guest at Malverne Manor. Strange how she changed her mind about the visit," she murmured, her eyes fixed on the lemon sauce she was whipping vigorously in a bowl. After a few more turns of the spoon, she glanced up. "What caused her to change her plans?"

"Well, Amy is a rather impulsive, adventurous girl," I said, turning my face aside to admire the dishes displayed on the sideboard because I didn't trust the expression she might read on my face. "I'm sure that when I return home there'll be a letter from Amy, explaining her whereabouts."

Now that I was more certain of the expression on my face, I turned around to meet Mrs. Hopkins' thoughtful gaze. "Yes," she said, "that's how it will probably turn out. You have no reason to concern yourself, Miss Atwood," she consoled me, then dropped the subject with "You will like the currant cake I made for teatime. The tart lemon sauce dresses it up nicely."

The remainder of the visit went smoothly enough. Amy was dismissed from the conversation. Sir Edmond was never mentioned. Mrs. Hopkins did most of the talking—about Lady Edythe's election campaigning, about the fine condition of the Malverne orchards, about Old Abner's pride concerning the orchard and what a pity the old man's eyesight and hearing should be so impaired. All safe topics. I thought she might make some reference to other servants and what happened to them. For a place the size of Malverne Manor, there was a conspicuous absence of servants. I rather expected her to make some comment about the servant girl who'd drowned recently in the pond. But Mrs. Hopkins remained mum on those topics. I was convinced that if I took the initiative on any touchy subject, my questions wouldn't go answered.

It soon became clear that if Mrs. Hopkins had an ulterior motive when she invited me into her kitchen, it was not because she wished to tell me anything, but, rather, that she'd hoped I would tell her something. Since our mutual reluctance to confide in each other reached an impasse, I was soon thanking her for the pleasant little visit and I left the kitchen.

It might have been the contrast between the kitchen, which was, perhaps, warmer than I thought, and the sharp breeze that once again whipped across the lawns, but I soon became uncomfortable. I decided to take Lady Edythe's advice and went up to my room to lie down for a while.

In a short time I felt so cold lying on the bed, I had to get up and put an extra cover over me. I could not drift off to sleep. The dismaying possibility that I might become ill only made me more restless.

I tossed and fidgeted but could not catch even the briefest of naps. The chills increased and, later, I was dimly aware that it was now almost teatime, but I did not care to go downstairs. A cup of hot tea would have been nice, but moving off the bed seemed like too much effort.

I knew my restlessness had worsened because a light rap on my door startled me. It was Mrs. Hopkins, inquiring if I was coming down to tea, that Lady Edythe was waiting.

When I told her I didn't feel up to it, she immediately promised to bring me some hot tea and I did not refuse the offer.

I was beginning to think she'd gone back on her promise because I waited a long time, but, finally, she bustled in with the tea and some of the currant cake she'd mentioned.

"I made you some of my special herb tea," she explained, "the kind I make for Lady Edythe when she's out of sorts and can't sleep. Now you drink it all up," she urged like a conscientious nanny, "and you eat every bit of the currant cake with lemon sauce. You will see that a little bit of nourishment and the soothing herb tea will do you wonderfully good. By dinnertime you will be chipper and bright-eyed after catching a nap."

She hurried out, explaining she was needed downstairs. I took a bite of the currant cake but found the lemon sauce too tart for my taste, almost sour, and put it aside. The tea had a bitter taste which I supposed was typical of herb tea, but it was hot and, in an odd sort of way, refreshing, so I drank it all.

After my unsuccessful attempts at sleep, I was astonished that the herb tea should relax me so quickly. A drowsiness came over me as soon as I placed the empty cup on the bedside table. The drowsiness deepened at an alarming speed into a heavy-headed grogginess. My head nodded and trying to keep it erect, or to keep my eyes open, was futile. When I tried to move my arm to a more comfortable position, I discovered I could barely lift it. I shifted my body into a more upright posture, struggling against the waves of sluggishness and, where a while ago I'd been troubled by chills, the room now seemed stuffy.

I tried to force my body to the edge of the bed so that I might get up and open a window for a breath of fresh air. The room had become stifling.

When I tried to move my legs off the bed, I couldn't manage them. They were leaden. The room began to spin; my head fell back on the pillow. When I opened my eyes slightly, the room was shrouded in swirls of gray. As I watched helplessly, the grayness turned to black then the blackness, like a smothering wool shawl, fell over me, and all sensation was gone.

When I opened my eyes again, it seemed to be much later. I turned my head slowly on the pillow and the small clock on the bedside table wavered and blurred before my eyes. I waited until the hands of the clock finally steadied themselves and I could see it was almost eight-thirty. I wondered dazedly whether it was the same day.

The drugged sleep, though lifting slightly, was still pulling me down. I turned my eyes back to the bedside table. What if I'd eaten the currant cake also? I remembered how sour the lemon sauce had tasted.

I was able to lift my legs but they moved with a leaden slowness. I tried to raise my arms. They barely moved off the bedcovers then dropped back limply.

Then I heard it again. The voices.

That was what had jarred me out of the sluggish sleep. Through the murky clouds of the drugged sleep that was now tapering off, I'd heard a loud, shrill voice, then an answering voice.

I heard it again, more plainly, and realized gradually that it was the blaring voice of Old Abner, shouting to someone who now answered the deaf old man in a loud, clear tone. The loud voices seemed to be coming from the orchard, directly beneath my windows.

Even with the windows closed, Old Abner's shrieking, deaf-man's shout penetrated into the room. The other voice was also raised so that the old man could hear.

The other voice. Sir Edmond's?

With an effort that astonished me, I forced my body into a sitting position and listened, thrusting my head forward, working my brain through the grogginess that still bound me. The other voice definitely was a man's and he was shouting to Old Abner that he was pleased the orchard was doing so well.

I started to grope my way out of the bed so I could pull a window open and call for help. My brain refused to function at my bidding and my legs wouldn't move. I lunged forward awkwardly, but with results, and after slipping to the floor, I pulled myself to a kneeling position and, finally, was able to crawl to the window.

I snatched at the window latch. My fingers were limp, useless. By placing one hand firmly over the other and pressing down, I could feel the latch slowly turning. Between my strugglings with the latch, I made futile attempts at rapping on the window glass, but my feeble efforts made practically no sound.

As I frantically worked the latch, I could still hear snatches of the loud conversation, the younger voice explaining to Old Abner that he had to leave now because of an urgent appointment, but he'd be back at the manor tomorrow, around five.

"Then, t'morra, Sir Edmond, 'ee be sure t' take a good look at the trees near the pond," Old Abner shouted and, to my dismay, while my clumsy, limp fingers still struggled with the tight window latch, I saw that the two men were now walking away from the house.

I finally unhooked the latch and pushed the window open. I opened my mouth to call out, but no words would come, only a faint, labored whisper. I tried to bang on the window glass, but my hand seemed lifeless.

Gripping the window sill for support, I forced one more feeble call for help from the partly open window. The sound I made was no more than a shaky whisper, but Sir Edmond turned around abruptly and my heart leaped. I thought he'd heard me. But no, he was merely gazing about, not even looking at the house. The next moment he was out of sight and, soon, Old Abner, trailing after him, couldn't be seen either.

I leaned my head wearily against the window. I didn't have the energy or inclination to return to the bed, but remained in the exhausted, slumped position against the window ledge.

After a while the stillness of the room was broken by the sound of footsteps in the hallway. I could feel my body thrust itself into an upright position and with a strength and speed that instinct commanded, I tugged at the window latch. I pulled the telltale open window shut then groped my way to the bed.

I'd just managed to pull the cover over me when my bedroom door opened quietly.

CHAPTER 5

I opened my eyes a tiny slit and saw that it was Lady Edythe entering the room, carrying a tray on which stood a cup and teapot.

I shut my eyes, hoping she would leave if she thought I was still asleep. I heard the rustle of her skirt and the clatter of teapot and cup as she approached the bed and placed the tray on the bedside table. I could now feel her breath on my face as she leaned over me, and when she did not move away, I opened my eyes.

She drew back into an upright position and stared at me for a moment. "Feeling better, Miss Atwood?" she inquired with a smile. "You seem improved. Your color is much better."

Looking up at her, I became aware that the drug was fast wearing off. That whiff of cool air at the window probably helped, too. Lady Edythe's face looming over me was quite distinct. I turned my head to look at the clock and, doing so, I discovered that my head moved more freely on the pillow.

"It's almost nine o'clock," I said in a voice that was beginning to sound normal. I knew very well it was about that time since I'd seen the clock a short time ago but I felt it was the safest opening remark.

"Yes, you've slept almost five hours. I was in twice to see if you were resting and you were sleeping quite soundly." She nodded toward the teapot. "I brought you more of Mrs. Hopkins' herb tea. You might want to eat your currant cake now with the tea. I can see that you've already had a fine sleep from the herb tea. It could very well be repeated. Then you will sleep well all night."

"Yes, the herb tea certainly did its work," I said, avoiding her eyes. "You said Sir Edmond was to arrive at the manor today," I added, turning to look at her. "When might I speak with him?"

"I'm sorry to have to tell you this, Miss Atwood, but Sir Edmond did not arrive today. I received a message informing me his business engagements in Edinburgh will delay his return to Malverne Manor by two weeks."

"Two weeks?" I repeated, turning my eyes away from her probing gaze. "I wish Sir Edmond had returned to the manor for even a short time," I went on, injecting the correct surprise and disappointment into my voice. "There are so many questions I would have liked to ask him."

"As I've mentioned to you before, Miss Atwood," Lady Edythe said with rising asperity, "the place to ask questions is in London, not here. The person to question is Amy, not Sir Edmond."

"Two whole weeks," I murmured, gazing absently at the windows. "How unfortunate that I shall miss seeing Sir Edmond."

"It couldn't be helped," Lady Edythe said, her tone brisk. I turned to look at her. She was reaching for the teapot to pour me another cup of Mrs. Hopkins' brew.

"Lady Edythe," I said, "would it be an imposition—that is, could Mrs. Hopkins serve me a light supper? After that sound sleep, I feel much improved. I've become quite hungry. Some nourishment would be more helpful toward a good night's sleep than the tea. Then, in the morning I would be truly fit for traveling."

I could see her eyes widen and hear her breath quicken at the news that I would leave the manor the next morning.

"Then you feel well enough to leave tomorrow morning?" she asked, the smile permeating her voice.

"Yes, I feel much better and have no chills," I said, sitting up in bed which I was now able to do. "I'd appreciate a light supper," I said, feeling quite secure the food would not contain any of Mrs. Hopkins' additives. If I intended to leave the following morning, I was no longer a threat. There'd be no reason to keep me hidden, under sedation, while Sir Edmond was at the manor.

"Why, certainly, you may have a light supper," Lady Edythe exclaimed, unable to hide the enthusiasm and relief in her voice. She picked up the tray with quick, eager fingers, placed the currant cake on it, and hurried to the door. "I'll have Mrs. Hopkins bring you some supper immediately," she said from the doorway.

When she was gone, I sat up in bed awhile longer. The room no longer swam before me. I moved my arms and legs about on the bed and they moved easily. I swung my legs to the floor and found I could stand, with only a hint of dizziness. Slowly, I walked to the window and looked out at the gathering darkness. Had I dreamt that I saw Sir Edmond in the orchard, heard him say he was returning to the manor the next day around five o'clock? No, that was real. I'd seen him—not very well because it was getting dark and Mrs. Hopkins' brew further dimmed my vision, but I'd overheard the conversation between Sir Edmond and Old Abner.

I went into the small bath, washed my hands, and splashed cold water on my face. I'd just returned to the bedroom when Mrs. Hopkins entered, beaming, carrying a tray.

"Ah, I am so delighted that you are feeling better," she exclaimed, setting the tray down, darting a side glance my way.

"Yes, I do feel better, but that was rather strong medicine, wasn't it?"

"No, no," she assured me as she bustled about, pulling the small table away from the wall and setting down my supper. "The tea is the way I always make it, miss. How it affects the person has much to do with the condition of the one drinking it. You see, miss," she explained, "you were all tuckered out, perhaps had not slept well the night before, so the herb tea went to your head with dispatch." She bobbed her head gleefully. "But you slept well and feel improved. It all worked out very well, did it not?"

"Yes, it worked out very well," I said, then, after a moment's thought, added, "For a while, though, I was afraid the sound sleep might have caused me to miss meeting Sir Edmond if he should return to the manor and then be on his way again. But Lady Edythe has told me that Sir Edmond did not arrive at the manor after all."

"That is true, miss," she said. "I suppose it is a disappointment to you, knowing you wished to speak with him about your friend." She shrugged and gave me a cheery smile. "But it couldn't be helped, miss. Lady Edythe said she received a message that the master would be delayed." She raised the silver cover off a succulent leg of roast chicken, filling the room with a delicious aroma. "Now you eat the supper I warmed up for you," she coaxed, "so you will be fit for traveling tomorrow."

I took my place at the table, eyeing the tasty-looking chicken, the warm, buttery rolls, the fresh green beans.

"Looks lovely," I said as I started to eat. "Thank you for taking the trouble, Mrs. Hopkins."

She lingered at the door, repeating that she was sorry I would be leaving the next day.

I thoroughly enjoyed the supper. There was no off-taste and I ate everything, down to the sweet, a creamy bread pudding with almonds.

While I ate, rambling thoughts of Sir Edmond threaded in and out of my head. Although I'd heard him plainly, I hadn't really seen him, no more than a blurred shadow. Was he young? He walked like a young person. His voice sounded strong and virile. But I couldn't be sure, not with the way my brain was boggled by that potent herb tea.

Afterward, when Mrs. Hopkins cleared away the dishes and I stood at the window for a while, I planned my strategy for the following day. I would definitely be leaving the manor in the morning. Lady Edythe would see to that. If possible, I would slip down to the cottage after breakfast to see Brian. What would I say to him? I would tell him only that I was leaving the manor. After that, what else I confided, would depend upon what he would tell me. If in the course of our conversation, I felt he was in collusion with someone at the manor, I wouldn't tell him I was staying at the Three Crowns Inn.

I wondered fleetingly whether Brian was related to anyone at the manor and it struck me suddenly that it was Mrs. Hopkins whom he resembled slightly—the roundish face, the pink fleshiness. Even the bright, sunny smiles were similar somehow. But then I began to see a slight resemblance to Lady Edythe, too. Nothing in particular, only a vague similarity. I stopped my guessing game when I realized I was so intent on knowing Brian's association with Malverne Manor that if I met Sir Edmond, I would see a resemblance there, too.

I turned my attention to the next day's plans. Shortly before five o'clock then, I would once more walk up the road from the inn to Malverne Manor. The particulars of how I would gain access to Sir Edmond escaped me for the moment, but by morning that part of my strategy would work itself out in my mind.

As I lay in bed, I started to consider various ways I might manage a meeting with Sir Edmond. This time I did not want to be turned away from the door. I didn't get far with my planning. Sleep—natural, this time—soon took over.

When I came to breakfast the next morning, Lady Edythe greeted me with a cordial smile, remarking about my radiant good health.

I assured her I felt fine and had slept well the past night, which was true.

"Well, you certainly look refreshed, Miss Atwood," she said, showing me to a chair at the table. We were having breakfast again in the cheery green and white oval room facing the rose garden.

The morning was warm, not breezy like the day before. Lady Edythe wore a lighter morning dress, pale-gray silk, which complemented the silver-white hair. Glancing at her across the table, I again thought of how much she looked like the lady of the manor. Only she wasn't that actually. This was Sir Edmond's property.

Amy would have been the lady of the manor.

The prospect of my departure from the manor enlivened Lady Edythe's spirits. Cheerfulness streaked through her conversation. There were flashes of good humor, and lively, entertaining tidbits about her encounters with Sir Edmond's constituents as she went about the county on her daily visits.

I tried to keep my mind on her sprightly talk, but my thoughts were suddenly moving along totally unexpected lines. I was gazing idly at the pleasant sunlit oval room with its honey-oak furnishings, then turned to look at the rose garden beyond the wide windows and at the pond shimmering in the distance.

I couldn't define my feelings. It was more than the pleasure of having breakfast in such delightful surroundings. There was an undertone of sadness. I realized gradually that after having been a guest—of sorts—at Malverne Manor for only a short time, I'd come to love the place and was going to miss it.

An unreasonable reaction. Now that Amy was no longer a part of it, Malverne Manor should have meant nothing to me.

I was convinced that Amy was, indeed, no longer a part of Malverne Manor. I refused to believe she was dead. I was not ready to accept that. But I was reasonably certain she was not in the manor house.

Before coming to breakfast, I'd searched the upstairs halls, rapping on doors, looking into empty rooms. I soon gave up the search. If Amy was somewhere in the vast house—which I now doubted—she was well-hidden.

Malverne Manor had no sentimental association for me. But as much as I tried to put aside my unreasonable attachment to it, the lovely sweep of the Malverne gardens skimmed through my mind's eye—the apple orchard, the morning sun touching the stone and brick walls of the manor house. I remembered every detail of the drawing room.

My strange reaction bewildered me. I was sad because I would never see Malverne Manor again. Except perhaps for a short while if I should be successful in meeting Sir Edmond.

Lady Edythe's voice broke through my skittering, confusing thoughts. I caught only the last part of her conversation.

"The coach doesn't leave the inn until noon," she was saying, "so you have three hours to rest up before your journey, Miss Atwood. You might wish to sit in the rose garden. It's a beautiful sunny day; no sharp gusts of wind like yesterday."

"I slept so well last night, I have no need to rest. I believe I will walk about in the gardens. Is Abner taking me to the inn?"

"No, he will be occupied. He is taking me to Wickham Place directly after breakfast. Mrs. Hopkins has graciously consented to take you to the inn. She will be busy in the kitchen the early part of the morning, but she will be free around eleven o'clock."

I thanked her, hoping I didn't betray my disappointment at this arrangement. I'd expected to ride with Old Abner, hoping the old man would let slip some vital information. A more disturbing thought crossed my mind. Was Mrs. Hopkins going to linger at the inn until she saw me safely aboard the coach which I had no intention of boarding? I wondered how I would manage, then put the worry aside. I'd deal with that problem when the time came. For the present, since I had about three hours, I would go to the cottage.

I encountered no difficulty about going unnoticed. Lady Edythe left with Old Abner immediately after breakfast. Mrs. Hopkins was not about, busy in the kitchen, probably, as Lady Edythe had indicated.

At first, I hurried. Soon I found myself stopping to look and listen, knowing that it was all farewell. Everything. The morning sun casting a warm, rosy glow on the stone and brick walls of the lovely manor house. The lushness of the lawns as they swept down to the pond. The flutter of bird wings in the many trees. As I continued toward the cottage, I kept looking about, taking it all in, reminding myself it was an unreasonable attachment yet unable to help feeling as I did.

Brian must have seen me through the cottage window because he was waiting for me in the doorway, the sun brightening the blondness of his hair. He smiled and came swiftly toward me.

"I was worried that you wouldn't come," he said as we entered the cottage. He swung me lightly at arm's length. "Claire, you look even more fetching than you did yesterday."

"There you go," I bantered. "More of that extravagant flattery."

"It isn't flattery," he corrected me good-naturedly. "Oh, it will be a marvelous portrait," he rushed on. He was snatching up things to be carried outdoors for the portrait sitting and I put a detaining hand on his arm.

"No, Brian, I'm sorry. There will be no portrait."

He wheeled about, dropping the brushes from his hand. "What do you mean? You are really leaving the manor?"

"Yes. Mrs. Hopkins is taking me to the inn for the noon coach departure."

"Claire, you can't. You simply cannot do that." His voice rose; his face clouded from its sunny appearance a moment ago.

He stood motionless, gazing at me in silence, then asked in a quiet voice, "Does that mean you will abandon your search into Amy's disappearance?"

"No, but I will have to alter my plan," I replied and he jerked his head back, regarding me with a wary expression.

Oh, he knows something, I thought, but for some reason he is not divulging what he knows, at least, not yet. I could see the muscles of his face contract, his mouth compress into a tight line as if he were weighing in his mind what he should say, if anything at all. Something was holding him back. He seemed to be on the brink of telling me something then withdrawing for some inner reason. I wondered whether in some way Lady Edythe had some hold on him. Or was it Sir Edmond he seemed to be protecting? Yet, looking at him then, I was again reminded of his slight resemblance to Mrs. Hopkins.

"What do you mean, alter your plan?" he asked finally.

"My plan to find out what happened to Amy."

He laughed suddenly and said in a light, careless tone, "Oh, Claire, you're making too much of it." He paused, placed his hand gently on my shoulder, and looked into my face. "Well, I'm glad you've decided to continue your search for Amy because you'd got my curiosity up. We'll make arrangements—you and I—we'll meet in London and begin our search from there."

He became silent again, his face betraying his unease. We were standing in the middle of the room, he still holding the palette in his hand, I still holding the paintbox he'd asked me to take outdoors.

I placed the paintbox on the table. "There's no point, of course, working on the portrait. I must return to the house to pack. As for meeting you in London, Brian, I just don't know."

He remained standing in the center of the room, lost in thought, and as I started to walk toward the door, he sprang into action and thrust out his arm, holding me back.

"Claire, you can't simply walk out of my life like that." He held me tightly by the arm and when I glanced up into his face, his eyes held mine with an imploring look. "Please don't laugh at me, Claire," he continued, "but you can't rush away with the chance I might never see you again." His face was close to mine and his voice dropped to a low, urgent whisper. "Will I never see you again? Claire, I'm not thinking of the portrait. I'll have the showing without it. And don't talk to me about flattery and that I'm talking nonsense. You may laugh at me if you like, but I've fallen in love with you." He was looking into my face, his hand tightening around my arm.

I moved out of his firm hold and stepped outdoors. "I expect we'll see each other again, Brian. But I must hurry back. It's a long walk to the house from the cottage."

After going a short distance, I looked back when I heard him shout from the doorway.

"Stop chasing about in circles, Claire. You're wasting time trying to track down your friend. Forget about her. Think of us. And I'm going to do that portrait, too. You aren't going to walk out of my life quite that easily."

Walking back to the house, I caught myself smiling. Despite all the worrisome thoughts about Amy that went in and out of my head, Brian's sudden heated declaration of love brought an amused smile when I compared Brian's instant and undying ardor to the plodding courtship that Walter Binson and I had trod these past two years.

I thought of Walter, toiling away diligently in the chemist's shop, waiting for me so that we might resume our sedate courtship until we finally changed that into a sedate marriage.

Did Walter Binson ever tell me my eyes were gray like the sea at dawn? Or that I looked even more fetching today than I did yesterday? Dear, hard-working Walter. I often said to him, much to his embarrassment, that he should marry the Milkins girl, that she'd always been sweet on him, and he shouldn't think he had to marry me just because he worked in my father's shop.

"I wish you didn't make light of serious matters," Walter would say. "As for the shop," he would add, "you and I will make a real success of it when we are married."

No, if Walter ever thought my eyes looked like the color of the sea at dawn, he kept that information to himself. "What I like about you, Claire," he'd often told me, "is that you're sensible." "Hasn't anyone ever told you that you're a beautiful woman?" Brian had asked.

I smiled, remembering the expression on Brian's face when he shouted his ultimatum from the cottage doorway, that I wasn't going to walk out of his life quite that easily. Even taken as flattery, Brian's words weren't exactly harsh on a woman's ears.

I quickly went up to my room and began to pack. It was almost ten-thirty by then and, before going downstairs, I lingered at the bedroom window, gazing down at the orchard—the trees frilly with the delicate blossoms, the heady scent drifting upward.

Then, with the traveling bag in my hand, I paused in the middle of the room that, in a short space of time, had become familiar. I crossed over to the mirror, set down the travel bag, and decided to run a comb through my hair. As I caught my reflection, Brian's extravagant praise about the gold highlights in my hair flicked through my mind. I smoothed down the bodice of my dress after I'd combed my hair and straightened the pearl brooch at my lace collar.

It was when I touched the brooch on my dress that I had the answer about how I would manage my second entry into Malverne Manor so that I might meet Sir Edmond. After all, there was supposed to be no reason for my returning here. I wasn't supposed to know Sir Edmond was returning to the manor around five o'clock.

The brooch solved my problem. I quickly removed it from my dress, wrapped it in a handkerchief, and tucked it into the drawer of the dressing table.

When I stepped out of the room, my gaze fell on the glass cabinet in the hallway. I placed the travel bag on the floor and walked over for a last look at the shepherdess figurine.

I turned round to look at the door of the Cream Lace Room. The door, as before, was not locked. I opened it and gazed about, my eyes roaming from the creamy lace counterpane on the bed to the small graceful writing desk at the window where the morning sun shone through the filmy lace curtains.

As I closed the door, I wondered what secret the room was hiding.

Mrs. Hopkins was waiting for me, standing by the large round table that was placed in the center of the vast entry hall. The large crystal vase now held an immense bouquet of hyacinth and daffodils. I remembered that yesterday there were roses in the crystal vase.

Mrs. Hopkins was impatient to leave and we were on our way with dispatch.

As the horse clopped along at a rather high speed over the uneven road and I tried to keep my balance on the narrow wooden seat of the trap, Mrs. Hopkins chattered on almost without pause. Twice, she slid Amy into the conversation, trying to elicit information from me, but I maintained a guarded attitude and she returned to her favorite subject —the culture and many uses of her herb garden. By the time the trap pulled up in front of the Three Crowns Inn, I knew a great deal about poultices, cough remedies, and herbaceous broths.

When we arrived, I jumped down from the trap, pulled my travel bag after me and, with a quick thanks and good-by to Mrs. Hopkins, hurried toward the inn.

To my dismay, Mrs. Hopkins followed me. What I had feared was, apparently, going to be the case. She'd wait—perhaps on Lady Edythe's orders—until she saw me safely aboard the coach.

"You needn't trouble yourself," I said, giving her a quick backward glance while hurrying ahead. "I'll manage."

"No trouble at all," she answered blandly and walked with me into the inn where she ordered a pint, then deposited herself at a table.

I looked at the clock on the wall. Eleven-thirty. I dropped the traveling bag to the floor and glanced at Mrs. Hopkins who was silently engrossed in her pint of ale. I turned to look at the lady innkeeper, but she was no longer leaning her elbows on the bar, watching us. I could hear her rattling pans in the kitchen.

"I'll walk outdoors awhile," I said to Mrs. Hopkins. "Maybe buy a souvenir at one of the little shops."

Mrs. Hopkins wiped the back of her hand across her mouth and gave me a quick look. "It's a short stop that the coach makes," she informed me rather sternly. "Don't wander far from the inn."

I stepped out and paused near the door, looking right and left. I was about to move away in the direction of the cluster of shops when a loud voice inside the inn made me pause. The lady innkeeper had come out of the kitchen and was addressing Mrs. Hopkins. It was the opening remark that made me pause.

"Nuther servant girl bein' sent packin'?" she shouted to Mrs. Hopkins. "They'm sure havin' trouble up there, keepin' 'em." She broke into a shrill splatter of laughter. "Di'nt this one like it up there neither?"

"It's a chore finding a proper servant girl, Mrs. Ploovey," Mrs. Hopkins answered in a prim, authoritative tone.

"Thought this 'un might stay. I saw her come off the coach yesterday. Plain sort," Mrs. Ploovey said and, after another shrill streak of laughter, added, "Not like that yellow-haired bit of pastry that arrived on the coach while back, eh, Mrs. Hopkins? Thought maybe the one who came on the coach yesterday might stay." There was a brief silence before Mrs. Ploovey, in a quieter tone, said, "Too bad it worked out like so for the yellow-haired one. Did her family come to get the body?"

It seemed like a long time before Mrs. Hopkins answered. "Yes, her brother came," she said, then, after another pause, added, "Yes, that was a sad thing to have happened and after that experience, we decided to be more careful. Malverne Manor, most likely, will not be hiring another servant girl for a while, not after all the trouble that one caused us. But, as I said, Mrs. Ploovey, a first-class servant girl is hard to come by."

"Well, I thought this one might do, being sort of plain lookin'," Mrs. Ploovey drawled, then laughed again. "With the likes of him up there, the plain ones 'ud be better off."

I quickly moved away from the door where the surprising conversation had immobilized me. I walked swiftly down the road toward the shops.

CHAPTER 6

I walked past the few shops onto a field path, away from the main road, in case Mrs. Hopkins should come tearing by in the trap, anxious about my missing the noon coach.

After wandering about in the fields for what seemed like an interminable time, I became concerned. It was well past the noon hour, but the coach still hadn't gone by. It struck me then that Mrs. Hopkins had persuaded the coachman to wait.

I decided I would have to roam a bit farther afield. The coachman, after all, would wait only so long.

Eventually, I heard the pounding of hoofs and then the swaying roof of the coach with the strapped-on baggage became visible as the coach rumbled by.

When I retraced my steps, I was relieved to see that the trap was no longer parked by the inn. I went inside, wondering now about the safety of my traveling bag but it was there, leaning against the table where I'd left it.

I dropped into a chair at the table and, out of the corner of my eye, I saw that Mrs. Ploovey, the innkeeper, was watching me from the kitchen doorway.

"The coach has left, dearie," she called to me and I turned to look at her. The broad, sweaty face creased into a grin and she winked at me. "Or wuzn't you meanin' t' get on it, dearie?"

She was polishing an enormous pewter meat platter, swirling the rag in wide, slow circles, and regarding me with a smothered grin. After a while she lowered her eyes and turned her full attention to the meat platter.

"Wuzn't goin' t' be shoved off that easy, now wuz you?" she said after a brief silence, her eyes sliding back to me, and I wondered what in the world Mrs. Hopkins might have said to her about me.

"I don't know what you mean," I said.

"Aah, now, is that the truth?" she chortled. "Y' wunt be the first one, y' know," she added. She darted a shrewd upward look at me then bent once more to the task of shining up the meat platter.

"Course," Mrs. Ploovey said after another sharp little silence, "might 've been better if y'd took the coach 'n left, dearie. Better off th'n staying up at that place." She jerked her head in the general direction of Malverne Manor. "After what happened t'uther servant girl . . . 'n a few other consid'rations t' keep in mind. It might——"

She let the words hang and resumed her polishing job.

"I did not go to the manor to seek employment," I said and she gave me a sly look. Then, since she seemed disposed to gossip, I continued speaking, hoping she might favor me with some information about "the yellow-haired bit of pastry" that arrived on the coach "while back" and drowned in the Malverne pond. The moment I'd overheard the conversation about the elusive servant girl, I wondered whether Mrs. Ploovey and Mrs. Hopkins were not actually discussing Amy, whether it wasn't she who'd supposedly drowned herself in the pond, whose body was taken away by someone posing as her brother.

"I did not go to Malverne Manor to seek employment," I repeated, and Mrs. Ploovey's polishing rag came to an attentive halt. Some of the doubt squeezed out of her face. "I went to the manor," I continued, "at the invitation of a friend. She was expected there as a guest and I was to join her."

"Wuz expected there as a guest?" Mrs. Ploovey mimicked when she'd roused herself from a brief circumspect moment. "'N you wuz t' join her?" The fleshy jowls rippled as she burst into a spasm of laughter.

I overlooked her hilarity and continued my labored explanation, hoping that she in turn would let something slip away from her vast store of village gossip. "It seems," I went on, "that my friend might have been detained in London and hasn't yet arrived at the manor. If she was delayed, she might arrive on the noon coach tomorrow, or the day after, so I've decided to remain here for another day or two."

Mrs. Ploovey heaved her hefty shoulders, pursed her lips and said nothing. She began to worry the rag over the meat platter in deep contemplative silence.

"I hope I didn't keep Mrs. Hopkins waiting about," I said, just to fill in the void.

"No, no," she answered absently. "She left soon's she finished her pint. Said she'd be baking and the dough riz t' the top o' the pans 'n she'd better rattle on t' the kitchen." That said, Mrs. Ploovey remained tenaciously positioned in the doorway, shining up the platter, eyeing me with curiosity. I wondered what I might say to her that would be safe enough to be repeated to Mrs. Hopkins. The woman's tiny dark eyes rarely strayed from my face and I wondered once more what Mrs. Hopkins might have said in my absence. Possibly nothing. Mrs. Ploovey might only be hoping to replenish her store of Malverne Manor gossip with any tidbit I might chance to let drop. Apparently, the goings-on up at

Malverne Manor piqued the interest of the local residents and "with the likes of him up there," the interest bordered on curiosity. It occurred to me now "the likes of him" might refer to Brian, not to Sir Edmond as I'd immediately presumed.

"Y'r expectin' t' stay hereabouts f'r a day or two?" Mrs. Ploovey inquired, with a pronounced hesitation in her voice.

"Yes, I'd like to have my room back."

She shook her head. "Not 'vailable," she declared.

I thought, at first, she was refusing me accommodations altogether but, after a long reflective pause, she informed me that she'd find something. If she still had some dark doubts about me, she, nevertheless, thought twice before she turned away a paying customer.

When she started to move out of the doorway, I quickly asked whether I could have some lunch and she nodded halfheartedly before disappearing into the kitchen.

While she served me the lunch—stringy beef streaked with fat and a mound of cold potato—she became talkative, placing herself at the table facing me while I ate.

Although I was willing to exchange vital news with the lady innkeeper, I soon learned our little chat would be very much one-sided, like my kitchen visit with Mrs. Hopkins had been. Mrs. Ploovey was steadfastly tight-lipped about anything she might know about Malverne Manor, but her little bursts of meaningless chatter always ended up, one way or another, with an inquiry as to the precise reason for my interest in the manor. Twice, she asked me if I wasn't a servant girl, as if I wasn't quite sure myself or would admit the fact when questioned further.

"You di'nt know him in London?" she asked and I replied I hadn't, not bothering to ask whether she meant Brian or Sir Edmond.

Our verbal parrying came to an abrupt end when a clatter outside the door announced the arrival of some patrons. Mrs. Ploovey heaved her massive body out of the chair and shuffled away. She soon became occupied with drinks and food and I was left to my stringy beef and cold potato.

Soon more people streamed into the inn and the place reverberated with raucous laughter and boisterous talk. I rather enjoyed the rowdy conviviality and dawdled over the meal which, in itself, did not encourage one to snap it up greedily.

After lunch, I decided on another stroll. I'd already done a considerable amount of walking about before lunchtime, but Mrs. Ploovey's leaden lunch now necessitated another stroll to walk off an uncomfortably heavy sensation below the rib cage.

Feeling considerably improved after the constitutional, I went up to the room which Mrs. Ploovey assigned to me, not the large comfortable room I'd engaged the day before, but, rather, a dismal dustbin of a room. The bed was lumpy but I stretched out on it and, as I gazed at the grimy walls and out the smeary window, I speculated about the innkeeper's opinion of me, since I'd been banished to these quarters. . . . *"Y' wunt be the first one,"* Mrs. Ploovey had remarked. *"—the likes of him up there."* Did she mean Brian or Sir Edmond?

After a brief and questionable rest on the humpy bed, I combed my hair, smoothed down my dress, and set off once more for Malverne Manor now that it was a little past four.

This time my walk was not threatened by rain. It was a glorious sunny day. My mood, also, was unlike the previous day's. Today I felt no apprehension. My purpose was clear-cut. I only hoped that Sir Edmond had not changed his plans, and would be at the manor, and that my ploy involving the "carelessly forgotten" pearl brooch proved successful.

Despite the uncertainties that marked my errand, I couldn't help but enjoy the pleasantness of the day. I lifted my face to look at the sky, a luminous azure, the puffy white clouds sailing along lazily. A lark soared high above, trailing a song in its flight.

I did not hurry. I wanted to enjoy the stillness of the country lane where the loudest sound was the song of the lark in a distant tree.

My eyes traveled from the tree where the lark sang to a field where hops grew on tall vines. In the distance, the white conical tips of the oasthouses rimmed the horizon and I wondered whether the hop fields were Malverne property.

At the other side of the road, behind the hedgerows, pastureland rolled away up a slight rise, then dipped into a green fold and rose up again into a knoll. There were lambs frisking about in the lush grass and I stopped to watch them. Yesterday's rain freshened the grass to a vivid green and the sweet grass scent filled the air.

I was about to move on when I thought I saw movement in the pasture. There was someone out there. He'd come around the side of a large shrub and was now heading for the road where I stood. He apparently had not seen me. He was taking his time, looking about, stooping to inspect a stone wall, then gazing off into a distant field.

Immediately, I wondered whether it might be Sir Edmond. I had no idea whether land this far away from the manor house might be his property.

He was still far from the road where I stood but, even from this distance, I knew it wasn't Old Abner. Could it be Brian? No, it didn't seem to be a fair-haired person.

I waited for the distant figure to come closer, but, unfortunately, he switched directions and started to walk farther away. Perhaps it was someone not at all connected with Malverne Manor, I decided, and continued on up the road.

When I saw the tops of the tall brick chimneys of the manor house, I came to a stop, remembering that the day before the chimneys were barely visible because of the low-hanging rain clouds.

As I walked along and the gray stone and pink brick of the walls came into view, I thought, how different the house looks today. Yesterday it was shrouded in dark gloom. Today, with the bright sun shining on it, it appears inviting and seems to beckon.

I was so intent on my approach to the house, going over in my mind how I would deliver my little recitation about the treasured pearl brooch I'd left behind, that I wasn't aware of someone approaching. The person was almost beside me when I, startled by his presence, whirled about to face him.

I knew immediately it was Sir Edmond.

He towered over me, a powerfully built man, his appearance of strength coming not so much from his height, although he was well over six feet, but, rather, from a sinewy hardness that showed in his face. The hair was coal-black. The black brows were drawn down over eyes, a startling blue because of their clear, cold color. His face, deeply tanned by the sun, had sharply cut features, the sharpness conveying an impression of arrogance and, possibly, even cruelty. The only softness about him was the incredibly thick black lashes which did not suit him in the least.

"What, may I ask, are you doing here?" he inquired and, although his voice was pitched low, there was an abrasive quality about it.

"Are you Sir Edmond?" I asked and he nodded slightly, the cold blue eyes appraising me with open boldness.

"I've come to see you," I said. "To find out what happened to my friend, Amy."

At the mention of Amy's name, the cool, annoyed expression—as if I were trespassing on his land—changed to a guarded look. He stood stock-still, staring down at me, then said, "Why do you put it that way? Why should anything have *happened* to her?"

"I have reason to be concerned. I'd like to know where she is."

"Don't make it sound so ominous," he said with a suppressed antagonism. "You haven't explained, by the way, who you are or what right you have to ask such impertinent questions."

"My name is Claire Atwood and I'm sure Amy mentioned my name to you. She was a friend of mine and I intend to find out what happened to her."

He lowered his head, looking directly into my face. His voice was as cold as the chilly glint in the blue eyes. "Stop insinuating," he said, "that something terrible has happened to her."

"I believe it has," I said. His belligerent attitude had caused me to feel a rush of anger and my voice now matched his in indignation.

I had not expected this kind of encounter with him. I'd hoped we would work together to unravel the strange puzzle, but I saw now that I was up against a solid antagonist. His attitude was more mystifying than Brian's or Lady Edythe's. If the others evaded the issue, Sir Edmond, it seemed, was going to crush my attempts to discover what happened to Amy.

Then I realized, all at once, that his attitude was partly my fault. If he was belligerent, I'd probably angered him with my alarming statements. It also occurred to me that, possibly, our similar reactions—anger and antagonism—might be only a cover-up for what we really felt—a secret fear that something terrible had happened to Amy.

I cast a quick glance behind me and decided that the manor house was too close for comfort. I wanted my meeting with Sir Edmond to be private and someone could have been watching us through a window. I started to walk away, knowing he would follow.

He walked beside me, not speaking, and after we'd gone some distance down the road, I said, "Amy wrote to me from Malverne Manor and . . ."

He came to an abrupt stop in the road. ". . . from Malverne Manor?" he repeated in an incredulous voice.

"Yes, she wrote me six letters from the manor."

He regarded me with a long wary look then said, "You're talking nonsense again. Amy never came to the manor."

"Oh, but she did. I am certain of that and not only because of the letters." I turned my face away from his intense scrutiny and continued walking.

For a moment he remained where I'd left him then, in a few long strides, he caught up with me.

"You had better explain yourself," he demanded. "No one at the manor ever saw Amy. My aunt, Lady Edythe, told me Amy had written to her, telling her she was coming to Malverne Manor, but she never arrived." He paused and his next words were spoken with quiet, emphatic firmness. "And I've never had reason to doubt Lady Edythe's word."

We walked on in an uneasy silence and I made a firm resolve to keep my emotions on an even keel. I would not permit the rush of anger and impatience that he aroused in me to ruin my expectations from this meeting. I needed this arrogant man's help. I'd have to watch my words, speak carefully, particularly when I spoke of Lady Edythe.

We'd come a long distance from the manor house and had wandered onto a path winding through the sheep pasture. I sat down on the smooth, sun-warmed top of a low stone wall. He sat down beside me and I waited for him to speak first.

"What you are saying is impossible," he said after a lengthy silence. "Amy could not have written you any letters from Malverne Manor, since she was never here. My aunt assured me Amy never arrived." His tone now showed no trace of hostility, but neither did his voice possess the unwavering assurance of a while back. There was a shade of doubt now, puzzlement, too.

"Didn't Amy write to you from the manor while you were in Edinburgh?" I asked.

He didn't answer my question. He was staring ahead, lost in thought, then, as if he hadn't heard my question, he turned to look at me. "I'm sorry, but I've forgotten your name. Amy mentioned it, of course, but . . ."

"My name is Claire Atwood," I answered and repeated my question, "Did Amy write to you from the manor while you were in Edinburgh?"

"She might have," he replied absently, "but there was a change in my plans and I was in Edinburgh for only two days rather than the two weeks I'd originally planned. After my short stay in Edinburgh, I was traveling about until I finally returned to the manor yesterday. If Amy wrote to me at the Edinburgh address, her letters haven't reached me yet."

After another lengthy silence he said, the impatience returning to his voice, "Besides, there was no need for letters." He got up from the stone wall and, as he stood over me, I once more became conscious of his tremendous height. He began to pace back and forth and then said, "I'm not much of a letter writer and Amy came to Malverne Manor—or was supposed to have come—in order to arrive at a decision as to whether she wished to marry me." He paused then added, "My writing to her wouldn't have been much help if she was to make a clear-cut decision of her own. And even after her friend, Lady Bellingford, could not accompany her to the manor, I knew Amy would be in good hands with my aunt, Lady Edythe, to take care of her."

He halted in his pacing and stood before me, leaning forward, fixing me with a hard, skeptical look. "Why do you insist that Amy did come to the manor? Why should I accept your wild guessing rather than the word of my aunt, Lady Edythe?" He made an impatient wave of his hand. "Yes, yes, I know. Amy wrote some letters to you from the manor."

He dropped down to the low stone wall, sitting with his head thrust forward, his hands gripping the edge of the wall.

"I don't believe your story, you know," he said after a while. "Not about the letters or—or anything." He gave me a sidelong look. "I'm sure Amy wrote to you from London. She must have told you that she wasn't sure in her mind that she wished to marry me." He paused and then continued, "She'd come to know a young man during the five months I was away from London, told me she hadn't much cared for him at first but had changed her mind and was seriously considering marrying him."

I admitted that, yes, she'd told me that in a letter from London, explaining that she was going to the manor to make up her mind which man she wished to marry, but in her very first letter from the manor she'd stated it was Sir Edmond she would marry. In fact, she'd seemed so inclined even while still in London. She'd also explained that Lady Bellingford had suggested that a stay at the manor would tell her whether she desired the life of a country squire's wife, which was quite different from life in the city.

"Had you ever met the other man?" I asked.

"Couldn't avoid him. He was a tenacious rival, believe me. Was always hanging about."

We'd fallen into a silence when I heard Sir Edmond say in a quiet, reflective tone, "I frequently wondered whether Amy would ever be happy in this country atmosphere. She seemed to thrive on the excitement of city life. My rival was very much the city type, as Amy appeared to be."

I looked about me, at the green and gold landscape. I listened to a thrush's song, the only sound on the quiet country air and I, too, wondered whether Amy would be happy here, remembering how she wrote with joy and exhilaration about her exciting life in the city. . . . "After being buried alive in that quiet little graveyard of a village," she'd written in her first letter from London, "I feel I'm now really beginning to live. . . ." That was why I was surprised when she'd written that she was considering marriage to a country squire. But living in the country with Sir Edmond, of course, would have made a difference.

I turned to look at Sir Edmond. He was still sitting on the stone wall, head thrust forward, gazing at the far-off field beyond the hedgerows. As I looked at him, I thought of his rival. I tried to imagine what superior attributes that young man possessed to cause Amy any hesitation in her choice. Could his being a city type have given him a tremendous advantage over Sir Edmond who was tied to the land? I couldn't imagine the other young man having a superior appearance. True, there was an air of arrogance and obstinacy about Sir Edmond that might have clashed with Amy's willful nature but one had to admit that Sir Edmond, at least, did not look ordinary.

Even now, dressed in simple country clothes, dark tweed trousers, and plain cotton shirt, he did not look ordinary. There was an air of authority about him, due partly to his height but mainly to an inbred self-assurance. For a large man, he moved with agility and I expected him to be an excellent horseman. I could visualize him in complete command of a bucking, snorting animal. I wondered for a fleeting moment whether he was also a cruel person. I was astonished that I should think such a thing, yet many times a look crossed his face suggesting unkindness, even cruelty.

Perhaps because I'd let my thoughts wander out of control and had permitted my imagination to cast this shadow of doubt and distrust, I caught myself looking at Sir Edmond in this harsh light, seeing only his arrogance, all of a sudden—his flashes of anger and highhandedness. Now all his evasions and smooth explanations stood out in a glaring light. I began to doubt everything he'd said.

I tried to shake off this disquieting, suspicious attitude but it persisted, bringing with it other disturbing questions that had been lingering at the back of my mind, not only remarks he'd made to me, but things Amy had written in her letters from London and from the manor. Knowing that sooner or later I would bring up the subject with him, I decided to have it over with then and there.

"I was puzzled at Amy's explanation," I said to him, "when she wrote me she was going to Malverne Manor to make up her mind which man she'd decide to marry, you or that young man she met in London. Struck me as rather extraordinary. Why such an elaborate arrangement? Couldn't she have made up her mind just as well in London?"

"No, she couldn't have," he replied sharply. "There was nothing so extraordinary about her going to Malverne Manor. After all, I was——"

He paused and I thought he was going to say, "After all, I was in love with Amy," but he did not.

"After all," he went on, "I was fond of Amy. I'm sure she told you of her accident with the horse, that she'd injured her shoulder and hurt her foot so badly she couldn't walk. There was no one to take care of her, only her friend, Lady Bellingford, who isn't exactly the nursemaid type. At Malverne Manor, Amy could have recuperated nicely with Lady Edythe and Mrs. Hopkins to take care of her. Besides, as I've already told you, I knew how much Amy enjoyed city life and how she had escaped to London from the country. By staying at the manor for a while, she would have had the opportunity to know if she cared for this kind of life. Also, Lady Bellingford, whose hospitality I'd frequently enjoyed, had often remarked she would like to visit the manor."

He thought a moment then said, "I'm leaving for London tomorrow. I'm not going to wait for a letter from Amy. I'll inquire at old Mrs. Alroyd's house. Lady Bellingford is in the South of France. I will contact Amy's other London friends. I will first seek out my rival, to learn if Amy simply hadn't decided to marry him rather suddenly and hadn't yet got around to letting me know," he said, and I thought of how lame his excuses sounded.

I was about to interrupt him but he raised his hand and quickly said, "Yes, yes, I know. You claim Amy had come to the manor, had written you some letters from Malverne Manor." There was a hint of triumph in his voice. "She might have written *about* the manor but not necessarily *from* it. Are you certain about the postmarks?"

"Well, no——" I began and he pounced on my words.

"There! You see. You are not truly certain she was here. You have only some letters posted from who knows where, listing details about Malverne Manor which she might have read in a book. There is such a book, you know. Or she was repeating things I'd told her."

"Not quite," I shot back. "To begin with, Amy is not devious." Lowering my voice, I added, "Besides, when I was a guest yesterday at Malverne Manor, I——"

"When you were—what?"

"When I was a guest yesterday at Malverne Manor," I repeated.

His eyes narrowed. I could not read the expression on his face, whether it was surprise, disbelief, or a carefully guarded look. "Lady Edythe," he said after a while, "never mentioned any such thing to me."

"Her failure to mention it to you doesn't disprove the fact that I was there."

"Now, look here," he said, getting up from the stone wall, the fury slowly rising in his voice. "You have persisted in making insinuations, about me and about Lady Edythe. You accuse Lady Edythe of denying that Amy was at the manor. Now you claim you, too, were a guest at the manor but, for some strange reason, Lady Edythe has chosen to lie to me."

"I didn't say she lied. But, obviously, she's failed to mention those facts. It's me you're accusing of lies."

He still loomed over me, the chilly blue gaze fixed on me. I gave him look for look and he finally sat down once more on the low wall.

"Oh, I don't know what to think," he said after a while.

"It might be helpful if you spoke to Mrs. Ploovey, the innkeeper," I suggested. "She seems to know something about a blond young lady who arrived on the coach about the time Amy was to arrive."

"I'm sure a number of blond-headed female passengers have reason to use the services of the coach," he said in an offhand way. "It might have been the new servant girl Mrs. Hopkins was expecting."

"Or," I continued, "you might ask Brian a few questions. I believe he knows something."

"Brian? Who the devil is he?"

"You know very well, who. The painter, of course."

He gave me an amused, sidelong glance. "Painter?" he asked in a mocking voice. "You mean pictures?"

"Don't be facetious. You know I mean pictures. I'm speaking of the painter who stays in the cottage by the pond."

At first, he regarded me with an indulgent smile then said, "The more you say, the harder you are to believe. Now you tell me a preposterous story about an artist who lives in the cottage." He lowered his voice to an emphatic whisper. "There is no artist living there. Never was. I am the only one who uses that abandoned cottage on a rare occasion."

"I was in that cottage yesterday," I answered hotly, "and I was there this morning. And an artist most certainly does stay there."

He swung off the stone wall and started to walk away. "Come with me," he ordered, waving a hand. "We'll go and talk to your mythical artist."

We walked in silence along the narrow footpath through the sheep pasture, he a short distance ahead, taking long, purposeful strides, I trying to keep up with him.

"You'll have to slow down," I shouted at him when he was getting too far ahead of me.

By the time I caught up with him, and we proceeded along the path together, his mood had softened, as if his aggressive stomping along the footpath had released some of his pent-up hostility.

"I hope you'll forgive my impatience and harsh manner," he said in a surprisingly gentle tone, "but ever since I returned to the manor yesterday, I've gone over and over in my mind why Amy did not come to the manor, why she didn't write to Lady Edythe and explain her change in plans about coming to the manor." He fell into a silence, then added, "To tell the truth, until you suddenly materialized, I'd become convinced that she'd simply decided to marry the other young man and that her letter explaining her decision hadn't reached me yet. Then you appear like a mischievous genie out of thin air and——"

"I'm sorry I upset you, Sir Edmond, but I've been worried about Amy. I wish, though, that we might have discussed the matter along less hostile lines."

He lifted his shoulders in a slight shrug and I added, "Well, I hope Brian can throw some light on the subject because on both occasions when I spoke with him, I got the impression that he knew something but was holding back."

He shook his head and when he spoke there was no trace of anger or mockery in his tone.

"But neither I nor Lady Edythe," he said, "knows of anyone named Brian."

The cottage was now only a short distance away and I quickened my steps. If Brian had refused to divulge any information to me, his being confronted by Sir Edmond would be quite another matter.

I rushed ahead and pounded on the cottage door.

Sir Edmond approached the door and waited for a moment. He glanced down at me, then threw the door open.

The cottage was empty. The easel was gone. There were no paint things about, no pictures propped against the chairs where I'd seen them only that morning. Even the dishes had vanished from the small sideboard and the cot in the corner of the room was stripped.

CHAPTER 7

Although I stood with my back to him, I knew he was looking at me with disbelief, curious as to why I should have concocted such a far-fetched story.

"I didn't dream it," I declared, whirling about to face him, seeing the skepticism in his face. "Why don't you believe anything I tell you?"

I gestured toward the small sideboard. "There were dishes on those shelves this morning. I had tea with Brian at that table. There was a red and white cloth on it." I swung round, pointing to a corner of the room. "The cot in that corner was made up. There was a pillow on it and a plaid blanket. An easel stood by the window and pictures were propped up against the furniture."

"This place is exactly as I left it," he said, his voice flat, toneless. I would have preferred he'd shouted his antagonism rather than face me with that suppressed fury.

He began to move leisurely about the barren-looking room, gesturing in an offhand way. "The cot was stripped just before I left for London. I carried the linen up to the house myself so it could be laundered. The objects on the desk are where I left them. As for dishes on the sideboard and the tablecloth, I don't hold tea parties here."

"Oh, stop it," I said. I sat down at the roughhewn table, now minus the red and white cloth.

He dropped into a chair the other side of the table, leaning his elbows squarely on the table, regarding me with waiting silence. I turned my face away, my eyes wandering about the empty-looking room. After a while I heard him shift his position in the chair.

"Perhaps we should stop fighting each other," I heard him say, and when I turned to face him, the belligerent set to his jaw and the cold mockery in his eyes were gone.

"Perhaps we should work together," he continued. "Then we might be able to puzzle this out." He stopped, thought a moment, then added, "But you see, Miss Atwood, until you appeared, I never considered Amy to be in danger. When I arrived at the manor yesterday and was informed she did not arrive, I had good reason to understand why she changed her mind about coming. When I invited her and Lady Bellingford, I'd almost precluded that Amy would marry the other young man and that her holiday at Malverne Manor would be only that, a holiday. Lady Bellingford had shown me hospitality when I was in London and I thought it was a reasonable gesture to invite her also and she could then be chaperone to Amy. Even when Lady Bellingford could not accompany Amy, I thought it would do Amy well to spend a quiet time at Malverne Manor regardless of whom she decided to marry."

He made a quick, impatient gesture. "Then you show up and intimate that something terrible has happened to Amy and someone connected with the manor is responsible for this crime." He darted me a sharp look. "You did, you know." He hesitated then added, more to himself than to me, "I cannot believe Lady Edythe would deny that Amy was present at the manor. In all the years she's been living at Malverne Manor, I have never known her to indulge in any form of deceit or intrigue."

I recalled my experience of the day previous, the drugged tea and Lady Edythe telling me Sir Edmond's return to the manor would be delayed by two weeks, telling me he had not come to the manor that evening when, moments before she'd entered my room, I'd heard and seen Sir Edmond in the orchard below my bedroom window.

But I said none of this to Sir Edmond. Not yet. If I were going to enlist his aid in unraveling the puzzle concerning Amy, I had better refrain from making disparaging remarks about Lady Edythe whom he blindly trusted and admired.

"How long has Lady Edythe lived at Malverne Manor?" I asked. "Mrs. Hopkins told me she'd been at the manor seven years. Did Mrs. Hopkins come with Lady Edythe?"

"Yes, Mrs. Hopkins came with Lady Edythe. She'd worked for her for many years. Lady Edythe has been living at the manor for seven years. She'd been a widow for about a year before she came to live here. She, at first, came to take care of my mother who'd become ill. Lady Edythe and my mother were second cousins. My mother, unfortunately, died as a result of her illness and Lady Edythe then returned to her house in London. But when my father died, only a few months after my mother's death, Lady Edythe then came here to live. I needed someone to run the house, someone more than a housekeeper." There was a slight pause, then he said with a quiet firmness, "In all the years she's lived at the manor, I've never had cause but to take her at her word."

I remained silent, giving my full attention to the lilac bush rustling its branches against the window.

Sir Edmond relaxed into his chair, stretching out his long legs. "It is just possible," he mused with a wry grin, "that Lady Edythe might have jumped to some alarming conclusions when she received the letters Amy and I sent her. You see, Miss Atwood, I'm involved at present in a county election." He made a sweeping gesture. "I've a great affection for my land and I like the people living hereabouts. I want very much to win this election." He smiled briefly. "But Lady Edythe is even more determined that I win the county seat. I know she would fight anything and anyone who might in the slightest way prevent my success politically." He gave me a quick sidelong glance. "Although Lady Edythe gives me credit for being a good landlord and believes in my political potential—no doubt, expecting me to become a member of the House of Lords, eventually, as her late husband was—but you see, Miss Atwood, from the time I was quite young, and she was coming to the manor only to visit, she frequently predicted that one day I would bring disgrace on this noble house, meaning that I would become unfortunately involved with some scheming young lady not worthy of me. My peccadilloes, she called them."

He paused; an amused smile flicked across his face. "However, I assure you, Miss Atwood, Lady Edythe has overestimated my prowess with young ladies," he said, and I wondered whom to believe, him or the all-seeing, all-knowing innkeeper, Mrs. Ploovey, who seemed quite knowledgeable about "the likes of him." I was convinced now it was Sir Edmond she'd meant, not Brian.

"When Lady Edythe came to live at the manor," he continued, "she even more frequently voiced her dark fear about my 'bringing disgrace on this noble house.' She always looked upon my trips to London as an embarkment on another of my peccadilloes. I can easily imagine her pouncing on the wrong conclusion when she received my hasty letter from London, informing her of Amy's arrival at the manor. I'm a miserable letter writer, Miss Atwood, probably stated things clumsily, left too many gaps for my aunt to fill in with her own alarming interpretations. My unexpected announcement that I was contemplating marriage to someone Lady Edythe had never heard of—well, I'm sure I alarmed the poor woman."

"And with the county elections coming up," I said, not caring that there was bitterness and sarcasm in my voice, "Lady Edythe decided that Amy's arrival was not the marital plans she had in mind for you and that you chose a bad time to bring disgrace on the house?"

He stared down at me, anger hardening his face, the lips pressed together tightly. He was visibly pulling himself into control, holding back the words he wished to hurl at me. We faced each other in silent rage for a time then, slowly, he turned his face away. "Sorry," he said after a while. "I suppose I had that coming."

After a lengthy pause he said, "If Amy did come to Malverne Manor as you've suggested, Lady Edythe might have convinced her that since she was so busy with my campaigning, it would be advisable for her to stay at the Colonel's place in Surrey till I returned from Scotland. The Colonel is my Uncle Leland. Everyone calls him the Colonel which he was in the Queen's army in the Crimea."

"And if Lady Edythe had persuaded Amy to stay at the Colonel's place," I said, not at all convinced of this possibility, "she wasn't going to tell you this until after the county elections?"

"Or until she's decided just how to bring up this matter with me. After all, I haven't been back at the manor all that long and it isn't as if Amy were being neglected. There are plenty of servants at the Colonel's place."

He got up from the chair and walked slowly to the open doorway of the cottage and I thought he looked as if he were considering still another explanation for Amy's whereabouts.

I'd guessed correctly because after gazing thoughtfully at the distant fields from the doorway, he said, "It's even possible that Amy arrived at Malverne Manor when Lady Edythe was away. She's been visiting county constituents of mine up in the north section and I know that on two occasions she's stayed with the Wickhams, acquaintances of ours, who live a short distance away to the north."

I was struck by this unexpected news. "Lady Edythe has been away from the manor on two occasions?"

He turned round in the doorway to face me. "Yes. But if Amy had arrived during my aunt's absence, Mrs. Hopkins would have welcomed Amy. Lady Edythe would have informed Mrs. Hopkins of Amy's arrival. I didn't question Mrs. Hopkins because until you appeared, I had no reason to ask questions. When my aunt told me Amy had not arrived, I was convinced she'd simply gone off and married my rival."

He turned again to gaze out the doorway and my thoughts skimmed back to the conversation I'd overheard between Mrs. Hopkins and Mrs. Ploovey about the "yellow-haired young lady" who'd arrived on the coach about the time Amy was due, and whom Mrs. Hopkins called a servant girl while remarking about "all the trouble that one caused us." I wondered now who exactly Mrs. Hopkins meant by *us*.

Lady Edythe, I suddenly realized, might have played no part in Amy's disappearance. Amy might have arrived when Lady Edythe was staying with the Wickhams. Then, when she returned to the manor, could Amy have somehow—I thought of the drugged tea—been prevented from encountering Lady Edythe? Was the person Amy took to be Lady Edythe an impostor? How did Brian fit into this because I was sure that in some way he did. I gazed around the stripped-down cottage, wondering about his sudden flight and why he was so careful to leave no traces.

The room had become very still. I turned my eyes to where Sir Edmond was still leaning lazily in the doorway, gazing out. No, I was grasping at straws, I told myself. Even what I considered a family resemblance between Mrs. Hopkins and Brian now proved a hasty conclusion on my part because I had to admit that the longer I was in Sir Edmond's presence, the more convinced I was that Sir Edmond and Brian resembled each other vaguely. I saw what I wanted to see.

As for all these new possibilities and explanations that Sir Edmond had presented, he was only trying to confuse me, or pacify me.

"Where do you expect to go tomorrow?" I asked Sir Edmond abruptly, wanting to put a stop to my scattered thinking. "Will you go to London or to Surrey?"

"I haven't decided. I must go to Wickham Place first, to see about some horses of mine that are stabled there." He stepped outdoors, waving an arm at me. "Come along. Let's walk about for a while." I was relieved to see he was walking away from the manor house. I did not wish to be seen by anyone there.

We walked at a leisurely pace, he modifying his long strides to my shorter ones. Occasionally I stole an upward glance at him. His eyes roamed the stretch of grainfields and orchards on one side of the road and the lush pasture beyond the hedgerows at the other side. He'd said a while back that he had an affection for his land. This now showed in his face. The puzzlement, anger, and tension caused by Amy's mysterious whereabouts and our subsequent discussions had given way to a look of contentment.

"This is good land," he said after a long silence. "I'm proud of it." He stopped, pointed to a faraway field. "That's where the Wickham property begins. It's even better situated than the Malverne land. The Wickham property is truly a superb stretch of land. Has fallen into disrepair but—" He didn't finish.

I brought up a subject which interested me more than Miss Wickham and her property. The question had been curling around in my brain for the past few minutes.

"You said you'd met this young man of Amy's," I began, and he turned to look at me, surprised at my sudden question. "Your rival," I said. "What was he like?"

"In many ways like Amy—personable, high-spirited, impulsive, adventurous. Oh, he was a formidable rival, considered me a bothersome intruder. One evening when I called for Amy, I found him there. Seems Amy had forgotten she'd made a previous engagement with him. He was quite adamant and wouldn't leave, insisting he had first claim on Amy. As it turned out, I found myself going alone to a dinner engagement and Amy went out with her fair-haired young man."

"Fair-haired?" The words came out in one breath. "Did he also have dark eyes?"

Sir Edmond stared at me, raising quizzical brows. "Yes, he was quite fair-haired. I don't know whether his eyes were dark-colored or not. He did glare at me with dark looks all the while I hung about that evening, waiting for Amy to make up her mind between us." He stopped and peered down at me. "You know this blond Adonis?"

I shook my head. "No—no—it's just that—that Brian is blond and has dark eyes, and he did say he'd been in London recently. It's only a wild guess."

"Yes," Sir Edmond agreed, "it's only a wild guess. If Amy chose to marry her London admirer, I am quite certain it is not your mythical artist that she has married."

Then, switching subjects so abruptly he took me by surprise, Sir Edmond asked, "You have absolutely no recollection about the postmarks on Amy's letters? The ones you claim she wrote from the manor?"

I said I did not, but that they were probably postmarked from the village, to which Sir Edmond said, "If, for some reason, Amy wanted the letters postmarked from the village, that could have been negotiated. Someone could have done it for her. I can't imagine, though, why Amy would have had any reason to resort to such intrigue."

"What about the many specific details concerning the manor house and gardens that she wrote about?" But as soon as I'd asked the question, I knew what his answer would be.

"Manors are often well-documented, Miss Atwood, as Malverne Manor is. As I told you, there is such a book. Amy might have found all those details in that book."

He broke off and his glance lingered. A smile stole across his face. "Why don't we stop our question-and-answer game for a while," he suggested. "We're really getting nowhere. Let's forget about Amy for a little while. I'd like to know something about you, Miss Atwood. Will you come and be my guest at Malverne Manor?"

He'd stopped in the road and was looking down at me, waiting for my answer.

I remembered suddenly the little recitation I'd rehearsed about the pearl brooch I'd left behind at the manor.

Misinterpreting my hesitation, he said, "I wish you would come, Miss Atwood. You would be most welcome. And I'll need your assistance in puzzling out this business about Amy."

"I'll come, but—well, since you and I have been talking more or less in circles from the moment we met, we may as well continue on that note."

He looked at me, baffled and slightly amused.

I explained briefly, but not too clearly, my plan to gain entrance at the manor front door so that I might meet him, how I'd tucked the pearl brooch into the dressing table of the room I'd occupied. "I was afraid that otherwise I'd be turned away and wouldn't get to see you," I concluded breathlessly, "and so, if you go on ahead to the house, I will appear shortly afterward to inquire about my forgotten brooch. You will then pretend you've never seen me before."

"Why in the name of heaven," he shouted, "do I have to go through that idiotic charade?"

"Because it is necessary," I answered stubbornly. "It is preferable that neither Lady Edythe nor Mrs. Hopkins knows that we've met previously. If the reasons elude you at present, you will come to know why I suggest this approach."

He glared down at me with speechless exasperation then flailed his arms in hopeless resignation. "Miss Atwood," he shouted again, "never in all my life have I met anyone who can try my patience the way you can."

We stood in the road facing each other.

"Oh, all right, I'll come in on cue," he grumbled and then stalked off.

When he'd gone, I went into the cottage, my eyes searching the room. If I could find some evidence of Brian's recent occupancy, Sir Edmond would have second thoughts about my "mythical" artist. Although the cottage was meticulously cleared of Brian's belongings, one telltale item left behind would be helpful.

I went first to the small sideboard and peered into the drawers, but, like the two open shelves where the cups and teapot had stood, the drawers were now empty. Since the room was almost barren, there were few places to investigate. There was a cupboard near the hearth, but the shelves were empty. I went to a storage chest the other side of the hearth and thought I'd found my evidence. I immediately saw what appeared to be drawing paper. On closer inspection, though, I saw it was ordinary stationery.

That left only the desk by the window. I pulled out the top drawer. It contained more of the same kind of plain writing paper. There was a pen, a ball of twine, and a pile of London newspapers. I stuck my hand under the stack of newspapers and felt a hard object jammed toward the back of the drawer.

I pulled out the bundle and discovered it was a book, wrapped in an old cotton shirt. I flipped absently through the yellowed pages which seemed crammed with uninteresting fine print. I clapped the covers shut and was about to wrap it up again in the shirt when my hand stopped in mid-air. The faded title on the gray leather cover caught my eye and I held the book closer to the window. The words became clear—*A Documented History with Detailed Descriptions of Malverne Manor.*

I turned to the Table of Contents where I saw an entry for The Manor Drawing Room. My fingers fumbled for the page indicated.

It was all there—the gold-colored brocade curtains; the Chippendale sofa covered in pale blue silk; the harpsichord with the ivory inlays; even the garden view from the windows—the stone wall with the rambling roses, the pond, the church spire in the distance.

I quickly skipped back to the Table of Contents and found another chapter heading, The Cream Lace Room.

There was a lengthy description of the lace counterpane, its Belgian history and acquisition minutely documented. The silk wallcovering was described, with full details about its shipment from Canton. There was a thorough account of "the small but superb Constable with its fine workmanship in the execution of the village scene with its small wooden bridge."

Slowly, I closed the book, wrapped it up in the cotton shirt and replaced it in the back part of the drawer under the newspapers.

All the way up the road to the manor house, I thought about the cottage and the book hidden in the desk drawer. Had Amy been here, I asked myself, not at the manor house but at the cottage?

CHAPTER 8

So once again I was standing at the front door of Malverne Manor, tugging at the bellpull, waiting for the now familiar soft tread of Mrs. Hopkins' footsteps and the jangle of the keys pinned to her apron.

When she finally opened the door, she did not greet me with the cheery smile she gave me previously. Instead, she gasped, throwing her hands to her face in a startled gesture.

While she continued to gape at me in stupefied silence, hands still pressed against her mouth, I began my rehearsed explanation about the pearl brooch.

There wasn't much for me to explain; nevertheless I stammered through my words with difficulty. The flabbergasted, struck-dumb expression on Mrs. Hopkins' face was enough to distract me; but glancing past her shoulder, I could see Sir Edmond quietly open the drawing room door and lean in the doorway with an amused smile to await his cue.

I quickly drew my eyes away from him and had to repeat my lines to Mrs. Hopkins because she either had not heard me or did not understand a word I'd said.

When, finally, Mrs. Hopkins' hands dropped limply to her sides and it seemed she'd recovered her voice and was about to speak, Sir Edmond stepped forward abruptly, further unnerving Mrs. Hopkins. She made a startled croaking sound and gaped at him in total confusion.

"What is this? What does the young lady wish?" Sir Edmond inquired in his best theatrical manner. Mrs. Hopkins gave him an anguished look. She tried to work her lips into a reply to his question, but the best she could do was stammer an incomprehensible jumble of words to Sir Edmond's stern inquiry and I then laboriously repeated my dilemma of the forgotten brooch.

"You left a pearl brooch here at Malverne Manor?" Sir Edmond said with feigned surprise, in a voice so loud Mrs. Hopkins shuddered. He then turned his stare from me to the befuddled Mrs. Hopkins and for a moment I felt a quiver of guilt that he and I should be enjoying our little theatrical performance when we both knew our ulterior purpose was anything but amusing.

But after our brief moment of comic relief, the seriousness of our purpose became heightened and I thought I saw this in his face too as he sternly dismissed Mrs. Hopkins, telling her that he would take care of the matter.

Mrs. Hopkins did not move away at his strict command. Her voice and presence of mind returned with a flash. She crossed her arms across her large bosom. "I cannot imagine," she said with an air of self-assurance, "what the young lady is talking about, Sir Edmond." Her eyes grazed me with a cool glance. "But if she believes a pearl brooch of hers is somewhere in the house, I will certainly go and look for it."

She instantly started for the staircase and I turned to Sir Edmond. "I don't wish to have her do all that walking and stair climbing," I said. "Would you get it, please?"

He saw the urgency in my face and I thought I detected in his expression an awareness as to why I suggested this method for my entry into the house. More than once he'd darted a puzzled look at Mrs. Hopkins.

Mrs. Hopkins was already scurrying up the stairs when he stopped her with a firm command.

"I will get the brooch, Mrs. Hopkins. You needn't trouble yourself."

Her shoulders jerked up at his command, and when she came back to where we were standing, her manner was timorous, the flash of self-assurance gone.

"You needn't trouble yourself, Mrs. Hopkins," he repeated. His voice now was pitched low, but the stamp of authority was there.

For a moment Mrs. Hopkins stood stock-still, confused, and I wondered whether she'd planned to say that there was no such brooch anywhere in the house and from there, would it follow that, like Amy, I'd never been there. I wondered, too, whether this possibility had crossed Sir Edmond's mind.

"That will be all, Mrs. Hopkins," I heard Sir Edmond say and, with a slight nod, Mrs. Hopkins hurried away. "And you will wait in here, please," he said to me, opening the door to the drawing room.

I stepped inside and heard him firmly close the door behind me. My eyes roamed about the room—the gold-colored brocade curtains at the high arched windows, the harpsichord between the windows. My gaze came to rest on the fireplace. It was a warm day and there was no fire in the grate. I recalled how welcome the fire felt the day before yesterday when Mrs. Hopkins led me to it after my rain-drenched walk to the manor.

I crossed the room to a window, remembering the rain-veiled beauty of the garden the previous day. This day the late-afternoon sun cast long shadows across the lawns. In the rosy, late-day sunlight, the rambling roses on the stone wall were a vivid pink. The pond glittered where the sun touched it; the church spire was clearly etched against the sky.

At first I thought only of the drawing room and the garden view being as lovely as I remembered them when the shadow of Amy fell over it all, leaving me sad.

The haunting question edged into my thoughts, Could she possibly have got all her information about Malverne Manor from a book? The one hidden in the cottage?

I'd become so engrossed in my thoughts, the sudden opening of the door made me start.

Sir Edmond approached the window where I stood, the pearl brooch in his outstretched hand. I reached out my hand for it, but he ignored my gesture and silently pinned the brooch to my collar. Our glances met for an instant and I quickly turned my face to look at the garden.

For a while we gazed out the window, standing some distance apart, not speaking.

"You still believe she's been here?" he asked after the silence.

"Yes, don't you?"

"No," he answered, "not here."

I tried not to read too much into his ambiguous statement, but the cottage leaped to my mind once more. "Yes, I still believe Amy stayed here—at the manor house," I declared. I found it necessary to emphasize the last two words; the cottage and hidden book were still very much on my mind.

He turned his eyes from the garden to look at me. I could see disbelief there, but not the challenging truculence he'd shown previously.

"Yes, I know Amy might have got all her information about the house and gardens from a book," I said, wondering whether I should tell him about the concealed book, considering that he would have a reasonable explanation for that as he had for everything else. However, before I could come to a decision about disclosing my discovery of the book, he spoke.

"There is a book called *A Documented History with Detailed Descriptions of Malverne Manor*. It was written by my great-grandfather. There are only six copies in existence. I'm sorry to say I own only one of them."

He moved away from the window and waved to me to follow him. "Come along, Miss Atwood. I'll show you the book. It's in the library. You may wish to read some portions of it."

"Who owns the other five copies?" I asked as I followed him along the hall, trying to keep up with his long strides.

"Two are owned by a canny book collector in Scotland. When I was in Edinburgh recently, I tried to persuade him to sell me the books, but he refused to sell even one. A book collector in London has one copy and he also refused to sell his. The Wickhams have a copy and the Colonel has one."

He threw open a door and as we entered the book-lined room I was conscious of the unusual lighting in the room. Looking up, I saw that it was due to a huge skylight in the high-domed ceiling. The late-afternoon sun, shining through the enormous skylight, tinted the entire room with a russet glow, like a waning sunset. It bathed the oak paneling and bookshelves with the soft light. It caught the shimmer of the leather bindings on the books and warmed the colors of the Persian rugs.

While I stood motionless, my eyes taking in this subtle play of color, Sir Edmond went directly to a bookshelf near the mantel. I had turned to look at a long slender window that framed a copper beech tree when I heard him make a disconcerting sound. He was pushing books back and forth on the shelf, then turned to me with a puzzled frown.

"The book isn't here," he said. "I haven't looked at it in some time, but . . ." He started to inspect other shelves. "Lady Edythe had been reading it but, by now, she's probably memorized every word. I doubt that she'd been reading it lately." He continued to search the shelves.

"I know where the book is," I said, and he swung around to face me.

"Miss Atwood, do you ever say anything that isn't startling or at least surprising?"

He dropped into one of the deep tapestry-upholstered chairs near a window and gestured to a cushioned window seat facing him.

I sat down and met his direct questioning look. "It's in the cottage," I said, and a light flickered behind the intense blue gaze as his eyes widened slightly. "I was looking around for some evidence," I continued, "something to show that an artist had indeed occupied the cottage and that was how I found the book."

His eyes didn't leave me and, as irrelevant as the observation was, I noticed how dark blue his eyes were in this light.

"Where is the book now?" he asked. "You put it back where you found it?"

"Yes."

"And you found information in the book," he went on in a strangely quiet voice, "similar to the details in Amy's letters?"

"Yes, but Amy also wrote about Lady Edythe and Mrs. Hopkins, so the book doesn't solve everything."

He looked past me out the window. A silence followed and I let my eyes travel idly about the room, waiting for him to say something about the concealed book, but when he spoke it was not about the book. My idle gazing about had come to a stop when my eyes lighted on the portrait that hung over the oak mantel. I was struck by the harsh, even sly expression on the subject's face.

"I see you don't approve either," I heard Sir Edmond say, and I turned to look at him. "It's Old Swyndon," he explained. "An ancestor but not a venerable one." He studied the portrait for a moment then said, "I'm not very proud to have him for an ancestor and I'd relegated his portrait to the attics, but when I returned to the manor yesterday, I discovered Old Swyndon hanging there. The portrait Lady Edythe had removed was far more decorative."

He looked away from the portrait which obviously displeased him. "The portrait Lady Edythe removed," he went on, "was of herself when she was a young woman, twenty-one to be exact. Even now in her later years, she is a striking woman. She'd be even more handsome, but the years she lived in India were injurious to her health and she still suffers relapses of jaundice and fever. When she was a young woman, she was a beauty, quite blond then, with marvelous good looks. I heard that from several people and the portrait attested to her good looks."

"Why did she remove her portrait?"

"To help finance my county campaigning. When I walked into the library yesterday and found her portrait gone, I confronted her and she explained her reason. She sold it. I made it clear she needn't spend her money to finance my campaign but she knows I've been pouring much money this year into improving the manor, and she was quite firm about her decision to help out financially. She wouldn't tell me to whom she sold the portrait so I wouldn't buy it back."

He swung his head round for another glance at Old Swyndon then quickly looked away, and I wondered what transgressions made Old Swyndon such a black sheep.

"Lady's Edythe's portrait," he continued, "is a very good likeness of her at that age I've been told. It was painted the year she was married and living in Malta. She was married to the Colonel's brother and like the Colonel he, too, was a military man, stationed in Malta then sent to India."

He'd been sitting and talking in a languid manner, the long legs stretched out, the voice quiet and lazy. Now he sat up; his voice became brisk, businesslike.

"And now, Miss Atwood, let us establish some rules to go by while you are a guest at the manor."

"A guest at the manor?" I repeated, and he gave me one of his side-long glances, catching the involuntary hesitation in my voice.

"How else are we going to puzzle out this business concerning Amy?" he inquired, and then continued, "I am inclined to agree with you that it is best if Lady Edythe and Mrs. Hopkins believe we met for the first time at the front door a moment ago. I thought at first our little charade was foolish, but I can see that it might have its merits."

His next words were in the nature of a command. "You do not say anything to Lady Edythe about your conviction that Amy had been here. Is that understood? You tell her nothing; you ask her nothing. I will not have her questioned or her word doubted. If you have anything to say or ask, you come to me and only to me. I am presuming you have the intelligence and good judgment not to discuss anything with the servants." He stopped and fixed me with an austere look. "Is that agreeable with you?"

"Yes, but only because it seems to be the only way I may continue my search concerning Amy's whereabouts, and if these house rules should not be to my liking, I would leave and pursue my search in some other manner. I will stay at Malverne Manor only so long as I wish to stay."

He gave me a surprised look, then, as he slowly drew his eyes away, a faint smile played on his face.

"Well, Miss Atwood," he said, turning to look at me, the smile still lurking on his face, "I am pleased that you have decided, nevertheless, to stay awhile at Malverne Manor and I promise you your stay will not be too unpardonably dismal." He rose from his chair and went to a bellpull near the mantel. "I will have Mrs. Hopkins ready your room and I will see you at dinner."

He was reaching for the bellpull when there was a knock at the door.

It was Lady Edythe and, as she crossed the room to where I sat, she showed no surprise or discomfort at seeing me again.

"Why, Miss Atwood," she said, smiling pleasantly. "Mrs. Hopkins has just informed me that you did not leave for home after all." She glanced at Sir Edmond. "Miss Atwood was a guest here yesterday, inquiring about that young lady who was expected as a guest," she said to him and, turning to me, added, "I hope you will stay with us awhile longer this time. You could occupy the same room. It's just as you left it."

"Perhaps Miss Atwood would like to go up to her room now," Sir Edmond suggested, crossing the room. "I will see you at dinner," he said from the doorway and left.

"Well, well," Lady Edythe said, facing me again. "This is a pleasant surprise. How fortunate that you left your pearl brooch behind." She started for the door, beckoning to me. "I believe Sir Edmond is right, that you might like to freshen up before dinner. Your room needs nothing done to it, so we can go right up."

As soon as we stepped into the room, Lady Edythe closed the door and sat down on the chair by the bed. The tense expression on her face indicated she was about to tell me something which distressed her.

"I believe, Miss Atwood, it is best if I am forthright, so I shall speak frankly." She pressed the palms of her hands together and darted a glance at me before averting her eyes. "I deceived you yesterday, Miss Atwood. I told you a falsehood because I thought it was the sensible way to meet the situation." She stopped and I could hear her take in a shallow breath, then she rushed on: "When I came to look in on you yesterday after Mrs. Hopkins had served you some of her herb tea, I became alarmed at how deeply you were sleeping. I'd had that experience once myself when I'd complained about an indisposition and Mrs. Hopkins served me some of her herb tea. When I saw you lying there practically unconscious, I knew Mrs. Hopkins had once again got carried away with her herbal medications and made your tea too strong. I was quite stern with her, but she assured me that was what you needed and, indeed, you did feel much improved."

She stopped, hesitated then continued: "I saw my opportunity. When you finally awakened, I told you Sir Edmond had not returned to the manor though he did for a short while. I further misled you saying he wouldn't return for two weeks." She lifted imploring eyes. "I thought it was for the best, Miss Atwood—that you would return home and there would be no embarrassment about your friend. I didn't wish to torment Sir Edmond any further. I was certain then, as I am now, that your friend is in London." She stopped again, nervously pressing her palms together. "I felt that your presence here, Miss Atwood, asking questions, making inquiries would only cause Sir Edmond more personal anguish and might have a detrimental effect on the county election."

"Then why don't we dismiss the subject, not speak of it any more," I said and her face brightened. The shoulders dropped in repose and her tightly clasped hands slowly unfolded.

She arose briskly from her chair and went to the door. The tightness around the eyes and mouth had smoothed out and her smile was brilliant. "Then we will see you at dinner, Miss Atwood. Mrs. Hopkins will be up shortly with some hot water."

As she placed her hand on the doorknob, she laughed softly. "What will Mrs. Ploovey ever think of us?" she said, turning to look at me, the soft laughter still in her voice. "As soon as you place your travel bag in a room at the inn, Old Abner goes down to collect it." She ended her remark on another ripple of laughter and after telling me dinner was at eight, she left.

I went to the window and looked down at the orchard. In the twilight, the flowering trees were quite lovely, the delicate blossoms appearing even more fragile by dusk.

I thought of the tree that grew near the window of the back room of the chemist's shop at home. I wished that were a flowering tree because I spent a great deal of my time working in that back room. That I should think suddenly of home surprised me because I'd hardly thought of home since I'd come to Malverne Manor. Yet, in a way, it wasn't so surprising because after my parents' death it no longer felt like home, not the house nor the village nor the shop.

Ours is neither a pretty nor interesting village. I had to agree with Amy on that count. With two loving parents I had reason to live there. When they were gone, the village and working in the chemist's shop became a drab existence. Looking forward to a life in the village—and shop—with Walter Binson did not fill me with joyful expectation. I'd never really decided to marry Walter. Somehow, gradually, it was being decided for me. Walter had great plans for the shop. "We will make a real success of the shop when we are married," he'd often say.

I'd even made a decision to follow Amy to London, but around that time her mystifying letters began to arrive, about her friendship with a Lady Bellingford, then her meeting with Sir Edmond, and her plans to go to Malverne Manor. When I told Walter that I should go to Malverne Manor because I didn't like the sound of Amy's letters and considered her plans to marry Sir Edmond foolish, he was very much opposed to my going.

"I need you here in the shop," was his firm statement. "What's more," he added, "you know what Amy is like. Two or three days in the country is all she will tolerate. You haven't forgotten, have you, how she disliked quiet village life and fled to London? Besides, this infatuation with Sir Edmond will wear off. You know how fickle she is."

He'd stopped, a half-smile forming on his face. "People like Sir Edmond do not *marry* village girls who worked in teashops."

"I don't picture my cousin, Amy, as—a village girl who worked in a teashop," I retorted. "And I'm sure Sir Edmond did not see her in that light either." I could see by the expression on his face that he'd interpreted my words differently from my intention and I became even angrier. "Besides," I said hotly, "Amy is not fabricating when she lays claim to aristocracy, she——"

He didn't let me finish. "Oh, I'm sure Amy has let Sir Edmond think she is impoverished gentry—if she mentioned the teashop at all." He gave me the patient half-smile again. "People like Sir Edmond do not marry the Amys of the world."

"Amy is not that kind of girl," I hurled at him.

He looked up from the mortar where he was preparing a headache powder. "What I mean," he said, his face reddening, "is that Amy has always been a silly, flirtatious girl. The romantic fling with Sir Edmond probably meant no more to her than it did to him." He turned his attention to the headache powder, pulverizing it in silence for some time then said, "Although Amy referred to her London admirer—the one she met while Sir Edmond was away from London—as an adventurer, I'll wager it is him she will marry. If she hasn't already done so. They seem well-matched, that is, they both thrive on the excitement of city life and transient joys."

This wasn't the first time Walter had dismissed Amy as a silly, flirtatious girl. Watching him crush the white headache powder in the mortar, I thought of the Milkins girl. It was she who would come to purchase the headache powder for her mamma. She came at least twice a week.

I often wondered whether her dear mamma had that many headaches.

Every time she came to collect the headache powder she flirted outrageously with Walter. Since I was usually in the shop, the flirtation began outside the shop. She always drove her ponytrap very slowly past the shop. Then came the inevitable difficulty with the trap, sometimes with the horse, sometimes a wheel on the trap was misbehaving. Walter always had to go to her aid.

Each time she sidled into the chemist's shop and I chanced to glance into the front part of the shop from the back room where I usually worked, the Milkins girl was fondly gazing up into Walter's flushed face while he explained in minute detail the symptomatic manifestations of migraine headache and that he was certain this new remedy would alleviate her mamma's distress. Her errand of mercy was then prolonged with questions about that violet-scented soap that was on order and when did he expect a new shipment of the lavender eau de cologne which Mamma liked to dab on her forehead when the headache raged.

Somehow, in Walter's eyes, the Milkins girl's flirtation was altogether different from Amy's flirtations and I wondered more than once whether Walter had been cruelly rebuffed by Amy.

It occurred to me that the following week was the first week of May. The church picnic was always held the first Sunday of May. When Mrs. Hopkins arrived with the hot water, I would ask her to bring me some letter paper and a pen. I would write Walter, telling him I might not be home in time for the church picnic and why not ask the Milkins girl. It would be perfectly all right, I'd assure him; it wasn't as if he and I were officially engaged.

In a short while I heard Mrs. Hopkins coming down the hallway and when she entered, she was her usual bustling, cheerful self, completely recovered from her stupefied shock.

"Ah, you gave me such a start, miss, when I saw you at the door," she said on a peal of laughter. "I was so surprised to see you again," she continued, the dark eyes snapping with good humor as she carried the hot water into the bathroom. "Why I couldn't make out even what you were saying," she said when she returned. "What lost pearls I asked myself. I was so astonished to see you I could not follow what you were saying."

She placed some folded towels and night clothes on the bed and then said, "But I am pleased to see you are with us again. I know how taken you were with Malverne Manor." She crossed her arms over her chest and gave me a direct look. "I got a little scold from Lady Edythe about the herb tea I served you." Her plump face creased into a smile. "Oh not a real scold. But Lady Edythe thought the dose was too strong." Her chin came out a little defiantly. "As I explained to you, miss, I knew how much dose to give."

"I'm sorry you got scolded," I broke in. "Everything worked out for the best, Mrs. Hopkins."

She flapped her hands down, smoothed her apron front with a gesture of relief and gratitude, and then went to the door. "Dinner is at eight, miss," she said, and as she opened the door I remembered about the letter paper.

"Be glad to, Miss Atwood. Old Abner can post the letter tomorrow morning when he stops by the inn for your travel bag."

I thanked her and went into the bathroom to freshen up for dinner. I had the feeling that now with the master returned to the manor, dinner might be on a splendid scale and I wished I had something more suitable than my green muslin walking dress. At least the color was good for me; it did nice things for my hair, bringing out the russet coloring.

I had guessed correctly about the dinner. The instant I entered the formal dining room and saw the equally splendid formal attire of Lady Edythe and Sir Edmond, I felt curiously out of place and wished once more I'd had something more elegant to wear.

The spacious dining room was paneled in a satiny, pale-colored wood, the panels enhanced by gold-leaf filigree that framed them with decorative gilt scrolls. A Venetian chandelier shimmered overhead; the tiny candles in the glass prisms cast a golden light on the table where the crystal and china sparkled. Fawn-colored velvet curtains at the tall windows seemed like the velvet lining of a jewel box and the room, with its golden reflected light, appeared like some exquisite topaz in a golden setting.

I was so moved by this unique room it was probably a while before I became aware that Sir Edmond was standing beside my chair, waiting for me to be seated. In the quick upward glance I gave him before taking my seat, I saw that slightly amused smile slip across his face, a touch of mockery behind the eyes.

I hadn't really looked at him then, but when he took his place at the head of the table, I was struck by how handsome he looked in his formal clothes and the ease with which he wore them. The white cravat intensified his dark good looks, the deep tan, and the crisp blackness of his hair.

I indeed felt a bit awkward in my plain green walking dress. Lady Edythe, wearing a diamond necklace, looked quite regal in a luxuriant chiffon gown the color of sapphires.

To my surprise the awkwardness I felt when entering soon dissipated, due mainly to Sir Edmond's high spirits and, undoubtedly, his knack for sensing my unease. He unerringly knew how to remedy the situation, and before I was hardly aware of it, I fell easily into the conversation and was soon talking and laughing along with him and Lady Edythe as if the three of us had known each other a long time.

Since by then I was familiar with Mrs. Hopkins' culinary expertise, I expected the food to be excellent, which it was. The roast pheasant was tender and rich in flavor. Knowing how lovingly Mrs. Hopkins tended her vegetable garden, I wasn't surprised that the accompanying vegetable should be tasty and properly cooked. The feast ended with a delicious apple charlotte served with clotted cream. By the time Sir Edmond suggested we go to the drawing room for our coffee, I no longer felt the least ill at ease. I'd enjoyed everything about the dinner.

For an instant I felt at odds when we entered the drawing room. All at once the room brought back to me the reason I was at Malverne Manor. Everything became all mixed up with Amy, but, again, Sir Edmond, as if sensing my unease, quickly dispelled my vague discomfort by the same sort of easy banter that had made me feel relaxed in the dining room.

Lady Edythe was also at her gracious best and while she and I enjoyed our coffee, Sir Edmond had his brandy and cigar. The conversation once again went smoothly. Amy was never mentioned.

I admired Sir Edmond's conversational skill. I could see his political potential along those lines. Like a wise politician he did not monopolize the conversation but, rather, tossed in topics and questions which encouraged others to do the talking. He was also a good listener.

It was obvious all through dinner, and later during coffee in the drawing room, that Sir Edmond was the unquestionable master of Malverne Manor. Although Lady Edythe basked in her role of mistress of the manor, it soon became evident that she sometimes felt a little unsure of her status. Her attitude toward Sir Edmond was timorous at times, almost obsequious, as if she knew she had better not arouse his displeasure, as if she knew that a more violent nature was hidden beneath Sir Edmond's charming façade.

This relationship between them became evident when Sir Edmond turned abruptly to Lady Edythe and informed her that Miss Atwood and he would take a stroll in the gardens and would she please bring Miss Atwood something to put across her shoulders.

If she'd been a servant, she could not have obeyed with greater dispatch.

When we stepped out into the garden, I was glad for the light wrap Lady Edythe had fetched. The evening was cool, but with the covering over my shoulders I was quite comfortable.

The gardens were on the brink of darkness. In the half-light, they had a dreamlike quality, hushed and softly shadowed. We strolled first in the rose garden, the air heady with the floral scent. The fragrance from the apple orchards drifted over on the evening air.

I looked up at the hazy outline of a moon shining faintly through the treetops and, all at once, I thought of the manor library with its enormous skylight and imagined how breath-taking that room would look when moonlight poured down from the skylight.

I was still gazing up at the treetops and the moon when I became conscious of Sir Edmond's eyes on me, and as I drew my eyes down, I caught his bemused smile. I could feel my face flush as if he'd read my foolish thoughts.

We walked along in silence and then he said casually, "We might stop by the cottage and see if it has been invaded again."

He said it so lightly, with such good humor, I could not take offense and we both laughed.

We were walking near the pond now and I thought of the servant girl who'd drowned there recently. I was tempted to ask him about this then changed my mind. That question, like some others I was going to ask him, would have to wait till later. For the present, my thoughts were concentrated on the cottage because its window was now visible and I thought I saw someone pass by the window.

When I thought I saw this movement at the window, I came to an abrupt stop in the path. Sir Edmond stopped too and gave me an inquiring look, but only because he wondered why I'd stopped.

"What's wrong?" he asked. "Did you hit your foot against a stone?"

"No, I'm all right," I answered and resumed my walking.

As we approached the cottage door, I saw that it was opened wide and I remembered distinctly having closed it. I wondered whether Brian had returned.

CHAPTER 9

There was no one inside, but the room had been disturbed. The chairs which Sir Edmond and I had left near the table were at the far side of the room. There were other little changes. The objects on the desk were rearranged and the window which I was quite sure had been closed was now open.

When I turned my attention to Sir Edmond, I saw that he too was looking about with a perplexed frown. "The room has been changed about," he mused then glanced at me. "Well, Miss Atwood, your fanciful talk about mythical artists and disappearing guests is infectious. Now I'm beginning to imagine that as we came near the cottage, I saw someone walk past the window."

"I saw it, too." I looked about. "And the room has been disturbed."

His eyes scrutinized the room, then he gave me a curious glance. "Unless you'd really ransacked the place when you were searching for evidence and found the concealed book."

"I did not ransack the place," I retorted. "This is not the condition in which I left the room."

He gave an apologetic wave of his hand. "Forgive me. I should not have put it that way." He went to the window and closed it. "Did you open it?" he asked and I said I hadn't. "I'm quite sure," he said, "that it was closed a while ago."

He lifted his shoulders slightly in a casual shrug. "Poachers. I've had trouble with them before. They prowl about. Well, Miss Atwood, where did you find the book?" he asked, and when I told him, he went to the desk and began to go through the drawers.

After he'd thoroughly gone through the drawers and turned around to tell me the book wasn't there, I wasn't at all surprised. I'd rather expected it.

"Seems our poacher is also a book thief," he said.

"Why would he be interested in the book?"

"For the money, Miss Atwood. He can get a good price for it." Then he shook his head. "No, that isn't likely. The book wouldn't be an easy thing for the poacher to dispose of." He dropped down into a chair, his eyes sweeping the room. "So, it's gone," he said. He sat in thoughtful silence for a moment. "Well, let's start back for the house, Miss Atwood," he said, getting up. He closed the door after us and then helped me place the wrap over my shoulders. It was dark now but the moon was bright, lighting our way.

"Do you suppose it was Old Abner hanging about?" I asked. "That it was him we saw pass by the window? But no," I checked myself. "Why would Old Abner take the book?"

"And since our intruder probably escaped through the window, that also leaves out Old Abner who's too old and crippled for such gymnastics." He paused, then added, "It might have been Lady Edythe who'd placed the book there and then removed it."

"Lady Edythe?"

He laughed. "Not for any nefarious purpose, Miss Atwood. Lady Edythe likes to take strolls about the manor. Sometimes she stops at the cottage to rest and to read. I found her here more than once, sitting in the wicker chair under the tree, reading the very book we're searching for. It might have been she who hid it, since she knows its value. Something tells me that when we return to the house, we will find the book back on the library shelf."

"Then perhaps it was only Old Abner we saw in the cottage," I said. "The poor old man might have simply got scared when he heard sounds outside and bolted out the door before we got there." Although I thought this might possibly have happened, I wondered, nevertheless, whether it might not have been Brian who'd bolted.

"Out of the question," Sir Edmond said. "Not Old Abner." He stopped and nodded toward the pond which shimmered in the moonlight, the rush of the water sounding quite loud in the night silence. "The cottage is off-limits as far as Old Abner is concerned," he went on. "He claims it's haunted by the ghost of a servant girl and he won't go near the cottage." He was still gazing at the pond. "She drowned in that pond."

"Yes, I've heard," I said.

"When I returned home yesterday, Abner told me a frantic, garbled story and Lady Edythe and Mrs. Hopkins then explained the situation. The blond young lady that you'd mentioned, Miss Atwood, the one who arrived a few days ago on the noon coach, was a servant girl who was to work at the manor. Mrs. Hopkins said that the young lady proved unsatisfactory from the first because the girl was, as Mrs. Hopkins put it, 'crazed.' "

"Crazed?"

"Yes, Mrs. Hopkins said the girl had weeping spells, was exceedingly absent-minded and, as Mrs. Hopkins described it, 'had a few tiles loose upstairs.' Lady Edythe disagreed with Mrs. Hopkins' diagnosis. She believes the girl was ill and terribly worried about something." He gazed quietly at the pond, then continued walking.

"Well, it turned out badly," he said. "When she was informed she was unsuitable for service and would have to return home, the desolate girl either deliberately, or by accident, drowned herself in the pond. Lady Edythe suspects it was suicide. She believes the girl had got herself into a family way at her previous place of employment and was desperately afraid to face her family."

"Was the body recovered?"

"Yes. The brother came and took the body home. He was a vicar. The father is one, too. Lady Edythe says the brother was terribly shocked, as if he, too, suspected his sister had committed suicide."

We didn't speak after that until we entered the house and Sir Edmond said, "If you will wait here a moment, I will take a quick look in the library to see if the book has been replaced."

I stood in the vast hall, not really seeing anything, hardly conscious of even the scent of the roses on the table in the center of the hall. My thoughts were still on the young woman who'd drowned in the pond.

Then I saw Sir Edmond return and he shook his head.

"No, it isn't there," he said and then asked, "You won't lose your way to your room, will you? The hallway is lighted."

"No," I said, going to the stairs. "I know the way."

I was almost at the staircase when I heard him say my name, then come forward.

He placed his hand lightly on my arm. "Miss Atwood, I know you've had much on your mind lately and perhaps a little diversion might be desirable. I have persuaded Lady Edythe to take it easy tomorrow, take a breather from this intense campaigning she'd been doing. She will remain at home, but I will visit a couple of my constituents and stop by the Colonel's place since it's on the way. Would you like to accompany me?"

"Yes, I would like that very much."

"Fine. We will leave shortly after breakfast." He paused, looked into my face, and it seemed he was about to speak but, instead, he quickly walked away.

"Good night, Miss Atwood," I heard him say.

"Good night," I answered, although I didn't expect he'd heard.

When I reached the top of the stairs and was about to turn into my wing, I heard a door open then close somewhere near my room. This was followed by quick, almost running, footsteps along the hallway.

I was still in such a bemused state, I did not realize immediately that those footsteps did not sound like Mrs. Hopkins' or Lady Edythe's. They were quick, youthful steps.

I broke into a run and as I rushed around the corner and into my wing, I saw a young woman running along the hallway which was lighted by two wall lamps, casting a dim illumination.

Although she was now far down the hallway, I could see that it was neither Mrs. Hopkins nor Lady Edythe. It was a young woman.

"Amy!" I cried. The name rushed out involuntarily.

She swung her head around but it was a swift movement and, with a scarf tied about her head, the ends flapping about, I could see little. The dimness of the hall further obscured her and she was so far along the corridor, I couldn't see the face.

"Amy!" I cried again.

She ran still faster and the next instant she disappeared into the adjoining corridor.

I raced down the hallway. I could hear her swift footsteps along the next corridor. I heard a door open then slam shut.

I plunged into the corridor and looked about frantically. There was no light here. I could dimly see doorways, but there was no sliver of light under any door.

"Amy," I cried softly, "was that you?"

There was no answer.

I stood motionless in the dark corridor and, all at once, the silent darkness became oppressive, vaguely menacing. I hurried away into the lighted hallway.

I hesitated at the door to the Cream Lace Room. It might have been the door to this room I'd heard open and close when I'd reached the top of the stairs. I opened the door and glanced into the room. It was empty, shrouded in silence and near-darkness.

At my bedroom door I hesitated once more, trying to decide whether I should go downstairs and look for Sir Edmond. In this huge unfamiliar house, where would I look for him or Lady Edythe or Mrs. Hopkins?

Before opening my door, I glanced over my shoulder at the door to the Cream Lace Room. It couldn't have been Amy that I'd seen. She wouldn't have run away from me.

CHAPTER 10

When I entered my room, I glanced around to see if anything had been disturbed. Nothing was out of place which was what I'd expected because I was quite certain the young woman had come out of the Cream Lace Room.

I remained standing just inside the door. Bewildering thoughts whirled through my head. Could it possibly have been Amy that I'd seen? The harder I tried to cast off the fanciful thought, the more tenaciously it clung. Once more I considered finding Sir Edmond or Lady Edythe or Mrs. Hopkins and informing them of what I saw. But, no, I didn't wish to wander alone about the vast, shadowy house. And didn't they always have a reasonable explanation for anything I said or asked?

I swung around to bolt my door. After all, I had no idea who the prowler was. As I prepared for bed, I tried to put the incident out of my mind, but I kept remembering how the girl raced frantically along the hallway, then vanished when she ran into that dark adjacent corridor. No, it couldn't have been Amy, I decided. But who was it?

I went into the bathroom where I saw that Mrs. Hopkins had left hot water for me. The water was by then barely warm, but I began to wash. By the time I'd finished, got into my nightgown and plaited my hair, I felt much calmer about the whole thing. With my door bolted, I was safe from prowlers. In the morning, the incident would be explained.

I felt quite wide awake and decided the time was as good as any to write that letter to Walter. I found the paper and pen Mrs. Hopkins had brought to my room, moved the lamp on the bedside table closer, and began to write: "I meant to write sooner, Walter, but I've been rather occupied since I arrived at Malverne Manor," then my pen came to a halt and it occurred to me that my letter might fall into someone else's hands and be read by some person at the manor before it got posted. I disliked this business of being constantly cautious, but nevertheless I continued the letter with that in mind. It could not be a confidential letter. . . . "But Amy is not at Malverne Manor," I continued writing. "Perhaps she is still in London, possibly married to the young man you'd mentioned." That much, I thought, Walter had already precluded. . . . "If there should be a letter for me from Amy," I went on, "do not forward it." I had the feeling that if any letter from Amy had arrived since I'd left home, it would be another of those cries for help from Malverne Manor and I did not want anyone at the manor reading the incriminating letter then destroying it.

"I will be home shortly," I concluded, "but I may not be home in time for the church picnic so feel free to ask the Milkins girl. You have my permission, Walter. After all, it isn't as if you and I were officially engaged. I'm sure the Milkins girl will be quite pleased if you ask her. I hope everything is going fine at the shop," I finished off and then sealed the envelope.

As I lay down to sleep, I made a firm resolve not to let the puzzling occurrence of the girl in the hallway interfere with my sleep. I purposely diverted my thoughts to everything and anything but that, deciding, in fact, to set aside the whole mysterious business about Amy. I wasn't going to think about it for a while. I would, instead, consider the pleasant aspects of my visit to the manor because, despite the unhappy reason for my visit, there admittedly were redeeming aspects.

Possibly because I'd so forcibly crammed far back into my mind all thoughts of Amy and the disturbing incident in the hallway, I dreamt about the entire strange experience. In my dream the fleeing girl was Amy. She wasn't racing along a corridor but running along a shore where waves swirled and washed up onto the land. As she ran, she kept calling my name. When I'd almost caught up with her, she turned her head for an instant and her face was so contorted I couldn't tell whether she was laughing or weeping. Then she whirled away and fled along the shore, disappearing out of sight until only the loud pounding of the waves could be heard.

I awakened with a jolt from the nightmarish dream when I realized that the loud pounding was someone banging on my door. I sat up, dazed, then snatched up my dressing gown and went to the door. It was probably Mrs. Hopkins with my hot water.

I stared in astonishment. A young girl whisked past me. She gave me a quick smile then placed my morning tea on the bedside table and took the hot water into the bathroom.

When she'd done that, she stood before me, her young face—she seemed about sixteen—shining with an eager, shy smile, her hands clasped behind her back.

"Good morning, miss. I'm Myrna," she said. "We returned to the manor late last night and——"

"We?"

"Yes, miss, we, the Farrises—that's us, miss," she stammered, "the whole of the Farris family. We work at the manor. I'm Myrna Farris." She brushed back a stray lock of soft brown hair with an awkward, self-conscious gesture. The sunny smile appeared again, deepening the fresh color in her cheeks.

"You see, miss," she went on, smoothing down the front of her apron, still with that self-conscious shyness, "my sister Floss was married last week. She used to work at the manor too, but she did not come back with us now that she's married. Floss is going to live with his people. So, besides my parents, there is now only me and my two brothers. My older brother helps in the gardens and my younger brother works in the stables."

"And you returned to the manor late last night?" I asked.

She bobbed her head. "Yes, miss. Lady Edythe was kind enough to let the whole of the Farris family have a holiday of two weeks. Lady

Edythe, you see, knew my sister Floss was planning on getting married come Christmas. After the holidays here at the manor, the whole of the Farris family has a four-day holiday and we all have a nice visit to my married sister's place in Sulpston. Lady Edythe came up with the suggestion that we all go up to Sulpston for two weeks and Floss could have her wedding now instead of waiting for the Christmas holiday. Lady Edythe was even kind enough to give Floss a nice gift, enough money for the making of a wedding dress and some left over to pay the fiddlers."

She paused in her rush of happy news. "It was a pretty wedding, miss. Didn't bother none having to make wedding arrangements sudden-like. Lady Edythe explained it would be all right for us to be away for two weeks. She was staying with the Wickhams, she said, and Mrs. Hopkins and Old Abner could keep an eye on the place, so to speak. The horses, all but two, were taken up to Wickham Place. The Wickhams, miss, are acquaintances of Lady Edythe and live nearby."

She turned now to straighten up the bedcovers and I said, "Myrna, was it you running along the hallway last night? Why didn't you stop when I called to you?"

She was fluffing up a pillow and I could see her back and arms stiffen. "Running, miss?" She did not turn around to face me but continued to pummel the pillow. "Running in the hallway?" she asked. "No, miss. I know nothing of that."

She then turned to leave. As she headed for the door, I was aware of the change in her face, the bright open smile gone, a clouded, almost furtive expression in the quick side glance.

"Will there be anything else you wish now, miss?" she asked, avoiding my eyes. Remembering the letter I wrote, I asked would she see it got posted and she promised she would.

I stepped forward and looked directly into her face. "Myrna, if it was you last night, I wish to know only because I was puzzled and frightened at seeing someone so unexpectedly, someone who ran away when I called."

She shook her head vehemently. The clear gray eyes widened. "No, miss," she murmured. "I do not know about anyone running along the hallway." She inched toward the door. "Is there anything else you wish, miss?" she repeated in an urgent voice and when I shook my head, she rushed off.

She left in such a flurry of embarrassment and confusion she'd forgotten to inform me about breakfast, and since neither she nor Mrs.

Hopkins came later with instructions, I went to the small dining room where I'd had breakfast before.

Sir Edmond was there, waiting for me, and rose to greet me with a cordial smile.

"Lady Edythe will not be joining us," he said as he held out my chair. "She awoke with one of her mean headaches."

Mrs. Hopkins bustled into the room, cheery as usual, doing herself proud with delicious little sausages and eggs poached in cream. There were deviled kidneys, too, and browned apple rings. The buttery muffins were excellent and the coffee, rich and fragrant.

"Unless there are many guests present at the manor," Sir Edmond explained, "I prefer to have breakfast served fresh at the table rather than lying about on a sideboard. I hope this arrangement is convenient for you, Miss Atwood."

I assured him it was quite convenient and we drifted into a casual conversation ranging from the expected cider yield for this year at the manor and the fact that the wool yield would be doubled. From there Sir Edmond got to talking about the Colonel, his military exploits in India and his home in Surrey where he had retired to a quiet life.

When there was a brief lull in the conversation, I broached the subject of the mysterious young woman I saw running along the upstairs hallway last night.

"Must have been one of the Farrises," Sir Edmond said in a light, unconcerned tone. "Probably Myrna."

"I asked her. She claims it wasn't she."

Sir Edmond lifted his shoulders in a faint shrug. "I'm sure it was nothing," he said in a tone indicating he wasn't interested, and the subject was closed. He then reminded me we should be on our way directly after breakfast. "I decided to stop by the Colonel's first. It'll be more convenient to visit two of my constituents on the way back from the Colonel's place," he said and I wondered whether he was actually expecting to find Amy at the Colonel's home.

"Do you mind if we ride in the curricle rather than take a driver along?" he asked and I said it was agreeable with me.

"Although the Colonel lives in the neighboring county," he explained, "the distance isn't far really. One of my tenants, in fact, lives nearer the Colonel's place than the manor."

When we arrived, the manservant informed us the Colonel was in the garden behind the house. Sir Edmond immediately asked the servant whether any guests were present. The answer was no, and Sir Edmond and I went to find the Colonel.

We found him working in his flower garden, quite an old gentleman, early seventies perhaps, very frail-looking. His movements, though, as he busied himself among the flowers were surprisingly brisk.

He looked up from the delphiniums he was staking when he saw us approach, and his thin, lined face lit up with a puckish grin.

"Well, well, my boy," he said in a voice as brisk as his quick steps when he came forward to greet us. "What a nice little surprise, Edmond, to have you visit." He cocked his head in my direction then nodded at Sir Edmond with a broad smile. "I always enjoy a visit from you, my boy, but, I say, you've brought along a lovely extra surprise today."

The Colonel turned his mischievous grin at me once more and Sir Edmond made the introductions, explaining me simply as a guest at the manor.

We followed the Colonel to some bamboo lawn chairs placed in the shade of a plane tree. The three of us soon slipped into a lively conversation with much laughing because no matter what mundane subject was mentioned, the Colonel had a knack for turning it into a witty entertainment. I liked the Colonel from the start. For a frail, aged little person, he was possessed of an amazing vitality. Before we'd got settled into the lawn chairs, the Colonel had Sir Edmond go into the house and fetch him a glass of port. The wine might have raised the Colonel's spirits and livened up his conversation but I got the impression that with or without the aid of port, the Colonel was jolly good company.

"Since you two have hit it off so well," Sir Edmond said after a while, glancing from me to the Colonel, "I'm sure you wouldn't mind if I excused myself for a short time." He rose from his chair and addressed the Colonel. "I'm sure you wouldn't mind being left in Miss Atwood's charming company while I make a quick trip to see one of my tenants who lives close-by." He then turned to me. "We'll be returning to the manor by a different direction and the two stops we make will be brief ones." He made a quick gesture of good-by and after a slight wave of his hand, hurried off.

"He's a fine lad," the Colonel said in a tender, affectionate tone as he watched Sir Edmond rush away. After a long, pleasurable sip of port, he cocked his head to the side and asked, "Well, Miss Atwood, how are you getting on with that vulture in dove's plumage?"

I sat up with a start and he made a brushing gesture with his hands and bobbed his head.

"Sorry," he muttered, "didn't mean to put you on the spot, Miss Atwood. No need to answer my impertinent question, but I'm sure you knew right off I meant Lady Edythe. How could anyone mistake her for anything else."

"Sir Edmond is devoted to her," I said lamely, feeling that I should say something.

The Colonel grunted into his wineglass. "In some ways my nephew is a clever fellow, Miss Atwood, but in some other ways he is oh so blind."

I was at a loss for words, afraid of saying the wrong thing so I decided to say nothing at all.

"Lady Edythe married my younger brother, Wilford," the Colonel went on. "We're an army family, Miss Atwood. I retired from the army some time ago. My brother, Wilford, served his country well, first in Malta as a major then he did himself honorably well in India. Ended up doing equally well in the House of Lords." He stopped then added in a grumbling tone, "And none of his accomplishments, thank you, were due to the woman he married.

"Oh, she was a beauty in her younger days," he conceded after a gloomy pause. "You could have seen how much of a dazzling blond beauty she was in those days if she hadn't sold that portrait of herself. It hung in the Malverne Manor library until a few days ago."

"I've been told about the portrait, that Lady Edythe sold it to finance Sir Edmond's election campaign," I said, and it occurred to me that if Lady Edythe had misconstrued Amy's and Sir Edmond's letters as he'd suggested, did Lady Edythe sell the portrait to pay off Amy so she would leave quietly and not cause a scandal?

The Colonel made a fierce, grumpy noise in his throat. "Lady Edythe need not go about taking any credit for Edmond's winning the county seat." He sniffed, the lined, gaunt face hardening. "As if her prancing about, shaking hands with tenants and constituents was doing any good. Edmond will make it on his own. He no more needs Lady Edythe's help than my brother ever needed it—or got it."

A brooding silence followed and before I could think of some polite remark to make, the Colonel continued in a slightly subdued manner. "In some ways Edmond is like my brother, Wilford. Not in appearance, but he has Wilford's keen mind and winning ways. I was disappointed at first that Edmond did not choose an army career, but Edmond has this fine sense for land and he's done remarkable things for Malverne Manor and his tenants are pleased with him. I suppose Edmond knows where his talents lie."

The Colonel drained the last of his port, stared glumly into the empty glass for a while then said, "Miss Atwood, would you mind if we continued our little visit while I finished up my gardening chores? I've very little left to do. The sweet peas and delphiniums are drooping badly."

I got up from my chair. "Don't mind at all. May I help?"

"Oh, would you?" he said, popping up from his chair and trotting to the garden with those quick, jaunty steps.

We worked silently for a short while and soon I guessed the Colonel was thinking of Lady Edythe again. He was handling some delphinium stalks a bit roughly as if letting loose his anger on the plants.

"If Edmond would only use some good sense," he sputtered, "and clear that woman out of his house. But he's blind, I tell you, absolutely blind on some matters. Feels sorry for her because she's a poor lonely widow and that she does an excellent job as temporary mistress of the manor. Rubbish! Of course, when I go to visit at Malverne Manor, I pretend to get on with the old girl but that's only because I like Edmond and I know he'll come to his senses one of these days."

The Colonel lapsed into a glum silence after that and we worked diligently on the sweet peas and delphiniums. After a while, I felt obliged to say something to break the heavy silence.

"How long did you serve in the Indian army?" I asked, hoping it would get him off the subject of Lady Edythe.

"I was in India for only three years," he replied in that booming voice. "My brother, Wilford, was there much longer. He liked it there, but Lady Edythe didn't. She pretended to be deathly ill from the climate. Left him, just like that. Went back to Malta to stay with friends. Came back to India the following year when she heard rumors my brother was up for the House of Lords."

Feeling impelled once more to draw the conversation away from Lady Edythe, I remarked about the gardens at Malverne Manor, how beautiful they were.

The Colonel wouldn't be diverted. This, apparently, was the day he chose to say all the things he'd been saving up about Lady Edythe and he evidently decided it was best to say it to a stranger. My remark about the Malverne gardens only served to point up yet another grievance he had concerning the lady.

"Lady Edythe would have you think she is responsible for Malverne Manor looking so prosperous," he said with a wry smile. "Not so. It is all Edmond's doing. And the Farris family. The Farrises wouldn't stay on if it were not for their devotion to Edmond. Abner is too old for anything to matter. But it's Edmond who made Malverne Manor into a success. It was in horrible shape when he inherited it seven years ago. My youngest brother—Edmond's father—was a good enough fellow but had no head for business. Didn't like the military life either and left that, but he was a charming, likable sort."

He stopped speaking and gave the sweet peas and delphiniums an over-all glance. "Well, that finishes the garden chores and I thank you, Miss Atwood, for helping out. Now let us go sit in the shade for a spell."

As soon as he was seated in the lawn chair, he leaned forward and peered into my face. "Have you met Miss Wickham?" he asked, and I shook my head.

He leaned back in the chair and thoughtfully fingered the empty wineglass on the table beside his chair as if he wished the glass were filled again.

"They're hoping," he said with a lopsided smile, "Miss Wickham and her papa, that is—with Lady Edythe's blessing, naturally—that Edmond will marry Miss Wickham and do for that ruin of a Wickham Place what he did for Malverne Manor."

"Then you don't know about Sir Edmond's intention to marry a young lady named Amy?"

He nodded. "Yes, I know about that."

"That was why Sir Edmond and I came here. He thought Amy might be here."

"No, she never came here. Fact is, she never came at all, not to Malverne Manor either."

"You're sure?"

He nodded once more. "I went up to Malverne Manor the day after that young lady was to have arrived. Edmond had written me from London telling me when this Amy acquaintance of his would arrive." He shrugged. "She never came."

He paused, thinking, then added, "I even went back a couple of days later to see if the young lady had arrived by then but, no, there was no such guest there. I wasn't too surprised, though, that she hadn't come."

"Why do you say that?"

"Oh, little things Edmond let slip in his letters to me. I don't believe he had any real intention of marrying this Amy, no more than she had. It was a romantic whirl for Edmond. No more. And I got the impression there was another chap in this Amy's life, too, sort of waiting in the wings, you might say."

I was surprised that the Colonel's remark should make me think of Brian. "Have you met Brian?" I asked.

"Brian? Brian?" he repeated. "Never heard of anyone by that name." He closed his eyes and leaned back comfortably in the lawn chair. "You spoken for, Miss Atwood?" he asked, peering at me through half-closed eyes.

I drew back at the astonishing question and he looked at me with a mischievous grin. "Well, are you?" he demanded, leaning forward in his chair.

"Yes, I am, to someone back home. Why do you ask?"

He sighed and dropped back into his chair. "A pity you should be spoken for, Miss Atwood. The minute I saw you walking alongside Edmond I thought, now that is the girl for Edmond."

After staring gloomily into space for a while, he rose friskily from his chair. "Come, Miss Atwood. Let us go into the house and have our midmorning tea." We entered a large, dark-looking house completely lacking in Malverne Manor's sunny pleasing appearance.

"Come with me into the library," the Colonel said. "I will ring to have our tea brought there. I want to show you some portraits, of Edmond's parents and my brother, Wilford."

The library was a musty, dreary place and I was shown first the portraits of Edmond's parents. Looking up at the portraits, I could see where Sir Edmond got his good looks. His father was a dark-haired, strikingly handsome man with the devilishly bold look I often saw in Sir Edmond's demeanor. The mother was a gentle-looking woman with sweet, delicate features, and eyes the same dazzling blue as her son's. I could see that Sir Edmond's fleeting moments of gentleness and the sometimes tender look about the mouth were inherited from the mother.

"And this is my brother, Wilford," I heard the Colonel say, and I turned to gaze at two portraits side by side, very much alike but for the manner of dress. In both portraits he was the austere soldier, but despite the military stance and circumspect expression, some of the Colonel's affability and good humor came through as a family trait. Not even the dignified robes and impeccable military uniform could hide it.

I mentioned this observation to the Colonel and he was pleased, adding that he missed his brother because they'd always been good friends.

When I looked away from the portraits, my glance fell on the books stuffed haphazardly onto shelves and I remembered that the Colonel owned a copy of the Malverne Manor book. I asked him if I might have a look at the book and he quickly produced it.

"Why don't you make yourself comfortable in that chair while you look at the book, Miss Atwood." He gestured toward a large shabby-looking upholstered chair. "The chair is older than I am but comfortable no end." He went to the door. "While you do that, I'll go and see personally about the tea things. That way I won't keep interrupting you while you glance through the book. I expect Edmond will be back shortly and have tea with us." He stopped, gave me a direct look. "What's your young man's name?"

"Charles Binson."

"Too bad. The moment I saw you and Edmond together, I knew you were for him." He scowled and hurried away.

I seized upon the book, eagerly reading snatches here and there, trying to discover the particular significance of the book, why it should have been hidden in the cottage then snatched away. From the first, I had a strong intuition that the book was somehow related to Amy and to her mysterious disappearance.

But I could find nothing in the book to throw light on the puzzle. It was a thick volume and in the little time I had, plus not knowing what to look for, my skimming through the book proved fruitless.

When I heard Sir Edmond's voice in the hall, I quickly slipped the book onto the shelf, asking myself why I should do this the instant I heard Sir Edmond, as if I didn't wish him to catch me studying the book. Nor did I say anything about the book while we had our tea and when it was time for Sir Edmond and me to leave, the Colonel asked me to visit him again. I, of course, could not promise any such thing, knowing my visit at the manor would end shortly.

"You and the Colonel got along well," Sir Edmond remarked as we rode away.

"Yes, I became rather fond of him. He's a spry old gentleman. Quite entertaining."

"I'm rather fond of him myself. He's all alone now that he's a widower. I'm sure he gets lonely in that dark, dreary house. He broods too much about his wife who died a year ago, and he misses his brother, Wilford. They were close. I'd like to have the Colonel at Malverne Manor more frequently, but he isn't too keen on Lady Edythe and now, in his old age and with his brooding spells, he's resurrected all his old grievances against her and keeps adding new imaginary injustices. I'm sorry to say the Colonel and Lady Edythe don't exactly see eye to eye."

No, not exactly, I thought.

After we'd gone a short distance, Sir Edmond pulled the curricle to the side of the road and hailed a man walking along a nearby field path.

"That's Will Hockinson," Sir Edmond informed me as the man now started to come forward. "One of my constituents and the person who first urged me to run for the county seat."

Sir Edmond jumped down from the curricle and held his arms up to help me down. "Come along. I'd like you to meet some of my people."

Will Hockinson, a tall, lanky man, about forty, his smiling face quite sun-browned, was now standing at the side of the road. He greeted us with a hearty handshake and open friendliness. I soon sensed the mutual respect between the two men. Before I was really aware of it, they had drawn me into their spirited discussion.

I'd only listened quietly at first, but then became so interested in what they were saying, I caught myself making comments and asking questions. I'd expected to be a silent, disinterested bystander and to my astonishment I got swept into the conversation. I found myself agreeing with Will Hockinson's remarks concerning Sir Edmond's proposed measures to help the people living in the county. The comments I made and questions I asked were not dismissed as mere politeness. Both men seemed interested in what I had to say.

"Well, you are a delightful surprise, Miss Atwood," Sir Edmond said to me with a pleased smile as we returned to the curricle. "You've got a head on your shoulders. I believe I will appoint you my publicity manager," he laughed.

"I don't know what came over me," I said, and I could feel my cheeks flushing. "I should have kept quiet. I've never done anything so forward in my life."

We were standing by the curricle. He put his hand on my shoulder, smiling down at me. "And why shouldn't you come forward and show you're interested and have a brain in your head?"

"Stop teasing me," I said and he laughed, then playfully pressed my hands lightly in his as he helped me back onto the curricle.

He was in rare high spirits as we rode to the next farmhouse. He whistled softly part of the time and when he spoke of his constituents it was with affection and respect.

When we stopped at the farmhouse, the farmer's wife also came out to greet us. I reminded myself to keep in the background, that it was still the prudent behavior but I wasn't able to keep my word. Once more I felt myself being drawn in, particularly since the farmer and his wife immediately included me in the conversation and Sir Edmond was no help at all. He behaved as if I'd already been appointed his publicity manager.

On our return to Malverne Manor, I fell into Sir Edmond's light-hearted mood. We talked and laughed in a carefree way and soon the tall, pink brick chimneys of Malverne Manor rose into view.

As we neared the drive, Sir Edmond brought the curricle to a brief stop and looked up toward the front entrance of the house where I saw a carriage parked at the door.

"The Wickham carriage," Sir Edmond said. "Miss Wickham and her father have come to call."

CHAPTER 11

As we approached the front door, I did not expect Sir Edmond to maneuver me into a meeting with the Wickhams; I most certainly had no reason to be included in such company. Remembering, though, how he'd commandeered me into a meeting with his tenants, I was prepared to make a quick departure up the stairs to my room if he should suggest I meet Miss Wickham and her father.

My being poised for a swift getaway did me no good. The moment Sir Edmond and I entered the house, Lady Edythe spotted us. She was in the drawing room with the Wickhams. The drawing room door was open and when she glanced into the hall and saw us, she hurried out to us. The next instant she had me firmly by the arm and was leading me into the drawing room.

"I'd like you to meet some acquaintances of ours, Miss Atwood. You heard me speak of the Wickhams of Wickham Place."

She stopped before a chair where a corpulent, sallow-faced man, late sixties perhaps, sat. A thick woolen coverlet was placed over his legs; a woolen scarf was wrapped about his neck. His large, puffy-looking hands lay limp in his lap.

Lady Edythe made the introductions. Mr. Wickham did not speak, only nodded. His eyes, as he glanced up at me for an instant, conveyed no interest in the meeting.

Lady Edythe lingered at his chair, but when Mr. Wickham lowered his head and began plucking at the fringe of the wool coverlet, I was steered away. Miss Wickham now came forward from the window where she'd been standing and covertly studying me.

Unlike her taciturn father, Miss Wickham greeted me with a winning smile. "Why don't you and I," she promptly suggested, "stroll in the garden." And before I had a chance to decline her invitation, she'd taken my arm which Lady Edythe now released to her.

As I was thus being led out, I caught a glimpse of Sir Edmond lounging against the mantel, observing Miss Wickham's officious greeting. There was an amused smile on his face. I threw him a malevolent look that he should be so delighted at my discomfort.

"My father is an invalid," Miss Wickham explained as she rushed me outdoors. "He prefers to be indoors with windows shut tight." She beamed another smile at me. "You and I can have a little chat while we enjoy the lovely Malverne gardens."

While she meticulously pointed out every shrub and tree, listing the Latin nomenclature, I did not observe the greenery so much as I observed Miss Wickham who, according to Lady Eydthe, was destined to become the mistress of Malverne Manor.

She was quite tall. I came only to her shoulder and I am above average height. She appeared even taller since she was extremely thin. The face was long and narrow. The elongated nose and jutting, pointed chin gave her face a sharpness which wasn't softened when she smiled which she did frequently. Her dress, pink, with tiny flowers embroidered on the bodice, was fashioned in a demure style with many ruffles and bows, as if to offset her gauntness, to give her a soft, girlish look. Still, she did possess a marvelous air of self-assured gentility.

Miss Wickham was explaining the average growth per year of a flowering shrub when she cut short her discussion with, "I hear you are a friend of Amy's."

I looked up at her in surprise and she added, "Lady Edythe told me about her." There was a slight pause, then she went on. "I was told she'd met Sir Edmond in London about five months ago and that she was to be a guest at Malverne Manor but that she'd changed her plans and didn't come after all."

She lowered her voice and said almost in a whisper, "Sir Edmond is like that." An understanding, conspiratorial smile crossed her face. "Sir Edmond has a wild streak in him, makes fleeting friendships with almost anybody. He sends guests to the manor at the oddest moments. Lady Edythe, fortunately, can take that sort of thing in her stride and——"

"——Amy was not one of those 'almost anybody' people," I broke in. "Sir Edmond and Amy were considering marriage. Amy did not come here to visit for a few days. She came here to be married and to live here."

It wasn't till I'd started to speak that I realized how furious I was. My voice trembled and I was sure my eyes blazed.

"Oh, Miss Atwood," Miss Wickham cried, touching my arm lightly, "you have completely misunderstood my words. I have nothing against the poor thing."

"She isn't a poor thing."

Miss Wickham's distress mounted. "Oh, I'm dreadfully sorry, Miss

Atwood," she murmured. "I seem to be using the wrong words. I did not mean it the way you've interpreted it." She looked down at me with an anguished expression. "As a matter of fact, Miss Atwood, I have been quite worried about the whole thing, wondering what might have happened to her. Lady Edythe said your friend, Amy, was very definite in her letter concerning her intention to visit at Malverne Manor, even indicating the exact day she was to arrive on the noon coach that stops at the Three Crowns Inn."

Miss Wickham hesitated then continued in a dropped voice. "I am deeply concerned about the matter and only hope she has not met with any harm." She stopped and gazed toward the pond. "I hope your friend has not met with some sort of misfortune. Seeing the pond, reminds me of the terrible thing that happened to one of the manor servant girls—that is, she'd come here to be employed at Malverne Manor."

She continued to stare sadly at the pond, then turned to face me. "Poor thing. She took her life, drowned herself in the pond. It happened about the time your friend, Amy, was to come to Malverne Manor."

Miss Wickham resumed walking, her sad gaze still on the pond. "I wasn't too surprised when I heard the dreadful news," she said with a slight shrug. "When I met her she certainly seemed like someone who might do something like that. Still, what a dreadful thing to do, to take your own life."

"You met this servant girl?"

We'd come to the formal gardens and she indicated a garden seat near the pool. We sat down. "Yes, I met her," Miss Wickham replied. "I saw her twice. Lady Edythe requested that I speak with the girl, see if I could draw her out, discover what was troubling her. Lady Edythe was distressed. The girl had come to Malverne Manor to be employed as a servant and she arrived so ill and so distraught that Lady Edythe did not have the heart to send her packing."

"The girl was ill when she arrived? Did Lady Edythe send for a doctor?"

"Lady Edythe wanted to, but the girl wouldn't hear of it, became hysterical, and explained that she'd been to see a doctor at her last place of employment. The girl insisted she would soon be over her indisposition. She showed Lady Edythe some medication the doctor had given her for her condition."

Miss Wickham paused and mournfully regarded the lapping water in the pool then shook her head sadly. "Lady Edythe was ever so kind to the girl. She refused to put her to work, in her condition, and decided she would simply wait till the girl was improved before she sent her home. She even let her stay in the Cream Lace Room hoping that——"

"The Cream Lace Room?" I said, hoping I did not betray my alarm.

Miss Wickham nodded. "Yes, it is an unusual name for a room, isn't it? But if you saw it, you would see why it is so-called. It's the loveliest room in the house. There was plenty of room for the girl in the servants' quarters because the Farrises were away, attending their daughter's wedding. But Lady Edythe let the girl stay in the Cream Lace Room, hoping that the lovely room would hasten the poor girl's recovery."

"That is where you saw this—this servant girl? In the Cream Lace Room?"

"Yes, on both occasions. She was confined to bed. The medication she'd shown Lady Edythe was a sedative of some sort for her highly nervous state. Both times that I saw the girl she was under the influence of this medication. She'd open her eyes for a while and stare at me from the bed, then she'd drop off to sleep. I tried to talk to her but it was no use. The best she could do was mumble a few incomprehensible words. On my second visit, my father, despite his being an invalid and finding stairs extremely difficult, also came up to talk to the girl, but when he saw her stuporous condition, he didn't even attempt a conversation."

"You said she did utter a few words. What did she say?"

Miss Wickham compressed her thin lips, thoughtfully considering my question then replied, "It was senseless muttering, nothing more."

"Oh, there must have been something, perhaps a few random words."

Miss Wickham slowly turned all the way around on the garden seat and regarded me full-face. "No, Miss Atwood," she said, biting off the words, "it was nothing more than senseless muttering. Why should you be so concerned about the stuporous mumbling of a servant girl?" She drew herself stiffly upright and added with a slight twist to her mouth, "Of course, I'm inclined to agree with Mrs. Hopkins' opinion, that the girl had disgraced herself at her last place of employment, had got herself in a family way. Lady Edythe said that the girl's condition caused her to have nervous hysterical spells. That was why she took that sedative. Mrs. Hopkins claims the girl's hysterics were due to her shame and guilt for—for getting herself into that disgraceful condition."

"Would the doctor have prescribed a sedative if she were in a family way?"

"Miss Atwood, I did not say that—that was the girl's problem. I did not know the nature of her indisposition. I am merely inclined to agree with Mrs. Hopkins who is quite wise about such matters." She brushed down the skirt of her dress then rose from the garden seat.

"Perhaps Lady Edythe had the correct impression about the girl," Miss Wickham went on. "She told me that as soon as she met the girl she got the impression the girl was—was unbalanced. That type is prone to such dreadful behavior, including suicide."

She started to walk away from the garden seat, gesturing to me that I follow, and as I fell into step with her, I asked, "What did this servant girl look like?"

"Like nothing."

I wasn't going to be put off. "What color was her hair, for instance?"

"I haven't the slightest recollection and, really, Miss Atwood, what does it matter?"

"A terrible thing like that happening right here at Malverne Manor? Of course, it matters. One can't help but be curious."

"It's not the first time, Miss Atwood, that some poor servant girl disgraced herself then couldn't live with her shame and guilt and took her life." She stopped and plucked some blossoms from a bed of daffodils and began to roll and pinch the petals into tiny wads. "I feel more sorry for her family," she said after a while. "I was present when the girl's brother came for the body after it had been recovered from the pond. The brother is a vicar. The girl's father is one, too. It was no wonder she was so distraught about her disgrace. She must have been a problem of sorts while living at the vicarage. I remember how grief-stricken the brother was when he came to claim the body and how he sadly repeated that he wished she'd never left home."

She tossed away the torn bits of flower petals. "Thank heaven," she exclaimed, with a sigh, "that the whole dreadful episode occurred while Sir Edmond was away in Scotland." She brushed her hands together with a couple of sharp slaps, ridding herself of the last shreds of flower petals that clung to her fingers. The desolate tone left her voice and she once more began to speak of the Malverne gardens, drawing my attention to a lush shrub which, unfortunately, she informed me, was quite susceptible to mealy bugs.

I heard little of the dissertation on horticulture. My mind was still on the puzzling episode of the servant girl who'd occupied the Cream Lace Room. I recalled the conversation between Mrs. Hopkins and Mrs. Ploovey at the Three Crowns Inn when Mrs. Ploovey had remarked about the blond-haired young lady who'd arrived on the coach and Mrs. Hopkins' comment that Malverne Manor would not be "hiring another servant girl for a while, not after all the trouble that one caused us." I wondered then whether they were actually talking about Amy just as I wondered now whether Miss Wickham was knowingly or unknowingly also talking about Amy.

"You would really appreciate the lovely appearance of Malverne Manor," Miss Wickham was saying, "if you could have seen it when Sir Edmond inherited it seven years ago from his parents. It was in a rundown condition then, the house and the land. With Lady Edythe's help, Sir Edmond has made a remarkable improvement in the manor."

We were approaching the house and Miss Wickham let her eyes wander lovingly across the stone and brick walls, up at the arched windows shining in the afternoon sun, then her gaze swung to the verdant lawns sloping down to the pond.

"No one, myself included," she said with a lingering smile, "ever believed that Sir Edmond would do all this for Malverne Manor." Her gaze returned to me, a candid glint shining in her eyes. "Sir Edmond, as I told you, has an inclination for a high-spirited, irresponsible sort of life, but, with Lady Edythe's guidance, he finally began to take an interest in his property. The orchards are doing exceptionally well this year. Shall we take a stroll through the orchard?"

I agreed, hopeful that since she was in a conversational mood, she might shed some more light on the servant girl who had been confined to the Cream Lace Room. I had the feeling Miss Wickham knew more than she'd divulged. Suddenly I remembered about Brian and asked her whether she'd ever met the artist who sometimes stayed at the cottage.

My expectations rose when I saw the flash of alertness on her face, but after a brief puzzled frown, she said, "An artist staying in the cottage? You're mistaken, Miss Atwood. No one uses the old cottage. Oh, Sir Edmond uses it on rare occasions, but that is all."

After that we walked in silence until we reached the apple orchard. Then Miss Wickham spoke and with such suddenness and sharpness that I drew up with a start.

"Miss Atwood," she said, "you haven't forgotten, have you, that Sir Edmond and I are virtually betrothed?"

"Forgotten? Not at all, Miss Wickham. Lady Edythe has so informed me."

She attempted a smile. "I thought that during your brief visit here at the manor, you might be reading too much into Sir Edmond's common courtesy."

"I have read nothing at all into Sir Edmond's common courtesy."

Miss Wickham flushed slightly. "It's just that this friend of yours, this Amy—she apparently read too much into—well, as I explained to you, Miss Atwood, Sir Edmond is of a rather impetuous, frivolous nature."

She gave me a little flustered smile. "It will be different, of course, once we're married," she said, then added, "I simply didn't want you to make the same mistake that your friend, Amy, made."

"No, Miss Wickham, you may rest assured I will not make the same mistake Amy made."

She placed her hand lightly on my arm as we walked along; the narrow, thin face warmed with a tremulous smile. "I'm so glad we understand each other," she murmured, pressing my arm then drawing her hand away.

We had reached the orchard and I stood under the canopy of blossoming apple trees. I breathed in the heady fragrance.

"I am sure that when Sir Edmond and I are married, he will do for Wickham Place what he's done for Malverne Manor," Miss Wickham said, and I remembered the Colonel's indignation when he spoke on the subject that morning when I visited with him. How furious the old man had become at the mere thought of Sir Edmond's marrying Miss Wickham and, as a result, doing for Wickham Place what—with Lady Edythe's alleged assistance—he'd done for Malverne Manor.

"But if Sir Edmond went to live at Wickham Place," I said, sounding almost as indignant as the Colonel sounded this morning, "what will happen to Malverne Manor?"

"Lady Edythe will live here. She's extremely fond of Malverne Manor. It's been her home for seven years. Lady Edythe will probably marry again. She's still a handsome-looking woman."

She turned abruptly to leave the orchard and as we retraced our steps toward the house, I said, "I can't imagine Sir Edmond's ever leaving Malverne Manor."

She smiled down at me. The gaze lingered. "Oh, can't you, really, Miss Atwood?" She began to walk faster. "We had better hurry back. My father, being an invalid, tires easily and, no doubt, wishes to return home."

We'd come to the back door, the one I'd used once before when I went to fetch the shawl from my room. I said good-by to Miss Wickham and went toward the door.

"Oh, Miss Atwood," Miss Wickham said as I started to enter the house, "is it you who works in a shop or was it Amy? I somehow have got a shop mixed up in my mind with one of you."

"Amy worked in a shop," I answered, turning round. "The family teashop. I also work in my father's chemist's shop."

"Oh, you do? Well, how nice for you." She threw me a smile then slowly walked away.

Although I was relieved to escape from Miss Wickham, I was, never-theless, thankful that I'd learned so much from her, perhaps more than she'd intended.

Yet, as Sir Edmond would have been quick to point out, the puzzle concerning Amy was not solved; only more pieces had been added to the jigsaw.

I made my way up the backstairs and along the upstairs hallway. When I turned the corner into my wing and approached the door to the Cream Lace Room, I slowed my steps.

When I reached the door, I hesitated, recalling Miss Wickham's story about a servant girl who'd occupied it. I turned to look into the tall glass case at the little shepherdess figurine which Amy had admired. . . . "There's a glass display case facing my bedroom door. . . ."

I started to move away, to go to my room, when I thought I heard a slight sound behind me, as if coming from the Cream Lace Room.

I swung around and listened intently, moving closer to the door.

There was a faint sound again then another, as if someone were qui-etly moving about in the room.

I knocked and the soft sounds came to a dead stop.

"Who's in there?" I whispered through the door.

There was no answer, but there was another faint sound from the room. Someone had moved abruptly. Then there was silence again.

I knocked once more on the door, then I tried the door and it opened.

When I stepped inside, I saw no one, but I knew I was not alone in the room.

CHAPTER 12

I looked around the room for any sign of the slightest movement.

"I know you're in here," I said, hoping my voice did not betray my mounting apprehension. "I'll soon find you, so you may as well come out."

My sweeping glance came to rest on the bed where the floor-length counterpane trembled slightly.

I stepped quickly to the bed. I lifted the counterpane. A startled face peered up at me.

The face was unfamiliar. For a while we stared at each other in speechless surprise, then she scrambled out and stood before me, eyes blazing. She was about Myrna's age, a bit older perhaps, but quite un-like Myrna, olive-skinned, with dark glossy hair which tumbled to her shoulders in luxuriant ringlets. The eyes were a deep lustrous brown. She stood before me now, hands on hips, legs wide apart, a slow insolent smile creeping into her face.

"Who are you?" I demanded. "What are you doing here?"

She looked me up and down with disdainful silence before she replied.

"I'm Corinne. I work here."

"Oh, are you one of the Farrises?" I asked. "Myrna's sister?"

The smirk slid off her face. The dark eyes burned briefly with a flash of annoyance.

"No, I am not her sister." The words were chipped off icily, one word at a time.

"You're the young lady I saw running out of this room last night," I said. "It was you who ran down the hallway. Why didn't you stop when I called you?"

She flung back her dark hair with a contemptuous gesture, the glossy hair rippling around her shoulders. She walked away, pausing briefly at the door, letting her eyes slide over me with a quick side glance then swept out of the room. I could hear her running swiftly along the hallway.

I stood in the middle of the room, trying to comprehend the encounter. My eyes went back to the bed. Seeing that I'd wrinkled the lace counterpane when I pulled it back, I automatically went to straighten it out.

As I patted it into place I asked myself, why, if she worked at the manor, did she find it necessary to hide? And why in this room? I felt a wave of revulsion for the girl who, in the short space of time I was in her presence, conveyed a wanton air. It was more than the bold look in the dusky eyes, the half-smile. I quickly checked my hasty condemning judgment of her but the impression lingered.

I forgot about the girl, Corinne, but a little later when Lady Edythe sent for me to join her and Sir Edmond for tea on the terrace, Corinne was serving.

Lady Edythe, although extending the girl every courtesy due a servant, could not conceal her displeasure with the girl. Corinne, obviously wise to Lady Edythe's pretended courtesy, repaid her with cool contempt, shrewdly careful not to let her feelings show too openly.

I tried to overlook the unspoken, thinly disguised hostility between them and concentrated on the tea and the gardens off the terrace. The subtle interplay between Sir Edmond and Corinne was not so easy to ignore. I had to keep reminding myself that I must pretend not to notice. Miss Wickham's remarks of a few moments ago came to mind, that Sir Edmond had an inclination toward a frivolous sort of life. But that sort of thing would end when she and Sir Edmond were married, Miss Wickham had predicted.

Corinne, one couldn't help but observe, found it necessary to pass by Sir Edmond's chair innumerable times, slowing her languorous steps each time she was near him. When she placed anything on the table, the flashing dark eyes always swept up across his face, lingering for the briefest yet very noticeable moment.

If Sir Edmond had in some way politely discouraged the girl's bold behavior, it would not have been half so obvious as his determination to ignore the girl so completely. He was careful never to meet her glance and pretended that she was not present.

It might have been Corinne's undaunted flirtation that prompted Sir Edmond to excuse himself rather hurriedly, not staying for his usual second cup in order to linger and talk.

As soon as he was gone and Corinne had also left, Lady Edythe dropped her mask of patient courtesy.

"That hussy," she said in a small, tight voice. She folded up her napkin and tossed it on the table. "I simply cannot abide that girl."

"Is she an upstairs chambermaid?" I asked, thinking that might explain partly the girl's presence in the Cream Lace Room.

"No, she works in the kitchen, helps Mrs. Hopkins."

I drank my tea in silence and wondered whether Lady Edythe knew that Corinne prowled about the upstairs rooms, particularly the Cream Lace Room? The next time I saw Myrna I would try to get some explanation from her. When I'd asked Myrna whether it was she I'd seen running along the hallway, Myrna had given me a guarded look, as if she knew it had been Corinne. For some reason Myrna did not wish to discuss Corinne, but I had to know if Corinne knew anything about the young woman who'd occupied the Cream Lace Room. The young woman, I was convinced, had been Amy.

I asked Lady Edythe if I might be excused since teatime was apparently over. She roused herself from her preoccupation and nodded with a smile.

I went to the library to choose a book to read. I even had hopes of finding the missing book about Malverne Manor.

When I stepped into the library, I was once more struck by the interesting play of light in the room. The glowing rays of sunlight spilled down from the immense skylight, touching everything in the room with a soft, mellow sheen.

I first went to the shelf where Sir Edmond had expected to find the Malverne Manor book, but it wasn't there. I glanced around at the walls of books and, though I knew it was almost pointless to look for the book, I attempted a search anyway. There simply were too many books, too many unreachable shelves and I gave up the search. I found a copy of *Barchester Towers* and left the room.

I took the book into the rose garden where I found a comfortable garden seat in the shade of a rose arbor.

I'd barely started reading when I saw Corinne come out of the house carrying shears and a flower basket. She threw me a chilly glance as she passed by and went to a far corner of the garden where she set to work cutting roses.

I found myself looking up from my book occasionally. Corinne stood with her back to me and even from that position, she suggested the sensuous, voluptuous impression—the rounded body, the languorous gestures, the luxuriant dark hair tumbling to her shoulders.

I felt a prick of conscience, not liking my hasty judgment of the girl whose sultry appearance might belie her true nature. If she cast admiring glances at Sir Edmond, she wasn't the only one who'd succumbed to his handsome looks and charming ways. Probably all young ladies, servants included, couldn't help but fall under his spell. Corinne was perhaps only clumsily obvious about her infatuation.

When I'd thoroughly convinced myself that I'd wronged the girl in my judgment of her, reminding myself how indignant I could become when someone drew such erroneous conclusions about Amy, I put my book aside and approached Corinne, intending to make amends for my first brief but unfriendly meeting with her.

She threw me a quick, curious glance and continued cutting the roses.

"Corinne," I began, "I'm sorry if I sounded unfriendly when I found you in the Cream Lace Room, but I——"

"It is none of your concern," she cut in. She stopped in her task and looked directly into my face. "What I do is none of your concern," she repeated.

I debated for a moment whether I should make another attempt. She darted me a quizzical look and I said, "Corinne, it isn't that I wish to pry but——"

She again cut into my words and, though she spoke quietly, the mocking tone shaded her words. "I have no time now for conversation," she said. "I must have these flowers done for Mrs. Hopkins." A slow secret smile passed over her face, then she turned her back on me.

I left her and returned to my book. I knew there would be no point in lingering and I had no desire to be a victim of her ill manners.

Later, in my room, I decided that when Mrs. Hopkins came with my hot water so that I might freshen up before dinner, I would ask her to send a tray to my room. I wanted to be alone for a while, away from Lady Edythe, away from Sir Edmond. Corinne would probably be serving dinner and I did not wish to see her for a while either.

It was Myrna who brought my hot water, along with fresh towels. Seeing her rosy-cheeked face without a trace of guile, I thought, how different she is from Corinne. Myrna put me in mind of a sunny meadow of dew-fresh field flowers. Corinne was a dark, shadowy garden, heady with lush, jungle plantings.

"Dinner will be at eight, miss," Myrna said with her quick, bright smile as she carried the hot water and towels into the bath.

"I would like to have a tray sent to my room, Myrna, if that wouldn't cause an inconvenience," I said when she returned to the bedroom.

"Oh, but, miss, they are expecting you down to dinner." She paused; her face lit up with pleasure. "It's ever so much nicer, miss, to have dinner in the golden room." She giggled softly. "That is what I call the dining room, miss, the golden room."

"An appropriate name, Myrna. That was my impression, too, when I had dinner there yesterday."

"Then you will come down, won't you, miss?" she said, going to the door.

"Would you wait a minute, Myrna. I would like to ask you something and please don't be offended. I am not asking out of mere curiosity." As I spoke I could see her sunny, beaming face cloud up. She knows I'm going to ask her about Corinne, I thought.

"I met Corinne," I said, "and I'm quite certain she's the young lady I saw come out of the Cream Lace Room last night and run away from me when I called."

The soft contours of Myrna's face tightened visibly. She slowly lowered her eyes to gaze at the floor.

I was afraid she was going to excuse herself and rush away because my inquiry was obviously causing her embarrassment, so I quickly asked, "Myrna, did Corinne stay here at the manor while you and your family attended your sister's wedding?"

"No, no, miss," she replied, turning wide eyes on me. "She went with us." She hesitated for an uncomfortable moment then continued, "Corinne is not a Farris, miss. She is my cousin and—well, my mum—you see, miss, Corinne's mother is my mum's sister—and—well, miss,

my mum thought it would be a good plan if Corinne came to work at
the manor." She gave me an eager, emphatic nod. "Corinne came with
us. She came to my sister Floss's wedding. Lady Edythe gave Corinne
the two-week holiday also."

"So Corinne is your cousin," I said. "I thought at first she was your
sister."

"Oh, no, miss. She is not." Then, realizing perhaps she'd disclaimed
Corinne too emphatically, Myrna made a fumbling gesture and hastily
added, "Mrs. Hopkins is quite pleased with Corinne, says she's a good
worker in the kitchen."

"Thank you, Myrna, for telling me about Corinne. I wanted to know
if she was at the manor while you and your family were away."

The guarded, uncomfortable look returned to her face. "No, miss,
Corinne was given holiday. She came to Floss's wedding." She started
to open the door. "And I do not know why she would have been in the
Cream Lace Room or—or running away from it." She gave me a slight
smile. "Don't forget, miss. Dinner is at eight," she reminded me, then
scurried away.

The dining room appeared just as dazzling to my eyes as it had the
first time I'd seen it. As Myrna had remarked, it indeed was a golden
room. The brilliant chandelier was lit again; the tiny candles glowed in
the shiny glass prisms, their shimmery light glancing off the gold leaf
in the wall panels. The long table once more bore the two lighted
candelabra, bringing out the shine and sparkle of the elegantly set table
of crystal and china.

As Sir Edmond held out my chair for me and my glance swept across
the room, my eyes catching the velvet curtains at the windows, I was
again reminded that the room was like a brilliant topaz in a velvet jewel
box.

It was at dinner that I met Mr. and Mrs. Farris, though not actually.
Farris was the butler, a portly, neat man, in meticulous swallow-tailed
coat and crisp white shirt, his movements discreetly silent and efficient,
his bland face, impassive.

Mrs. Farris, although the equal of her husband's unobtrusive effi-
ciency in serving, did not possess the bland, expressionless face. Farris
never so much as glanced in my direction, as if whom he served never
meant anything personal to him. Mrs. Farris, on the other hand, frequently shifted her eyes in my direction.

I couldn't help comparing her with Mrs. Hopkins whose smiling,
bustling cheerfulness could lend a happy air to a meal. Mrs. Farris was
grim. Her stone face held no warmth. She moved like an automaton

who'd been dressed in clean, starched clothes. Only her eyes betrayed a human quality. They kept glancing off me, as if she were trying to puzzle out my presence at Malverne Manor.

Her covert glances at me, if curious, at least, were not the darkly disapproving ones she frequently darted at Corinne.

Corinne was aware of Mrs. Farris's watchful eyes and conducted herself in an aloof, impeccable manner. Under Mrs. Farris's grim surveillance she had altered her personality like a chameleon, performing her duties with a demure-like obeisance, not once letting her eyes wander to the place where Sir Edmond was seated.

Corinne's modified behavior permitted Lady Edythe to be at her gracious, relaxed best. Sir Edmond, too, was in excellent spirits, as if relieved of Corinne's unwise boldness.

The food was superlative. I wondered for a moment how much of the dinner was due to Mrs. Hopkins' skillful touch, now that the Farrises had returned. The roast capon had the subtle hint of rosemary from Mrs. Hopkins' herb garden. The accompanying vegetables suggested Mrs. Hopkins' deft touch, not a shade overcooked. The meal was finished off with an airy, apricot-flavored soufflé.

Not only was the food excellent, the conversation was lively, good-humored. Lady Edythe and Sir Edmond were exceedingly gracious, treating me like an honored guest. When the dinner conversation turned to the county election, I realized, somewhat to my surprise, that I was now interested in the subject. Part of my interest, I knew, was due to Sir Edmond's enthusiasm for his land and "his people." It was infectious. Then, having met some of his tenants, I was pulled further into the election fever. Nevertheless, I was aware of the fact that I was an outsider, merely an interested spectator.

It was for that reason that I demurred when Sir Edmond casually informed Lady Edythe that I was going to the campaign meeting tomorrow.

"No," I said to him. "I would serve no purpose. I would feel out of place."

"Nonsense," he answered. "Of course, you'll go. In those two brief meetings with my tenants earlier today, you showed a surprising flair for such matters. I could see that Will Hockinson was impressed with your sensible questions and comments. No one will make you feel out of place, so don't talk nonsense."

I cast a quick look from Sir Edmond to Lady Edythe. She was smiling indulgently at him, but there was a constrained annoyance in her expression.

"Miss Atwood is properly concerned about the impropriety, Edmond," she said after a while, "particularly since the Wickhams will be attending." She turned her cool smile on me. I could see that her tightly reined displeasure was beginning to desert her. "Miss Atwood is right," she added. "Her presence would serve no purpose and would most certainly be out of place."

Sir Edmond waved aside her curt argument and in the commanding tone that came easily to him, said, "We'll all attend the meeting—that means you, Lady Edythe; Miss Atwood; the Wickhams. The Colonel will also be there. And the Raynords will attend. I met them yesterday, paid a call, and they're quite interested in the election."

There was a short, sharp silence then Lady Edythe said, "Edmond, would you mind terribly if I did not attend?"

"Of course, I'd mind. I cannot imagine your missing the most important meeting of the campaign. Now so much for that," he finished off and turned the conversation away from the subject.

Lady Edythe became quietly thoughtful, barely following what Sir Edmond was saying. Although she no longer protested about the meeting, the subject still seemed to be on her mind. I decided that later I would speak privately with Sir Edmond and explain that I wished him success in the election, but it was not my place to attend the meeting. Surely he'd observed Lady Edythe's intense disappointment at his suggestion.

But I had no opportunity to tell him this. He excused himself immediately after dinner and I did not see him again until the following day when Myrna came to tell me the master wished to see me in the drawing room.

When I entered, Sir Edmond was there with Lady Edythe and a pleasant-looking middle-aged couple who, Sir Edmond said, were Mr. and Mrs. Raynord. The Raynords, a cheerful, talkative pair, promptly drew me into the conversation. Encouraged by the Raynords, it became a foregone conclusion that I was going to the meeting, and we were soon on our way, stopping first to collect the Colonel who was to accompany us. Once or twice I stole a glance at Mrs. Raynord in the coach, recalling that I'd gained admittance to Malverne Manor because I'd been mistaken for her.

The meeting was held in a parish hall adjacent to the village church. A large crowd had assembled and was milling about, engrossed in noisy discussion and argument. Miss Wickham and her father were present, removed somewhat from the boisterous crowd, sitting silently in a far corner. When Miss Wickham saw us enter, she came forward, clasping

Lady Edythe with both hands. Her glance in my direction did not conceal first her astonishment then her annoyance that I should be present.
After murmuring a polite greeting to me, she collected her father and
joined Lady Edythe in the row of wooden seats directly in front of the
speaker's platform where Sir Edmond was now greeting a group of men.
The Colonel directed me and the Raynords to the front row of seats
and the meeting began immediately.

Occasionally, out of the corner of my eye, I could see Miss Wickham
dart a chilled look my way, but I paid scant attention to her. I was more
interested in what Sir Edmond was saying from the speaker's platform
and the replies he gave to questions addressed to him.

A social hour with refreshments followed the meeting and I then
gave Miss Wickham even less attention. She remained seated during
the social hour, fussing interminably with the coverings on her father's
legs. I was drawn into a round of sociability. The Raynords had appointed themselves as my mentors. Although new in the county, they'd
already made friends with many of Sir Edmond's constituents. The
Colonel also knew everybody. I was soon thoroughly enjoying myself.

My enjoyment, I knew, would be short-lived. Even as I met these
people and was pleased that they should accept me, there remained the
ever-present reminder that it was all fleeting. It was just a matter of
courtesy shown a guest of Sir Edmond's. Catching Lady Edythe's
and Miss Wickham's outraged glances brought home the message that
I was "out of place."

After the social hour, the Raynords remained at the parish hall to
discuss something with Will Hockinson, Sir Edmond's campaign manager. The Wickhams declined Lady Edythe's invitation to have dinner
at Malverne Manor and returned to Wickham Place because, Miss Wickham explained, Mr. Wickham was overfatigued. The Colonel, though
not invited by Lady Edythe, came with us to the manor and stayed for
dinner.

I asked to be excused from dinner, preferring a tray in my room, but
the Colonel wouldn't hear of it and Sir Edmond readily agreed with
him.

Farris served, but Mrs. Farris was absent. Mrs. Hopkins replaced
her. Her bustling cheerfulness was a welcome change from Mrs. Farris's
grim face, but with Mrs. Farris's watchful eyes no obstacle to her now,
Corinne reverted to her sultry gazes at Sir Edmond, lingering at his
chair, always brushing ever so lightly against him.

Sir Edmond, as before, made quite a point of avoiding the girl's
glances. Corinne's flirting game was not lost on the Colonel. The first

time he caught her playful flirtation, a flabbergasted expression crossed his face. After that, he surreptitiously observed the performance, sometimes with a puckish grin, sometimes with a raised, puzzled brow.

Mrs. Hopkins, bustling about in her usual flurry of activity, was either unaware of Corinne's behavior or did not consider it worth her attention. Lady Edythe watched once more in silent, repressed outrage.

If Corinne had unnerved her at dinner, Lady Edythe's sensibilities were further assailed when we adjourned to the drawing room where the Colonel now proceeded to try Lady Edythe's patience, making all sorts of statements and remarks, mischievously determined to rub her the wrong way. He cleverly refrained from open insult and outright malice, but the sly mischief was devastating. It seemed enough offense to Lady Edythe that he should be present at the manor. Nevertheless, she conducted herself in a faultless, ladylike manner.

Despite the Colonel's mischief, the drawing room conversation moved along smoothly, due mainly to Sir Edmond's diplomatic parrying, but the atmosphere became charged when Sir Edmond casually informed Lady Edythe that, the following day, he would be leaving for London to make inquiries about Amy's whereabouts.

There was an audible gasp from Lady Edythe.

"In my absence," Sir Edmond explained, "Will Hockinson and the Raynords will take charge of the meeting at the north end." He glanced at me. "The Raynords have requested that Miss Atwood accompany them." Turning to Lady Edythe, he continued, "I'd like you to rest up a day or two. You've been driving yourself with this campaigning. I don't want you to become overtired."

Lady Edythe stared at him, pale-faced. She parted her lips, then compressed them. Finally, able to speak, she said in a small, strained voice, "But, Edmond, I wish to continue with the campaigning. I should be attending the meeting in the north end. I—I've barely become acquainted with the Raynords and—and I've worked with Will Hockinson." She swept a glance past me. "Wouldn't it be far more feasible, Edmond, if Miss Atwood entertained the Colonel here at the manor and I accompanied the Raynords to the meeting—" Her words faltered. For an instant, she stared at Sir Edmond, speechless, then the words rushed out. "Oh, Edmond, why go to London now? Why now at this critical time? And it's such a foolish, pointless thing to do, rush up to London all because of that shopgirl." As if regretting she'd let the last word slip out, Lady Edythe fumbled nervously with her hands, lowering her eyes skittishly.

After a short, sharp silence, Sir Edmond quietly but firmly repeated his intention to go to London.

Another silence followed. Lady Edythe was sitting across from me in the same chair she'd occupied when I'd first entered the drawing room that rainy afternoon. The stricken look I saw on her face now was the same anguished expression I observed when I'd first mentioned Amy's name to her. She was again nervously working her fingers over the silk covering of the chair arms. For one instant, her eyes lifted and she looked at me as if she were thinking, You started it all, Miss Atwood. If you hadn't come, there would be no problems.

"Now, don't distress yourself, Lady Edythe," I heard Sir Edmond say. He was gazing languidly over his brandy glass and winked at the Colonel. "A day or two away from the strain of campaigning, Lady Edythe, and you will fuel up nicely for the finishing line. You know how that malaria trouble recurs when you get overtired. I must go to London and wind up this puzzling business about Amy to ease my mind and"— he gestured toward me with his brandy glass "—and Miss Atwood's. Will Hockinson and the Raynords will keep everything under control the short time I'll be away."

Lady Edythe pulled herself erect in the chair and, her voice, self-assured and slightly authoritative now, made another attempt at persuading Sir Edmond to forego the London trip and permit her to accompany the Raynords to the meeting. Sir Edmond's reply was swift, almost echoing the tone he'd used on Mrs. Hopkins when he'd commanded her to return to the kitchen while he retrieved the pearl brooch I'd left in the guest room.

Lady Edythe shrank back, her eyes flicking past the Colonel who had made a curious rumbling noise in his throat. Then, all at once, her face brightened; her hands fluttered up in an exuberant gesture.

"On second thought, Edmond," she said lightheartedly, "your suggestion is fortuitously convenient for me." Her voice rose, trailing into a ripple of laughter. "Now, you know very well that your election victory is a foregone conclusion. Why don't I begin making preparations for the Victory Ball?" She paused, smiled. "And why not make the Ball the occasion to announce your engagement to Miss Wickham? You know everyone is waiting for the official announcement."

The Colonel, who'd begun to doze over his brandy, stirred abruptly.

"Edmond married to that simpering, whey-faced creature," he bellowed. "Never!"

Lady Edythe uttered a startled gasp, then glared at the Colonel who continued to squirm in his chair, sputtering and muttering into his brandy glass.

Sir Edmond, unperturbed, a smile playing on his face, sipped his brandy, stealing a glance at me over his glass.

"No, Lady Edythe, no victory balls of any sort," he said after a while. "Not with this Amy business not cleared up yet. And you never know about county elections."

Lady Edythe appeared crushed. She sat slumped in her chair, only her fingers still working the chair arms. Soon she was excusing herself, explaining she planned to retire early.

The Colonel, strangely silent, stayed for one more brandy, then also excused himself, saying he would go to bed shortly since he wished to rise early.

"I'm sorry, Miss Atwood," Sir Edmond said when we were left alone. "Sorry you had to be witness to a family squabble."

"But I am responsible for the squabble," I said. Our eyes met and I found myself looking away from his intent gaze. "I must leave Malverne Manor," I said; yet even as I uttered the words, I knew that the answer to the puzzle concerning Amy was hidden here at the manor, that it was tied to something—or someone here. What would I accomplish by running home? Or by staying at the Three Crowns Inn?

I sat very still, my face turned away from him because I knew that seeing him made it all so much more difficult. Yet, that was another reason I had to leave. I didn't like the way his very presence affected me, causing me to forget about Amy and why I was here at the manor. Or that he was presumably betrothed to Miss Wickham. And there was someone named Walter Binson at home, waiting for me to return so that we might be married this summer.

"No, I must leave," I repeated. "It's you who should stay here, continue with your campaigning, and I should go to London and make inquiries about Amy. You're surely aware that Lady Edythe is unhappy about my presence at the manor and my becoming involved in your election campaigning. I must go away." I still could not bring myself to look at him as I spoke.

"Don't talk nonsense," I heard him say, his anger rising. "And look at me when I speak to you."

I turned my head and as our glances met, the fiery look in his eyes gentled all at once. For a while neither of us spoke.

"Lady Edythe," he said after a while, "does not decide matters for me, not whom I marry, nor who my guests shall be, nor who helps me in my election campaigning." He gave me a brief, reassuring smile.

"Lady Edythe is not distressed with you. You're being oversensitive. She is distressed with the Colonel. Lady Edythe is always uncomfortable and quick-tempered in his presence. He sets her off. Don't misunderstand me. I'm not making excuses for either of them. I don't take their little spats seriously. I told you they don't see eye to eye. If the Colonel had not been present, Lady Edythe wouldn't have been so fidgety and quick-tempered. And I'm not trying to take anything away from her. I admire her greatly. She's taken excellent care of my house since my parents' death. As for the Colonel, I like him equally well."

He paused, regarding me quietly for a moment, before saying, "Besides, you came here expressly to discover what happened to Amy. I presume you're still convinced she's been here at the manor, so this is where you should pursue the search."

"And you? Do you now believe that Amy came to the manor?"

He shook his head. "I believe what Lady Edythe said, that Amy wrote that she was coming but never arrived. For a while, after hearing your strange story, I began to wonder but, after discussing the matter thoroughly with Lady Edythe, I am assured Amy never came to Malverne Manor."

"I'm surprised to hear you say that. I thought that by now you were convinced she'd been here."

"Convinced? The only thing you have to go on," he reminded me, "are details you say were in her letters describing Malverne Manor. As I told you, Miss Atwood, Amy could easily have got that information from the book about Malverne Manor."

"She also wrote about Lady Edythe," I began, but he waved that aside.

"She didn't have to be present at the manor to know that Lady Edythe lives here."

I felt defeated. No matter what argument I'd present, he'd fling it down with some apparently reasonable explanation.

"The book about Malverne Manor," I said. "Has it turned up?"

He rose from his chair. "Come along. We'll take another look in the library. It may have been put back." We were out in the hall now, I trying to keep up with his long strides. "I asked Lady Edythe about the book," he continued, "told her I'd looked for it in the library. She was surprised it wasn't there."

He gave me a quick discerning look as he opened the door to the library and paused in the doorway. "I did not tell Lady Edythe that you'd found such a book concealed in the cottage. I didn't think you'd have wished me to disclose the fact that you'd found it necessary to search the cottage. And I did not tell her about your mythical artist who inhabits the cottage. I wanted to spare you any awkward questioning." He then stood aside and I preceded him into the library.

A full moon was shining down through the huge skylight. It touched the entire room with a shimmery silver glow. I made a hushed exclamation of delight as I entered.

Sir Edmond heard and turned to look at me. "Striking, isn't it?" he said with a smile.

I nodded, my eyes wandering about the room where the pale moon-glow cast a fantasy of soft light and shadow over everything; the leather-bound books glimmered in the soft light; the colors in the Persian rugs seemed woven of glittery threads.

I was vaguely conscious of following Sir Edmond to the shelf where he'd previously looked for the book, but with my eyes and full attention on the breath-taking moonlit room, I was not aware that he'd come to a stop and consequently I fell against him.

I am not quite certain what exactly happened next. I recall looking up at him suddenly, that he was smiling down at me and that in the moonlight he looked even more attractive than usual. I know I was about to excuse myself for jostling against him, but I don't believe I got the words out. All at once his arms came about me and he was kissing me, gently at first then with such intensity, I withdrew my arms from him and turned my face away.

We stood together quietly for some time, with the moonlight spilling down on us from the glass roof. Neither of us spoke. He held me close and I could hear his heartbeat as he held my head against his chest.

The unexpected joy that soared through me hovered on the brink for a moment, then it vanished as quickly as it had possessed me. I lifted my face to his.

"It isn't right," I murmured, and he replied by kissing me softly on the mouth.

"It isn't right?" he said afterward. "For us to fall in love with each other? You know very well why you haven't left Malverne Manor. It's more than your desire to puzzle out Amy's whereabouts. You are in love with me and you know I have fallen in love with you. That is why you have stayed here."

"But you and Miss Wickham—" I began and got no further. He placed his lips lightly on mine to still my words, then said, "I am no more in love with Miss Wickham than you are with that Walter Binson you mentioned to the Colonel."

"But Amy—" I began again and he once more silenced me with a kiss.

"I've told you once before. I was never really in love with Amy. And she was never in love with me. It was a short-lived infatuation for both of us. It was the other fellow that Amy was in love with and whom she's probably married to by now. As for Miss Wickham, can you imagine my being married to her?"

"That's not for me to say."

"Then it is for me." He drew me close again and after kissing me gently said, "So don't talk to me about leaving Malverne Manor. You will not leave. I won't have it." He brushed my cheek softly with his lips then turned to look for the book, but it wasn't there.

"The Malverne book will eventually turn up," he said, "and it isn't that important a matter anyway." His eyes swept across the walls of books. "And we aren't going to search through all that."

We went to the door and, as he opened it, we both stopped in the doorway for a last look at the moonlit room, his hand lightly holding mine.

When he closed the door and I turned to leave him, to go to my room, Lady Edythe suddenly stepped into the hall from one of the nearby rooms. She was dressed in a long velvet dressing gown. She stopped, looked at us with a faint smile, her gaze lingering on me.

"I thought you had retired by now, Miss Atwood," she said, the smile curling her lips. "I couldn't sleep," she went on, her eyes still on me, her expression the same as when she watched Corinne hovering about Sir Edmond. "I came down to ask Mrs. Hopkins to brew me some of her soothing herb tea."

I could hear Sir Edmond take in a quick, sharp breath. I started to move further away when I suddenly realized his hand was still holding mine. His fingers now gripped mine even more tightly.

Lady Edythe's eyes moved up abruptly from our clasped hands when Sir Edmond, in a firm, even voice, said, "Good night, Lady Edythe. Sleep well."

For a confused moment she stood motionless; the little smile drained from her face. I broke away from Sir Edmond and rushed toward the staircase.

As I raced up the stairs, I could hear Lady Edythe speak to Sir Edmond in an urgent, subdued voice; then Sir Edmond, in a clear, loud tone, bid her good night once more, and the next instant I heard him taking the stairs behind me two at a time.

He caught up with me as I rushed into the wing where my room was located. His hand reached out, caught my shoulder, and spun me around.

I knew there were tears on my face. I'd felt them welling up in my eyes as I escaped up the stairs. I knew I hadn't misread the look in Lady Edythe's eyes, as if she were asking, "What right have you, Miss Atwood, to censure Corinne when you are no better?"

Sir Edmond pulled me close with one hand and wiped the tears away with the other.

"How can you be so oversensitive?" he said in a low, laughing voice. "Lady Edythe meant no offense. It's just that she's got this fixation about my being promised to Miss Wickham." He gently brushed back a lock of hair that had fallen against my cheek. "And she's all steamed up because I suggested that she not attend the campaign meeting tomorrow. Pay her no mind."

"It's—it's all so—so confusing," I said. "Oh, I just know I should——"

He stopped me. "Don't tell me again that you plan to leave Malverne Manor. Don't even start on that. I won't hear of it." He kissed me, a long, lingering kiss then said, "Good night. I won't see you tomorrow morning. I'll be off for London by the time you get up. Take good care of the Colonel for me while I'm away. He might want to go to the meeting with you and the Raynords tomorrow."

He tilted my face up, gave me a quick good-night kiss, then hurried away.

I prepared for bed in a dreamy preoccupied way, my thoughts weaving in and out, my hazy impressions all mixed up with that extraordinary moonlit room and how, all at once, the touch of his hand on my shoulder and the soft kiss on my mouth had made known what I'd secretly felt for him from the start, what I'd tried to deny to myself.

The lovely dream, the realization that I was in love with him, darkened when the shadow of Amy fell upon it. I tried to convince myself that Sir Edmond was speaking the truth, that Amy was never in love with him, nor he with her, that it was only a brief infatuation, that Amy was really in love with someone else, and she was not dead but married to the man she truly loved. "I am no more in love with Miss Wickham," Sir Edmond had said, "than you are in love with that Walter Binson. . . ."

All the while I was getting ready for bed, I tried to cast aside the disturbing, conflicting thoughts. I tried to forget Lady Edythe's accusing look. I would bear in mind what Sir Edmond said, that I was in love with him and he was in love with me.

On that note I drifted off into a dreamless sleep, not awakening until I heard a knock on my door, telling me Myrna had arrived with my morning tea and hot water.

I hurriedly got into my dressing gown and opened the door. It was Mrs. Hopkins, an envelope in her hand.

"Good morning, miss," she said, her sunny, pleasant face beaming with a broad smile. "I will have your tea and hot water up in a jiffy, miss, but a letter came for you by special messenger. Might be important so I thought I'd bring it up to you prompt-like."

She handed me the envelope and called over her shoulder as she hurried away, "The Colonel will be having breakfast in an hour, miss, if you should like to join him."

I thanked her, quickly shutting the door. I was surprised that the handwriting on the envelope was not Walter Binson's. Although I'd asked him not to write to me at the manor, I thought he'd found it necessary to overlook my request. I did not recognize the handwriting and ripped open the envelope, realizing that Walter Binson hadn't yet received my letter.

It was a brief, one-page letter, and my eyes first went down to the signature.

The letter was from Brian.

I went to the window where the light was better and began to read:

My dear Miss Atwood:

I'm sorry I disappeared from sight so suddenly but it was necessary. When you spoke to me of Amy and told me of her strange disappearance from Malverne Manor, I had to pretend to you that I knew nothing of the matter. When I see you and explain, you will understand why.

I've just returned from London and, as much as I dislike communicating this sad news to you, Amy is dead. Even more distressing is my discovery that Sir Edmond was responsible for her death.

Tell no one the contents of this letter and meet me this morning at the Three Crowns Inn. Tell no one about our meeting. I'll be at the inn about ten o'clock.

Brian.

CHAPTER 13

When, a few minutes later, I heard a knock at my door letting me know that Mrs. Hopkins had arrived with the hot water, I was still standing at the window, the letter gripped in my hand, my brain still trying to comprehend the full meaning of Brian's startling news.

I moved mechanically away from the window, hoping Mrs. Hopkins would not importune me concerning the contents of the letter. As I opened the door, I wondered whether I should ask her who the special messenger was. But I wouldn't know the person anyway.

It was Myrna at the door. She scurried inside, her bright, sunny face with its cheery smile like a shaft of clear sunlight, whisking away momentarily the dark shadow that engulfed me.

"Oh, miss," she exclaimed as she carried the hot water into the adjoining bath, her voice bubbling with excitement. "You have come to visit at Malverne Manor at the very right time. There is going to be a grand ball very soon, miss," she rushed on when she returned to the room. Her voice dropped a little, as if we were sharing secrets. "It's all on the quiet sort of, miss, but there will be a grand ball."

"You mean a Victory Ball, Myrna? The county election?" I asked and she nodded. "But, Myrna, there's no assurance Sir Edmond will win the election. There's the little matter of the people's votes."

"Oh, miss, everybody is very fond of the master." Her voice trilled into a soft giggle. "He is sure to win the election." She again lowered her voice to a confidential whisper. "Besides, miss, there is talk that the master's engagement to Miss Wickham will be announced. Miss Wickham lives not far from here, miss, up at Wickham Place. Everybody knows that the master and Miss Wickham will marry one of these days. The grand ball to celebrate the engagement to Miss Wickham and the election victory is sort of a big secret because"—she shrugged "—well, just in case the master should not win the election." She smiled and flapped her hands in a quick gesture. "But there will probably be a grand ball anyway, to celebrate the engagement announcement." She once more flapped her hands against her apron and made a quick shrugging gesture, as if the whole matter were now settled. "So you see, miss, there still will be a grand ball. An engagement party could not be held at Wickham Place, which is not beautiful like Malverne Manor, and it is in a rundown condition what with Mr. Wickham being sickly."

She hurried to the door, the mounting anticipation about the upcoming ball shining through her face. "Oh, I almost forgot, miss," she added, in her flurry of excitement. "The Colonel is having breakfast in a few minutes and has requested that you join him."

When she was gone I reread Brian's letter, then went into the bath-dressing room to wash and dress.

Before leaving my room, I debated about what to do with Brian's letter. I didn't wish to leave it in my room lest it be found and read nor did I wish to destroy it. For some reason not quite clear to me at that moment, I believed I should keep it.

I tucked the letter securely into the waistband of my skirt where a ruffle from my blouse hid it from view and went down to breakfast.

At the foot of the curving marble staircase, I came to an involuntary stop, my eyes resting on the door to the library. In one sharp painful wrench I remembered last night, how the moonlight, filtering down through the skylight, turned the room into a fantasy of soft glowing light, how handsome Edmond appeared, how his arms suddenly came round me and . . . Words from Brian's letter pounded through my brain . . . *Amy is dead . . . Sir Edmond was responsible for her death.*

I turned away quickly and hurried toward the small dining room. It was when I'd almost reached the dining room that it occurred to me I must not betray myself, not show any unease or anxiety because of the letter or because I was meeting secretly with Brian. I must not encourage any inquisitive questions, particularly from Lady Edythe. Surely Mrs. Hopkins would not mention the letter, not even in a casual way, while she served breakfast.

But Mrs. Hopkins was not serving. When I walked in, Mrs. Farris was pouring the Colonel's coffee. Lady Edythe was not present.

"Lady Edythe is confined to her room," the Colonel explained when Mrs. Farris left to get my breakfast. "After that tantrum she threw last night, it's no wonder she has a sick headache. I think she's just ashamed to show her face. More likely, she's closeted up in her room, secretly planning Edmond's engagement party, knowing she'll bring him around, convince him it's time his betrothal to that simpering Miss Wickham became official. Edmond will probably listen to her, too. Rotten shame how Edmond lets Lady Edythe lead him by the nose."

When Mrs. Farris returned with my bacon and eggs, I noticed a difference in her demeanor, less stone-faced, almost cheerful. I soon discovered it was due to the Colonel's presence. She seemed at ease with him, as if they were old trusted friends. After the Colonel's introduction of me as a special friend of his, Mrs. Farris unbent a little toward me. Her wary, inquisitive glances became less frequent now that I had the Colonel's approval. Once she even went so far as to smile at me briefly. Although she still maintained a guarded, slightly curious attitude toward me, with the Colonel she was talkative, even confiding.

"I see Corinne is back at the manor," the Colonel said to her with a wheezy chuckle.

Mrs. Farris's face drooped into a gloomy frown. She wagged her head back and forth. "I can see," she moaned, regarding the Colonel with a weary expression, "thut it haint been the right decision for me t' make." She emitted a long ragged sigh and her shoulders drooped as she returned to the kitchen.

"Corinne," the Colonel explained, "is a bit of a problem. Corinne's mother and Mrs. Farris are sisters and it seems Corinne is too much for the mother to handle. Mrs. Farris, as a kindness to her sister, brought Corinne to work here at the manor but . . ." A puckish smile worked at his mouth. The wrinkled old face furrowed into deep folds as the smile slid into a roguish grin. He leaned across the table. "With her hot eyes and fetching ways, Corinne could be a problem anywhere. The sooner they marry her off the better. You can't keep that kind of healthy energy bottled up." He grinned again and began to lavish butter on his muffin.

I was not interested in Corinne's "healthy energy," but I was mystified that Lady Edythe should permit Corinne to remain at Malverne Manor when she was unhappily aware of the girl's behavior around Sir Edmond. Or was Lady Edythe only fulfilling the master's wishes? I drove the accusing thought from my mind. How could I trust my own judgment of Edmond so very little? How could I condemn him simply because some foolish servant girl seemed infatuated? It was Brian's letter, of course, that caused me to believe the worst. Why should I want to believe Brian rather than Edmond?

I concentrated on my breakfast, trying to dismiss all of the disturbing, perplexing thoughts from my mind. One thought, however, kept edging its way back. I still would have liked to know why Corinne was hiding in the Cream Lace Room. Then, something Myrna had said crossed my thoughts, that Corinne had attended Floss's wedding. But had Corinne been with the Farrises all during the two-week holiday? Or had Corinne returned secretly to Malverne Manor?

The Colonel had also lapsed into a silence, enjoying his breakfast, particularly the buttered muffins which he was now heaping with marmalade. My eye caught the unusual walking stick hanging on the back of his chair. The handle of the walking stick was a beautifully carved ivory elephant head. The Colonel looked up, saw me admiring it.

"Belongs to Edmond," he explained. "Lady Edythe gave it to him, brought it from India. I often borrow it when I visit here. Thought I'd take a little stroll in the gardens after breakfast. I don't go walking without it, nice to lean on. Edmond, in fact, always takes it with him when he prowls about the manor. Not that he needs to lean on a stick, but he uses it to poke around, you know. By the way, what do you plan to do with yourself until it's time to leave for the afternoon meeting? I've decided to go to the meeting. Felt a bit out of sorts last night but I feel fine this morning.''

I checked my inclination to read too much into his curious gaze when he asked the question and it occurred to me now that I might have difficulty meeting with Brian. The shocking contents of his letter consumed my thoughts so completely, I overlooked the problem of getting away from the manor without arousing suspicion.

"I might write some letters," I answered lamely, "then, later, I might take a walk, see some of the countryside.''

"Don't overdo the walking, Miss Atwood. You'll do plenty of that later. If I know Will Hockinson, he'll have us tearing up and down the countryside, visiting every constituent in his north end of the county. And the Raynords, I hear, move at quite a pace.''

He paused, sighed heavily. "Too bad all this about that young lady, Amy, had to come up now with Edmond having to be away at such a critical time in his campaign. He left very early this morning, was already gone when I got up.'' He hesitated, lowered his eyes, and fiddled with the silverware. "I hear your circumstances are somewhat similar to Amy's.''

I sat up with a start. "What do you mean, similar circumstances?''

"That she had no family," he said, shifting the silverware back and forth restlessly, "only a stepfather who doesn't seem to matter. That you also have no family, only that young man, Walter Binson, who works in the chemist's shop.''

"It's true that my parents are dead," I said, wishing I didn't sound so insecure and defensive, but his question unnerved me. "But I have many acquaintances in my village," I added as if this information were of vital importance. Then, all at once, I relaxed into my chair, realizing I was doing exactly what I'd cautioned myself I must not do. I was looking for hidden meanings and threats in every corner, all because of the letter I'd received this morning.

"Have you had any news about your friend, Amy?" I heard the Colonel ask and I steeled myself for a direct, noncommittal reply.

"Nothing new," I answered.

There was a sharp silence, then the Colonel reached for the elephant-head walking stick.

"Well, I will take my little garden stroll," he said. He was leaning heavily on the stick and, with the sunlight from the windows shining directly on him now, he appeared terribly old, the face thin, frail-looking, lined with deep wrinkles. His shoulders were stooped as he hunched over the walking stick and I wondered how he expected to tear up and down the county this afternoon.

"Don't forget about the meeting, Miss Atwood," he said over his shoulder as he went toward the french door that led into the garden. He stopped in the doorway. His thin face creased into a broad smile. "I'm quite pleased you're staying at the manor, Miss Atwood. Don't rush away," he said, then went out, and I found myself puzzling over the word, *meeting*.

I watched him go, slowly at first, using the walking stick. After a while, as if he'd picked up momentum, his steps became surprisingly brisk. He jabbed the walking stick ahead of him with quick strokes.

I encountered no problem getting away from the manor. Lady Edythe was not about nor was anyone else. The entire place, as I slipped out a side door, seemed deserted. The only sounds came from the stable, the neighing of horses, and someone pounding on metal.

I hurried down the gravel drive and was soon on the main road, remembering, at once, the first time I'd traveled it from the inn to the manor, how I'd got caught in that thunderstorm.

As I approached the inn, I felt uncomfortable about Brian's choosing it as a meeting place, yet he might have done so only because he knew its location was familiar to me. But I wasn't looking forward to seeing Mrs. Ploovey, the innkeeper, again, her shrewd eyes lighting on me, plying me with questions about "them, up at the manor" especially about "the likes of him." Surely she wouldn't be bold enough to hang about while Brian and I talked.

When I neared the inn I was pleased to hear an interminable racket inside, indicating the place was overflowing with patrons. Then Mrs. Ploovey would be too occupied. She might not notice me or even remember me.

But Mrs. Ploovey noticed me the instant I set foot inside. Remembered me, too. I glanced around the packed tavern, looking for Brian. Out of the corner of my eye I could see Mrs. Ploovey staring at me. I pretended not to see her, my eyes avoiding her as I searched the crowded room. My displeasure with Brian for selecting the inn as the meeting place mounted. I could hear slurry remarks directed at me from a couple of whiskey-sodden patrons. I'd attracted considerable attention all around. Mrs. Ploovey was now sidling toward me, her broad fleshy face, sweaty and flushed, was creased into smiling expectancy.

"Why lookee here," she cried, "if it baint the young lady from up t' the manor." She thrust her grinning face forward. "Spectin' t' meet someone, dearie?"

I started to back slowly toward the door. "I—I had an appointment with someone," I stammered, scanning the crowded room once more. "But my—my friend isn't here."

She followed me to the door, waving a hand at some raucous patrons who were demanding her attention.

"Did yur friend," she inquired eagerly, "arrive t' the manor? The friend o' yours, the young lady from London?"

I shook my head and she followed me tenaciously as I tried to make my way to the door through the noisy crowd.

"Too bad," she muttered almost in my ear. "About the servant girl I mean. Drownding herself and all."

"Yes," I agreed. "Too bad."

"Is he up there now?" she persisted, following me outdoors. "The master, I mean."

"No, he isn't there."

She peered at me, grinning, then, turning to go back into the inn, she flung her head around and shouted, "Too bad yur gentleman friend dint show up, dearie."

I raced up the road, my face burning with fury and indignation. It was all a hoax, a cruel joke. Brian never intended to be there.

I started to walk back to the manor at a rapid, furious pace, finding it necessary to walk off my anger and humiliation.

After I'd gone a short distance, my temper cooled and reason returned. I stopped in the road, feeling slightly foolish. I'd become so unsettled at meeting up with Mrs. Ploovey again, with her crafty, jeering face bringing back the entire Amy episode into sharp focus, the remarks about the "servant girl," who'd drowned, reawakening my suspicions about who the victim actually was. And with the whiskey-smelling, caterwauling crowd surrounding me, I'd become even more upset. I wondered for a moment what sort of rowdies Mrs. Ploovey was entertaining now. The last time I had been there, the place had become crowded and noisy, but the men had not been like that gang.

I glanced at my watch and saw it was not quite ten. I sat down on the smooth boulder near the road, deciding not to re-enter the inn. Brian, after all, might be just a little late for the meeting. I pulled out his letter from my skirt waistband to check if I'd made a mistake about the time or day of the meeting.

I'd made no error about that and settled back to wait. From where I sat, I could see Brian if he approached the inn.

I waited and waited, but he did not come. I had to tell myself again that the letter and the proposed meeting were a hoax. By whom? Brian? Had Brian, for that matter, written the letter? If not, then who?

After a while I got up and slowly started up the road toward Malverne Manor when I heard my name being called. I looked back. Brian was running up the road, waving to me.

"Claire, I'm so sorry I'm late," he said, a little out of breath. He took me lightly by the arm and we began to walk back to the inn. His face lit up with pleasure, the smile almost caressing. "I was afraid you'd leave, Claire, that I'd miss seeing you." There was a slight impulsive pressure of his fingers on my arm. "Oh, I'm so glad to see you again. You look lovely, Claire."

I murmured a thanks for the spontaneous praise then said, "Let's not meet at the inn, Brian."

"You've got a point," he agreed readily. "The lady innkeeper is not to my taste. I chose it only because you'd mentioned it, knew where it was." He indicated a footpath leading off the coach road into a pasture where sheep were grazing.

"I know you're anxious to hear what I have to tell you," he said when we'd found a felled tree trunk and sat down, "so I'll get right to it. When you met me at the cottage and told me about your friend, Amy, and her mysterious disappearance from Malverne Manor, I had to pretend I knew nothing. I had to be cautious. Well, for one thing, I didn't know your true connection in the case and——"

"Speaking of connections, Brian," I interrupted, "what exactly is your connection with Malverne Manor?"

He was gazing ahead at the grazing sheep in the distance. Now he turned his head and looked directly at me. I waited for him to speak, but he only regarded me with a slightly amused smile.

"Don't you see the connection, Claire?" he inquired after a while, but I continued to gaze at him in puzzled silence.

Then just as I was about to say that I did not understand, I uttered a gasp of surprise and stared into his face. "Good heavens, yes," I exclaimed. "I see the resemblance now." I recalled now that at one time I'd thought he resembled Mrs. Hopkins, mainly because of the similarity in their sunny disposition and a certain likeness in the smile. Later I sensed a resemblance to Lady Edythe, slight, but the suggestion was there. Now, looking directly into Brian's face with the strong sunlight on it, I saw that he resembled Sir Edmond. I hadn't spotted the resemblance at first because Brian was blond with brown eyes, and Sir Edmond had black hair and blue eyes. But the family likeness was there.

"Yes," Brian said with a light laugh. "I am a poor relation, Claire.

It's not surprising that you didn't catch the resemblance immediately. Edmond is much taller than I, and slimmer. Then, with his black hair and blue eyes, it sort of throws the whole thing off."

I was still studying his face. "There certainly is a family resemblance," I admitted. "You even resemble the Colonel in some ways. Lady Edythe, too. Because they're old, the similarities are a little blurred, but the family likeness is noticeable."

Brian nodded. "My mother and Sir Edmond's mother were related. I bear a stronger resemblance to Lady Edythe than to the Colonel. In fact, I most resemble Lady Edythe but because of her age, the gray hair in particular; the likeness is not so sharp." He picked up a twig and began to toy with it. There was a mischievous glint in his eyes. "Well, as I said, I am, nevertheless, a poor relation, not really welcome at Malverne Manor." He darted me a gleeful look, the dark eyes still shining with mischief. "But I descend on them occasionally like the plague. Edmond and I don't get on at all. I refuse to be a hypocrite. I dislike Edmond. I also distrust him. I cannot abide that arrogance, all that surface charm, his insatiable obsession with property, land and more land at any cost. Now this obsession about the House of Lords, to work his way into Parliament." He shrugged. "That's not my idea of life—money, property, ambition. I prefer a different kind of contentment." He paused for a thoughtful moment, then laughed amusedly. "To Edmond, I don't even exist. And Lady Edythe barely tolerates me, but because she knows I will annoy them with my occasional visits to the manor, she sometimes sends me a reluctant invitation to come for a brief visit when Edmond is away.

"One such invitation arrived at my London lodgings about a fortnight ago," he went on. "When I received this tender little invitation from Lady Edythe, I smelled a sense of urgency, even panic. When I arrived at the manor, Lady Edythe was in a tizzy, wailing about dear Edmond bringing disgrace upon the noble house because of some scheming shopgirl——"

"By the way," I cut in, "how did Lady Edythe know Amy had at one time worked in a teashop?" I remembered Lady Edythe's conversational slip in the drawing room yesterday, when in a fitful rush of words she'd referred to Amy for the first time as a shopgirl.

Brian thought a moment, then said, "She must have learned that from a couple of letters Amy had written,"—which I thought was unlikely— "or perhaps Edmond mentioned it to Lady Edythe."

"Go on," I said. "So you came to Malverne Manor two weeks ago at

Lady Edythe's urgent call because Amy was scheming to become the mistress of Malverne Manor. Then what?"

"Lady Edythe related that this Amy person had had the effrontery to write her, informing her that she was coming to the manor to marry Edmond. Lady Edythe immediately laid out her plans—would I dash up to London, catch up with Amy before she left for the manor, bargain with her? She mentioned a large sum of money for my trouble, an even larger sum for Amy. She also suggested I talk to Edmond who was in London then."

"Did you see Amy in London? Did you talk to her?"

Brian shook his head. "When I got to Mrs. Alroyd's house, where Amy was companion to the old woman—Amy's return address was on her two letters to Lady Edythe—well, Mrs. Alroyd informed me Amy was gone. She wouldn't say where. I got the feeling Edmond had requested Mrs. Alroyd to say nothing."

"Did you see Edmond?"

"Yes, I knew where he stayed when he was in London. When I confronted him, he denied everything, said he knew no one named Amy."

"Then you returned to Malverne Manor but Amy wasn't there?"

"Right. But I became suspicious, smelled something tricky going on. Lady Edythe promptly informed me that Amy, after writing exactly when she'd expected to arrive at the manor, had not come after all, that Old Abner went to meet the coach the day Amy had indicated, also the day after in case she'd arrive late, but Amy never came." A sharpness edged into Brian's voice. "Lady Edythe," he went on, "is a cool, clever schemer, but I detected too guarded a manner in her explanation; there were chinks in what struck me as a carefully executed plan."

"That servant girl who arrived about the time Amy was due, the one who drowned," I began and Brian swung around to face me, the dark eyes alert, questioning.

"Servant girl?" he repeated in a hoarse whisper. "Servant girl who drowned?"

"Yes, drowned in the Malverne pond."

"Where did you get that information?" The puzzled expression on his face deepened.

"I overheard it at the Three Crowns Inn, a conversation between Mrs. Ploovey and Mrs. Hopkins. I wondered immediately whether they weren't actually discussing Amy; wondered, too, whether the drowning was accidental. Earlier, Lady Edythe had briefly mentioned the drowning when she cautioned me that the pond's banks were hazardous at some spots. Miss Wickham also told me about the drowning; said she was present when the girl's brother, a vicar, came to claim the body."

There was a prolonged silence from Brian. He sat hunched forward on the felled tree trunk, head thrust forward, the lines of his face hardening into a severe expression and, incongruously, I thought, how, in profile, his face sharply resembled Edmond's.

"Well, well," Brian murmured after a while, turning to face me now, a rueful smile touching his face. "That puts a different light on things."

"You believe it was Amy who was drowned?" I asked. "And not accidentally? I wondered whether she wasn't murdered, then thrown into the pond," I added, noting the shock on Brian's face.

"What a gruesome development," Brian said in an almost vicious tone, visibly upset. "But you know, Claire," he said after a reflective moment, the shock in his eyes lessened now, "we might be talking about two separate things. I know servant girls come and go frequently at Malverne Manor. Lady Edythe is quite the martinet and Mrs. Hopkins not much better. A servant girl could very well have come to the manor about the time Amy was due and drowned accidentally. And Amy might have been murdered by Edmond which has nothing to do with the drowning." I flinched at his casual statement, calling Edmond a murderer, his sounding so definite that Amy was dead. I had to will myself to listen as he continued.

"Piecing together the information I've gathered," he went on, "from Edmond's acquaintances when I talked with them yesterday in London and listening to what some people here in the county had to say when I spoke with them this morning—" Brian paused and gave me a quick look. "Not everyone in the county is Edmond's friend. He's made some enemies because of his highhanded ways and his obsession about property. Well, I'm convinced that the Amy murder plot is something separate from this servant girl's drowning incident," Brian concluded.

"When you returned from London, that other time, when Lady Edythe sent you there to pay off Amy, did you find Sir Edmond at the manor?"

Brian made an emphatic gesture, hurling away the twig he'd been toying with, some of the indignation returning to his voice. "That, Claire, was why I was hiding out in the cottage when you first met me. When I'd returned from that previous visit to London, on Lady Edythe's orders, Lady Edythe said Edmond was in Scotland, but I had a strong suspicion he was secretly present at the manor, that it was he who'd sent the servants away, all but Mrs. Hopkins and Old Abner. Lady Edythe gave me some story about one of the Farris girls getting married and so the whole Farris family, at her largesse, she said, were given a two-week holiday to go off to some relative for the wedding festivities."

"Myrna Farris told me about the holiday, that her sister, Floss, was getting married at this relative's home."

Brian grinned. "A convenient opportunity for Edmond." He shrugged, the grin slipping into a grim look. "Well, to get back to what I was saying, when I'd returned to the manor after my fruitless journey to London, not finding Amy and with Edmond denying everything, I listened patiently, at first, to Lady Edythe's explanation that Amy never came to the manor then—I don't recall where our conversation took an unexpected turn—but, all at once, Lady Edythe and I were having a deuce of a row. Words flew fast and hard because I knew I was being taken for a gullible fool. After a considerable amount of shouting, when I'd made it clear I wasn't going to go away quietly, as if the whole thing were settled, Lady Edythe finally admitted that Amy had come to the manor—while Edmond was supposedly in Scotland—and after being offered even more money than I'd been commissioned to offer, Amy had agreed to go to Malta to have her child."

"Child?" I gasped. "Edmond's?"

Brian shrugged and said nothing.

"Why Malta?" I asked, still shaken by his news.

"Lady Edythe used to live in Malta, has friends there who she said would take care of Amy."

A silence fell upon us. I tried to make order of the chaotic thoughts whipping through my brain. Brian picked up the twig he'd hurled away a while ago and began to finger it with slow, lazy movements, as if waiting for me to get over my shock of his last statements, about a child, probably Edmond's child.

"Did Lady Edythe say whether Amy went alone to Malta?" I asked when I could bear to speak.

"No, not alone. There was some young man, she said, whom Amy had known in London. With all the loot Amy had acquired, Lady Edythe insinuated, he was quite willing to go to Malta with Amy and marry her there." Brian stopped and looked at me. "I know you're shocked about the news about a child, but remember, Claire, that's only Lady Edythe's story, all that about Malta. She was probably instructed to say that, at Edmond's orders. The more shocking thing is the truth, that Amy was murdered and Lady Edythe is covering for Edmond."

"You never believed the story about Malta?"

"No, I did not."

"That was why you disappeared so mysteriously from the cottage and went up to London again?"

"Yes, to talk to Edmond's acquaintances, to check if he'd really been intending to go to Scotland."

"And on this trip you learned that Amy is dead, that Edmond is responsible for her death? And some people here in the county also have their suspicions?"

"In London I learned that Edmond, indeed, knew Amy and that he never spoke of going to Scotland. After talking this morning to people who live hereabouts, everything points to the fact that Amy was done away with and that Edmond was at the manor at the time. At present, my information is still sketchy but damning nevertheless. Lady Edythe is still sticking with her story about Amy's escape to Malta with a bagful of money. Pretty soon, I suppose, Edmond will inform you that he's received word that Amy is in Malta," he added bitterly, and I wondered whether, indeed, that would be Edmond's news when he returned from London.

Brian was staring thoughtfully ahead, the gentle contours of his face hard and grim once more. He did not speak for some time. When he finally did, his voice was barely audible. He grasped both my hands and, even in the quick movement, his touch was gentle. How different from Edmond, I thought, whose touch, even his embrace, always bore a roughness.

"Claire, you must leave Malverne Manor." His tone was quiet but intense. "You must. You're in danger there."

"Because of Lady Edythe?"

"No, not because of her. She's a shrew but——"

"——because of Edmond?" I finished for him. "Because he may murder me as he did Amy?"

He'd been holding my hands loosely. He pressed my fingers briefly, then let my hands drop into my lap. He looked away, shaking his head. "I can't believe that you, too, could surrender to that surface charm of Edmond's," he said vehemently. Before I had a chance to protest, he went on speaking. "Claire, I wish I knew for certain about Amy. It's all been so cleverly covered up. I'll admit I dislike Edmond, but murder—" He stopped, looked into my face. "But you must not stay at the manor. It's too dangerous for you."

He placed his hand lightly over mine. He smiled faintly. "Claire, there just might be something to this story about Amy going to Malta. It just could be true after all. Perhaps it was a servant girl who drowned accidentally in the pond." His voice rose, his face brightened as he rushed on. "Perhaps if you went home—yes, that's it—you should return home. You might find a letter from Amy—from Malta. She might have thought you'd receive the Malta letter before you rushed down to Malverne Manor or she might have written from London telling you she was going to Malta. She might have married someone else, the young man Lady Edythe mentioned. It may be his child, not Edmond's."

I listened to his eager explanation and all the while snatches from Amy's six letters from Malverne Manor skimmed through my head. . . . "I know it is Sir Edmond I wish to marry." She'd also stated that in a letter from London before she went to the manor. The repeated remarks in her letters from Malverne Manor . . . "As soon as Edmond returns from Scotland, I want you to come to Malverne Manor to be my maid of honor." But I recalled the letters from London during those five months while she waited for Edmond to return, stating that she'd "almost decided" to marry the young man she'd called an "adventurer." Did she go to Malta with him? With "the loot" Lady Edythe had bribed her with? Was he the father of the child, not Sir Edmond? If she was with child, which I did not believe.

"If you believe that Edmond—that he—that he murdered Amy and that the murder plot was carefully covered up, who helped Edmond? Only Lady Edythe? Anyone else?" I asked.

"I hear the Colonel would do anything for Edmond."

"That old man? I find that hard to believe."

"Don't underestimate him. He has quite a reputation in the county, including his liking for the bottle."

"And Corinne?" I said after a while. "What about her?"

Brian smiled knowingly. "Ah, yes, Corinne," was all he said.

"Miss Wickham told me she and her father visited this—this servant girl in the Cream Lace Room, that she was ill and lying in bed."

"It wouldn't be difficult to fool Miss Wickham, judging from what I've heard about her. Her papa isn't much smarter and he is senile and myopic besides. Also, Miss Wickham will believe anything Lady Edythe wishes her to believe. As for Mr. Wickham, the only invalid that interests him is himself. I doubt that he so much as glanced at the invalid in the Cream Lace Room."

"What about Mrs. Hopkins? How much does she know?"

"You can't get blood out of a turnip," was Brian's cryptic reply. "And Old Abner," he added, "doesn't count. He's practically blind and soft in the brain. The Farrises, though, had to be cleared out. Floss's wedding was a fortuitous event."

"Myrna said Corinne had attended Floss's wedding, but that doesn't mean that Corinne was with the Farrises the entire length of the holiday."

"No, indeed, it does not," Brian agreed and I saw that knowing little smile creep into his face once more. "Corinne might be a little more than scullery maid at the manor."

His words stung. I stared down at the ground. I could feel the hot flush on my cheeks. After a moment I got up slowly. Brian rose also and we walked silently up the road.

"Brian," I said after we'd walked for some time, "I believe you're mistaken about Edmond."

He gave me a quick, impatient look. "Oh my God," he muttered. "Can't any woman resist Edmond's charm?"

"I have not succumbed to Sir Edmond's charm," I retorted, straining to keep my voice on an even keel. "It's just that——"

I felt his gentle touch on my arm. His voice was equally gentle. "I'm sorry, Claire. I shouldn't have said that. Forgive me. Although you make light of it, I have fallen very much in love with you. I know you don't believe me or it doesn't seem to matter to you, but I have hopes that —that—" He smiled at me, his clear blond good looks quite attractive in the bright sunlight. "I'll go on hoping, Claire," he said, kissing me lightly on the cheek, then added, with that rising urgency in his tone, "Will you promise me, Claire, that you will leave the manor? I'm afraid for you." He glanced up the road. "I'll have to leave you here. I don't want anyone from the manor seeing me. I must continue looking for the truth about Amy, and both of us must work in secret." He looked intently into my face. "Will you promise me you will leave the manor?"

"Yes, I'll leave," I murmured and he appeared pleased and enormously relieved. "But before I leave," I added, "I wish I could find that lost Malverne Manor book."

He'd turned to leave and now he swung round, his eyes widening with astonishment. "Malverne Manor book?" he repeated.

"Yes, I found it hidden in the desk in the cottage. Now it's missing," I said, then seeing the excited expression on his face, asked, "You know about it?"

"I know that Lady Edythe is quite concerned that it is missing. You say you found it in the cottage? Did you find something in it that ties in with Amy's disappearance? Perhaps—well, something placed into the book?"

"I found nothing placed into the book."

He thought a moment, obviously shaken at my news. "You didn't see any possible connection between the two—the book and Amy's disappearance?"

"No, but apparently you believe there is. I only glanced at the book, read a few lines about the Malverne gardens and some details about the manor house."

"That's all?"

"That's all." I continued to look at him curiously. "How can there be a connection?"

He made an impatient wave of his hand. "Oh, there probably isn't, Claire. I don't see how there could be. It's just that Lady Edythe is so frantic about its being lost. I should have remembered that a book detailing her beloved Malverne Manor would be important to Lady Edythe." He pushed aside his original concern. "I'm simply clutching at straws. Looking for any possible clue." He stopped, stood quite still, thinking, then said, "But the book might be important in some way and it might have been returned to the cottage by now. Tell you what, Claire. I'll try to get to the cottage later today. I'll look for the book, all through the cottage. Will you try to get to the cottage secretly before dinnertime? I may also have some additional information. There are some people living nearby I'll be talking to. Will you try to get to the cottage later today?"

I said I would and made a move to leave, then turned and said, "I still believe you're mistaken about Edmond."

"I hope so, Claire," he said in a quiet voice, looking back at me, "for your sake because I know you've fallen in love with him. I know. And I know I'm flimsy competition against Edmond's winning ways and fabulous wealth. All I could offer you, Claire, is my love for you and that I would do anything for you, anything to make you happy." He smiled, a brief, wistful smile, then quickly turned and walked away.

CHAPTER 14

Walking back to the manor, I tried to close my mind to what Brian had said. He could be mistaken, might have let his animosity toward Edmond influence his thinking. I'd wait to see what news Edmond brought from London.

But Brian's suspicions and accusations persisted, weaving insidiously through my hectic thoughts. I began to wonder whether I should believe what Edmond would tell me when he returned from London. On the other hand, I was quick to remind myself, why believe Brian so readily?

By his own admission, Brian called himself "a poor relation," and his accompanying laughter might have been a cover-up for his true feelings. He spoke derisively of Edmond's wealth, his charm, his social position. Then anything Brian had said could be nothing more than a betrayal of his deep-seated jealousy.

And didn't my heart tell me anything? Could I be so much in love with Edmond if he were a—a murderer? A cold shudder touched me at the monstrous suggestion. Edmond could never be a murderer.

I quickened my steps, driving the tormenting questions from my mind. A glance at my watch told me it was almost time to leave for the election meeting. My steps faltered, then I stopped altogether in the road and asked myself why I was hurrying to a meeting concerning a county election that had nothing to do with me. This isn't my home county. These people are Edmond's people—and Miss Wickham's—and it doesn't concern me. I thought of the secret preparations for the upcoming ball, to celebrate the election victory and Edmond's official announcement of his engagement to Miss Wickham. Was I foolish enough to delude myself into thinking that Edmond had no intention of marrying Miss Wickham? That, instead, he would marry me? That only proved how muddled I'd become about things. I recalled with painful clarity the letter I'd written to Amy in London, scolding her for being muddled, for imagining that Sir Edmond intended to marry her. Miss Wickham might be as simpering as the Colonel said she was, or even as stupid as Brian claimed she was, but Miss Wickham was gentry, I reminded myself, and I was trade. Just you remember that, Miss Atwood, I went on admonishing myself. True, my mother was French aristocracy, but surely I wasn't going to drag that qualification into the proceedings—as Amy had done.

As for that afternoon's election meeting, I recalled Lady Edythe's blunt remark that my attendance would be "out of place." Well, she was right. I wouldn't go.

Now that I'd let myself see some things in a clear, candid light, another disturbing question crossed my mind. Why did I remain at Malverne Manor? Ostensibly to solve the mystery concerning Amy's disappearance. That much I understood. Amy was like a sister to me, but even if she'd been a mere acquaintance, I wouldn't ignore a question of murder. Yet, truthfully, what had I accomplished? The more I probed, the more I complicated things. I no longer knew whom to trust. Who was my ally? Who was my enemy? My potential murderer? I should be in London at this moment, not Edmond. I should have gone to Mrs. Alroyd's house where Amy had lived. I should have questioned the people Amy had come to know in London. Perhaps Lady Bellingford had returned from the South of France.

I had to face up to the fact that it was no longer only Amy's disappearance that was keeping me at the manor. It was this futile emotional entanglement with Edmond. I would have to leave Malverne Manor, regain my sense of perspective. I could not leave today because I'd already missed the noon coach departure from the Three Crowns Inn. But I would leave tomorrow. Edmond would be back from London by then and I would know what he'd found out.

I walked leisurely now, dawdling really, feeling pleased with myself that I should be able to cut across a lot of emotional chaos and arrive at such a neat, clear-cut decision, beginning with my refusal to attend the election meeting.

I still had half the distance to go before reaching the manor house and I purposely slowed my pace even more, so that by the time I'd reached the house they would have already left.

But as I turned off the main road into the drive, all my fine resolutions about the meeting went up in thin air. The Raynords and the Colonel were waiting for me at the front entrance and in a flurry of haste and excitement, because we were somewhat late, we were on our way. It would have been ill-mannered and decidedly awkward to refuse, particularly since they showed no impatience with me for keeping them waiting. They rushed me into the carriage and we were off.

My surprise that, after firmly resolving not to attend the meeting, I should be going after all was slight compared to the surprising developments that occurred once I got there.

The meeting was again held in a parish hall, a much larger one this time. A huge amount of food was displayed on long tables placed against the walls and people were helping themselves. The room reverberated with assorted sounds, loud voices, the clanging of dishes, good-natured arguments. The Colonel and Mr. Raynord immediately got lost in the milling crowd. Mrs. Raynord, with a firm hand on my arm, led me to the lavish serving board. We then took our plates to one of the small tables scattered about the hall where people were already eating—enjoying their loud discussions as heartily as they were enjoying the bountiful food. At the front end of the hall was a small stage which would serve as speaker's platform where today Will Hockinson would preside since Edmond was in London.

I turned to speak to Mrs. Raynord when my eye caught Will Hockinson standing near the stage where he was talking to Edmond.

At first I stared in amazement then, asking Mrs. Raynord to excuse me for a moment, I approached the speaker's platform. Edmond saw me and quickly came forward.

"I didn't go to London," he immediately explained, drawing me over to a corner of the meeting hall. "I received a letter early this morning," he rushed on and pulled a letter out of his pocket, handing it to me. "I got the letter quite early today. I didn't want to awaken you so early in the morning to tell you about the letter, knowing I'd see you at the meeting. Because of the letter, I didn't have to go to London and was able to meet with Will Hockinson early this morning. We got a great deal of work out of the way."

I barely heard what he was saying. My attention was on the letter he'd handed me. It wasn't Amy's handwriting. I saw that immediately. And it did not resemble the handwriting of the letter I'd received this morning. I glanced down at the signature of a man's name, unfamiliar to me. I started to read:

Dear Sir:

I had been debating about writing to you and have decided that I should do so. You do not know me, of course, but you have been acquainted with Amy, the young lady my brother married recently.

Amy unexpectedly came into a small inheritance and consequently she and my brother decided on the spur of the moment to go to Malta and be married there. My brother has a small property in Malta which he now plans to sell and, along with Amy's inheritance, they intend to emigrate to Australia where my brother hopes to increase their joint fortune.

Amy decided—wrongly, I believe—that she would write you from Australia and explain her decision to marry my brother rather than you. Since you might be wondering, possibly worrying about her whereabouts, I decided that her irresponsibility—and my brother's—should be rectified and so I have taken the liberty to write to you.

Hoping this reaches you, that I have been given the correct address, I remain,

Respectfully,
Charles Coombes

Even as I read the letter, Brian's prediction of only a few hours ago, whipped through my mind—*Pretty soon* . . . Brian had said, *Edmond will inform you that he's received word that Amy is in Malta.*

"I don't believe it," I said when I'd finished reading.

Edmond took the letter from my hand with a swift gesture, ramming it into his pocket. His face tightened; the eyes blazed with a cold blue light.

"What do you mean, you don't believe it?" His voice was a low, angry whisper. He'd turned his back completely on the milling crowd so that no one in the hall might see the livid fury in his face.

"May I see the envelope?" I said, my voice faint, unsteady, because of the fierce way he was staring down at me. "I would like to see from where the letter was posted."

For a long time he continued to stare at me, hot anger contorting his face. The veins at the temple quivered slightly.

"Since I did not expect to be disbelieved or interrogated," he said in a surprisingly calm, expressionless voice, "I did not bring the envelope to serve as evidence." He hesitated, his eyes narrowing. "Are you implying I had a friend write the letter? Or that perhaps I wrote it myself?"

I did not answer. I was conscious of the cold silence between us, of the milling, noisy crowd behind us, the clatter of dishes, the bursts of laughter, the din of voices.

"You didn't answer me," I heard him say, "and I've got to get back to the speaker's platform." Then all at once his face relaxed, his voice altered and he spoke in an almost loving tone. "We'll talk about it later," he said. "Mrs. Raynord, I see, is looking for you." He took me by the arm, his fingers digging into my flesh and, smiling and greeting people along the way, he led me to where Mrs. Raynord was standing, her eyes searching the hall for me.

"Here she is, Mrs. Raynord," he said in his most engaging manner, flashing his most disarming smile. "Will you see to it that Miss Atwood helps herself to some of that fine lunch."

Mrs. Raynord beamed at him; they exchanged a few cordial words which I didn't care to follow and as Edmond rushed away, Mrs. Raynord and I returned to the table where I'd left my food untouched and which I no longer wished to eat.

For me, the remainder of the meeting was a meaningless blur. I tried to follow Mrs. Raynord's chatter, not wishing to offend her cordiality since she had nothing to do with my misery. Then Edmond's voice, pleasantly warm and engaging, came from the speaker's platform. There was much applause from everyone and I applauded also because to do otherwise would have been conspicuous. What remarks from Edmond drew the applause I had no inkling of nor did I care. It was enough that I keep up a semblance of normalcy with Mrs. Raynord and with the Colonel and Mr. Raynord who'd joined us.

The meeting seemed to drag on interminably. Not even the Colonel's wit nor Mrs. Raynord's unflagging cheerfulness could awaken any enthusiasm in me. I was careful not to draw attention to myself by appearing sullen. I had to put on a good show.

Finally, the meeting came to an end and Mrs. Raynord went in search of the Colonel and Mr. Raynord who'd wandered off again. I stood at the table, waiting for Mrs. Raynord to return when my glance caught sight of Miss Wickham. Edmond, his face partly turned away from me, was leaning over her chair. They were talking and laughing together. Mr. Wickham appeared quite pleased. I could see Miss Wickham's face clearly. She was sitting not far from where I stood. There was a glow of animation on her face as she gazed up at Edmond. I was struck by how different she looked. Like a woman aglow with the happiness of love?

I quickly turned my head away. I thought of all the talk I'd just heard about land and property. Well, now Sir Edmond could add the Wickham property to his own. I remembered his telling me that the Wickham property, though rundown at present, was an even better property than Malverne Manor. Consequently, he could be an even greater man of property.

But that silent, acid comment gave me no comfort and I could feel a burning under my eyelids. I blinked my eyes hard to hold back the foolish tears. I straightened my back, set my mouth into a hard, stubborn expression, and stalked off. I heard Mrs. Raynord calling to let me know she'd found Mr. Raynord and the Colonel and that we'd be leaving now.

Edmond was not returning with us, the Colonel said. "Edmond said he was able to get a considerable amount of visiting out of the way earlier," the Colonel further explained. "That'll spare us the trouble of racing all over the county this afternoon. Edmond, I suppose, is going to Wickham Place," he said, his eyes glancing off me.

All the way back to Malverne Manor I was aware that I was talking and laughing too much, but neither the Colonel nor the Raynords seemed to mind. My determined gaiety was infectious. Anyone passing by our carriage would have said that every one of us was having a wonderfully good time, especially the young lady laughing the most.

My laughter and gaiety died abruptly when I reached my room. I'd begged off from the social hour when we reached the manor house. The Colonel had proposed we all have some brandy—or tea—but I was able to make my escape to my room without any awkwardness.

I stood at the open window of my bedroom, gazing absently at the soft beauty of the flowering apple orchard below and breathing in the heady fragrance of the apple blossoms. I recalled the two decisions I had made when I'd walked up the road after my meeting with Brian, first, that I would not attend the campaign meeting. Well, I'd had no choice about that. To have refused would have been a rudeness to the Raynords and to the Colonel. As it turned out, it was a stroke of luck that I did go. I learned much.

The contents of the letter that Edmond showed me ran through my mind. Australia, indeed. Edmond had decided to add a further twist to the Malta story, to put Amy even farther away from my reach.

I closed my eyes, not wanting to think of anything at all for a while, especially not about Malverne Manor, but the tantalizing aroma of the apple orchard assailed my senses, stirring up recollections of the manor. In my mind's eye I could see the lovely drawing room with its serene comfortable colors, the high arched windows looking out on the gardens. And what a lovely way to start the day, to have breakfast in the small oval dining room that overlooked the rose garden. The library. How the sunlight had streamed down from the vast skylight. And later. The moonlight shining down, touching everything with a silver glow. I thought of the Cream Lace Room with its hidden secret which I might never know.

But I would have to leave it all. Not that I would abandon my search for the truth about Amy, but I knew by then that staying at the manor was out of the question. If I'd had a cold premonition when I first saw Malverne Manor that rainstormy day when I rushed toward it, I was now certain of a real, ever-present danger. It was no longer a vague premonition.

I must leave this place, I told myself.

The words repeated themselves in my mind and a disconcerting sensation settled on me. Is there a point in one's life where we change and there's no going back? When there is no escape into a more secure past? When things will never be the same? Will I, after having met Edmond, ever be the same again?

I whirled away from the window and left the room. I wasn't going to have any of that kind of foolishness take hold of me. Of course I was going home—to Walter Binson and the chemist's shop and a sensible uncomplicated life in the village I'd known all my life.

I hurried down the back stairs into the garden, hoping the way would be clear so that I might talk to Brian. He might have already come to the cottage. I did want to see him once more before I left. I didn't have to believe everything he told me—and perhaps that was my gravest error, not believing everything he told me. Anyway, I wanted to know if he'd learned anything more. And if he'd found the Malverne Manor book.

When I came into the garden I saw Corinne heading for the kitchen garden, a basket swinging from her arm. She wore a bright, fringed scarf on her head. She saw me and threw me a dark scowl. With her flashing dark eyes, olive-hued skin, and the head scarf, bright red with splashy yellow flowers, she had a sultry gypsy look about her. Her dark scowl rested on me for a prolonged moment, then she swung her head away and stalked off.

I walked toward the pond, but saw that the way to the cottage was not clear. Not only would Corinne be coming out of the kitchen garden at any moment, but Old Abner was standing near the pond and might see me going by.

"Baint it a pity, miss?" he said to me immediately when I reached him. He was peering sadly at the rushing pond, shaking his head. "She was sech a young 'un. T' die like such. T' go and drownd 'erself."

"Then you'd met this servant girl?" I said to him. He stared at me dumbly and I remembered that he was quite deaf. I repeated my question loudly and he nodded, shaking his grizzled head.

"Yes, miss. Mrs. Hopkins and myself went t' the Three Crowns Inn in the ponytrap t' fetch the young lady." He paused, regarding the pond. His voice rose excitedly when he spoke again. "Her ghost haunts the stone cottage, miss." He turned to look at me, the dim watery eyes staring out of his wrinkled old face. "I saw her again yestiday, miss," he shouted. "The ghost, I mean. Saw her go past the window of the cottage. Seen this many times, but don't go near the place no more, I don't. First time I saw the ghost, miss, I figgered it was them poachers again. Nobody uses the cottage no more, miss. Only the master onct or twice a year mebbe. But that weren't no poacher, miss. I saw this shape flash by the window and when I come up to the cottage door, there weren't nobody there. No person come to the door. It was her ghost and when I come into the cottage, miss, it were gone, the ghost I mean. I seen this ghost again yestiday."

I knew it was Brian he'd seen come and go, probably escape through the window when he saw Old Abner approach. I wanted to ask him about the servant girl, but he spoke first.

"She was a pretty young 'un," he was saying, gazing at the pond once more. "Hair like cornsilk. Dint look like a servant girl. She was homesick. I used t' post letters for her when I went t' the village. Was a secret, she said and I wuzn't t' tell no one about the letters." He nodded emphatically. "Twas a secret."

I was listening to the old man, too startled to speak, then just as I started to form my question, I heard Corinne's voice behind us.

"Abner," Corinne shouted, "Mrs. Hopkins is askin' to see you."

The old man became flustered and muttered under his breath. Corinne stood waiting.

"She wants t' see you this minute," Corinne commanded, and the old man, still muttering, shambled away.

Corinne remained standing still, the dark smoldering eyes fixed on me; then, as she lifted her hands slowly to pull a tighter knot in the bright-red head scarf, the scowl on her face slid into a faint mocking smile before she walked away.

I waited, looked around. The way was clear now and I hurried to the cottage. Soon Edmond would return to the manor from Wickham Place. Brian thought he was in London. I must warn him. But as I approached the cottage, I debated about this. Perhaps it was time Brian and Edmond met face to face. Then the truth would out.

Brian was waiting for me in the doorway. "I saw you through the window," he said, ushering me inside. "You've come much earlier than I expected." He quickly sat down at the roughhewn table, facing me, leaning his elbows on the table. He smiled but I could see he was in an agitated state. The bright look of alarm was in his eyes, their color a dark glittery brown, almost black. He took hold of my hands across the table, holding them in that characteristic light, gentle manner which seemed so much a part of his nature.

"Now listen carefully, Claire, because I don't have much time. Edmond, I hear, did not go to London," he said and I wanted to ask him how he'd found out, but he wouldn't be interrupted. "I must leave. I would have gone already, but I had to see you first." I could feel that slight pressure of his hand around my fingers as his voice tightened with alarm. "I learned more disturbing things since I saw you this morning. It seems that Amy did go to Malta, but she was tricked into going there. She didn't go there to be married, but to be murdered. You must leave Malverne Manor. Edmond has come to realize you are a threat to him. His next move will be to tell you the Malta story, probably lure you there so you, too, can be eliminated by a paid killer."

I stared at him in speechless horror. I wanted to tell him that Edmond had already told me the Malta story but something inside stopped me. The words jammed in my throat. I could not say them. My head whirled with confusion, conflict. Whom should I trust and believe? my mind and heart cried out. No answer came. I did not speak.

Brian's steady gaze was on me, his face clouded with worry and deep concern.

"I will leave the manor," I said after a while and Brian sighed aloud, then smiled with joyful relief. He leaned across the table and kissed me softly on the cheek. His tension suddenly gave way to carefree laughter. He stood up and waved his hands about. "I searched every possible hiding place, Claire, and I did not find that book, but I'm convinced it has nothing to do with Amy. There can't possibly be any connection. Lady Edythe is worried only because the book deals with her beloved Malverne Manor."

I got up from the table and went to the desk. "But why don't I look around?" I suggested and Brian readily agreed.

"Good idea, Claire. You found it the other time. You have a knack for that sort of thing. I'll help," he offered and together we began a hurried inspection of the entire cottage beginning with the desk.

"Tell me how you discovered Sir Edmond did not go to London," I said as the two of us rushed about, prying into shelves and drawers.

"Well, as I told you, Claire, I am a poor relation and must restrict myself to kitchen visits most of the time. I am permitted to enter the other part of the house only when Edmond is away and Lady Edythe is in a generous mood. When I stopped in the kitchen a while ago I encountered Corinne. She was alone and thus a little more communicative. I didn't even have to ask her whether Edmond was about or soon would be. I knew that by the look in her eyes and that little smile that constantly lurks at her mouth when Edmond is in residence. After a little prodding, Corinne let it out that the master had a pressing engagement early this morning, but not in London, and that he would be returning to the manor before teatime."

"Corinne surely knows, doesn't she, that Sir Edmond is going to marry Miss Wickham? Surely she doesn't expect——"

"Expect to marry Edmond?" Brian laughed. "Corinne isn't very bright, but she isn't stupid either. Edmond won't be the first of the landed gentry to have a rich, respectable wife and an accommodating servant girl." He stopped suddenly and came to me, taking me gently by the shoulders. "I'm sorry, Claire. I keep forgetting that——"

I moved abruptly out of his hold and began to rummage in the drawer in the table. "That what?" I snapped, tears blinding me. "That I'm infatuated with the master of Malverne Manor? I'm not," I flared, slamming the drawer shut and going to a narrow cupboard door near the hearth to search there for the missing book.

I started to pull open the cupboard door when I felt Brian's hand on my arm. He turned me around with a light yet firm gesture, like a caress. For a little while he regarded me quietly, drawing me close, but still holding me gently, a little apart.

"Claire, don't reproach yourself for being attracted to him. After a while you'll realize it was a passing thing for you, but don't in any way reproach yourself." He saw the shiny wetness under my eyes, the escaped tears, and with a quick yet tender movement of his fingers, he wiped away the tears. A smile came to his face and with his arm round my waist, he led me to the door leading out of the cottage. "I'd hate to have anyone find us here, Claire. I expect you to take the noon coach tomorrow and I'll see you at the inn tomorrow around ten. Try to be there then."

My eyes went to the cupboard door where I'd meant to have a look inside. "Since I've looked everywhere but in that cupboard," I said, "let me have a look there, too."

"Oh, certainly. But I looked there, Claire. It's empty. Only some old newspapers."

He opened the cupboard door and, indeed, the narrow shelves were empty. Only the stack of newspapers.

"Forget about the book," Brian said as he rushed me back to the door. "Lady Edythe is concerned only because of its subject matter."

"Where are all your things?" I asked. "The paint things, the pictures and all?" I persisted as he urged me out the door.

Brian smiled. "I know of a secret culvert nearby. I hid everything there." His expression became urgent once more. "You'd better leave now, Claire. And if you value your life, make sure you are on that coach tomorrow. I'd strongly advise you to stay at the inn tonight. It would then be easier for me to see you before you take the coach. Now you'd be wise to get back to the house before Edmond comes looking for you. Corinne hinted he's meeting his political cronies in the cottage. He sometimes does that."

"I have a better suggestion, Brian. I believe the three of us should meet together, you and I and Edmond."

"Claire, that would be the worst thing to do. You've been safe at Malverne Manor up till now only because Edmond believes you're ignorant of what actually happened to Amy. He may have some doubts about you by now, but he hasn't anything definite to go on. If you tell Edmond about me," he was saying, and I realized I'd already revealed that to Edmond, "well, if you do, all will be lost.

"Don't say anything to Edmond that might give you away," Brian warned, and it also occurred to me that, although I'd carefully avoided telling Lady Edythe or Mrs. Hopkins about Amy's letters from the manor, I had confided in Edmond.

I started to move away when he reached out his hand and drew me back. He held my hands in his, our glances met. After a little silence he said, his voice light and playful, "I wish that you were at least half as fond of me as I am of you." He tenderly touched my cheek with his hand, then kissed me softly on the mouth. "I'd settle for less than half," he said. "Now hurry back before they miss you. I'll manage somehow to see you at the inn tomorrow morning before you board the coach."

On my way back to the house, I looked about frequently to see if anyone might be around, but I saw no one. Brian had sounded so emphatic when he'd warned that Edmond might come looking for me and that he might be planning a meeting in the cottage, I almost expected to encounter him. My eyes searched the grounds as I hurried along, but no one was about.

Soon my steps slowed. A nagging thought edged its way into my mind. That stack of newspapers in the cupboard. Was that alarm that I'd detected in Brian's eyes when I inquired about the cupboard? He'd certainly rushed me away from it and to the door. Was there something in the newspapers he didn't want me to see? I remembered the London newspapers stuffed into the desk drawers. Brian had not been the least perturbed when I'd scanned them while rummaging through the desk. Was it only the papers hidden in the cupboard that Brian did not wish me to see?

I dismissed the thought. If the newspapers were incriminating, they'd have been destroyed. I forgot about the matter and hurried toward the house.

But the nagging suspicion returned. I came to a stop and glanced back at the cottage. What harm was there in my going back to look? Even if Edmond should come to the cottage, Brian would probably be gone. It struck me now that even should Edmond come to the cottage, it wasn't him I feared. It was Brian. There was something questionable about Brian's tactics. He most assuredly wanted me to clear out of Malverne Manor, using Edmond as the threat. And, yes, he had become alarmed when I inquired about the cupboard. He'd shut the door on those old newspapers in very much of a hurry and rushed me out of the cottage.

I again tried to dismiss the whole thing from my mind and continued on toward the house. I'd almost reached it when I turned and raced back to the cottage, wondering now whether the papers would be gone.

I ran to the cupboard, pulling its door open by the wooden handle.

The papers were there, stacked on the bottom shelf. I snatched a few off the top and took them to the table where I scanned the pages, searching for some vital information.

There was nothing of consequence in the first batch and I rushed back to the cupboard for another stack.

I was in a crouching position near the cupboard, pulling together a handful of papers that had fallen on the floor when all at once a sharp painful blow on my shoulder made me cry out and fall forward.

I heard something clatter to the floor beside me and instinctively turned my head. It was the elephant-head walking stick. I tried to reach it, knowing it might be used on me again. As I groped for it, a foot was placed squarely on my back, pressing my body to the floor. I saw the flash of a hand scoop up the walking stick.

The second blow was so vicious my teeth clenched in a spasm of pain. As I cried out from the pain and tried to raise myself up, a strong hand gripped me by the shoulder and thrust me to the floor. In a half-conscious state I was dimly aware of someone closing the cupboard door then running out of the cottage.

CHAPTER 15

After the wave of semiconsciousness left me, I gazed about, wondering where I was and what had happened to me. Slowly the answers came. A throbbing forehead told me I'd severely bumped my head when I'd fallen forward onto the cottage floor. I pulled myself up, wincing from the pain in the shoulder where the walking stick had struck me.

I dropped into a chair by the table, sitting there in hunched exhaustion until I felt I could manage the long walk to the house.

When I finally arose to leave the cottage, I was surprised I didn't feel worse after the ordeal. The forehead still throbbed. When I cautiously drew my finger over the sore spot, I could feel the light swelling. My shoulder ached from the two blows from the elephant-head walking stick, but they must have been only glancing blows. It was the fall to the floor, bumping my head, that did the greatest harm, making me lose consciousness for a time. I glanced at the cupboard door but did not feel equal to rummaging through the newspapers.

About halfway to the house, I encountered the Colonel who greeted me cheerily, explaining he was out for a stroll. My gaze automatically lowered in search of the walking stick, but I realized immediately that if it had been the Colonel who had struck me down—which I doubted—he would hardly be carrying the weapon.

Apparently, my harrowing experience hadn't left any mark noticeable enough to draw an immediate comment from the Colonel. My hair covered the bruise on my forehead.

"The Raynords and the Wickhams have left," the Colonel was saying, as I gingerly fell into step with him. "The Wickhams brought Edmond home in their carriage. Didn't stay long. Edmond is planning a meeting, something to do with the election."

I stopped, looked at him. "Meeting? In the cottage?"

He'd stopped too, giving me a quizzical look. "In the cottage? Why—why, I don't actually know. He sometimes does that but—" He broke off and peered at me. "Miss Atwood, is something wrong? Did you fall? Your cheek seems——"

"I was attacked in the cottage," I broke in. "Someone struck me from behind."

His shaggy white brows shot up, then he vigorously shook his head. "Sounds like the Cheslick gang is at it again. They're three brothers, Miss Atwood, who own a raggedy farm a short distance away. After some kind of land dispute with Edmond, they've become his mortal enemies, bent on harassing him, especially now with the election coming up. Edmond had some nasty trouble with that gang a short while back, caught them poaching, even trying their hand at horse stealing. One of the Cheslick boys attacked the Farris boy in the stables recently."

"No," I said when he finished, "the Cheslick gang wouldn't have struck me down with the elephant-head walking stick."

He swung his head, gaped at me. I could see his face constrict. There was a sharp silence then, his voice tinged with defiance, he said, "How do you know it was the elephant-head walking stick? You said you were struck from behind."

"I saw it. It fell to the floor right beside me. The attacker picked it up and struck me with it a second time," I said, then, seeing the dismay my implication had aroused, I added, "Is that walking stick kept in such a place where anyone might have access to it?"

The Colonel shook himself out of a circumspect silence and then muttered that, well, he supposed anyone could pick it up, that, well, he didn't actually know. He drifted into silence again then, in a firmer voice, asked, "Miss Atwood, what were you doing in the cottage? It's only a dusty old abandoned place. No one ever goes near it. Only the Cheslick boys invade it occasionally. Oh, yes, Edmond holds tenant meetings there once in a while." He gave me a searching look. "What were you doing there?"

For a split second I debated about telling him about Brian then thought the better of it. "You remember my asking you about the missing Malverne Manor book?" I asked and he nodded. "I'd hoped to find it in the cottage," I went on, which established a reason for my being there. "I'd found the book there once before."

"Oh, the book," he murmured, resuming his walk toward the house. "Do you need assistance walking, Miss Atwood?" he inquired as I once more fell into step with him.

"Thank you. I can manage. But would you walk slowly, please."

He laughed. "At my age, Miss Atwood, it's the only way," he assured me, and I recalled the quick running footsteps out of the cottage after I'd been struck. Not like an old man's. But I also remembered seeing the Colonel through the dining room window only this morning when he energetically sprinted across the Malverne lawns. But why should I suspect this charming old man? Then I recalled Brian's remark that I shouldn't underestimate the Colonel. "He'd do anything for Edmond," Brian had warned. Even harm me if I got in Edmond's way?

"So the Malverne Manor book is still missing," the Colonel mused as we neared the house. He darted a glance at me. "And you are anxious to read it, Miss Atwood?" A faint amused smile played on his dry, wrinkled face. "You are quite interested in Malverne Manor."

"I would like to read the book," I said.

He again gave me a quick look and as he turned his head away, I detected a sly grin on his face.

"Then I will bring you the book, Miss Atwood."

"Thank you and could we keep that a secret between us?"

He grinned impishly. "I understand, Miss Atwood. Lady Edythe could become quite alarmed at your devoted interest in the manor, especially now that she's surreptitiously planning Miss Wickham's betrothal announcement. But you remember my telling you, when I first saw you and Edmond together, that you were the woman for him."

Ordinarily, I would have protested, but I only smiled, grateful that he'd misconstrued my motive. I was spared going into details not quite clear in my own mind. It was just that I had this strong intuition about the book, that somewhere between its covers, lay a clue to Amy's disappearance.

We'd reached the house and I said, "Could I also prevail upon you to keep the cottage attack a secret for a while?"

"But don't you need someone to look in on you?"

"Would you ask Myrna to come to my room?"

He nodded and I went to the back entry, which I always used to get from the gardens to my room.

Myrna arrived almost on my heels and I explained my difficulty, stating only that I'd gone into the cottage and was struck down by some unknown person from behind.

Myrna quickly recovered from her shock and went to work making me comfortable, tucking me into bed with a cold compress on my bruised forehead and a hot-water bottle on my painful shoulder. The odd combination of hot and cold plus the comfort of the bed soon relieved much of my discomfort.

"It's one of that Cheslick gang," Myrna declared, affirming the Colonel's suspicion. "They done the same to my brother, miss, knocked him down in the stables. They're troublemakers. Now they have formed sort of a pack, pulling in other mischiefmakers."

On her way out, after I'd been ministered to, she inquired if I would like some hot beef tea.

"I'd like that very much, Myrna. There is something else I wish you would do for me. Two things, really. Would you keep the cottage incident quiet and would you ask perhaps your father or brother to bring me the newspapers in the cottage cupboard?"

"Newspapers, miss? In the cottage cupboard?"

"Yes, and let's keep that a secret, too."

For a moment she gaped at me then shrugged. "I will ask my father, miss. If he is busy, I will have my brother fetch them."

But when she returned with the hot beef tea, she informed me there were no newspapers in the cottage cupboard.

CHAPTER 16

While I drank the hot beef tea, I went over in my mind what had occurred in the cottage and wondered who'd removed the newspapers. Was it Edmond? Had he approached the cottage because of that meeting he was to hold there and discovered me scanning the newspapers? I'd already discounted the Cheslick gang. The attack on me was connected with Amy, not with some local animosities.

Why were the papers kept about the place? I asked myself. Why hadn't they been destroyed if they were incriminating?

I couldn't bear to suspect Edmond as my attacker and my suspicions leaped to Brian. Had he gone to that secret culvert he'd mentioned, then returned to the cottage and found me there? No denying he'd rushed me away from that cupboard, and away from the cottage, when I became curious about the newspapers.

I refused to consider the Colonel as having had anything to do with this. I instinctively trusted him. There would have to be a strong suspicion directed at the Colonel to cause me to fear him. If he "would do anything" for Edmond, it was merely a sign of his affection for a favorite nephew. Not complicity in violence—or murder. I refused to believe that.

Could the distinctive elephant-head walking stick have been dropped deliberately so that I should suspect Edmond? Or the Colonel? But my attacker could have been a woman. Corinne? Possibly. Lady Edythe? No, I couldn't picture her indulging in an overt act of violence. She would prefer subtle torture. She might have resented me and wished me away from the manor but I doubted that her patrician hand would have clubbed me with a walking stick. It wasn't her way of doing things. My suspicion returned to Brian. He could have gained access to the walking stick, hoping to throw suspicion on Edmond.

I could arrive at no answers to my questions, but on one matter I'd become settled. I would lock my bedroom door that night and the following morning I would leave Malverne Manor. I would pursue my search concerning Amy's disappearance, but I dared not remain at the manor. If it were not for my confused feelings toward Edmond, I would have sought the help of the authorities, but I could not bring myself to do this. On one point I agreed with Brian. I was in grave danger if I remained at the manor. Besides, a letter from Amy might be waiting for me at home. What an irony that would be if a letter had arrived from Malta—or Australia—and Amy had capriciously decided to marry the other young man. But, no, if a letter from Amy had come, Walter Binson would have so advised me.

And then, with a twinge of guilt, I thought of Walter, conscientiously minding the chemist's shop, waiting for me to put aside this foolish search for Amy, waiting for me to come home so we could be married. I supposed it was too much to hope for, that in my absence Walter had established a firmer association with the Milkins girl. Well, I would know tomorrow when I returned home.

Having made the firm decision to leave the manor the next morning a composure settled over me and I drifted into a restful sleep.

When I opened my eyes and glanced at the window, the sky was darkened and I next realized it was the knock on my door that had awakened me. Before opening the door, I fluffed my hair over the bruise on my forehead should it be someone other than Myrna at the door.

As I got into my wrapper, I was relieved to discover that my shoulder, though still painful, no longer hurt as much as it had.

It was Mrs. Farris at the door with hot water so that I could freshen up before dinner which she said would be served in a half-hour.

I did not beg off eating dinner downstairs. After Myrna's tender ministrations, plus the nap, I felt equal to it. I would watch and listen at the dinner table, perhaps learn something.

I attempted light conversation with Mrs. Farris, remembering that at breakfast that morning, she'd softened a little toward me. For some reason she'd resumed her stony countenance, averting her eyes when I spoke to her. My mind snatched at the farfetched possibility that it was she who'd struck me in the cottage, but I promptly dismissed the impulsive thought. Mrs. Farris was apparently stewing in some private worry of her own—Corinne, possibly. I recalled her worrisome comments to the Colonel at breakfast that morning.

On her way out Mrs. Farris reminded me that dinner would be served in half an hour. She turned her face away when she addressed me. How fortunate, I thought, that I'd decided to leave Malverne Manor tomorrow. I could now look upon Mrs. Farris's furtive behavior with cool indifference.

I was afraid that when I went down to dinner and saw the formal dining room for the last time I would begin to feel saddened about leaving the manor. I remembered my delight the first time I saw it, how it had glowed like an exquisite jewel with its brilliant topaz colors.

But when I entered the room, I realized I need not have worried. I experienced no parting sorrow. It was only a lovely room to behold, nothing more. The glistening crystal chandelier was lit, its soft illumination from the candles suffusing the room with that shimmery topaz light—just as I remembered it. The fawn-colored velvet curtains at the windows once more reminded me of the velvet lining of a jewel case.

I could look at the room and admire it with no personal attachment just as I could now regard the people around me with cool objectivity. Not even the unexpected presence of Miss Wickham and her father dismayed me.

Sir Edmond was strikingly handsome in his dark suit, the white cravat intensifying the dark good looks of his face. He was in high spirits, stiffening slightly only when Corinne hovered near his chair when she served him. His attention was divided between his two guests, Miss Wickham who sat at his right and Mr. Wickham at his left.

Miss Wickham was considerably animated, talking and laughing gaily with Sir Edmond who seemed to be telling her many humorous anecdotes in a low private voice. The radiance on Miss Wickham's face outshone the diamond and sapphire tiara she wore.

Mr. Wickham, a light shawl draped over his shoulders, did not speak, but nodded frequently when Sir Edmond addressed him.

Just as Sir Edmond and the Wickhams seemed content to carry on a private conversation at their end of the long table, I was content to have the Colonel, chipper and chatty, on my left, and Lady Edythe, hospitably loquacious, seated at my right.

Lady Edythe, though smiling and talkative, appeared tense and haggard. Her face, bearing an unwell, jaundiced coloring, sagged repeatedly into deep anxious lines which not even the frequent smiles dispelled. Her gown of pale gray silk suggested repose, but the ruby necklace appeared like daubs of blood around her neck, due partly to the oblique lighting in the room and partly to her unnatural, jaundiced appearance.

The Colonel's wit was sharp. He was in his element, keeping me and Lady Edythe constantly entertained. Occasionally we made courteous conversational exchanges with Sir Edmond and his guests but soon Sir Edmond and the Wickhams slipped back into their private conversation and we into ours.

The food was superb. Roast guinea hen done to a succulent turn and Mrs. Hopkins' specialty, her particular way of preparing potatoes with just the right addition of cream and a hint of cheese and herbs, all done with a light, deft touch. The fresh vegetables from Mrs. Hopkins' garden were bright-colored, their delicate taste not ruined by careless overcooking. Although the Farrises were doing the serving, it seemed the food preparation was solely Mrs. Hopkins' province.

It was while we were enjoying the hazelnut cake that the Colonel remarked that long ago he used to pick hazelnuts near the Malverne pond which suggested to him that the next morning he would go swimming in the pond.

"It's deep enough," he explained to me, "down near the cottage and I will take a dip tomorrow. I suppose you don't swim, do you, Miss Atwood?" he inquired and I told him I did not.

"A pity," he said, "that so few women indulge in that pleasure."

Lady Edythe protested mildly about the Colonel's intention to go swimming, reminding him of his lumbago.

"Nonsense," he retorted. "The days are warm now and it is excellent exercise." He turned to me. "Too bad you never learned to swim, Miss Atwood. It is most refreshing."

"If Miss Atwood does not swim," Lady Edythe said, "perhaps she plays chess and might favor you with a game tonight."

The Colonel brightened at the prospect. "Oh, do you, Miss Atwood? I'd surely like a game tonight."

"I often played chess with my father," I answered.

"Splendid," the Colonel exclaimed, beaming with pleasure.

As the meal drew to a close, I caught myself several times studying Lady Edythe's face, struck now by her resemblance to Brian. I'd often questioned his story about being "a poor relation," but now I certainly could discern a family likeness. It wasn't an obvious similarity, due mainly to the age difference, and, at times, like tonight, Lady Edythe appeared much older than her years. Brian's youthfully pinkish face with its rounded contours, at first glance, seemed unlike Lady Edythe's aging face. His eyes, a dark, brilliant brown were unlike Lady Edythe's which had faded into a murky tan color, but that certain expression was there. The hair, too, was different, Brian's a bright blond, Lady Edythe's gray. Still, the family resemblance was there, as I'd observed previously.

I turned my gaze to the Colonel. Brian's features were in the old man's face, hidden partly because of the advanced years.

With Sir Edmond, although he was close to Brian's age, the likeness was harder to see due to Sir Edmond's black hair and blue eyes. Sir Edmond's lean, dark looks, as against Brian's inclination to pink fleshiness, further blurred the family resemblance, but, even there, in Sir Edmond's face, I could see that Brian was indeed "a poor relation."

My eyes scanned the exquisite, topaz-gold dining room and I wondered whether Brian, the poor relation, was eating in the kitchen and, if so, had they served him roast guinea hen, also.

After dinner, as we entered the drawing room, I felt a hand on my arm. It was the Colonel, gallantly leading me to a chair, the one I'd sat in when Mrs. Hopkins had bustled me into this room and up to the blazing hearth, helping me off with my rain-drenched shoes. She was in the room now, bustling over the coffee tray.

"Don't forget your promise about a game of chess," the Colonel reminded me before trotting off to serve himself some brandy.

While I drank my coffee I glanced around the room. Tonight, by lamplight, the drawing room looked different. All the colors appeared richer. The gold-colored curtains were now a deep amber hue. In the subdued light, the landscapes hanging on the walls appeared lush. The graceful Chippendale sofa was an intense blue rather than pale and I remembered, with a wrench, Amy's remark that the sofa's color was the same shade of blue as a dress of hers that she and I had sewn. . . .

"Remember, Claire, how we labored over that embroidered blue sash?" she'd written in one of her letters from the manor.

Unlike the arrangement in the dining room, we were now one convivial group. Sir Edmond was still in high humor and the Colonel's good cheer increased in proportion to his intake of brandy.

Lady Edythe, though never shaking off that restless anxious expression, did her best to appear gracious and seemed to enjoy the rapidly moving conversation, as if it were precisely the diversion she needed to distract her from whatever was causing her to lapse occasionally into tense preoccupation.

I was thankful, too, for the diverting conversation. It gave me little opportunity to ponder on other matters. I didn't even mind listening to Miss Wickham's ebullient chatter, confined exclusively to two subjects, horses and what "my dressmaker said."

The momentum of the after-dinner talk affected even Mr. Wickham, the brandy possibly having a little to do with it. Soon the shawl, like a protective cocoon around his shoulders, slipped away, and he regaled us with anecdotes about his days at Harrow and the summers he frequently spent on the Scilly Islands.

The drawing room rang with cheerful hospitality. Only once did a cloud descend on the bright gathering, when Corinne entered to help Mrs. Hopkins serve the coffee. I tried to hold my attention to Miss Wickham's details about her horse's grazed fetlock, but the little drama Corinne was enacting was more interesting. Corinne was a bit more subtle now, yet each time she crossed the room and passed by Sir Edmond's chair, she, ever so lightly, brushed her hand against his arm. Sir Edmond again pretended he did not see her.

When I turned my attention back to Miss Wickham, who was now detailing something additional her dressmaker had said, I was struck by her being so blissfully oblivious to the not-too-subtle interplay between Sir Edmond and Corinne. She'd ignored it at dinner also, as had her father, and it occurred to me that perhaps the Wickhams never looked at servants, not actually, that is.

But Lady Edythe was not blissfully oblivious concerning her servant's presence. A swift glance at her and I saw the same repressed outrage I'd seen on two previous occasions when she silently observed Corinne's flirtatious behavior.

As I averted my eyes, I caught a glimpse of the Colonel gazing speculatively over the rim of his drinking glass. His shrewd eyes shifted from Corinne to Sir Edmond. He lowered his head and smiled into his brandy when Corinne finally left the room.

When Miss Wickham completed her account of what her dressmaker said, the conversation dwindled to a halt and I reminded the Colonel of our chess game.

Lady Edythe uttered a sigh of relief at my suggestion and immediately rose from her chair, explaining that she would take Mr. Wickham to the greenhouse, since he'd expressed a desire to see the orange tree. Miss Wickham promptly requested Sir Edmond to stroll with her in the rose garden.

"I will have to speak to my nephew about some of his servants," the Colonel sputtered as we set up the chessboard.

I refused to be drawn in and remained silent. The table where we were going to play stood by a window. The lamps in the room illuminated the garden near the house. I could see the curving stone wall with the rambling roses. In the clear, moonlit night the pond was visible. The church spire pierced the sky beyond it.

We were now ready to play, but the Colonel was still complaining in a blustery tone that he could not, for the life of him, see why Lady Edythe tolerated it. "And that addlebrained Miss Wickham," he muttered. "She's blind as a bat." He gulped a mouthful of brandy. "By the way, Miss Atwood, how do you feel after your unfortunate experience in the cottage? I observed at dinner that you seem to have recovered well."

"I can still feel the bruises, but, on the whole, I'm happy to report that, with Myrna's help, I feel much improved."

"I'm glad to hear that, Miss Atwood. I have done as you wished. I've told no one. Well, let's try to finish our game before I must leave for home," he added, explaining that the Wickhams were dropping him off at his place on their way home.

"Then you've changed your mind about tomorrow morning's swim in the Malverne pond?"

"No, no, not at all. I have some urgent business to attend to early tomorrow and must be at home, but I will return to Malverne Manor later in the morning."

After that we played with such concentration that we didn't know Lady Edythe had entered until she spoke.

"I've come for Mr. Wickham's shawl," she explained when the Colonel and I looked up. "Since he has trouble walking, I offered to get it for him. He's become quite interested in the greenhouse but has complained of a slight chill."

She was on her way out when the Colonel asked abruptly whether Sir Edmond's copy of the Malverne Manor book had been found.

She had her back to us when the Colonel spoke, and her back arched at the question. She remained motionless for an instant, but when she turned around, her face was composed.

"No, it's still missing," she answered. "I'm concerned about its loss. You know what a valuable, rare book it is aside from its family importance." Her eyes flicked from me to the Colonel. "Why do you ask?"

The Colonel shrugged. "Just wondered. Heard it was lost and, as you say, it has its value."

"I'm sorry to say it is still missing," she said, reaching for Mr. Wickham's shawl. "I must hurry back before Mr. Wickham catches a chill," she added, rushing out.

When she left, the Colonel and I resumed our game, but it soon became evident that the Colonel was not playing well, due probably to his generous enjoyment of the wine at the dinner table and the brandy after dinner. Consequently he appeared greatly relieved when Sir Edmond entered and brought the disastrous game to an aborted end.

"The Wickhams are leaving soon," Sir Edmond said to him. "If you are to travel with them, you will have to stop your game."

The Colonel clambered immediately out of his chair. He stopped at the doorway. "Edmond, why don't you take Miss Atwood for a stroll in the gardens? By the way, I will return to the manor early tomorrow morning. I plan to have a swim in the pond." Then to me, "It's a pity you do not swim, Miss Atwood. You women are missing a fine pleasure by not taking up swimming." He was about to leave then added, "I will bring you the Malverne Manor book tomorrow if I don't forget."

"Malverne Manor book?" Sir Edmond said to me when the Colonel left.

"Yes, I'd like to read it."

"So, you do not swim, Miss Atwood," he said with a light laugh. "Well, it isn't the usual feminine pastime. But come, let's take that stroll in the garden."

Are you going to take the walking stick with you? a demon voice within prompted me to ask, but I quashed the absurd suggestion.

He noted my hesitation and I got up from my chair.

When we entered the darkened garden, he took my hand in his. It was such a hard, almost rough grasp, I tried to draw my hand away but couldn't, his clasp was so firm. I was immediately reminded that his touch was always so, even his embrace, a firm, grasping hold, as if gentleness was not a part of his nature. How different from Brian, whose touch was always light and gentle.

It's only his way I told myself. He probably doesn't even realize how firm his grasp can be. I once more tried to release my hand from his firm grip, but he held it fast. The hard pressure of his hand made his presence all the more known to me. I could feel my pulse racing. When he inclined his head and smiled down at me, I hoped that in the half-darkness of the garden he could not see the rising excitement in my face, the flush I could feel on my cheeks.

I made some inane comment about the fragrance from the apple orchard simply for something to say because as the silence between us lengthened, I became even more conscious of his nearness.

He said nothing. His hand tightened even more, then gradually eased.

We'd come to a small garden bordered on two sides by tall shrubbery. It was well illuminated by the lamplight streaming from the windows behind us. We sat down on a stone bench and, a short distance ahead, I could see the formal garden where the moon shone on the reflecting pool. The air was drenched with the aroma drifting over from the apple orchard and the rose gardens.

Another silence had come between us. We were sitting a short space apart, but with the deep silence enclosing us, I once more became intensely aware of his presence.

As if he, too, felt this, he turned suddenly, leaned over, cupped his hand under my chin and the next instant I felt his lips on mine.

At first, the overwhelming emotion blotted out everything but the touch of his lips on mine and what his sheer presence did to me. But, all at once, I drew away from him and when I heard him say, "Claire, darling—" I cut across his words.

"Don't call me endearing names," I said, the words rushing out in a choked whisper. "How can you when you're soon to marry Miss Wickham and . . ." I was in such a state of emotional turmoil, I was about to blurt out Corinne's name also but I stopped myself in time.

He took advantage of my coming to a sudden confused stop and roughly pulled me close. His voice was harsh.

"That's not what is causing you to fret. You've got yourself into a state because of your unnecessary fretting about Amy. You've been like this all day. You didn't believe that letter I showed you at the meeting this afternoon, did you?" he demanded.

"No, I did not," I answered, my voice now as cold as his. "I do not believe that she's happily married to someone else in Malta and that she and her husband are going to Australia to seek their fortune." The words came in a burst of released tension and anxiety. I couldn't have stopped myself if I'd tried. It was as if my pent-up suspicions and frustrations could no longer remain stilled. I surprised myself at the outburst, but I couldn't help myself.

"I don't believe that letter," I said in a low, bitter voice, "any more than I believe that Amy has never been here at Malverne Manor. You know as well as I that she's been here, but you keep denying it. She was murdered, then her body was thrown into the pond, and she was passed off as a disgraced servant girl who'd drowned herself."

"My God," he exclaimed, his voice seared with anger. "You still believe she—she was murdered." His eyes blazed in the half-darkness. "Murdered by me, Miss Atwood? Or by Lady Edythe? Or, perhaps Lady Edythe and I planned it together?"

He'd lowered his voice, but it sounded all the harsher. It made my skin prickle and tighten. I could feel the cold beads of perspiration form on my forehead. All at once a taunting whisper of guilt and betrayal assailed me, that I should have given in to his passionate kiss a moment ago. A disloyalty to Amy.

"Perhaps we've hidden the body somewhere," I heard him say. He was in shadow. I could not see the cold fury in his face, but I felt it in his voice. Thrusting his face forward, he looked directly into my eyes. "Is that what you believe? That I am a murderer? Or is Lady Edythe? Perhaps you have someone else in mind also."

His eyes held mine. I couldn't speak. The words jammed in my throat. After a while I turned my gaze downward. "You know Amy has been here," I said in a low spent voice, "but for some reason you choose to deny it."

I expected him to answer me with seething anger and when he replied in a smooth, calm voice, it was somehow more unnerving than if he'd shouted in a rage.

"I have no reason," he said, "to believe anything different from what I'd told you before, what Lady Edythe told me. You've pieced together irrelevant things and you've let your imagination play tricks on you."

"And, of course," I said, my voice, like his, pitched low in icy fury, "there is no such person as Brian. He also is a trick of my imagination. At least, I imagined him to resemble you. He does, you know. Resembles Lady Edythe too. And the Colonel. Oh, he's part of the family all right and your denying him will not cause him to disappear—from my imagination. Brian spends a considerable amount of time at the cottage and here at the manor house, too. You couldn't possibly not know of his existence."

If I'd struck him, his reaction could not have been more electrifying. I could see his body tighten, the shoulders draw back, the muscles of his face pull taut. My previous mention of Brian had prompted only mild amusement from him. His reaction now was altogether different. He continued to stare fixedly ahead. After a prolonged silence, he seemed about to speak, but he clamped his lips into a tight line and turned his head aside.

"Why is there so much mystery about Brian?" I asked, but I could tell he hadn't even heard me. "And that book about Malverne Manor," I went on. "Why all the mystery about the book?"

He turned to look at me. "Book?" he said absently. "Oh, the Malverne Manor book?"

"Yes, there seems to be as much secrecy about that book as there is about those newspapers in the cottage cupboard. Is that why I was attacked in the cottage? With your elephant-head walking stick? Because I was not to read something incriminating in those papers?"

"Attacked? What in God's name are you talking about?" There was naked shock and concern in his eyes. My remark was news to him. It would have been extremely difficult to feign the astonishment he showed at my statement.

"Why didn't you tell me?" he said in a demanding tone. "You had better tell me. Everything."

So I told him. Everything. I'd been holding back too long. That might have been why I was getting nowhere concerning the mystery surrounding Amy. At last, I was ready to risk something in order to gain something. I told him details of Amy's six letters from the manor which proved that she'd been here and that she feared for her life, that Lady Edythe showed resentment toward her. I told him all about Brian, my secret meetings with him, his admission that he was "a poor relation," that he often stayed secretly at the cottage and knew much about the goings-on at the manor. I told him about the newspapers in the cottage cupboard.

"There's no denying that Brian is a relative, probably a close one," I finished. "Most important of all, Brian knows too much about Amy's disappearance. Brian claims Amy did not go to Malta to be married but to be . . . to be murdered by a hired killer."

Edmond sat hunched forward on the stone bench. I could see his face in profile. The shadowed half-darkness did not hide the grim, taut lines. He'd clasped his hands into a tight fist and was staring fixedly ahead into the formal garden.

My gaze idly followed his and I found myself blankly studying the ripples in the reflecting pool, wondering now in a wave of doubt whether

I should have divulged everything, whether I shouldn't have maintained a circumspect silence.

I was taken aback when at last he spoke. All the shock and tension was out of his voice. His face had changed too, had softened into a tender, smiling expression. I looked closer into his face, thinking the shadowed darkness only made it seem so, but, no, he was smiling and when he spoke his words were soft and gentle. He reached for my hands and held them in that firm grasp so characteristic of him. I looked into his smiling face and wondered why I was afraid. The smile on his face sent a chill along my spine.

"Claire, darling," he said in a low, endearing tone which somehow seemed all wrong. His eyes caressed my face. "Now that you've told me these things, I do believe you. You're on to something." His fingers tightened around my hand, then he dropped my hand and got up. "We're going to talk about this and plan what to do. But it's getting a bit cool. I'm going in to get you a wrap of some kind and a cushion for that stone bench." He started to walk away then came back, bent down and kissed me, a long tender kiss. "I'll be back shortly," he said then hurried away.

The tears that overwhelmed me the moment he left took me by complete surprise. They welled up all of a sudden and washed down my face. I bent my head, trying to stop the foolish tears, wondering why exactly I was weeping. All the tension I'd held back rushed at me, my body trembling, then I sensed a surge of relief. At last I was freed of the locked-in fears and emotions. To have unburdened myself of growing apprehensions and doubts was an enormous comfort. I could now openly admit I was in love with Edmond. I knew he was in love with me. I could trust him. Together we would solve the mystery concerning Amy.

The tears stopped as abruptly as they'd begun. I turned my gaze once more to the reflecting pool in the formal gardens, but no longer staring blankly as I'd done previously. I was at ease.

I turned my head when one of the lighted windows behind me became darkened, plunging the place where I sat into deeper shadows. I saw someone moving about in an adjoining room where the lamps still burned. It looked like Mrs. Farris or perhaps Mrs. Hopkins. I couldn't tell. She now extinguished the lamps in that room, leaving the garden in complete darkness. Although I had no particular fear of the dark, I wished Edmond would hurry. He was taking an awfully long time finding that wrap. I considered leaving. The deep stillness of the dark garden made me uneasy. I put aside my impulse to flee and continued to wait for Edmond to return.

After a while I heard footsteps nearby. Edmond had finally arrived. I quickly dabbed at my eyes, hoping that because of the pitch dark, he wouldn't see I'd been crying.

It seemed as if two people were coming toward me. I swung around to look. I saw no one. I became alarmed about the muffled sound of footsteps behind the shrubbery. I quickly rose from the bench and began to hurry away.

It happened so quickly I had no time even to cry out. Someone jumped directly at my back and with one swift, sure stroke, thrust something soft, like a cloth, across my mouth. I could feel a tight knot being pulled at the back of my head.

I thrashed wildly, flailing my arms, trying to scream through the choking rag against my mouth, trying to pull it off.

A hand whipped past my face. Another rag was now pulled across my eyes. At the same time, someone else was roughly tying my hands behind my back. The cord cut into my flesh.

I could hear swift movements behind me and in a blur of pain from the still-sore shoulder and forehead, I was half-aware of being carried, then pushed into water that swirled over my head.

I tugged desperately at the cord that bound my hands. My forceful churning action undid it and I began to pull frantically at the tight rag pressing against my eyes. Not being able to see made the nightmare all the more horrifying. Not being a swimmer, I became conscious of panic rising at an alarming speed as the water swept over me. I discovered that the water was deep. My feet could not touch bottom. I kicked my feet and lashed out with my hands, but there was nothing to hold on to.

I tried to reach the side of the pool, but the wet knots in the blindfold and mouth gag wouldn't come loose when I struggled with them, and I didn't know if I was headed in the right direction. I tried to pull the rags over my head, but I couldn't because they were pulled so tight across my face. I knew that the two people were still at the pool's edge. I could hear their scuffing about. Then, just as I managed to rip the coverings away from my face, I saw two indistinct figures, like flashing shadows, disappear behind the shrubbery.

I began to scream with all my might. I felt my body bobbing wildly in the water. As I scrambled toward the pool's edge, sheer instinct commanded me to relax my body, try to float.

My attempts to float were in vain and I began to thrash in uncontrolled panic, hoping to gain the pool's edge by sheer force.

I thought at first it was only panic that made me think I heard footsteps pounding toward the pool. I'd become so exhausted from terror, I could barely move my limbs. The paralyzing fear was now causing me to sink deeper into the pool. The water rushed into my mouth and I thought my lungs would burst. I was sure now I'd only desperately imagined I'd heard approaching footsteps.

But the next moment, I heard someone plunge into the pool and soon strong hands were pulling me out of the water. I looked up, expecting to see Edmond, but it was Lady Edythe.

She placed me on the lawn beside the pool and when my panic and terror subsided and my eyes began to adjust to the near-darkness, I saw that Mrs. Hopkins was also bending over me, the same horrified expression on her face as on Lady Edythe's.

I hadn't been in the water long. It was mostly shock that left me prostrate for a time. With Lady Edythe's and Mrs. Hopkins' quick action, I was now able to lift myself to a sitting position. I was still dazed. My whole body ached. I trembled from the cold.

Lady Edythe, drenched and disheveled, was looking at me with a worried expression, then her glance shifted suddenly to the pool. Her reaction became so agitated, I turned to look. There was something floating near the pool's edge. In the clear moonlight it was quite visible. It was the cloth I'd torn away from my face.

Lady Edythe quickly bent down to snatch it up. She hurriedly rolled it into a ball and held it tight in her hand, but even in the half-light I saw it was Corinne's bright-colored, fringed head scarf.

CHAPTER 17

As we approached the house, with Mrs. Hopkins and Lady Edythe supporting me, there were hurrying footsteps nearby. Turning my head, I saw it was Edmond.

He came to a halt for a surprised second. I could hear and see he was considerably out of breath as if he'd been rushing about or had run a considerable distance. After his stunned immobility, he sprang forward, swiftly bundled me into the wrap he was holding and carried me into the house.

Placing me on the sofa in the drawing room, he turned to Lady Edythe and demanded, "What happened? Make it quick."

"I was entering the house after the Wickham's carriage pulled away," she answered, tugging nervously at her drenched clothing, "when I heard someone screaming. The screams were coming from the vicinity of the formal garden. I quickly summoned Mrs. Hopkins and we found Miss Atwood struggling in the pool."

Edmond turned to Mrs. Hopkins who was hanging back, gaping at me with frightened, blinking eyes. "Mrs. Hopkins," he said in a voice so gruff, she looked up with a jolt, "find Farris. Tell him to have one of his boys saddle a horse and get Dr. Pryor."

She raced out of the room, muttering, "Yes, yes, the doctor" and Edmond swung to face Lady Edythe. "Fetch Myrna. Tell her to bring dry clothing."

Lady Edythe shook herself out of a daze when Edmond's severe look fell on her and she rushed out of the room, nodding her head vigorously.

"What the devil happened?" he said, his voice sharp with impatience. "I can't believe you tumbled into the pool."

I was only half-aware of the question, and the brusque tone of his question further confused me. "This beautiful sofa," I murmured dazedly. "I'm ruining it with——"

"Damn the sofa," he snapped, then brushing his hand distractedly through his hair, quickly added, "Sorry. I didn't mean to shout at you. It's my fault that this happened. I thought you were safe in the garden. There was plenty of light there from the windows. But I shouldn't have left you for so long. Like a fool, on impulse, I raced down to the cottage to see if this Brian person might be there. There was no one there. Although I ran as fast as I could, I was gone too long." He got up suddenly from the sofa and brought me a glass of brandy.

"Drink it," he ordered. "Not too fast."

He helped me to a sitting position and I took a swallow, shuddering as the brandy burned my throat. He made me drink it all. Almost at once I felt glowingly warm despite the soppy clothes clinging to me. Even the pain across my shoulder subsided some.

"Now," he said, setting the empty glass aside, "until Myrna arrives with some dry things, tell me what happened."

"I remained sitting on the bench," I explained, "waiting for you. I became uneasy when the lights were extinguished in the windows behind me. It got pitch dark. Shortly afterward I was attacked from behind, like in the cottage, but now there were two persons. I was blindfolded, gagged; my hands were tied behind my back and I was thrown into the pool, which is surprisingly deep, and I can't swim."

"Yes, I recall your saying you can't swim." He sat thinking for a moment then said, "Sounds like the Cheslick boys are at it again."

"Is Corinne in with them?" I asked, and he stared at me, dumbfounded.

"What makes you say that?" he asked when he'd recovered.

I was about to answer when Myrna burst into the room, clutching an armful of clothes and coverings, her startled eyes darting from Sir Edmond to me.

"Will you hurry it up, Myrna?" he said to her and she nodded frantically. "I will be waiting outside the door," he said to me. "I want to hear the rest of that before Dr. Pryor arrives."

"It's them Cheslick boys," Myrna kept muttering as she swiftly, but gently, peeled off the wet things and put on the dry ones. "They are a mean lot, miss. It was a vicious attack they made on my brother. They are hoping the master will bow out of the election. That is why they are doing this."

I remained quiet, not wishing to discuss the Cheslick gang which I believed had nothing to do with this.

"The doctor will soon be here, miss," Myrna said as she gathered up the wet things and hurried out.

"What makes you think Corinne was involved in this?" Edmond inquired the moment he re-entered.

"Because I saw her head scarf floating in the pool. Even in the half-dark and although the scarf was wet, the brilliant colors were still distinguishable. There was no mistaking it, particularly with that long fringe that bordered the scarf. It was what I'd pulled away from my face after I'd untied the cord from around my hands."

It was a while before he spoke. "I doubt that Corinne is involved in this," he said at last. "If she were, she wouldn't be foolish enough to use her head scarf." He hesitated again as if what he wished to say next was difficult. "Corinne has—well, she has her annoying little faults but —no, she wouldn't do anything like this." Another sharp silence followed before he continued. "As you've no doubt observed, she moons over me like a lovesick juvenile. This distresses Mrs. Farris because she feels responsible for the girl. She brought her to work here at the manor when Corinne's precocious ways became too much for her mother to handle. Mrs. Farris has become terribly embarrassed and says the girl must be sent back to her mother. Corinne's mother is Mrs. Farris's sister. I don't believe it is necessary to send the girl away," he said, his expression indicating that he disliked discussing the subject. "Lady Edythe is considerably distressed by the girl's behavior, but I'm sure Corinne will soon get over her juvenile infatuation if I continue to ignore it."

"A lot you know about women," I said. "Corinne interprets your silence as assent."

"You see," he said good-naturedly. "I told you Lady Edythe—and some others—have grossly exaggerated my prowess with women."

I wanted to tell him I did not share his humble opinion on that subject, but I remained silent.

"But now," he was saying, "it seems that Corinne might have to leave the manor after all."

"Oh? Why?"

"Mrs. Farris has become even more distressed now that she's learned that Corinne is a thief. I myself caught Corinne at it yesterday. I was on my way to rap on your door because I wanted you to accompany me to Hammond House to pay a call on the Raynords. You weren't in your room and as I turned out of that wing, I heard footsteps. It was Corinne. She ran into the Cream Lace Room. I caught her rushing out, carrying a silver hairbrush. She tearfully explained she only wished to borrow it. But Mrs. Farris said she'd found Corinne in that room once before, trying to make off with something. Corinne seems drawn to that room. I suppose that sort of room would appeal to a young woman," he said, and I felt a wave of anger that he should speak of the room so nonchalantly. I'd confided to him only a short time ago in the garden that Amy had occupied that room. "And there are all sorts of bibelots in the room, things that Corinne finds enchanting," he was saying.

"I don't believe for a moment," I said, cutting into his words, "that the Cheslick gang had anything to do with the attacks on me. They're being blamed for an awful lot of mayhem not of their doing."

He stared at me speechless, his eyes narrowing. "Surely," he said after a while, "you don't think Corinne and I did this to you."

"Whoever did it, wishes, then, to implicate you and Corinne. First your walking stick now her head scarf."

He seemed at a loss for words. He gave me a long look then slowly turned his face away. "I know what you're thinking," he said in a dry, flat voice. "That Lady Edythe planned it. You've suspected her of all sorts of mischief from the start." He waved his hand impatiently. "Corinne I won't even discuss. As for Lady Edythe, I do not consider her a paragon. She has her shortcomings. Who hasn't? This I do know about her, that she was incapable of attacking you because she recoils physically from any sort of violence and suffering. It goes back to her having witnessed her husband's death when he was trampled by a horse. From that time she can become horribly ill at the mere sight of pain or violence. She even blames herself for that servant girl's drowning in the pond," he said and I was about to say, "How can you still go on believing that a servant girl had drowned in the Malverne pond?" But I checked myself. It would be useless.

"The servant girl, I've been told," he continued, "had become such a trial for the short while she was here that Lady Edythe went to stay with the Wickhams for a couple of days just to get away from it all. It was while she was at the Wickhams that the girl drowned herself. When Lady Edythe heard about it, she became very ill. She still maintains that if she'd stayed at the manor, the dreadful thing wouldn't have happened. She still suffers anxiety over it." He slowly shook his head back and forth. "No, Lady Edythe has nothing to do with any of this."

"Who, then? Brian?"

He looked away. "What I'm going to suggest is preposterous but after what you'd told me about this Brian person, I can't help but wonder whether—whether perhaps Amy knew Brian, whether somehow this whole puzzling business isn't some—some scheme devised by Brian and Amy." He made a helpless gesture with his hands and shrugged. "It is a preposterous suggestion but . . ."

In the silence that followed I sensed he expected me to agree or, more likely, vehemently disagree. His "preposterous" suggestion did not seem so unlikely to me. Although I said nothing out of my loyalty to Amy, my mind echoed back to the number of times I, too, had wondered about just such a preposterous scheme.

He was still waiting for some kind of response from me, but I could not bring myself to express aloud such a condemnation of Amy. I recalled her stepfather's accusations. No, I refused to believe it.

"Amy was incapable of such devious tactics," I said, hoping my tone conveyed as much conviction as I tried to put into the words. "She was impulsive, sometimes foolish, but never wicked," I added.

A stillness fell on the room. I stared blankly at the droplets of water on the Aubusson carpet where Myrna had momentarily dropped my wet clothing. Once I glanced up to see Edmond gazing idly into space. It was as if each of us was waiting for the other to speak first.

We were spared by the blustery entrance of Dr. Pryor.

Edmond rose and, after greeting the doctor and introducing me, explained briefly that I'd been attacked by the Cheslick gang.

The doctor, a small, white-haired elderly man with quick energetic movements, nodded vigorously. "The news is about that they're going to stop you from winning that election one way or another. Seems your victory would put a stop to some of their peculiar and illegal operations."

"I will be back shortly," Edmond said to me as he left. "You are in good hands, Miss Atwood. Dr. Pryor will do all he can to make you comfortable."

Dr. Pryor surveyed the situation, then declared that the bruised shoulder was the worst of it. I told him of my previous attack and that tonight's incident aggravated the trouble.

"They are a terrible lot, those Cheslick boys and their cohorts," the doctor declared. "Now they've even taken to attacking the guests at Malverne Manor," he muttered and I did not disagree with the good doctor.

"That forehead bruise will be an annoyance for another day or two," he said. "The shoulder will be a nuisance for a while longer. Tomorrow try to keep the shoulder moving a bit so it doesn't stiffen up on you. I'll leave a sleeping draft with you, Miss Atwood, in case you should be unable to fall asleep," he said, and I wondered idly whether his sleeping draft was as potent as Mrs. Hopkins'.

He promised to look in on me the next morning, wished me good night, and as he hurried out, Edmond returned, carrying an envelope which he handed me. He also gave me the letter which I recognized as the Charles Coombes letter, the one he'd shown me at the campaign meeting, the letter that neatly explained Amy's whereabouts, that she'd married Charles Coombes' brother, that the happy couple had gone to Malta and would soon emigrate to Australia.

"Look at the postmark," I heard Edmond say. "That is the envelope you demanded to see when I showed you the letter. You will see that the handwriting matches."

I looked up from the postmark. "The name of the town is unfamiliar to me."

"It isn't to me. It's nearby. A small port town. I doubt there is such a person as Charles Coombes. This Brian person might have written me the letter."

"No, the handwriting is altogether different."

"You speaking of the letter Brian wrote you, requesting that secret meeting at the Three Crowns Inn?"

"Yes. I kept Brian's letter. You can go to my room to get it if you wish. It might be a good idea to compare the writing."

He got up and when I explained how I'd hidden the letter, that I'd folded it into a small square and hidden it in the hem of a brown skirt hanging in the wardrobe, he smiled with amusement at my subterfuge.

"There's a tiny rip in the hem. You can reach the folded-up letter from there," I instructed, and he shook his head in wonder as he left the room.

He soon returned and we compared the writing, quite dissimilar.

"Although the letters seem to have been written by two different people," Edmond said, "I'd guess that Brian and Charles Coombes know each other." He hesitated then added in a dry, tight voice, "And, possibly, they both know Amy. Yes, I know, I'm accusing Amy but——"

He quickly pocketed the two letters and the envelope. "What was the postmark on Brian's letter?"

"There was none, only a sealed envelope with my name written on it."

"Tomorrow morning I will go to this port town. I might be lucky and come across something—or someone. In the meantime, you do as the doctor said. Myrna will take care of you while I'm gone."

"I want Myrna to sleep on a cot in my room tonight and I want her to prepare all my meals."

He smiled, then shrugged. "If you wish."

He turned to leave, then came back and sat down on the sofa's edge. "I will not try to extract any declaration of trust in me from you. I know you will not trust me until I've brought this Amy episode to a close. But I wish you did trust me. And Lady Edythe," he said, and then hurried out of the room. When he left, Myrna entered and helped me up to my room.

I did not need Dr. Pryor's sleeping draft. I was so exhausted I fell asleep almost immediately. Myrna's reassuring presence on the cot helped to induce restful sleep.

I awakened to a glorious, sunny morning. I sat up in bed, still stiff and sore but somewhat improved over the previous night. I drank the morning tea Myrna brought me and luxuriated in the warm sunshine streaming into the room. The scent from the apple orchard drifted in through the opened windows. I could hear Old Abner's loud conversation some distance away and I asked Myrna whether Sir Edmond was present at the manor.

"No, miss, he left very early this morning. Was in much of a hurry. Suppose with the election so close, he is a might busy. Will you be staying in bed all day, miss?"

"No, I couldn't bear that. I will go downstairs later."

Myrna gazed at me. "Might be you should rest in bed for the morning, miss. Not go downstairs till the afternoon."

"The doctor said I should move the shoulder so it won't become stiff. It isn't as painful as it was yesterday. You were a great help to me, Myrna. I feel much better this morning."

"Thank you, miss. You take care of yourself. Anything you wish, miss, you tell me."

"After I've had my breakfast, I'll walk about the room for a while, then sit in a chair rather than take to my bed. Later, if I feel up to it, I'll go downstairs, perhaps sit in the garden."

"Yes, miss. It is a bright sunny day," Myrna said with a nod toward the open windows as she gathered up the tea tray. "I will soon be back with your breakfast, miss," she said from the doorway.

Shortly after breakfast, washed and combed, with Myrna's help, and sitting in the chair by the window, I heard clattering footsteps in the corridor. I knew it wasn't Myrna's light step. A number of people seemed to be approaching. When I answered the rap on my door, it was Lady Edythe with Mr. and Mrs. Raynord in tow.

"The Raynords came to see Sir Edmond," she explained with a warm smile, "but he is away. When I told them of your unfortunate accident last night, they expressed a wish to visit with you."

"My dear," Mrs. Raynord cried, bounding into the room. "What a frightful experience. I was shocked." She pressed my hand affectionately, her eyes searching my face with concern. "How do you feel, my dear?" She was dressed in riding clothes which gave her an odd, over-clothed, rumpled appearance. Her red hair was windblown; the plump cheeks shone with exuberant good health.

"I feel surprisingly well, considering," I replied.

"How fortunate that Mrs. Hopkins and Lady Edythe heard your cries and rescued you," Mr. Raynord declared, stepping solidly into the room, his riding boots clattering on the wood floor. He, too, managed a similar bulky, rumpled look in his riding clothes and, like Mrs. Raynord, his round, pleasant face also beamed with glowing good health.

Lady Edythe quietly followed them into the room but stood back somewhat timidly while the Raynords dominated the room with their presence. Her brows quirked when the Raynords plopped onto the edge of the bed and the springs squeaked with an agonizing protest. She then placed a chair next to mine and sat back quietly while the Raynords continued to exclaim about the dreadful accident.

"Sir Edmond must do something about those rascals," Mr. Raynord blustered. "That Cheslick gang mustn't be allowed to go about beating up people."

"Let's not distress Miss Atwood by rehashing the nasty business," Mrs. Raynord decided with a wide sweep of her hands. "Let's talk about something pleasant to take her mind off the dreadful experience." She leaned forward, smiling broadly. "In fact, my dear, Mr. Raynord and I were saying at breakfast this morning that you must come and stay with us for a few days. Why not come for dinner tonight, Miss Atwood? Do you feel up to it, my dear?"

"It's not a question of how I feel. I expect to be leaving for home tomorrow morning. I'm sure the doctor will permit me to travel." As I spoke, I was aware of Lady Edythe's sudden stirring in her chair. Out of the corner of my eye, I saw the flash of a pleased smile on her face. Did I only imagine a faint sigh of relief accompanying the smile?

"Home?" Mr. Raynord said. "That shouldn't present a problem. Surely you live nearby?"

"No, I live some distance away, in Clisty. My father's people have lived there for generations."

"Clisty?" Mr. Raynord repeated, jutting out his lower lip. "Yes, I remember. You remember, too, do you not, my dear?" he said, turning to his wife. "It's a small village we pass through on the way to your mother's."

Mrs. Raynord thought deeply then shook her head. "No, I cannot say that I recall it. Is your mother's family also from Clisty, Miss Atwood?"

"No, she wasn't English."

"Wasn't?" Mr. Raynord inquired. "You lost your mother?"

"Both my parents are dead."

"I'm sorry to hear that, my dear," Mrs. Raynord said. "You say your mother was not English?"

"She was French."

"Where in France had your mother's family lived?" Mr. Raynord went on. "Mrs. Raynord and I have traveled extensively in France. Perhaps we know the place."

I hesitated before replying, conscious of Lady Edythe's alert attention, knowing she would consider my reply the same sort of foolish, wishful thinking Amy had indulged in.

But when I briefly explained my mother's family background, that her home had been the Château du Montellarais, I knew by Lady Edythe's lightning change of expression that not only did she believe me, my news disturbed her. Until the Château had entered the conversation, she'd gazed at me with an affable smile, particularly from the time I'd stated my intention to leave for home the next day. Now her mouth twitched, the eyes stared blankly ahead.

The Raynords happily cried out together at the mention of the Château du Montellarais. Indeed they did know of it. Who would not? They insisted upon discussing the Château, prodding me with questions which increased Lady Edythe's restlessness and soon she was excusing herself, saying with a stiff smile that she would leave us to talk over the happy news, that she had some house matters to attend to.

When she left, I tried to keep my mind on what the Raynords were saying but I kept wondering intermittently what about my mother's heritage had disturbed Lady Edythe so greatly. Did she still consider me—now even more so—a threat to usurping the role of mistress of Malverne Manor? Had I now become a more formidable threat to her plans than Amy had been?

Her anxiety was needless. I would leave the manor tomorrow.

I put aside Lady Edythe's anxieties and enjoyed my visit with the Raynords who stayed for quite a while. I liked them. The conversation rambled along, first about the Château, then about my parents. The chemist's shop caught Mrs. Raynord's interest. She explained her father's people had been in textiles for years and years. She didn't mind discussing trade.

When the Raynords finally left it was firmly decided—by them—that I would visit them later that day. I made no promise yet they evidently presumed I would stay on in order to have dinner with them that night, then extend my visit at Hammond House.

"Yes, my dear," Mrs. Raynord decided, "you seem quite recovered from last night's ordeal. I do want you to visit with us at Hammond House and stay for a few days."

Mr. Raynord, following her to the door, added, "We will call for you later in the day, Miss Atwood."

When they left, Myrna came up to tell me the Colonel had arrived and was asking for me. "He's in the rose garden, miss. Says he plans to take a swim in the pond and wishes to speak with you before he goes."

Then he'd brought the Malverne Manor book.

Myrna helped me downstairs where we learned Dr. Pryor had also arrived. His visit was brief and optimistic. I was doing well; I could stroll in the garden now; I could even travel home later.

Although I felt able to navigate all by myself, Myrna insisted upon assisting me. We found the Colonel sitting in a garden chair, clutching a bundle under his arm.

"I brought you the book," he said as soon as Myrna left.

"Thank you." I sat down in a chair beside him, began to unwrap the bundle. "I won't be able to get around much today, so reading will take care of the time."

"Yes, Mrs. Farris was just telling me about the ruckus that occurred last night soon after I left with the Wickhams. How do you feel?"

"Could be worse. I certainly am getting knocked about during my stay at Malverne Manor. I had better leave while I'm still able."

The Colonel sat quietly, watching while I idly paged through the book, then asked, "Anything in particular about the manor that interests you? I could probably answer your question. I know the manor very well."

"There seems to be some secret or mystery about the manor, which I hope the book will reveal."

"Mystery? Secret?" He peered at me, the shrewd wizened face puckered into a frown. "You speaking about this friend of yours, this Amy? You make some connection between her disappearance and this book? But how?"

I shrugged. "I'm hoping the book will supply the answer."

He uttered a sharp little laugh. "Now, Miss Atwood, don't tell me you suspect the poor girl's body is hidden in some secret place on the manor. There are no more secret places at Malverne Manor. Not any more."

"Not any more?"

"As with many of these manors, Miss Atwood, there was the hidden priest's hole and the secret chapel. Like a number of families in this vicinity, Edmond's family was Catholic and had to practice their faith secretly under penalty of property confiscation and even death. But the priest's hole was sealed up years ago," he went on. "It was Edmond's grandfather who bricked up the priest's hole that led to the underground chapel. He discovered that poachers were using the disused chapel as a convenient storage place for their pilfered goods. The servants found it to be a handy trysting place. Edmond's grandfather disapproved of that also."

"This—this underground chapel," I began. I could feel the pulse hammering in my throat as I spoke. "Where is it located?"

"In that old abandoned cottage," he replied and, no doubt, seeing the excitement in my face, he laughed again. "Come now, Miss Atwood. You surely do not suspect—oh, impossible. The chapel entry has been bricked up for years."

"This bricked-up entry—is the priest's hole hidden in the cottage cupboard?"

"Yes, but—now you stop getting such wild notions, Miss Atwood," he said, getting up from his chair, gazing up at the sky. "A lovely, warm, sunny day, a fine day for a swim in the pond," he said and started to walk away, then, with a backward glance, added, "After your sad experience of last night, Miss Atwood, you had better take it easy. Don't exert yourself tramping all the way to the cottage to peer into a dusty old cupboard. There's no priest's hole there now."

When he was gone, I pounced on the book, turning quickly to the chapter about the cottage. Since the book was written when it was then safe to mention the secret chapel, I found a detailed report, including how the chapel was entered through the cupboard by pressing against the bottom shelf. The back wall then swung away. When I'd briefly handled the Malverne Manor book previously, I'd skipped over the chapter about the cottage, not knowing its importance. Now I carefully read every word.

As I continued to read the details about the disused chapel, I gradually realized that my sudden suspicion was unwise. Why would anyone go to the trouble of knocking out the seal in order to hide the body in the underground chapel, then have to reseal the entry to keep the secret? There certainly were more expeditious ways of disposing of a dead body. I again wondered about the so-called brother in cleric's collar who'd come to take the body away. If that was indeed Amy's body that the impostor—I was quite certain he was that—if this impostor had taken the body away, there was no need to hide it on the manor.

I continued to read, turning to other parts of the book, forgetting for the moment about the cottage. I'd become so engrossed in the details about the gardens, I sat up with a start when a loud voice startled me. It was Old Abner.

"Baint it the miss," he exclaimed in his shrill voice, squinting at me with the faded blue eyes, the mouth agape in a toothless smile. "Why, miss, I hears you wuz in a bad way yestidday, almost drownd."

"I was rescued in time," I answered.

He stared at me dumbly. I saw I had to repeat my answer in a louder tone.

"You wuz lucky, miss," he then said. "Coulda drownd, like t'other one." He continued to lean over me, the faded, blinking eyes riveted on me, the grin widening, expecting the chat to continue.

"Did you see anyone prowling about the manor last night?" I asked, remembering to speak out.

"Yes, yes, I seen him," he responded promptly. "None strangers like, miss, but I seen him." He covered one side of his mouth and lowered his voice slightly. "I seen him, miss," he said in a wheezy whisper. "The ghost."

"You don't mean *him*," I said, "you mean *her,* the ghost of the servant girl who drowned."

He shook his head vehemently. "No, no," he cried. "It was him. The priest ghost. I seen *him.*"

"Priest ghost? What do you mean?"

"I seen him," he repeated belligerently, jutting out his bristly chin.

"Tell me about the priest ghost you saw," I said, and he immediately shook off his sulk. His shoulders drooped into a relaxed stoop. His eyes glistened with delight at the prospect of telling me about it.

"Onct, long ago, miss, a priest wuz killed by the Queen's men. They found him in the secret chapel, so the story goes. His ghost still haunts the place. That is what made the girl drownd herself, miss. She seen the priest ghost and got crazed, ran into the pond and drownd. The priest ghost now has no peace, miss. Comes to the cottage most every night. I hide by the trees. I see him come and go, goes into the chapel under the cottage."

"Yes, Abner, I've been told there is a chapel under the cottage and that Sir Edmond's grandfather sealed up the priest's hole in the cupboard."

Old Abner burst into a wheezy laugh. His shoulders shook with laughter. "Miss," he shouted at me, "ghosts have no need of doors. Brick walls do not stop them." He shook his head at me, as if wondering at my utter stupidity.

"Yes, yes, I see what you mean," I said, then asked, "Tell me about this blond-haired servant girl, the one you and Mrs. Hopkins picked up at the Three Crowns Inn, the one who drowned in the pond. Did you see her frequently? Did she walk in the garden?"

"I seen her. Not much round the gardens, miss. She stayed most in an upstairs room, wuz sickly and wuz lame. Dint stay here long." He flashed a bright grin. "But I posted letters for her," he said, and I remembered he'd told me about the letters previously.

He leaned over me again and whispered, "Twas a secret, miss. I told none 'bout the letters. I posted them in the village."

"Nobody knows? Not even now?"

He drew his stooped body into a half-erect position and gave me a mortified stare. "Miss, 'twas a secret."

"Yes, yes, Abner, of course. You wouldn't give away a secret," I said and as I glanced past him, I saw Corinne come out of the house. When she saw Old Abner, she came to a halt.

"Corinne is looking for you," I said to him, pointing to Corinne who stood waiting, hands placed on hips.

He turned, muttered, and shambled away.

When he was gone I tried to forget about the secret chapel and the priest ghost. Moreover, I wanted to cast aside the wild notion that Amy's body was hidden in the chapel. I purposely concentrated on the book, reading determinedly about the grand ballroom in the manor house which I hadn't yet seen.

But it was no use. I had to go and see for myself, enter that cupboard and press my hands against that bottom shelf. I hesitated, telling myself my wild suspicion was as foolish as the Colonel had indicated. And it was a long walk to the cottage. I did not feel up to that kind of exercise. Yet I recalled how Brian had rushed me away from that cupboard. Not from the newspapers on the bottom shelf but from the secret of the cottage cupboard?

My inner protests soon gave way and I started for the cottage, carrying the book with me since I felt responsible for it.

On entering the cottage, I dropped the book on the table and went directly to the bottom shelf of the cupboard, pressing hard with both hands. I gasped with astonishment when the back wall of the cupboard swung away. For a stunned, unbelieving moment, I stood gaping at the dark hole in front of me.

"How simple," I said aloud in still-unbelieving amazement. Then an alarm went off in my head. Simple? Too simple. I swung around, fully expecting to see either the Colonel or Old Abner grinning in the doorway of the cottage. There was no one there and I felt a wave of guilt that I should be so quick to condemn them.

I stepped outdoors, debating what I should do. I could hear the Colonel splashing in the pond. I sat down in the wicker chair, thinking back to the time Brian made me sit there while he started on my portrait. That seemed so long ago.

I decided to wait till the Colonel was through with his swim. Then I would tell him of my discovery. I didn't wish to venture into that dark hole alone. If the Colonel did not wish to brave it, he could wait in the cottage room. That would be some assurance.

After a long agonizing wait, the temptation became unbearable. I went back into the cottage.

I peered down the dark, musty hole. Dank cold air washed up. Gradually the blackness took shape. I could see narrow steps set against the stone wall. From where I stood, I could see only the stairs and the wall, nothing of the chapel.

I wanted to go down, at least partway, but reason won over impulse and I drew back. After all these years of disuse, those stone steps were probably loosened. I didn't care to acquire still more bruises.

I stood there, gazing into the shadowy, musty passage. The mysterious stillness below beckoned like a conjurer's wand. I swiftly turned away and walked outdoors before my curiosity won over common sense. I'd wait until Edmond returned to the manor. Yes, that would be best. But that would be hours away. Then I could, at least, wait for the Colonel. I wouldn't let the old man risk the stone steps. He could wait for me at the cupboard entry.

I returned to the wicker chair and waited again, but the splashing in the pond went on and on. I got up, finally, deciding to return to the manor house and wait for Edmond.

After I'd gone a distance, I remembered I'd left the Malverne Manor book in the cottage and, in my preoccupation, I'd also left the cupboard entry yawning open. I returned to the cottage.

My hand stopped in mid-air as I started to pull the cupboard entry shut. I stared into the mysterious darkness below. I could no longer resist going down a couple of steps.

Cautiously, I tested the top step. It seemed substantial. I went down another step. Then another.

It was no use any more telling myself I must be sensible. I felt that not to go down all the way would be only a sign of cowardice.

The chill air made me shudder. I clutched the rough stone wall as I made my descent. When I was halfway down, I stopped, looked around. My eyes had become accustomed to the murky darkness. The small dark chamber began to take shape.

Holding on to the stone step above me, I peered into the front part of the chapel. I saw a tiny window built close to the ceiling. An inside wooden shutter dangled from the window.

In the bleak light that filtered in through the window, I saw an altar and near it what looked like a heap of smashed statuary.

My eyes roamed the still, shadowy place. Except for the heap of broken statuary and the bare altar, the chapel was empty.

Slowly, I began to mount the stairs, planning to return later with Edmond for a thorough search, when my glance caught something protruding from around the corner of the altar.

What I'd thought at first was a fragment of the broken statuary now appeared to be something else. I stopped, held onto the steps with both hands and peered down at the thing. As I continued to stare at it in the faint light I saw that it was not stone but cloth.

The recognition of what I saw sent such a cold whipping shudder through my body that I had to grasp the stone steps more firmly, or I would have plunged down the stairs.

At first I had to wrench my eyes away. Then, slowly, I looked back. It was a sash from Amy's dress; one I'd helped her make. My eyes, now quite adjusted to the thin light in the chapel, recognized the wide blue sash. I knew that sash well. Amy and I had taken turns embroidering the crimson and white flowers on it.

I groped down the stairs and inched forward, my eyes never leaving the blue sash that curled from around the corner of the altar.

For a stunned moment I stared at the empty space behind the altar where I expected to find Amy's body. There was only the broken statue.

After a while, I gazed about the cobwebby, stone-floored chapel. In a dark corner where practically no light penetrated, I saw a framed picture turned to the wall. Without giving it much thought, and expecting it to be a religious picture of no consequence to my search, I turned the picture around.

The thin ray of oblique light from the high window on the opposite wall illuminated only the eyes and a small portion of the hair. My first thought was that it was a self-portrait of Brian. The dark luminous eyes that stared up at me were his eyes. The little I could see of the hair appeared golden blond.

I picked up the portrait and brought it closer to the window. I saw then it was a portrait of a woman. It came to me all at once. It was the portrait of Lady Edythe, the one she'd removed from the Malverne Manor library and said she'd sold to finance Sir Edmond's campaign. It was done when she was young, twenty-one, I think Edmond said. I was struck by her resemblance to Brian.

I leaned forward for a closer look when a voice behind me said, "You see the resemblance now, don't you?"

CHAPTER 18

The portrait dropped from my hands. I spun round to where the voice came from.

In the dim light I could barely see him at the top of the stairs but I knew he was smiling. The smile was in his voice. The languid almost laughing voice made my body go rigid with fear, much more than if he'd angrily shouted the words.

He was now slowly making his way down the stairs. His lazy, deliberate descent sent a trembling through my body. My hands shook so hard I tightened them into fists. As he slowly approached, the smile still on his face, I moved back, one difficult step at a time.

With his eyes still on me, he reached for a candle and some matches near the stairs. I flinched when the candle spurted into flame and I saw the masked fury in his face which the grotesque smile intensified.

As he came toward me, holding the flickering candle high, I was jolted out of my paralyzed fear and began to move farther back. I felt the sharp corner of the altar jab into my back and I cried out. Brian's smile widened at my outcry. In the fluttering candle flame, his eyes glittered with a flash of brilliance.

He came closer, then sideswept me like an agile dancer and leaned casually against the altar.

"Yes, that is my dear mother, Miss Atwood," he said, gesturing toward the portrait. "She was twenty-one when the portrait was done, the same age I am now. Remarkable resemblance, wouldn't you say?"

He became silent, leaning lazily against the altar, gazing at the picture. My eyes flicked toward the stairs. In one lunge I rushed for the steps but was able to clamber up only halfway. His hand came down roughly on my bruised shoulder. He pulled me down the stairway to the stone floor of the chapel. I cried out, lightly touching the sore shoulder.

Brian chuckled. "That must be the shoulder where my dear mother whacked you before she and Mrs. Hopkins trussed you up and tossed you into the pool in the formal gardens."

I looked up at him. He was still holding the candle. The shadows danced crazily across his face. "But mother's little plan about drowning you didn't come off," he went on. "I told her it wouldn't work. But I saw she was getting desperate. You could have spared yourself all this, Miss Atwood, if you'd simply gone home when Lady Edythe first suggested it, or, at least, when I later suggested it to you. You shouldn't have been such a snoop." He made a clucking noise with his tongue. "Last night's failure with the drowning routine has made my dear mother unhappy, Miss Atwood. She'd so counted on being finally rid of you, then placing the blame on the Cheslick boys." He laughed, a deep rumbling roar. "My, how they are being blamed for everything." The laughing tone switched to petulance. "I didn't like my dear mother throwing suspicion on Corinne also. She's a harmless little bitch, special friend of mine."

He waved his hand, the lighted candle making queer arcs of light across the stone walls of the chapel. "Well, the plan didn't work after all. But, you see, when Lady Edythe saw you through the window, sitting alone in the garden and was informed by Mrs. Hopkins that dear Edmond was seen racing toward the cottage, the two dear ladies thought they'd have enough time to carry out their plan. Unfortunately, dear, swift Edmond returned too soon and my dear sweet mother and her assistant had to become your rescuers." He wagged his head back and forth, the rumbling laughter drumming off the stone walls.

I decided to play for time. He was in a talkative mood. Perhaps I could keep him talking. Then, if the Colonel should glance into the cottage— Would the Malverne Manor book be on the table where I'd left it? No, Brian probably had removed it. And had closed the cupboard entry also. Nevertheless, the instant I heard the slightest sound above, I would scream with all my might on the chance it might be the Colonel entering.

Or I might succeed in distracting Brian while he talked. I was near the stairs. One brief lapse in Brian's watchfulness and I could escape up the stairs.

I looked up at Brian. He was idly watching the candle that he'd flung to the floor when hot wax burned him a moment ago. The candle flame hissed and flickered against the stone floor, then the flame died. The chapel was plunged into darkness.

"You say Lady Edythe is your mother," I said to him, voicing the first thing that came to my mind, anything to break the eerie, dark silence. Now, with the candle out, the enclosing darkness made my flesh creep. "She's much too old to be your mother," I rushed on. "I can see a slight resemblance but——"

I was aware of an abrupt movement then his fingers dug into my arm. He pulled me up from the floor. In the shadowy gloom, I saw he'd thrust me in front of the portrait. There was another swift movement behind me and I next realized he had relighted the candle. In the wavering flame his face looked distorted. His eyes gleamed as he shifted his glance from me to the candle in his hand.

"These candles, Miss Atwood," he said, resuming the soft laughing tone, "were stuck into the most elaborate silver candlesticks I've ever seen. Brought me a nice sum in a London shop." The smile went out of his voice and he kicked savagely at the heap of broken statuary on the floor. "I took one of those pious statues to the shop also. The man laughed at me, wouldn't give me a shilling for it." He kicked again at the pieces. "At least, I had the pleasure of smashing this one to pieces."

He snatched my arm with his free hand and thrust me in front of the portrait, closer than I'd been.

"Look closely, Miss Atwood, and you will see that there is no doubt that Lady Edythe is indeed my dear sweet mother. You can see the uncanny resemblance to me because, you see, at twenty-one she looked quite different from the haggard bitch she is now."

I gazed at the similar faces. Looking at the portrait was like looking at Brian's face. Still intent on keeping him talking, I said, "This is the portrait she removed from the manor library, isn't it? The one she said she'd sold to finance Sir Edmond's election campaign?"

Brian made a clucking sound with his tongue and shook his head. "Is that what she said?" He snickered. "No, Miss Atwood, I removed the picture the very same day I found that handy little book on the window seat of the manor library, the book that conveniently told me all about the manor, gave me all the details about this chapel, even how to enter it." He stopped, grinned at the portrait. "The picture is sort of my insurance. My dear mother thinks this is a copy. I am an artist of sorts, not that galleries show my pictures. I do good copy work. Some people call them forgeries. That was how I eked out an existence." He shook his head. "No, Miss Atwood, this is the original. I never found the time to duplicate it, but my dear mother doesn't know that. Even if she should suspect that this is the original, there is nothing she can do about it. It is my little insurance policy."

"In what way is it insurance?"

"For a small sum of money, Miss Atwood, I assured my mother I would keep both the portrait and myself out of sight. Dear Edmond, you see, rarely saw Lady Edythe when she was at the age when the portrait was painted. If he knew about that phase of her life, he'd change his mind about her. She was living then in Malta and in India. Lady Edythe is hopeful that after a while Edmond's recollection of the portrait will fade. That's all he's got to go on to notice the striking resemblance. With age, Lady Edythe will look even less like me. You must admit the likeness to me in that portrait is startling. I warned my sweet mother that unless she pays up, I will make a dramatic appearance before Sir Edmond, portrait in hand."

"You mean," I broke in, "Sir Edmond has never seen you?"

"Don't you remember my telling you at our little secret meeting at the Three Crowns Inn that Edmond doesn't even know I exist? I was proud of that little witticism, particularly since you did not catch on at all." His voice dropped to a sullen whisper. "Until two years ago, I did not know of my mother's existence. Then when I found out about her, I had to lead a skulking non-existence while she paid me little honorariums to remain anonymous. For the past two years, Miss Atwood, I've visited Malverne Manor on the sly, hidden away in the attics and most recently I have been relegated to this fetid chamber."

"Why must you stay hidden?"

"Because I am Lady Edythe's bastard son. She disowned me at birth." He held the candle higher and scowled at the portrait. "I would be an embarrassment." He gave me a sidelong glance. "I was the result of a little dalliance of hers in Malta. I didn't know what an interesting past history I had until two years ago when Uncle Philip died. He told me everything. Deathbed confession, you know. Eased his conscience."

He leaned more comfortably against the altar and silently watched the candle sputter. A bitter smile played around his mouth. I was afraid for a moment he would stop talking which was my only safeguard. I was about to prompt him when he spoke.

"You know, Miss Atwood, he wasn't even my uncle, just someone my dear mother paid money to, to keep me out of the way. But dear Uncle Philip told me everything finally, even who my real father was. I went to see him. My father—my dear mother's lover—was kind enough to give me a whole hour of his time. He didn't deny anything, but he saw no reason for my coming around again. Said it was all so long ago, that my sweet mother—foolish woman he called her—had left her husband in India and had come to Malta. He said it was all a mistake, her coming to Malta. And though he didn't say it outright, I was the biggest mistake of all."

He became quiet, lounging against the altar, studying the portrait and, wishing him to go on talking, I said, "Aren't you afraid that Lady Edythe, with Mrs. Hopkins' help, might murder you? It would solve Lady Edythe's problem."

He grinned. "You forget that I am Lady Edythe's son. I have inherited some of her traits. No, for the present, she needs me as much as I need her. What's more, Lady Edythe knows now that Mrs. Hopkins is my ally more than she is hers. Mrs. Hopkins will do anything for a price. Between the two of us, we keep Lady Edythe in line."

All at once Brian spat out a blast of profanity. He threw the candle on the floor, beating at his hand where the hot wax had dribbled. He gave the candle stub a vicious kick, then grabbed my arm and threw me against the wall with such force I shrieked with pain. I'd fallen into a hunched position. My limbs were so stiff from fear and the chilling air, I had considerable trouble easing myself into a sitting position. When I looked up, Brian was sitting on the bottom step of the stone stairway, watching me. Now that the chapel was in darkness again, he was just a hulking shape against the stone wall. Only his eyes were distinguishable.

"Good old Uncle Philip," I heard Brian cry out triumphantly. "I owe him much. It was he who told me of my dear mother's whereabouts. My loving father, the pompous beast, wouldn't tell me. Lady Edythe! Malverne Manor! You can imagine my surprise when Uncle Philip told me. Here was I, a nonentity, living in a hovel with a rum-soaked old seaman, and my mother was lady of the Manor. There was another little matter Uncle Philip kept babbling about. I got the impression Uncle Philip was confessing that he'd helped my sweet mother dispose of her husband. I intend to hunt down my hunch about the gentleman's sudden death. Might prove lucrative. Lady Edythe doesn't know I know. For the present I must pretend to be her ally. As you pointed out, Miss Atwood, she might put me out of the way if I don't watch myself. That sweet girl, Corinne, serves me well, keeps her ear to the ground."

He lapsed into silence and knowing that so long as he went on talking, I had time on my side, I said, "Lady Edythe is at least sixty years old. How could you——"

He pounced on my words. "I know what you're going to say, Miss Atwood. That she's too old to be my mother. No, my loving father told me the facts. Lady Edythe didn't have her first child—by her husband, not her lover, he made that quite clear—not until she was thirty-one years old. Imagine. An old hag of thirty-one. Then, after all the bad time she went through, the brat died on her. Then came that big love affair in Malta and I was born. By then my sweet mother was the overripe age of thirty-nine. Add it up, Miss Atwood. Lady Edythe is sixty. You guessed correctly. I played a nasty trick on my mother. Unlike the other brat, I lived."

I could hear him get up from the stairs and pace restlessly, his boots scraping against the stone floor. "My skulking days are over with. No more living in rotting poverty. My sweet mother is going to pay for all the misery she's caused me."

He continued to pace back and forth like a caged animal, his head hanging low. Ever so slowly, my eyes on him, I pulled myself up from the floor and inched toward the stairway. He went on pacing, his head still lowered. I'd almost reached the stairs when his hand shot out. He gave my arm a vicious twist and slammed me against the wall.

I clenched my teeth against the stab of pain in my back and where my head had hit the stone wall. When I opened my eyes, I saw him drop casually onto the steps and stretch his legs out comfortably. After a while, I could see more distinctly in the near-darkness. Even without the candle flame, I saw the gleeful smile on his face as he watched me trying to pull myself to a standing position. As I tried to lift myself from the stone floor, it seemed, for a confused moment, that the stones under me rocked slightly and I gave a start.

I glanced down confusedly at the wobbly stones and I heard him laugh.

"You feel the loose floor stones, Miss Atwood?" he said, soft laughter running lightly through his words.

I sprang up from the floor and stared down at the stones. Brian's soft laughter became a deep rumble, filling the small dark place, rising in crescendo until I thought my head would burst. I continued to stare in horror at the disarranged rectangle of uneven stones, a rectangle the width and length of a human body. I flung my hands to my mouth. I wanted to scream and couldn't. The scream died in my throat.

"I'm not quite through with that part of the floor," I heard Brian say in a quiet drawl. "That's why you can tell it's a grave. I'll take care of it later."

I wheeled about to stare at him. I opened my mouth but words wouldn't come. My throat was so dry and tight, the only sound that came forth was a moan.

"I did it for my dear mother, Miss Atwood. I thought at first I might only frighten away your little friend, but she became stubborn and troublesome. Lady Edythe would have you believe she didn't want me to go so far as murder, but that isn't so, Miss Atwood. She went to visit the Wickhams for a couple of days, instructing me she wanted the business finished while she was away." There was a little silence then he laughed. "So I finished it."

I turned my face away, leaning it against the moist wall. I wanted to tell him what sort of vicious criminal he was, but that would only prompt him to "finish me off." I could no longer save Amy. There was still a small chance I might save myself.

"You remember my telling you, Miss Atwood," I heard him say, "that Lady Edythe occasionally sent me reluctant invitations to visit secretly at the manor when Edmond was away."

I turned to face him and he continued, "You remember my telling you that when I arrived at the manor a fortnight ago, at Lady Edythe's urgent invitation, I knew my sweet mother had a very special favor to ask of me. The whole Farris family had been sent away on holiday. Corinne, too. Only Mrs. Hopkins and Old Abner were about. I wasn't hidden away in the attics that time. My mother promptly informed me she would pay me a nice sum if I did something about a scheming young lady named Amy who, with Mrs. Hopkins' help, was temporarily kept under sedation in a cloying, ruffly room called the Cream Lace Room. I soon realized it had to be a permanent solution. Murder was the only way out."

I could no longer keep still. I had to tell him what I thought of him and his unspeakable crime. But he cut me off at the first word.

"Now, don't scold me, Miss Atwood," he said with a pout. "That might upset me."

He'd lapsed into a sulky silence, then resumed speaking in a light, conversational tone. "Good thing I discovered the secret of this underground chapel. Lady Edythe thought at first that Amy's body, she was drugged, you know—something Mrs. Hopkins grows in her little garden —then she was thrown into the pond to drown. Well, Lady Edythe thought Amy's body was carted away by a friend of mine who pretended to be a cleric brother of a disgraced servant girl. That was Lady Edythe's ploy. She even had the impostor brother come for the body when those gullible imbeciles, Miss Wickham and her papa were at the manor. Sort of unwitting witnesses, you know."

He stopped. The sulkiness crept back into his voice. "But, you see, Miss Atwood, my sweet, scheming mother hadn't paid me yet for my trouble, so my friend secretly brought the body here. I placed it under those wobbly stones. That Malverne Manor book which I'd found in the manor library came in handy, the one you later found hidden in the cottage. I burned it. But I won't burn the Colonel's copy, the one you left on the table in the cottage before you foolishly ventured down here. Somehow I'll dispose of it. It's worth money. The Colonel was quite cagey about his copy, lending it to you yet refusing to lend it to Lady Edythe. She knew the Wickham's copy was safe from your curious eyes. But the Colonel hid his copy from her filching fingers.

"It was in that Malverne Manor book," he went on, "that I learned about this underground chapel and the seal in the cupboard. A most insecure seal. I had it knocked out in no time. Of course, I had to guard this place after I told Lady Edythe. I had to tell her. Make it clear the body would stay there till she paid me. She didn't believe me. I had to show her the body. She was foolish enough to think I would trust her to pay me after the body was disposed of."

His gaze wandered to the rectangle of stone, lingered there. "I knew Lady Edythe's patrician hand wouldn't dig up the stinking body. I was unsure of Mrs. Hopkins, but I soon found out she works for the highest bidder." He thrust his head forward to look at me. "I really began to worry about you yesterday, Miss Atwood, when you became terribly curious about the cupboard. I wondered whether the clever Miss Atwood was curious about the old papers, or had she learned about the secret chapel. I saw you return to the cottage after I'd steered you away from the newspapers. There you were, so conveniently hunched over the papers that had fallen to the floor. An opportune time, I decided, to use Edmond's filched walking stick on you. By dropping it deliberately, I'd hoped to throw more suspicion on dear Edmond, perhaps scare you away from him—and away from Malverne Manor."

He lounged back on the stone stairs. I could see him plainly. My eyes had become adjusted to the murky darkness. He began to move his head back and forth in a lolling movement. The light blond hair made dizzying streaks against the dark stone wall. Suddenly the room began to swim before my eyes. Brian's lolling blond head became pinpoints of piercing light. I realized I was becoming violently ill. Icy beads of perspiration pricked at my forehead yet my face burned hot, and I pressed it against the cold wall.

After a while the wave of sickness passed. I was slowly turning away from the wall when I froze with terror. Brian was standing near me, holding a knife. I stared at him, speechless with fright. He leaned forward, looked into my face, then straightened up and began to pick at his fingernails with the knife. He stood there a while then turned slowly and sat on the stone stairs. I could feel my body slump with exhaustion and relief against the stone wall. It was then I heard a faint sound above me, as if someone had entered the cottage. I thought of the Colonel. He'd finished his swim, stopped to see if I was in there. Slowly, I turned my head to see if Brian was aware of the faint sounds above us. He was placing the knife into his pocket, giving no indication he'd heard.

I was not mistaken. Someone was crossing the room above us. I darted a glance at Brian. He was gazing absent-mindedly at the tips of his boots.

There was a slight scraping noise at the top of the stairs. Someone was opening the cupboard door. I now heard the chapel entry sliding away.

I flicked a glance at Brian, stretched out languidly on the stairs, paying no heed to the soft noises above him. I took a deep breath, ready to shout for help, but at that instant Brian looked up to the top of the stairs, speaking to someone out of my line of vision.

"You've brought my lunch, I see. I have a guest," he said with a light laugh. "Would you be kind enough to bring Miss Atwood some lunch?"

CHAPTER 19

There was an abrupt movement at the top of the stairs as the person stepped forward then came to a stop. I still could not see who it was.

"I had to walk all the way from Bellesport," Brian complained sulkily, gazing up the stairway. Bellesport, I recalled hazily, that was the postmark on the envelope, the port town where Edmond went this morning.

"When I was almost at the cottage," Brian went on, "I had to duck out of sight. The Colonel was heading for the pond." He jerked his head at me. "Later, when I thought the coast was clear, Miss Atwood, a book clutched to her bosom, was making for the cottage. I knew immediately the enterprising Miss Atwood was carrying the Malverne Manor book and would soon discover the cupboard's secret. I thought I was mistaken because she soon came out but—" He cocked his head and grinned. "She went inside again and here she still is."

He got up from the stairs and lighted a candle which he somehow anchored to the stone floor then extended his hand up the stairs. "Let me have the lunch basket. It'll be a farewell lunch in this wretched hole. Tonight I seal up the entry to this fetid chamber and I'm off for parts unknown; my pockets stuffed with money. Let me see what's in the lunch basket."

Mrs. Hopkins came down the stairs, handed him the lunch basket, then turned to look at me.

"Is the Old Boy still splashing about in the pond?" Brian inquired as he rummaged in the basket.

"Yes, I heard him splashing about when I approached the cottage," Mrs. Hopkins replied, not taking her eyes off me.

"Here, have some meat pie, Miss Atwood," I suddenly heard Brian say over me. He thrust it at my face and I turned away. He spun my head around, forcing the food into my mouth. Waves of nausea washed over me as I, nearly choking, had to swallow it.

"I don't completely trust Mrs. Hopkins," Brian said in a deep whisper. "With her, one needs a food taster." He jammed another mouthful into me, then stood up, waiting a while before he returned to the stairs to finish the meat pie.

"I'll leave the Old Boy to your ministrations, Mrs. Hopkins." He grinned up at her. "You'll know what to do," he said, and she nodded.

"Close the chapel entry and the cupboard doors when you leave, Mrs. Hopkins, in case the Old Boy should peer into the cottage when he's through with his swim."

Mrs. Hopkins jerked her head at me. "What about her?" she demanded in a burst of annoyance. "I told you we should have done something about her the day she arrived. I should have put something a bit stronger into her tea the day Edmond returned to the manor." Her voice rose in pitch. She worked her hands convulsively. "I said from the beginning she'd cause trouble, even more than that one," she shouted, pointing to the grave. "We should have done something about this one before she could get to Edmond, before she had a chance to snoop around, cause trouble."

"Now, now, Mrs. Hopkins," Brian said in a soothing, cajoling tone.

"We will, we will. But let's not be inhospitable. Let's serve Miss Atwood some refreshment. A pot of tea would be ever so nice."

Their glances held for a moment then they laughed together.

"Now, you run along, Mrs. Hopkins," Brian murmured, "and brew a pot of your tea for Miss Atwood and tell my dear mother to bring it, will you?"

Mrs. Hopkins made a move to go, then twisted her head for a quick, scathing glance at me before leaving. The doors above pulled shut and for a long time the only sounds in the acrid, musty room were the spitting of the candle and the loud, wet noises Brian made as he continued to eat the meat pie.

"I never would have believed you capable of such cruelty—and murder," I said to him, and he looked at me with surprise changing into amusement.

"Blandishments will gain you nothing, Miss Atwood. I am what my loving mother made me. I will say this for her. She was doing you a kindness when she trumped up that business of having Mrs. Hopkins serve you the drugged tea. If you'd gone home the following morning, Miss Atwood, you would not be in this ticklish situation now." He thrust his head forward. "Now I must murder you also." The candle flame, leaping and shuddering up from the floor where he'd anchored it, cast distorting light and shadow on his face. At times the candlelight bathed his pink-fleshed, rounded face in a golden, cherubic glow. The next instant a shadow moved across his face, painting a hideous mask.

"I'm not certain yet how I will dispose of you. With Amy it was easy. She was fed enough of Mrs. Hopkins' brew to render her unconscious, then she was simply dropped into the pond until she drowned." He chomped thoughtfully on the meat pie for a while then said, "If I'm going to hang, I may as well hang for two murders. I can die only once." He shook his head, laughed gaily. "I won't hang."

"Have you forgotten that there will be inquiries about me at the manor and from my own people?"

"Don't lie, Miss Atwood. I know all about your people. Like Amy, you have no close relatives. I paid a call on your beloved, Walter Binson. Oh, he had no idea who I was. We had a nice chat over my purchase of some throat lozenges. He didn't strike me as very bright. Anyone else questioning your whereabouts would learn nothing. I'd take care of that. The same would have happened if you'd gone home when Lady Edythe suggested it. You'd have made attempts, investigating Amy's whereabouts, but you would have learned only what I expected you to learn. Don't take me for a fool, Miss Atwood. I'm no Walter Binson."

He removed an apple from the lunch basket and held it up. "I'm not going to share my apple with you. I doubt that Mrs. Hopkins would tamper with it." He concentrated on his enjoyment of the apple for a time then said, "I have a friend holed up in a dreary little port town called Bellesport. He's the chap who wrote dear Edmond that explanatory letter about Amy marrying some bloke in Malta and planning to emigrate to Australia. My co-operative friend is very adept at letter-writing and impersonations. He convinced Miss Wickham and her papa that he was the sorrowing cleric brother of the disgraced servant girl who'd drowned herself. Lady Edythe wanted the respected corroboration of the Wickhams just in case. My friend took the body away but only in a roundabout way. It was brought here to the chapel."

"This friend of yours? Is he still in Bellesport?" I asked, wondering what success, if any, Edmond was having and if he would learn anything in time.

"No," Brian answered. "By now, I expect he's on the high seas, off for Australia. That was a lucky break for me, that he was planning to emigrate to Australia. When my friend arrives there, he writes two more letters—different sort of handwriting, of course and posing now as a bereaved husband. One letter goes to Edmond, one to you, informing you of the sad news of Amy's death—natural death. He'll think of some convenient disease. Now, of course, he won't have to write to you. And with Edmond, Amy was only a brief reckless romance. He won't grieve long."

He'd finished his apple and crushed the core under the heel of his boot, twisting and smashing for a prolonged time as if it gave him pleasure.

"What makes you so sure he will write that letter to Edmond from Australia?" I asked.

"He doesn't get the money until Edmond gets the letter." He threw me a petulant look. "My friend is trustworthy. I'm particular about my friends."

"Perhaps you're overoptimistic about all the money Lady Edythe will give you. Where could she get all that money?"

"Where do you think my dear sly mother has been getting the money she's been doling out to me for the past two years? Even before I learned of her existence, she was paying that Uncle Philip person. Dear Edmond is clever about some things, but he's blind and stupid when it comes to his dear widowed auntie and how she manages the household accounts."

He tossed a backward glance at the portrait leaning against the altar. "How fortunate that I should have found such a striking resemblance to me in the Malverne library. I was afraid at first that Lady Edythe might destroy it once she knew it was here, but I knew that would not occur. The portrait is worth a lot of money. I know. I had it appraised. My sweet mother is greedy. Then there is her colossal vanity. I'm sure the dear lady spent a great deal of time admiring the portrait. When I disappear for good this time, the lovely portrait will once more grace the Malverne library and Lady Edythe will again be the lady of the Manor because the simpering Miss Wickham, though married to Edmond, will never be the real lady of the Manor. Amy wanted that honor and lived to regret it. Eventually Miss Wickham and Lady Edythe will persuade Edmond to turn his interests to Wickham Place, which is even larger and better-situated than Malverne Manor. Edmond is not only land-proud, he's land-mad. Soon the bridegroom will be performing miracles with Wickham Place. And Malverne Manor, which my dear mother has long coveted, will be hers."

He sprang up from the stairs, glaring up at the entry. "And where is the dear Lady Edythe?" he shouted. "The sly old witch."

He began to pace, then stopped abruptly and flashed a grin at me. "Do you know I owe much to that blowsy innkeeper, Mrs. Ploovey? It was she who gave me the whole idea about how to dispose of Amy. I stopped in there for a drink one day. Was a bit leary about it, afraid she might catch my resemblance to the eminent folk up at the manor. There was no problem. The old crone was prattling on and on—not to me but I overheard—about a yellow-haired, fetching bit of pastry who'd arrived on the coach the day before to be a servant girl at the manor. I knew she was talking about Amy. Thus was begun the sad little drama of the disgraced servant girl who'd drowned herself."

Brian resumed his pacing, kicking at the stones covering the grave each time he came by. "Had to pull up all those stones myself," he sulked. "My friend scurried off to Bellesport, said he'd promised only to write letters and impersonate people. I wrecked my hands and fingernails digging in that hard-packed earth. My hands still aren't presentable."

He wheeled about, eyes fixed on the chapel entry at the top of the stairs. He ran his hands through his hair. In the peculiar yellow light of the candle, the gold-blond hair rippled through his fingers like streaks of sunlight. He began to curse, first softly, then in a piercing rage. He swung round, regarding me quietly for a few seconds, then plunged again into his frantic pacing. The sound of his boots scraping against the stone floor and the hissing of the candle, now burned almost to the floor, combined to make a raw noise, grating and scratching at my nerves.

Crouching against the damp stone wall, I watched him through a haze of half-consciousness. Except for the dull pain radiating from my shoulder, I no longer had any other sensation. My body had become almost rigid from the creeping cold, from the mounting, paralyzing fear. I moved my eyes wearily from Brian to the stone stairs and the promise of freedom. If somehow I could escape up the stairs, ram open that door—I felt a wave of shame and cowardice that I had no fight left in me, that I did not make a rush for the stairs no matter what the consequences. I would die later anyway. But I no longer had the will or the daring to make the effort.

I raised my head when Brian halted his pacing. I heard it, too, the overhead noise as someone pulled the cupboard door open. Then the sliding sound as the chapel entry was forced open.

I looked up and saw Lady Edythe descend the stairs.

I could see only her face, framed by the silver-white hair. It was as if her face were suspended in air and I gradually realized she was wearing a black cloak with a hood. She came to a stop midway. I then heard a muffled, jangly sound. I could not identify the sound yet my heart began to pound like a drum the instant I heard it. It wasn't till Mrs. Hopkins came down the stairs to stand behind Lady Edythe that I recognized the sound. Mrs. Hopkins was carrying the housekeys, the ones that were usually pinned to her apron. I remembered with a sickness at the pit of my stomach how Amy had reason to dread that sound. Had she, too, heard it just before she died? Had she dreaded that sound when she lay in the Cream Lace Room and knew Mrs. Hopkins was approaching?

A stillness fell on the place. Only the faint jangle of Mrs. Hopkins' keys was heard when she moved slightly. I drew my eyes from the two women to Brian, expecting him to tear into a rage since he'd suffered the torment of a long wait for Lady Edythe.

It was Lady Edythe who broke the silence.

"You despicable, blundering fool," she said to Brian in a quiet, controlled voice. "You are exactly like your father, a cock-of-the-walk blundering fool." She slowly turned her face away from Brian who'd backed up against the wall, pressing his shoulders against the stones. His eyes seemed huge as he gazed up at her, speechless.

Lady Edythe's gaze slid from me to the stones covering the grave. "You ingrate," she said to Brian, her voice still low, calm, "you haven't covered your tracks for the first murder. Those stones were to look no different from the rest of the floor. When you tricked me and brought the body here, I said it may remain here provided the floor doesn't look tampered with."

I could hear Brian make a shuffling noise as he changed positions against the wall. When he spoke, I barely recognized his voice; it was thin, wispy. "I'm sealing up the chapel entry today. Nobody will be coming down here."

"Of course you will seal up the chapel entry today," Lady Edythe said with a little smile. "But before you do that, those stones will look like all the others in the floor."

Brian shot away from the wall. His voice trembled. "I wrecked my hands and fingernails pulling up those damn stones, digging in that hard earth and I——"

"And you will finish the job or you don't get a farthing," Lady Edythe interrupted, glaring down at him from the stairway. "Edmond left early this morning," she continued, "claiming he and Will Hockinson had some election business in the north end. But I know Edmond is on to something." She threw me a scathing look. "Something she said to him. Probably has something to do with that letter your accomplice in Bellesport wrote to Edmond."

"You told me Edmond believed the letter about Amy marrying Charles Coombes's brother in Malta then going with him to Australia," Brian cried, his voice shaking.

"He did," Lady Edythe replied. She looked at me. "Until she got to him. Every time I was assured Edmond was pacified and convinced, the inquisitive, obstructive Miss Atwood came up with a new twist to get him wrought up, even trying feminine wiles, hoping herself to become the mistress of Malverne Manor." She stopped, then added in a voice so low it sounded like a hiss, "Miss Atwood has been more trouble than her ambitious little cousin, Amy.

"And you—you blunderer," she said, turning on Brian, raising her voice for the first time. "I told you a letter from nearby Bellesport was a mistake. Your accomplice could have written that letter from some non-existent London address, posted it from London. That's where Edmond went, to Bellesport."

"Edmond will discover nothing," Brian declared, drawing himself up to a confident height from the shrunken posture he'd slipped into. "He wouldn't know where in Bellesport to look or whom to look for. Charles

Coombes is a name my friend made up." A swagger crept into Brian's tone. "Besides, my friend is on the high seas by now, heading for Australia."

Lady Edythe regarded Brian with speculative silence then turned to Mrs. Hopkins. "We may still have a chance," she said to her.

Mrs. Hopkins smiled and nodded.

The two women then proceeded to descend the stairs, Lady Edythe carefully holding up the long black cloak she wore, Mrs. Hopkins carrying a basket.

"Remove the stones from the grave," Lady Edythe commanded Brian in a precise, authoritative tone.

Brian gaped at her. When he spoke, it was a raspy whisper. "Surely you don't expect me to—" He jerked his hand at me. "I've been thinking about what to do with her," he rushed on, his voice rising. "I have a better solution, a quicker way."

He gazed at Lady Edythe, waiting for her to respond but she remained silent.

"You can't expect me to take out that foul-smelling body," Brian cried out in a pleading whimper, "and—and grub out a deeper hole and——"

Lady Edythe's hand flashed out. She struck him so hard across the face, he reeled back.

"Yes," she said as Brian caressed his cheek, "that is exactly what I expect you to do." She flung me a quick glance. "Mrs. Hopkins has brought some of her special brew. Miss Atwood has had some experience with it, only this is considerably stronger. By the time Miss Atwood awakens, she will already be buried alongside her friend, Amy."

"No!" Brian shouted. "I won't do it. I will not go through that grubby digging business again," he whimpered. "I've wrecked my hands and fingernails to the bone doing it once. I won't go through that again. It takes hours besides."

His last words jolted Lady Edythe into an alert standstill. Her lips compressed, her eyes wandered from me to the stones over the grave.

Brian stared at her wide-eyed, mouth hanging open. "Edmond may be home shortly," he said on a quick, bright note. "Digging in that hard-packed earth is quite time-consuming. My method of disposing of Miss Atwood is more expedient."

Lady Edythe turned to face him and Brian continued in a light, laughing manner. "Miss Atwood is drugged, I carry her to the cliff road, toss the body over the cliffside. That steep drop will surely kill her. Then

Edmond is told about Miss Atwood's unfortunate fall when she went out for a stroll. Who can prove anything?"

Brian thrust his head forward, waiting, while Lady Edythe regarded him silently then, turning to Mrs. Hopkins, she said, "We must be quick about this."

Mrs. Hopkins nodded and the two women approached me.

A moment ago I thought all the fight was out of me, but the instant they laid hands on me, I was like a wild animal, fighting for its life. I kicked, scratched, and fought so violently that Brian rushed forward to assist the women.

It was the excruciating grip of Brian's hands that became too much for me. His fingers dug into my temples as he held my head back in a viselike grip. I could feel more and more of the bitter fluid sliding down my throat until, soon, I no longer saw their faces hovering over me, no longer felt Brian's fingers digging into my flesh.

The drug's potent effect worked on me intermittently. At first complete unconsciousness overcame me. The obliterating blackness gradually became a wavering gray mist through which I was able to distinguish the stone stairway where I heard ascending footsteps.

There was a rattle, a scrape. The door at the top of the stairs was pulled shut. I was imprisoned in an oppressive lonely silence.

The wavering semidarkness began to change to a thick, smothering cloud, pulling me in. I struggled against it, scrambling to my feet. I managed to pull myself to a standing position, my gaze all the while fixed on the stone stairs which curled and swayed then disappeared from view altogether.

I tried to move forward. My legs trembled. I could feel my body go limp. I fell back against the gritty, cold wall and then slid uncontrollably to the stone floor. An enveloping blackness soon shut everything out.

When, later, the drug once more altered its effect, I became aware of the musty damp smell of the underground place. The acrid choking smell of the burned-out candles bit at my nostrils. I lifted my hand to my face to wipe away some of the cold perspiration that had formed on my forehead. It was then that I thought I heard a sound somewhere in the chapel.

I peered into the shadowy corner from where the faint noise had come. I heard it again. I could not make sense of the sound. Somewhere in my drug-scrambled brain I was certain that they'd all gone up the stone stairway, leaving me alone in the chapel. I knew then I was not alone. Someone had entered the chapel while I had lost all consciousness.

My eyes roamed the silent, shadowy chamber. Although I could see no one, I had the chilling knowledge I was not alone.

Holding my eyes open took enormous effort. The drug was pulling me into sluggishness once more. I thrust my head forward and continued to stare into the dark corner where I'd heard the flutter of sound. I now saw a thin shaft of light, a blur of movement.

The next instant a cloudy form approached me.

A different sound came to me. Fighting against the waves of insensibility that swept over me, I knew it was laughter that I heard. Someone was standing over me, laughing softly.

Now the hazy shape looming above me assumed a more definite form and I saw it was Brian. I could see him with remarkable clarity, the gold-blond hair falling over his forehead, the half-smile on his pink-fleshed, cherublike face, the dark, luminous eyes gleaming with a wild, fiery brilliance.

"The drug will soon take full effect," he said, his face almost touching mine. I could feel his breath on my face. "Before you go totally unconscious again, I want to tell you the most important part of this little episode. I want you to know the truth about Edmond. He and I are not enemies."

Brian smiled, shook his head as I stared up into his face. "Not at all," he said with a burst of laughter. "Edmond and I are in this together. Lady Edythe only thinks she's masterminded everything. Edmond and I let her think so. She was useful. All this is Edmond's plan and I helped him carry it off—for a price. We thought we were finished with it all when we got rid of ambitious little Amy, but you foolishly intervened, so Edmond and I realized we had to eliminate you also."

"I—I don't believe you," I managed to say in a choked whisper. I could feel my body lurch into an erect sitting position. "This is—is only your last bit of torment."

Brian clicked his tongue, then grinned. "Edmond did not go to Bellesport. There's no one there to find. He went to Wickham Place. He should be here just about now. He wants the pleasure of carrying you to the cliff road and dropping your unconscious body over the cliff. You've caused him an immense amount of trouble."

"No, no," I cried, my voice breaking into a convulsive sob. "You mean to torment me. It's a lie. A lie."

In a fierce thrust of effort I raised my hand to strike him, to cry out that no, I did not believe that about Edmond and why must he torment me so. But my hand dropped lifelessly. My mouth went slack. No words would come. I was dimly aware of my body toppling to the side from its tense sitting position. With a sudden, trembling seizure, I lost all consciousness.

What seemed like much later, I felt someone's presence near me. I had the unclear sensation of being lifted, then carried.

Somewhere from the deep primitive recesses of my mind I cried out and struggled against the person with astonishing force. As dulled as my brain was at present, I remembered for a terrorized moment what Brian had said—when the drug took full effect, I would be carried to the cliff and my body would be thrown over the cliffside.

Then a more terrible recollection seized me—that it was Edmond who wanted the pleasure of carrying me to the cliff road and hurling my body over the cliff.

Terror sharpened my wits, offsetting the pull of the drug, and I knew someone was now carrying me up the stone stairway out of the chapel.

I made feeble attempts to struggle out of the firm grasp of my murderer. Due to the darkness of the chapel and the blinding effect of the drug, I could not see who it was. I raised my hands to beat at the unseen face, but my arms dropped lifeless to my sides.

I felt a gust of cold air. We were out of the cottage. It was night. Pitch dark. I could hear the crunch and grab of boots against gravel as he hurried along. He spoke to me, but I could not understand him. I continued to make futile efforts to escape from his gripping hold on me. He was speaking to me once again, but his words, like his face, were lost in the blackness of the night and the darkness of my drugged brain.

When he'd carried me for what seemed an interminable distance, the blindness lifted momentarily and I was able to see faint outlines of trees all around me.

I looked up and saw it was Edmond who was carrying me.

CHAPTER 20

When I recovered somewhat from my horrible discovery, I began to struggle desperately against him, but he only held me in a still tighter grip. The struggle exhausted me completely and with the drug now overpowering me once more, I soon lost all sensation.

With awareness once more drifting back, before I even opened my eyes, I was confusedly imagining I was in a familiar place. The scent of an apple orchard surrounded me. I no longer felt strong arms grasping me tightly. I seemed to be lying on something soft, comfortable. I heard

Edmond's voice again. Although I still could not comprehend the words, I no longer feared him, no longer fought him.

I opened my eyes and stared at what, in my imagination, appeared to be curtains billowing at an open window. The aroma of apple blossoms was stronger now. I turned my head when I felt a hand placed over mine. The face bending over me wavered then steadied. It was Edmond and I now understood him when he spoke.

"You're safe, dear," he said. "You're in your room at Malverne Manor."

My eyes held his, then I gazed about me. The room came into clearer focus.

"I—I'm not imagining it all?" I murmured, looking into Edmond's face.

"You're not imagining it." He smiled, kissing me gently on the forehead. "Don't exert yourself. Don't try to talk."

Slowly, I shook my head. "No, I want to know. How—how did you find me?" I tried to raise my head from the pillow, but the room suddenly clouded then darkened. I could no longer see Edmond or hear him.

When I opened my eyes, Edmond was still there. Standing beside him was Dr. Pryor.

"You didn't answer my question," I said to Edmond and he laughed, along with Dr. Pryor.

"Before I had a chance to answer you," he replied, "you went back to sleep—for nine hours."

Dr. Pryor stepped forward to take my pulse. After peering into my eyes, he declared I had finally slept off the drug and should continue to improve daily.

"Then Miss Atwood may have visitors?" I heard a familiar voice inquire from the doorway. It was the Colonel. The doctor nodded approval and the Colonel entered, followed by Myrna, wide-eyed, on the brink of tears. Behind her was Mrs. Farris, a hesitant, friendly smile on her face. Even Farris's impassive countenance showed genuine concern. Old Abner shuffled in, peering at me in wonder. The procession's rear guard was taken up by the Raynords who approached the bed in solemn silence but soon burst into jolly well-wishing when they'd scrutinized me and considered me none the worse for wear.

"Oh, my dear," Mrs. Raynord murmured, her plump hand squeezing mine. "Oh, such a terrible, terrible experience." She smiled, nodding. "But I'm so happy you'll be all right. You do look fine, my dear."

"Yes, you've certainly managed to come out of it unscathed," the Colonel declared. "A couple more days and you'll be yourself again."

After the exuberant greetings toned down, Mrs. Farris inquired of Dr. Pryor if I might have some light nourishment, that she and Myrna would be happy to prepare it. I knew then, as the Colonel had predicted, I would soon be myself again because the suggestion of food pleased me. I was hungry.

Dr. Pryor gave his approval and Mrs. Farris and Myrna hurried away with a promise of something special and delicious.

Confusion and babble resumed, with my remaining guests wanting to know all the details of my ordeal, but Dr. Pryor put a halt to the torrent of questions.

"This will have to be a brief, quiet visit," he ordered. "The questions will have to wait. Besides, Sir Edmond has already explained most of the details to you."

The visit settled down to a calmer level, but, even so, the doctor was soon dismissing everyone with the promise they could drop by later. Only Edmond was permitted to remain.

When the doctor, too, left, Edmond gathered me in his arms and for a long while I was content to rest my head comfortably against his shoulder and simply feel his presence. After a time he held me at arm's length and gazed at me as if he couldn't believe he was seeing me.

"Edmond, I feel up to it," I said. "I want to know how you found me. You went to Bellesport?" I asked and he nodded.

"Brian, as a last bit of torment," I said, "wanted me to think you did not. Brian wanted me to believe you were in league with him."

"What a diabolical creature he is," Edmond said, "and what a surprise it was to learn that not only was there such a person as Brian but that he was Lady Edythe's illegitimate son." He shook his head in disbelief. "When you told me Brian bore a family resemblance, I decided he might be some distant relative I knew nothing of. But Lady Edythe's son. That was astonishing news. That Uncle Philip person whom Lady Edythe was paying certainly kept her secret until the death rattle. Brian's friend who was hiding out in Bellesport answered all questions thrown at him in the hope of saving himself, even volunteering information."

"Then you found Brian's friend in Bellesport?"

"Yes, finally tracked him down, quite by accident. I was inquiring at all the taverns and inns in the territory. At one tavern, when I mentioned Australia, thinking this so-called Charles Coombes person might have spoken of Australia, that possibly he was actually going there, someone at a nearby table overheard my remark. The fellow informed me he'd heard someone boasting of that very thing, that he'd come into a little money and was going to Australia to double his fortune. I gave the fellow a fistful of coins and he willingly led me to the tavern where the young man came frequently. We waited for so long in that tavern I began to think it was a hoax or wild-goose chase, but our man eventually showed."

"So Brian's partner in crime talked freely?"

"Not immediately, of course, but when the tavernkeeper got my signal and the constable arrived, the fellow became so scared of being involved in actual murder, he soon spilled out much information. He insisted his friend, Brian, had hired him only to write three letters and to play the part of a brother who'd come to take a body away for burial, that he'd committed no criminal act, no murder."

"He admitted writing you the letter, calling himself Charles Coombes, pretending to be a brother of someone Amy supposedly married in Malta?"

"Yes, and that Amy and this fictional husband would emigrate to Australia. The plan, of course, was that when he himself went to Australia he'd write two more letters, one to you, another to me, using another assumed first name, pretending this time to be Amy's husband, explaining in a disguised handwriting that Amy died of natural causes."

"Only a letter to me was no longer necessary. Did you bring this so-called Charles Coombes here from Bellesport?"

"Yes, with the help of the constable."

"And then?"

"When we arrived at the manor, Farris greeted us with considerable agitation, explaining that you had gone for a stroll long ago and that Lady Edythe was upstairs beside herself with worry because you'd been gone a long time. I left the Bellesport fellow in the care of the constable and went up to Lady Edythe's room. I already knew, of course, about Amy's murder and Lady Edythe's and Brian's part in it. The Bellesport chap had refused to tell where he'd taken Amy's body, said only that he'd delivered it to the care of Brian."

"At that time, when you'd arrived at the manor with the fellow from Bellesport, I was in the chapel, Brian's prisoner."

Edmond nodded. "When I got upstairs, Lady Edythe greeted me with a grief-stricken face, explaining, with a catch in her voice, that you'd gone strolling near the cliffs.

" 'I believe Miss Atwood went to look for Amy's body along the cliff-side,' she ran on, 'and has probably fallen to her death off the cliff road.'

" 'You told me Amy had never come to the manor,' I said to her. She turned pale but recovered quickly, stating that 'No, Amy never had come to the manor but Miss Atwood seemed to think so.

" 'You must go and look for Miss Atwood,' she wailed. 'She's probably fallen to her death. I tried to dissuade her from going there but she was adamant.'

"She began to wring her hands and weep. My next words stopped that.

" 'I've just returned from Bellesport,' I said to her. 'Someone who calls himself Charles Coombes told me everything.'

"I thought she was going to faint, possibly fall dead of shock," Edmond said. "For a long time she simply stared at me, white as a sheet, her body swaying back and forth. Then, all at once, she drew herself up and asked blandly who Charles Coombes might be.

" 'A friend of Brian's.'

" 'Brian?' she repeated with innocent surprise. 'And who is he?'

" 'Your son, your illegitimate son,' I said and she gazed at me in cool silence, then asked who'd told me such a foolish lie. She continued to deny Brian but when I confronted her with everything I'd learned in Bellesport, she went into a rage, blamed everything on Brian, that she'd disowned him when she realized he was evil, that he'd milked her and harassed her the past two years when he'd learned of her whereabouts.

" 'From whom?' I asked. 'From an old seaman, an Uncle Philip, whom you paid to keep your secret. This Uncle Philip's deathbed confession also included some remarks about the death of your husband, my uncle, that it was not an accident,' " Edmond related.

"She was thunderstruck but I went on. 'Oh, Brian's friend in Bellesport became quite talkative in order to save his skin and your old crone, Mrs. Hopkins, is no longer loyal to you, has become quite loquacious to save herself,' I told her." He stopped to ask if I was up to hearing more now. I said I felt fine and he continued.

"After that she became hysterical, shrieking over and over that she had nothing to do with Amy's murder, that she was at Wickham Place when it happened," Edmond explained.

" 'You planned it,' I said to her, 'partly because of your obsession about Malverne Manor but mainly because you aren't the person I for a long time thought you were.'

"I demanded she tell me where Amy's body was taken, but she insisted she knew nothing about it. I rushed downstairs and was met by the Raynords who'd come to take you to Hammond House for dinner, since you'd promised to go. When I told them what had occurred, the Raynords and I went in search of the Colonel to see what he could tell us. When the Raynords saw the constable, they thought the Cheslick gang was at it again. They, of course, had no part in any of this.

"When we found the Colonel in his room, I thought at first he'd had too much to drink, but I was suspicious of his stupor."

"He'd been drugged?" I asked. "Mrs. Hopkins' brew?"

"Yes, but he was beginning to come out of it and we managed to pry information out of him. He recollected your interest in the Malverne Manor book he'd given you before he went for his swim in the pond and that you'd become quite interested in the underground chapel. I feel like a complete fool about that, but I'd never suspected, ever considered that disused chapel. No one had ever so much as spoken of it in years. Well, it didn't take us long—me, the Raynords, the constable —we raced down to the cottage."

"And found me and Brian in the chapel?"

"When I slid open the chapel entry, Brian spoke up immediately, addressing Lady Edythe, obviously expecting her. He ran up the steps and right into the arms of the law. I've never seen a more thunderstruck expression as Brian had on his face, not even Lady Edythe looked more shocked when I informed her I knew about Brian."

"You then brought Brian up to the house?"

Edmond playfully ruffled my hair. "No, you silly goose, the others took him to the house. I brought you up to the house. My, how you fought me."

"Brian tried very hard to convince me that you wanted the pleasure of hurling my unconscious body over the cliff."

"A deranged, sadistic beast. If Mr. Raynord and the constable hadn't snatched him away, I'd have throttled him then and there. And you can imagine the revulsion I felt toward Lady Edythe who was responsible for it all. It was she, with Mrs. Hopkins' assistance, who kept Amy under sedation in that Cream Lace Room, spreading the tale of a disgraced servant girl, using the Wickhams as witnesses, convincing them the fellow from Bellesport was the grieving brother of the servant girl."

"Did Brian talk as freely as his friend in Bellesport?"

"At first he tried to play it clever, but when he learned we already knew much, he decided to wash his hands of the whole thing and blame Lady Edythe for it all."

"A pity," I said, "that he'd burned the Malverne Manor books, yours and the Colonel's, too, probably."

"No, we found both books. Brian was too greedy to burn them. He hoped to sell them."

"You know by now, of course, that Amy's body is buried in the chapel?"

"It was removed and is now in the village churchyard." He fell silent then said, more to himself than to me, "I could have spared Amy—and you—all the horror if I'd listened to the Colonel long ago. He'd warned me that I was blind and foolish in my trust and devotion to Lady Edythe. I thought the Colonel was only reflecting his personal animosity toward her, even accusing her of the fact that his brother, Lady Edythe's husband, had died under very mysterious circumstances. I believe that, secretly, the Colonel investigated his brother's death but learned nothing. Now, judging from what that fellow in Bellesport had babbled and what this so-called Uncle Philip had said, it seems the Colonel was right, that his brother was murdered." He stopped, looked at me, and heaved a sigh. "Thank God, the drug Mrs. Hopkins gave you and the Colonel merely induced stupor, that it wasn't poison."

"Did Corinne know what was going on?" I asked. "I mean about the murder plot? When Myrna explained that Corinne was also given the two-week holiday to attend the Farris girl's wedding, I got the impression Corinne was at the wedding but did not remain with the Farrises for the entire holiday. Had she returned to the manor? She seemed quite friendly with Brian."

"She was not at the manor while Amy was here. She was questioned thoroughly and her movements were checked out. After the wedding, she went to Bellesport, stayed with Brian's friend and Brian when he visited. Corinne, by the way, has left the manor. Before I had the opportunity to dismiss her, she herself expressed the wish to leave, to resume her job at a tavern near her home. I convinced Mrs. Farris she need not feel responsible for Corinne and when Mrs. Farris learned of Corinne's Bellesport holiday, she did not need much persuading."

"Corinne did cause her to worry. Mrs. Farris always seemed anxious and unhappy."

"You'll see quite a difference in her now, like she used to be before Lady Edythe and Mrs. Hopkins took over. She, of course, is terribly saddened about the recent events, but you will observe how relieved she is not to have Mrs. Hopkins and Lady Edythe about. She'd never liked either of them and repeatedly requested to leave the manor but remained only as a favor to me."

"What about the chapel? Has the entry been resealed?"

"Yes, securely," Edmond replied then, after a reflective silence, said, "Oh, how wrong I was about Lady Edythe. To think that all the time I was in Scotland I felt Lady Edythe was taking care of Amy. If I'd stayed in Edinburgh instead of traveling about, I would have received a letter from Amy, warning me of danger. Old Abner admitted he'd secretly posted letters for her." He stopped. "If Amy wrote to me at the Edinburgh address, I might yet receive a letter. It will be forwarded to the manor."

"She very well might have written you. She wrote secret letters to me from the manor, which Old Abner posted for her."

"Yes, I might get a letter," he mused, then said, "You recall my mentioning Lady Edythe's portrait? The one that hung in the library? I found it in the chapel. It was like looking at Brian's face. She was about his age when it was painted. I burned it. I wish I could burn all memory of her and Brian out of my brain."

"What will happen to Lady Edythe? Prison?"

There was a prolonged hesitation. His face tensed and he momentarily closed his eyes. "No need for prison," he said at last. "Between the time I'd left her in her room and when the constable went up to question her, she'd escaped the house." There was another sharp silence. "We found her body at the bottom of the cliff."

A hush fell on the room. It was some time before he continued speaking. "Brian, along with Mrs. Hopkins and the fellow from Bellesport, was taken away by the constable and his men."

We heard footsteps in the corridor and Edmond turned his head. It was Myrna with a delicious-smelling trayful.

"Chicken broth," she said, approaching the bed. "And the loveliest apple cake. And lots more." She gazed at me over the tray. "Do eat it all up, miss," she said, placing the tray on the bedside table, plumping up my pillow. She glanced shyly at Sir Edmond. "I brought you some apple cake and tea, sir, if you should wish to join Miss Atwood."

We thanked her and as she withdrew quietly, Edmond and I began to enjoy our treat.

The following day, with the doctor's approval, I was permitted downstairs to sit for a while in the drawing room where I again enjoyed the Raynords' visit. Old Abner came to inquire about my health. Mrs. Farris, Myrna, and the Colonel hovered over me and Edmond left my side only when election details demanded his attention.

The next day my improvement won me the privilege of sitting in the garden, even strolling for a short time in the rose garden, once with Edmond and again with the Colonel.

A week later I was allowed to accompany Edmond to Amy's grave. We placed white roses on the grave. I wept quietly. Edmond held me close but did not try to stop my weeping, knowing I could not hold back my grief. The following day Edmond learned he'd won the county election. Although he was pleased, there was no rejoicing.

For the two weeks that I remained at the manor, Mrs. Farris was particularly kind to me. As Edmond had indicated, there was a marked change in her. She became open and friendly, even taking me into confidence, expressing her relief that Corinne was no longer her responsibility. Sir Edmond had convinced her, she said, that Corinne was no longer a child and she, in turn, had convinced her sister, Corinne's mother, that Corinne should no longer be prevented from marrying the young man who worked in the tavern where Corinne now resumed her former job, adding with a knowing nod, that Corinne could do much worse than that.

Mrs. Farris never mentioned Lady Edythe or Mrs. Hopkins, but her contentment and cheerfulness reflected her feeling on that subject. Only once did Mrs. Farris, in her friendly little chats, speak of the Wickhams, informing me that now that Miss Wickham and her father had gone to live on the Scilly Islands, we would have fine new neighbors, that she knew of the people; they'd tried previously to buy Wickham Place. They will be fine neighbors, she declared, excellent people.

Three days before I was to leave Malverne Manor, two things occurred the same day. Early in the day, Amy's two letters to Edmond were forwarded from the Edinburgh address. In the first, Amy expressed alarm about Lady Edythe's attitude, a vague fear she had of her and of Mrs. Hopkins. She also questioned the dizzy spells and the sluggish sleep which frequently overwhelmed her and which Lady Edythe and Mrs. Hopkins assured her were probably due to her having struck her head when she'd fallen off the horse.

The second letter was almost incoherent, as if written under the influence of a drug. But anguish and desperation were clear. She feared for her life. She explained that Old Abner secretly posted her letters. She begged Edmond to come home. For the first time she mentioned Brian, that he was a visitor at the manor. He'd promised to help her, but she no longer trusted him.

Edmond lapsed into a quiet sadness after reading the letters. I held back my tears, waiting till he left the room, not wanting to increase the anguish and sorrow that showed so plainly in his face. I knew he blamed himself for Amy's suffering and death.

Later that same day we had a surprise visitor, the widow, Lady Bellingford. Expecting to find Amy happily married and mistress of Malverne Manor, Lady Bellingford became prostrate with grief when told of Amy's tragic death. She was so affected by the terrible news that Dr. Pryor had to be sent for.

The following day Lady Bellingford was improved and when she learned I was leaving Malverne Manor the next day, she expressed a wish to accompany me, declaring I should not travel alone.

I was pleased to have her accompany me. In the short space of time I knew her, I'd become quite fond of her. She was a delightful person. It was no wonder Amy had been so taken with her. It was evident she'd been fond of Amy. Much of her extreme grief over Amy's death was due to her blaming herself. "It was I," she lamented, "who encouraged Amy to go to Malverne Manor. I had no inkling of trouble. And then to be delayed because of my mother's illness." Edmond and I had to console her. Her grief was intense. She'd written Amy, she said, explaining her delay, asked Amy to write to her. Amy, of course, never saw Lady Bellingford's letter. Lady Edythe and Mrs. Hopkins saw to that.

Edmond was quite pleased with Lady Bellingford, as was everyone else at the manor. It was agreed she would accompany me home.

On my last day at Malverne Manor, Edmond and I visited Amy's grave in the morning, then we strolled through the manor gardens which were at their loveliest. The fragrance from the rose garden and the apple orchard perfumed the air. The memory of Amy hovered over the manor, but Edmond and I refused to slip into perpetual gloom and sadness knowing that Amy, vivacious and never wallowing in gloom herself, would not wish us to be unhappy.

I purposely requested a stroll in the formal garden. I did not expect to erase the frightening experience from my memory, but neither did I wish to dodge shadows. I was able to sit with Edmond by the reflecting pool and admire the sparkling water where the goldfish flashed in the sunshine. The long rows of daffodils and hyacinths blooming alongside the pool were a clear, fresh color. What had happened to me in this now serene setting seemed long ago.

At my request I asked Edmond to walk with me along the pond to the cottage. I wanted to banish hidden fears, to face them openly. As we strolled along the banks of the pond, I began to remember Amy as she looked when she smiled, laughed, with always some new adventure bringing a shine to her eyes. I noted that Edmond, too, was becoming less solemn, the tenseness in him giving way to acceptance, a determination that life must go on.

I paid my last visit to Amy's grave alone, at my request, just before Lady Bellingford and I left Malverne Manor. When I returned from the churchyard, they were all standing in the central hall waiting to bid me good-by. The entire Farris family was there, along with Old Abner. When the farewells eventually wound up, they all slipped away, leaving me alone with Edmond while Lady Bellingford waited for me in the carriage.

"Must we wait two whole months before we marry?" Edmond asked immediately, taking me into his arms.

"Yes," I said, "we must."

"I will be on your doorsill exactly two months from today," he said, holding me close.

But he came in two weeks, not two months, and would not take No for an answer.

With Lady Bellingford's help, I put together a modest trousseau. Walter Binson gladly bought the chemist's shop. I'd surmised from the day I arrived home with Lady Bellingford that he and the Milkins girl were anxious to marry and get on with making the chemist's shop a success.

Edmond and I were married quietly in the village church, Lady Bellingford my only attendant. She then returned to her town house in London, promising to visit us later, and Edmond and I went to my lovely new home, Malverne Manor.